A **BATPiG** BOOK

TOO PIG TO FAIL

ROB HARRELL

DIAL BOOKS FOR YOUNG READERS

DIAL BOOKS FOR YOUNG READERS

An imprint of Penguin Random House LLC, New York

First published in the United States of America by Dial Books for Young Readers,
an imprint of Penguin Random House LLC, 2022

Copyright © 2022 by Rob Harrell

Visit us online at penguinrandomhouse.com.

Library of Congress Cataloging-in-Publication Data is available

Manufactured in China

ISBN 9780593354209 • 10 9 8 7 6 5 4 3 2 1

TOPL

Design by Jason Henry

For Mr. Ackerson,
my middle school art teacher—
Thanks for the push, and I know you
would have loved this.

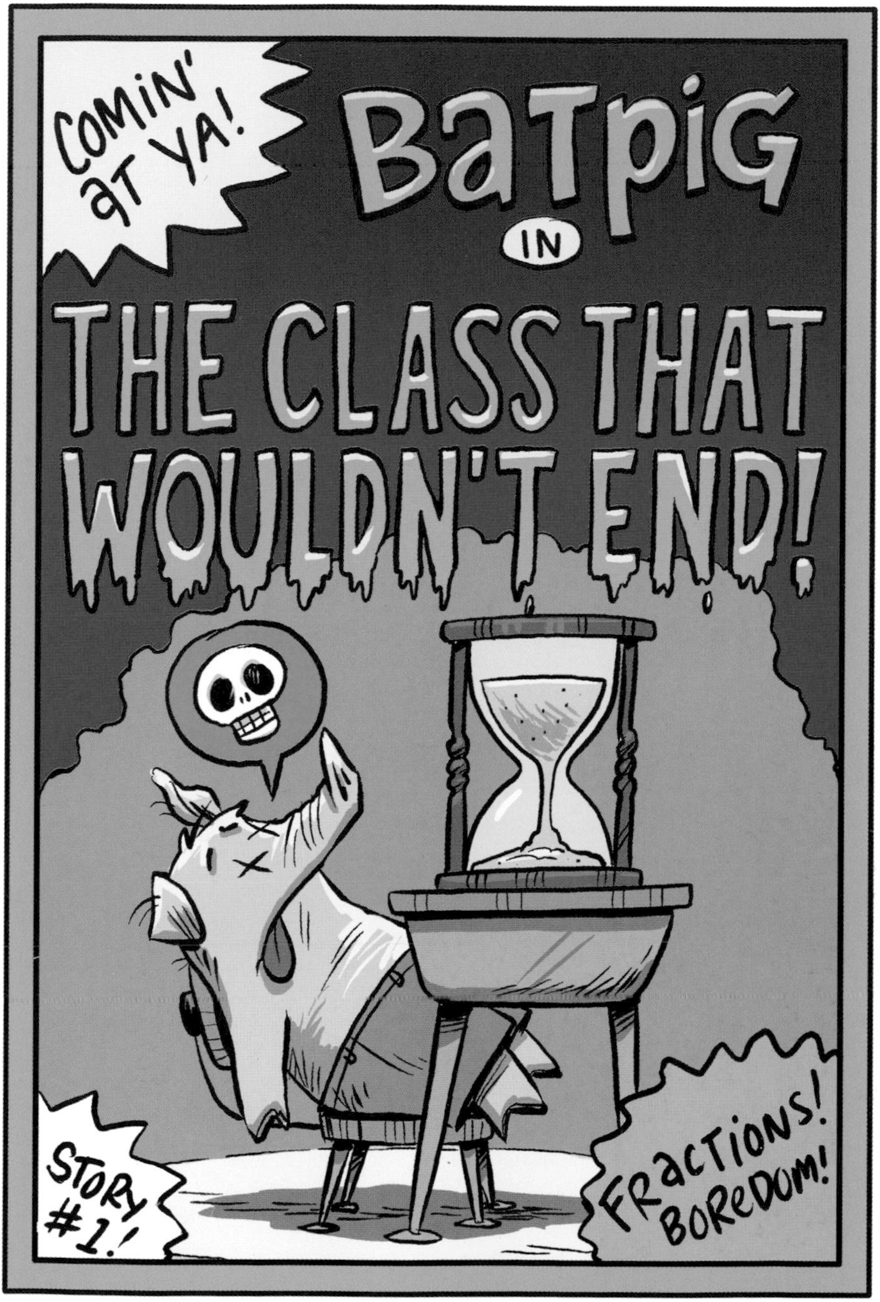
COMIN' AT YA!
BATPIG
IN
THE CLASS THAT WOULDN'T END!
STORY #1!
FRACTIONS! BOREDOM!

CHAPTER ONE

"Bad Sleep"

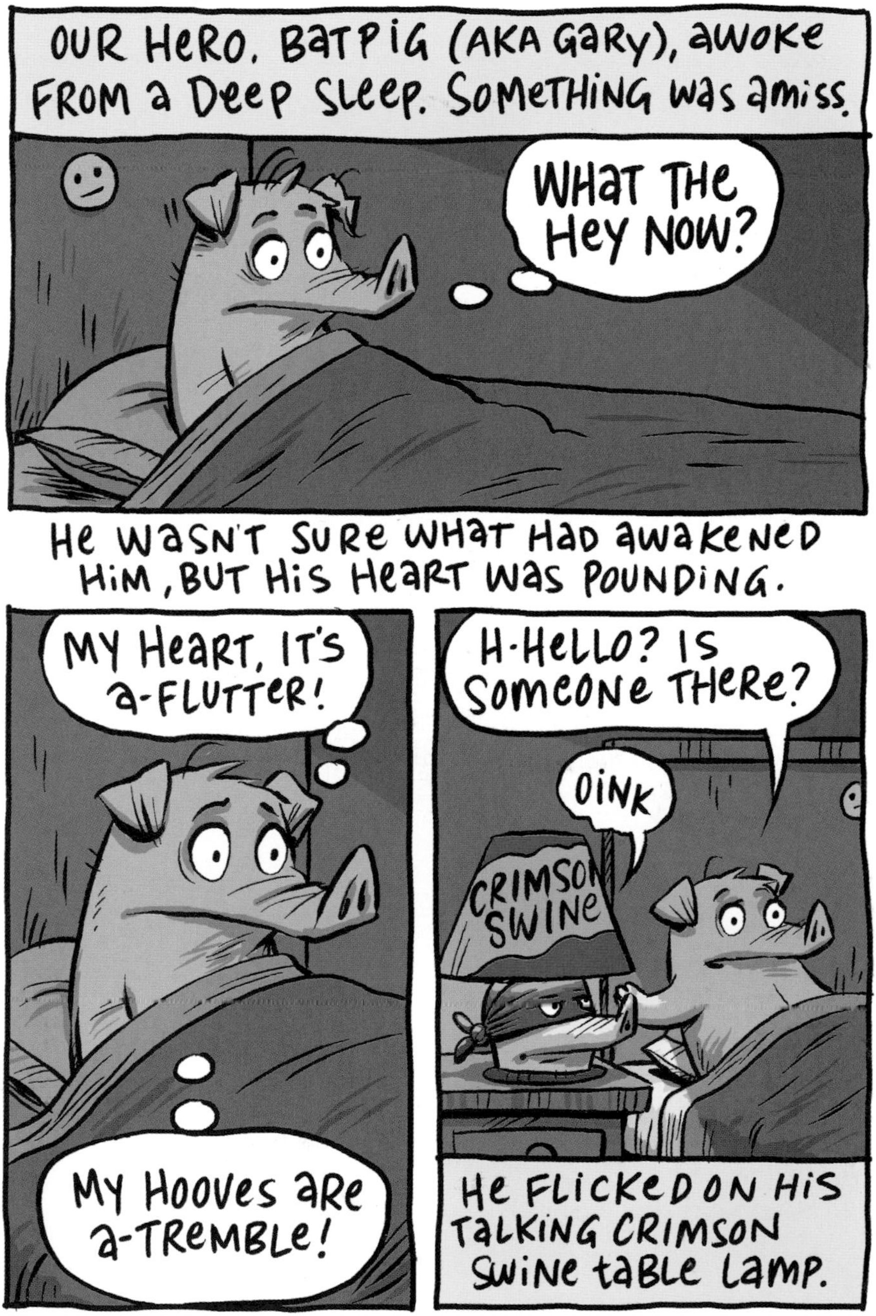
OUR HERO, BATPIG (AKA GARY), AWOKE FROM A DEEP SLEEP. SOMETHING WAS AMISS.
WHAT THE HEY NOW?
HE WASN'T SURE WHAT HAD AWAKENED HIM, BUT HIS HEART WAS POUNDING.
MY HEART, IT'S A-FLUTTER!
MY HOOVES ARE A-TREMBLE!
H-HELLO? IS SOMEONE THERE?
OINK
CRIMSON SWINE
HE FLICKED ON HIS TALKING CRIMSON SWINE TABLE LAMP.

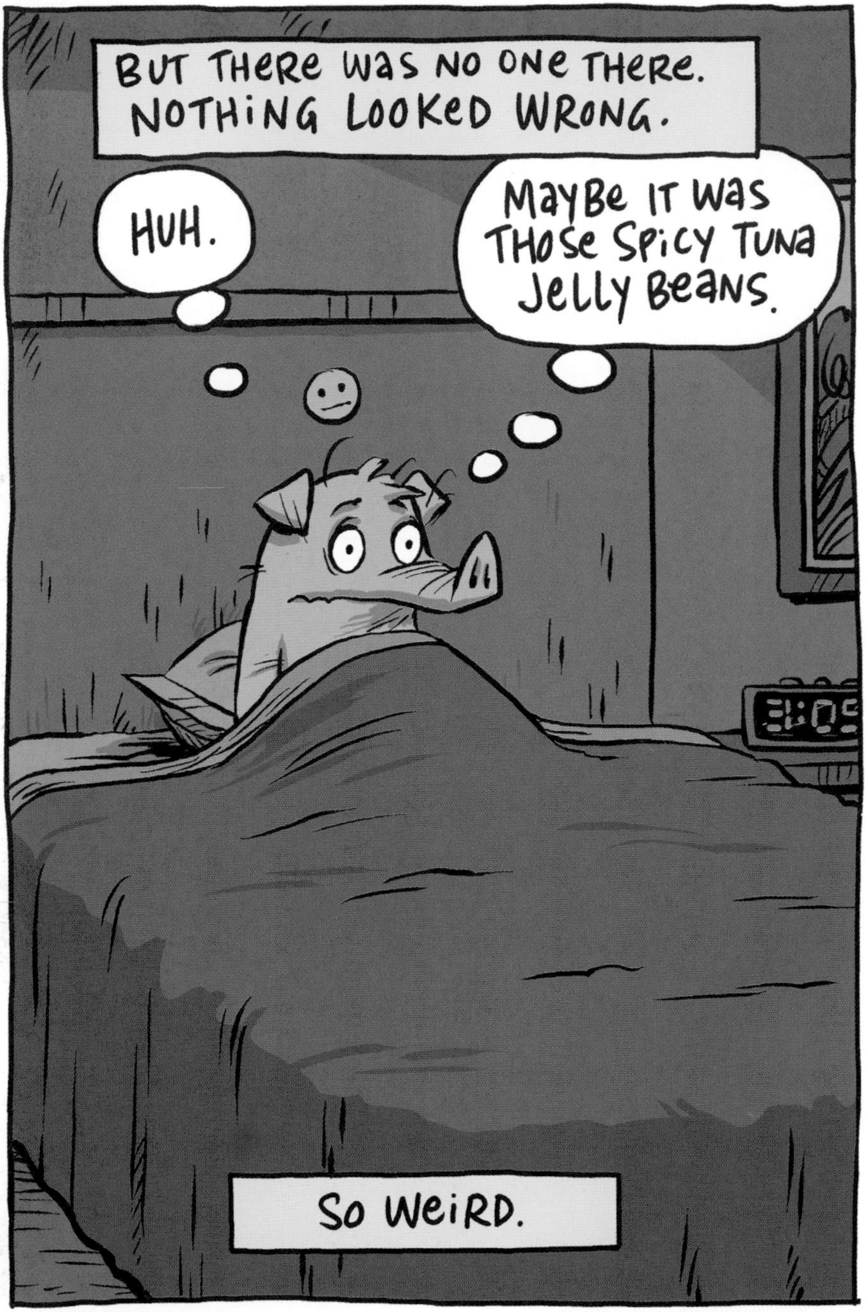
BUT THERE WAS NO ONE THERE. NOTHING LOOKED WRONG.
HUH.
MAYBE IT WAS THOSE SPICY TUNA JELLY BEANS.
SO WEIRD.

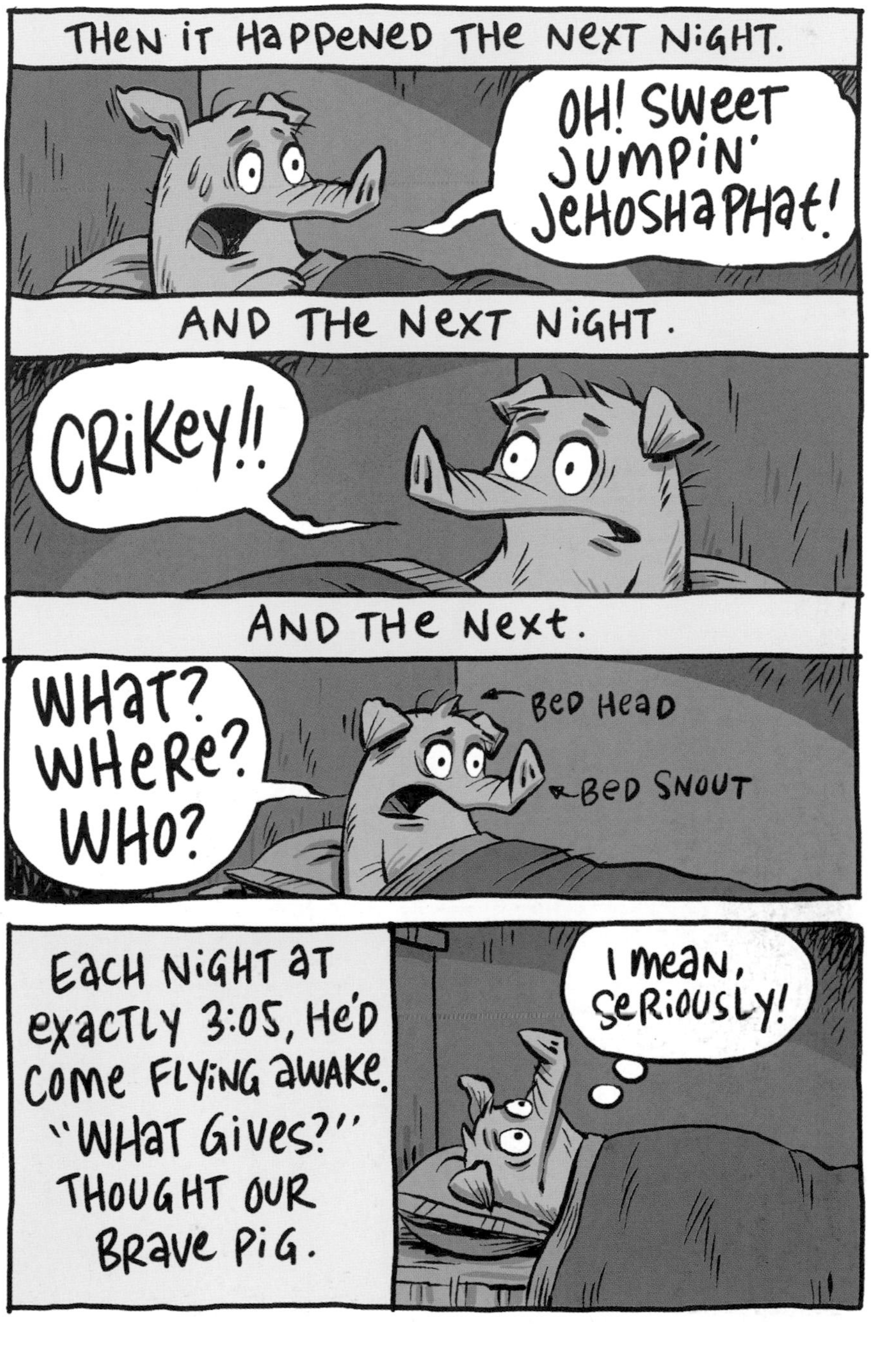
THEN IT HAPPENED THE NEXT NIGHT.
OH! SWEET JUMPIN' JEHOSHAPHAT!
AND THE NEXT NIGHT.
CRIKEY!!
AND THE NEXT.
WHAT? WHERE? WHO?
BED HEAD
BED SNOUT
EACH NIGHT AT EXACTLY 3:05, HE'D COME FLYING AWAKE. "WHAT GIVES?" THOUGHT OUR BRAVE PIG.
I MEAN, SERIOUSLY!

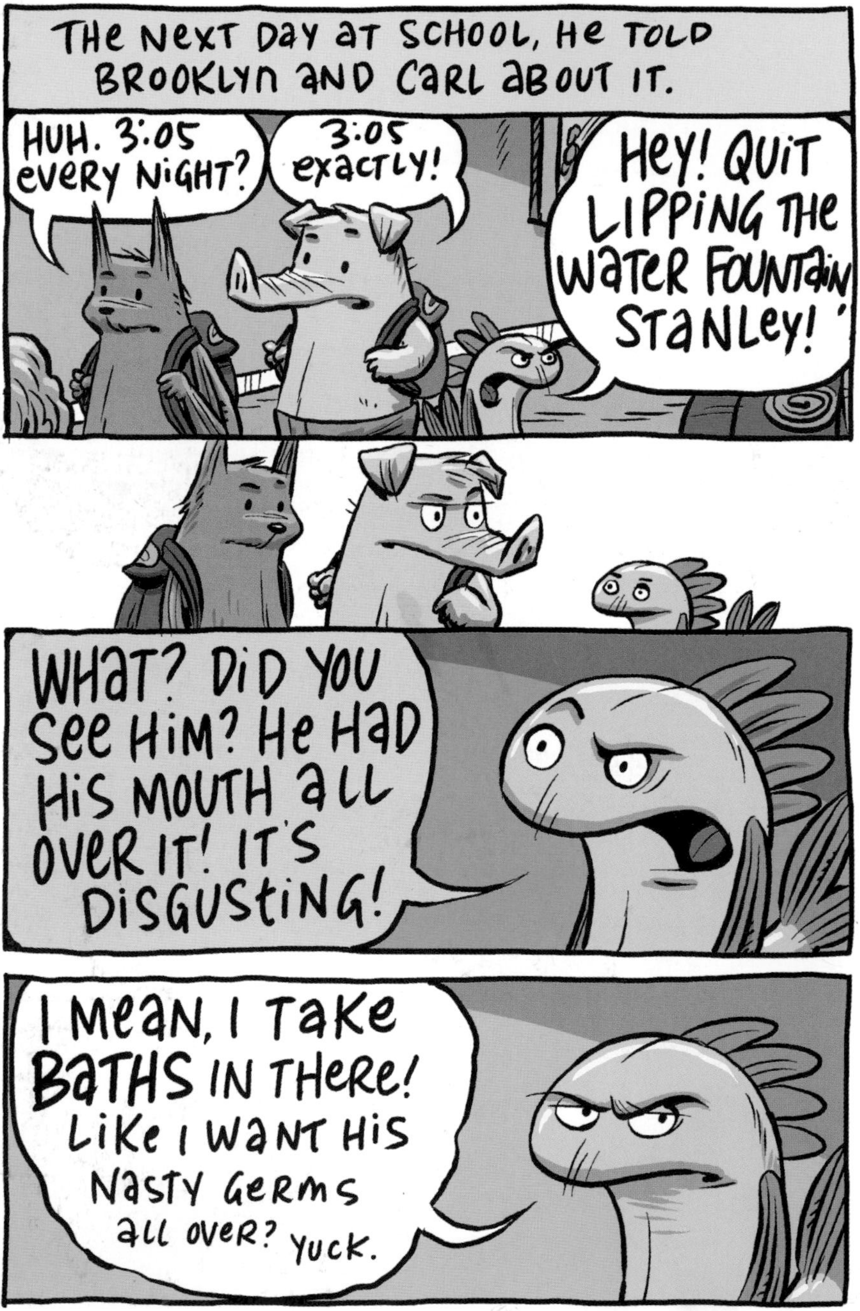
THE NEXT DAY AT SCHOOL, HE TOLD BROOKLYN AND CARL ABOUT IT.
HUH. 3:05 EVERY NIGHT?
3:05 EXACTLY!
HEY! QUIT LIPPING THE WATER FOUNTAIN, STANLEY!
WHAT? DID YOU SEE HIM? HE HAD HIS MOUTH ALL OVER IT! IT'S DISGUSTING!
I MEAN, I TAKE BATHS IN THERE! LIKE I WANT HIS NASTY GERMS ALL OVER? YUCK.

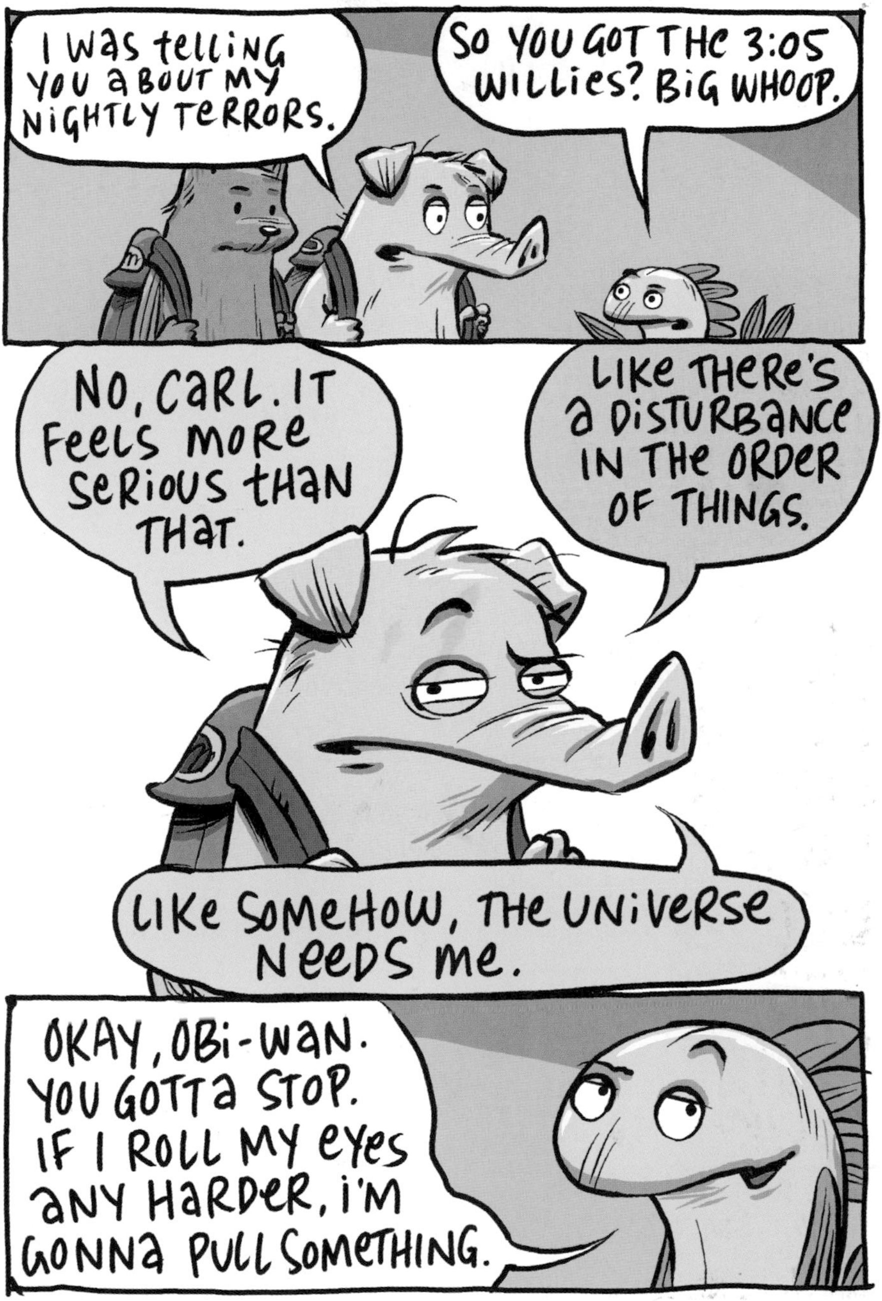
I WAS TELLING YOU ABOUT MY NIGHTLY TERRORS.
SO YOU GOT THE 3:05 WILLIES? BIG WHOOP.
NO, CARL. IT FEELS MORE SERIOUS THAN THAT.
LIKE THERE'S A DISTURBANCE IN THE ORDER OF THINGS.
LIKE SOMEHOW, THE UNIVERSE NEEDS ME.
OKAY, OBI-WAN. YOU GOTTA STOP. IF I ROLL MY EYES ANY HARDER, I'M GONNA PULL SOMETHING.

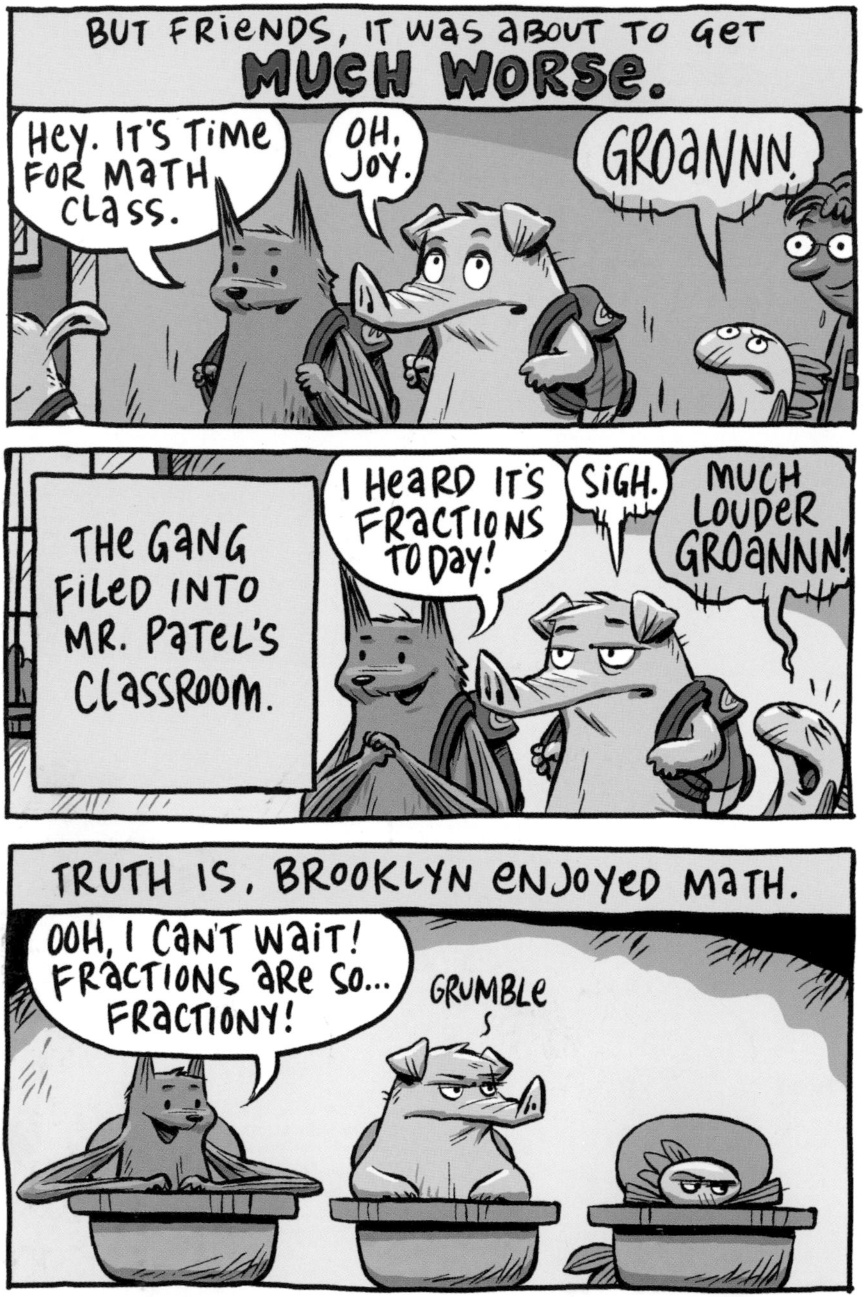
BUT FRIENDS, IT WAS ABOUT TO GET MUCH WORSE.
HEY. IT'S TIME FOR MATH CLASS.
OH, JOY.
GROANNN.
THE GANG FILED INTO MR. PATEL'S CLASSROOM.
I HEARD IT'S FRACTIONS TODAY!
SIGH.
MUCH LOUDER GROANNN!
TRUTH IS, BROOKLYN ENJOYED MATH.
OOH, I CAN'T WAIT! FRACTIONS ARE SO... FRACTIONY!
GRUMBLE

CHAPTER TWO

"SETTLE IN"

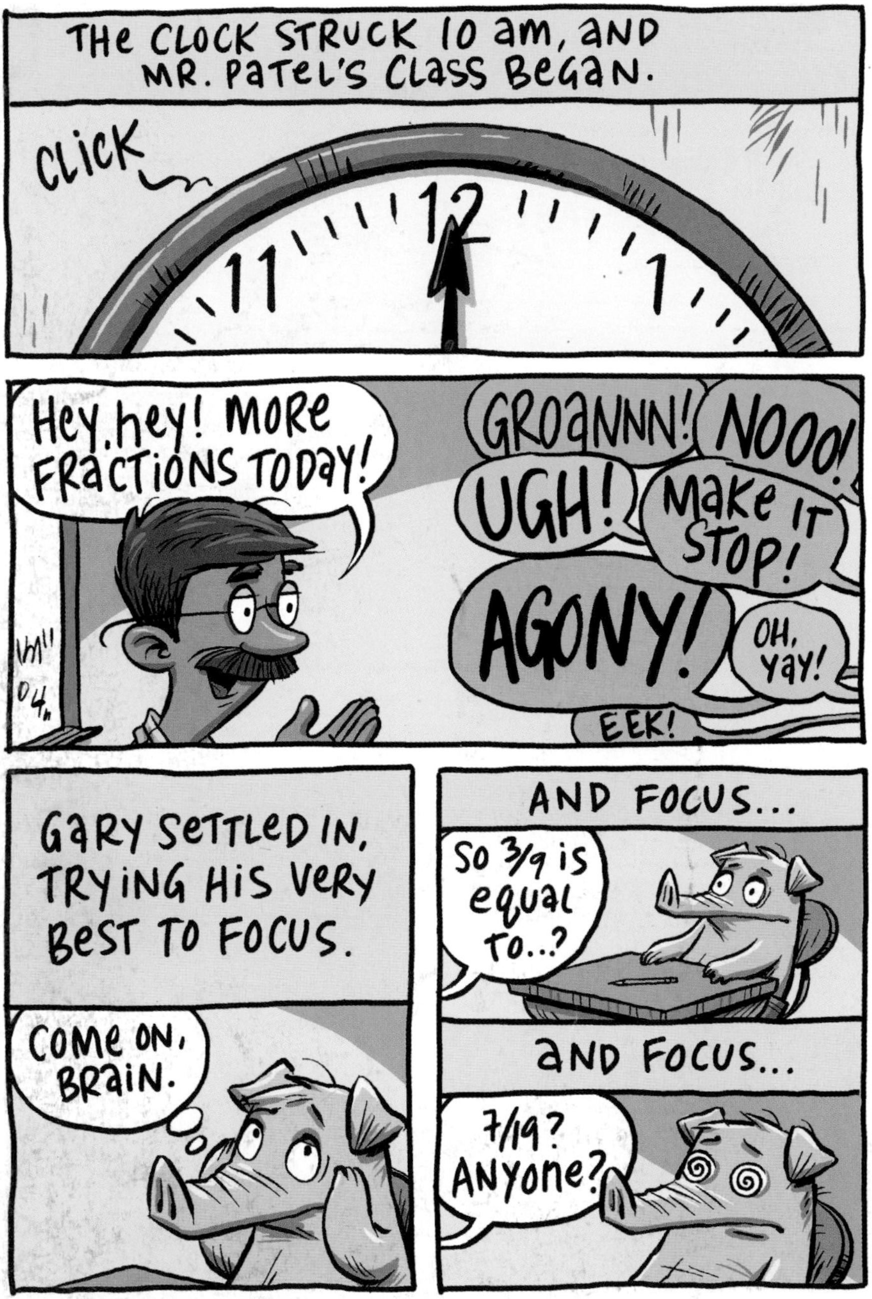
THE CLOCK STRUCK 10 am, AND MR. PATEL'S CLASS BEGAN.
CLICK
Hey, hey! MORE FRACTIONS TODAY!
GROANNN!
NOOO!
UGH!
MAKE IT STOP!
AGONY!
OH, YAY!
EEK!
GARY SETTLED IN, TRYING HIS VERY BEST TO FOCUS.
COME ON, BRAIN.
AND FOCUS...
SO 3/9 IS EQUAL TO...?
AND FOCUS...
7/19? ANYONE?

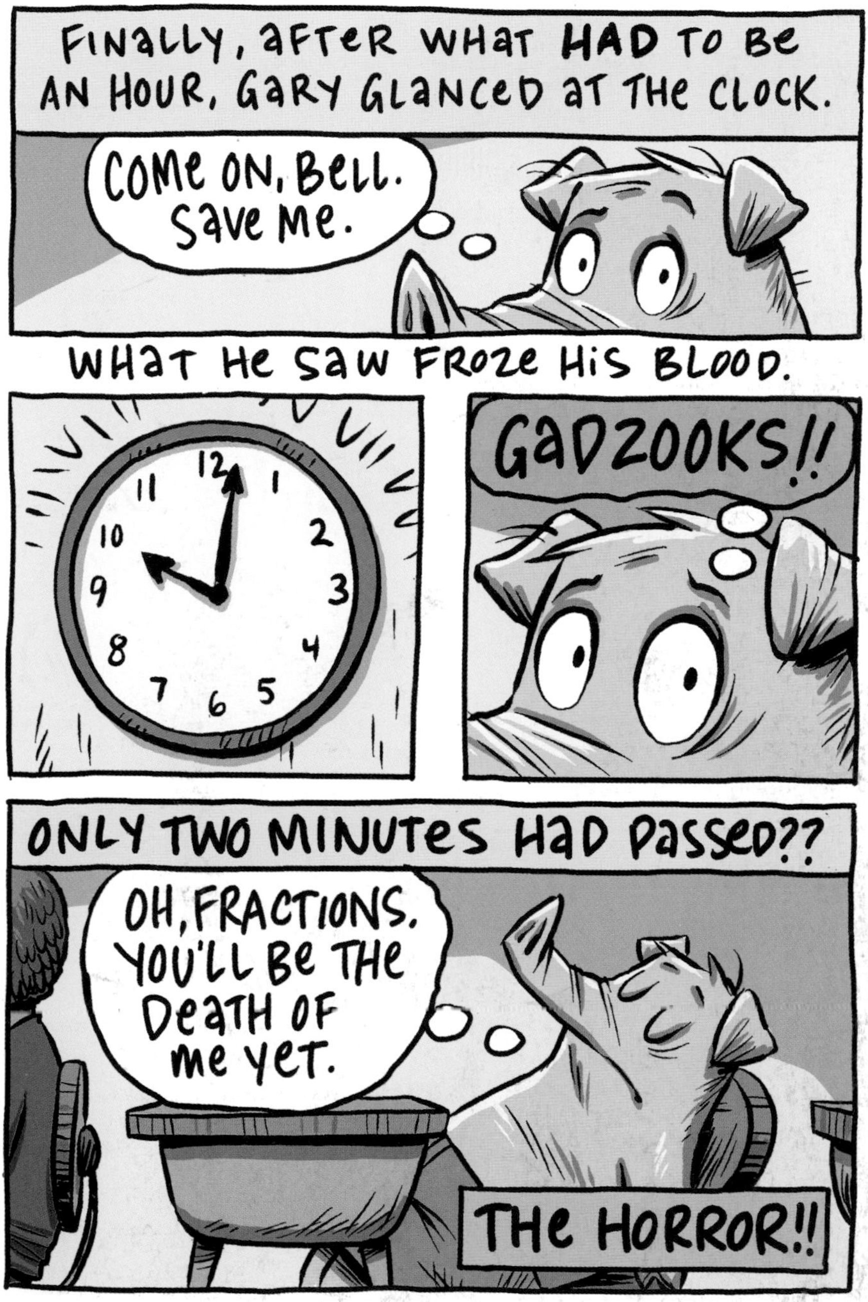
FINALLY, AFTER WHAT HAD TO BE AN HOUR, GARY GLANCED AT THE CLOCK.
COME ON, BELL. SAVE ME.
WHAT HE SAW FROZE HIS BLOOD.
12
1
2
3
4
5
6
7
8
9
10
11
GADZOOKS!!
ONLY TWO MINUTES HAD PASSED??
OH, FRACTIONS. YOU'LL BE THE DEATH OF ME YET.
THE HORROR!!

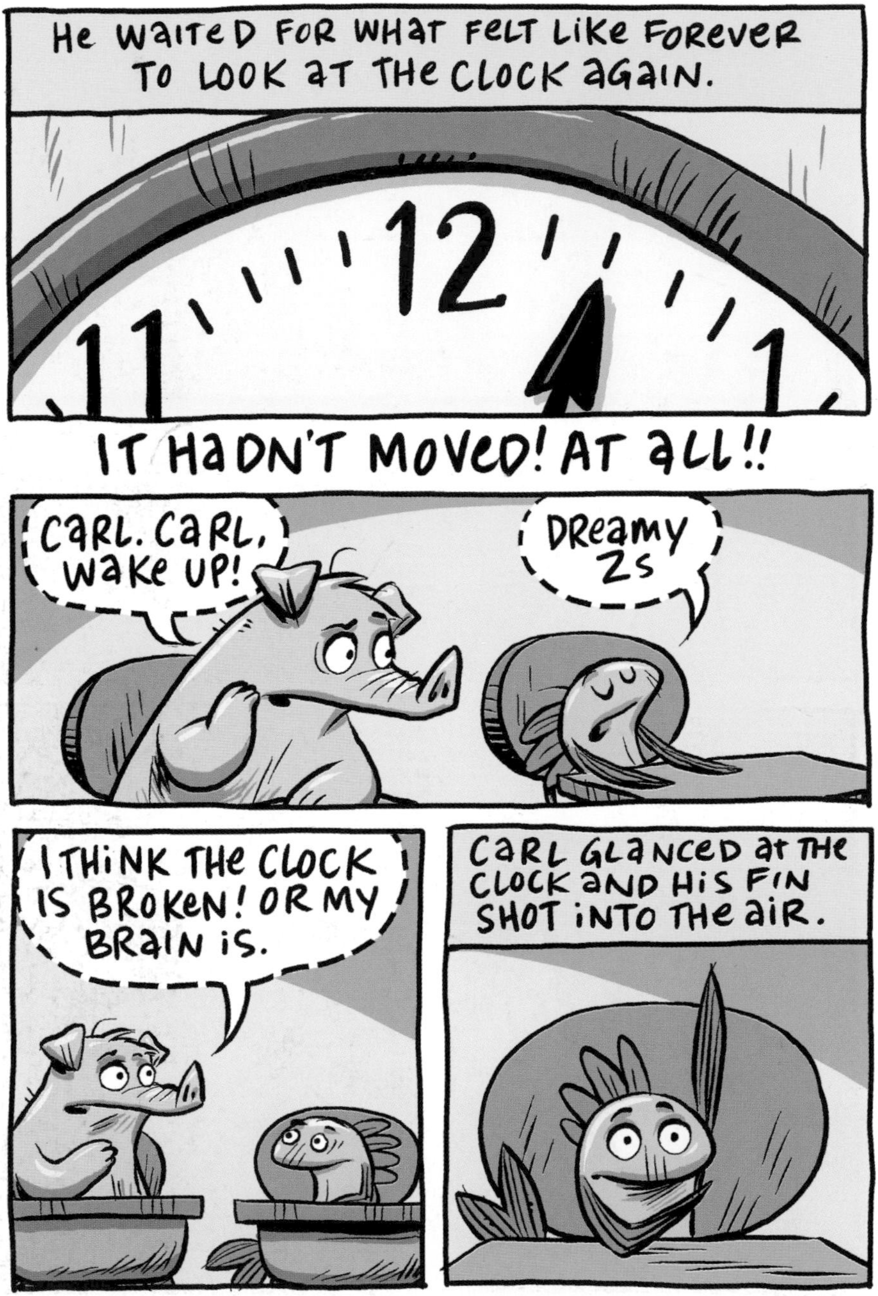
HE WAITED FOR WHAT FELT LIKE FOREVER TO LOOK AT THE CLOCK AGAIN.
12
11
1
IT HADN'T MOVED! AT ALL!!
CARL. CARL, WAKE UP!
DREAMY ZS
I THINK THE CLOCK IS BROKEN! OR MY BRAIN IS.
CARL GLANCED AT THE CLOCK AND HIS FIN SHOT INTO THE AIR.

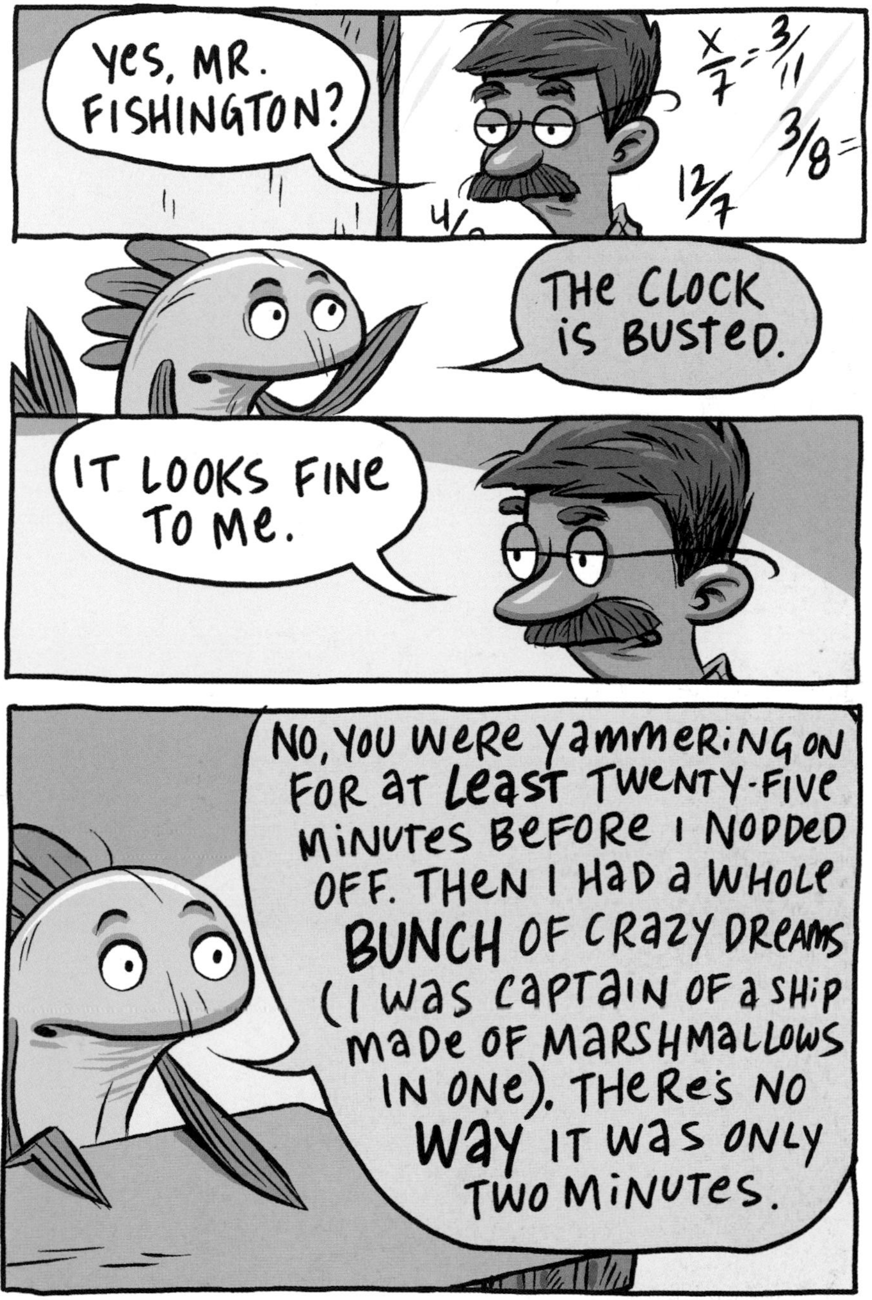
YES, MR. FISHINGTON?
x/7 = 3/11
3/8 =
12/7
THE CLOCK IS BUSTED.
IT LOOKS FINE TO ME.
NO, YOU WERE YAMMERING ON FOR AT LEAST TWENTY-FIVE MINUTES BEFORE I NODDED OFF. THEN I HAD A WHOLE BUNCH OF CRAZY DREAMS (I WAS CAPTAIN OF A SHIP MADE OF MARSHMALLOWS IN ONE). THERE'S NO WAY IT WAS ONLY TWO MINUTES.

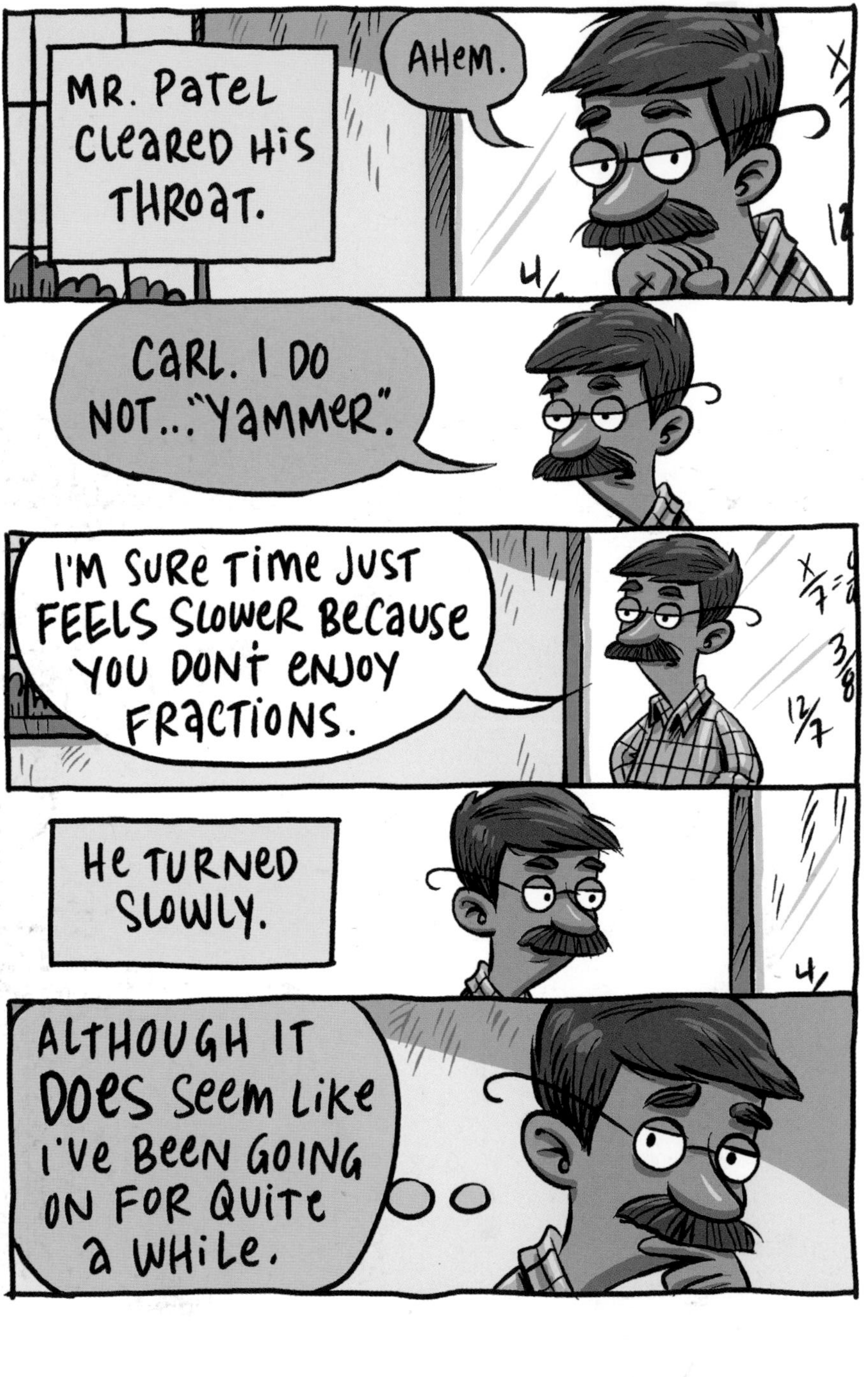
MR. PATEL CLEARED HIS THROAT.
AHEM.
CARL. I DO NOT..."YAMMER".
I'M SURE TIME JUST FEELS SLOWER BECAUSE YOU DON'T ENJOY FRACTIONS.
HE TURNED SLOWLY.
ALTHOUGH IT DOES SEEM LIKE I'VE BEEN GOING ON FOR QUITE A WHILE.

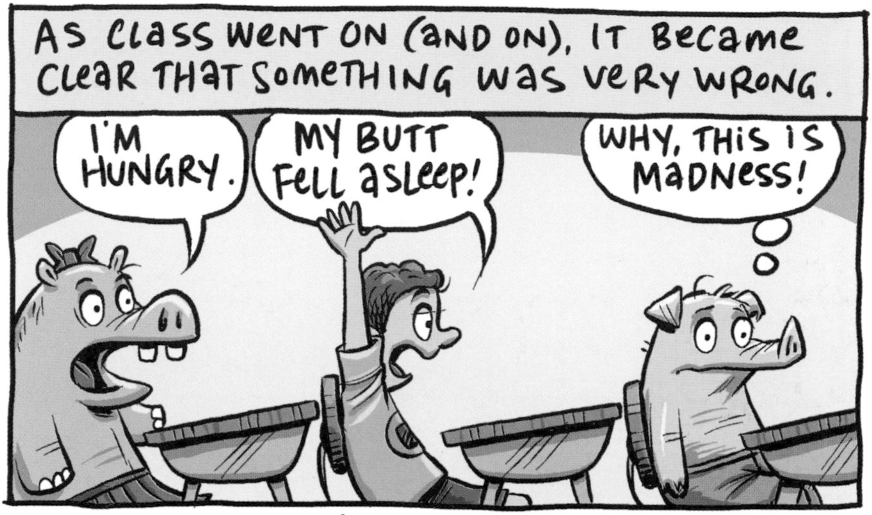
AS CLASS WENT ON (AND ON), IT BECAME CLEAR THAT SOMETHING WAS VERY WRONG.
I'M HUNGRY.
MY BUTT FELL ASLEEP!
WHY, THIS IS MADNESS!

ONE BY ONE KIDS STARTED NEEDING THE TINKLE PASS. (IT'S WHAT PATEL CALLED A BATHROOM PASS. IT'S WEIRD. I KNOW.)

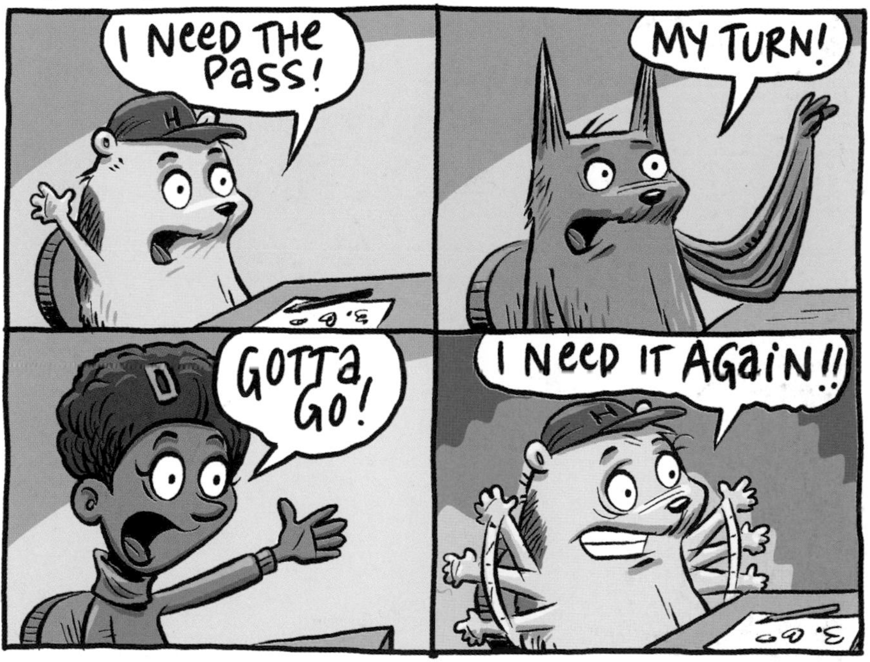
I NEED THE PASS!
MY TURN!
GOTTA GO!
I NEED IT AGAIN!!

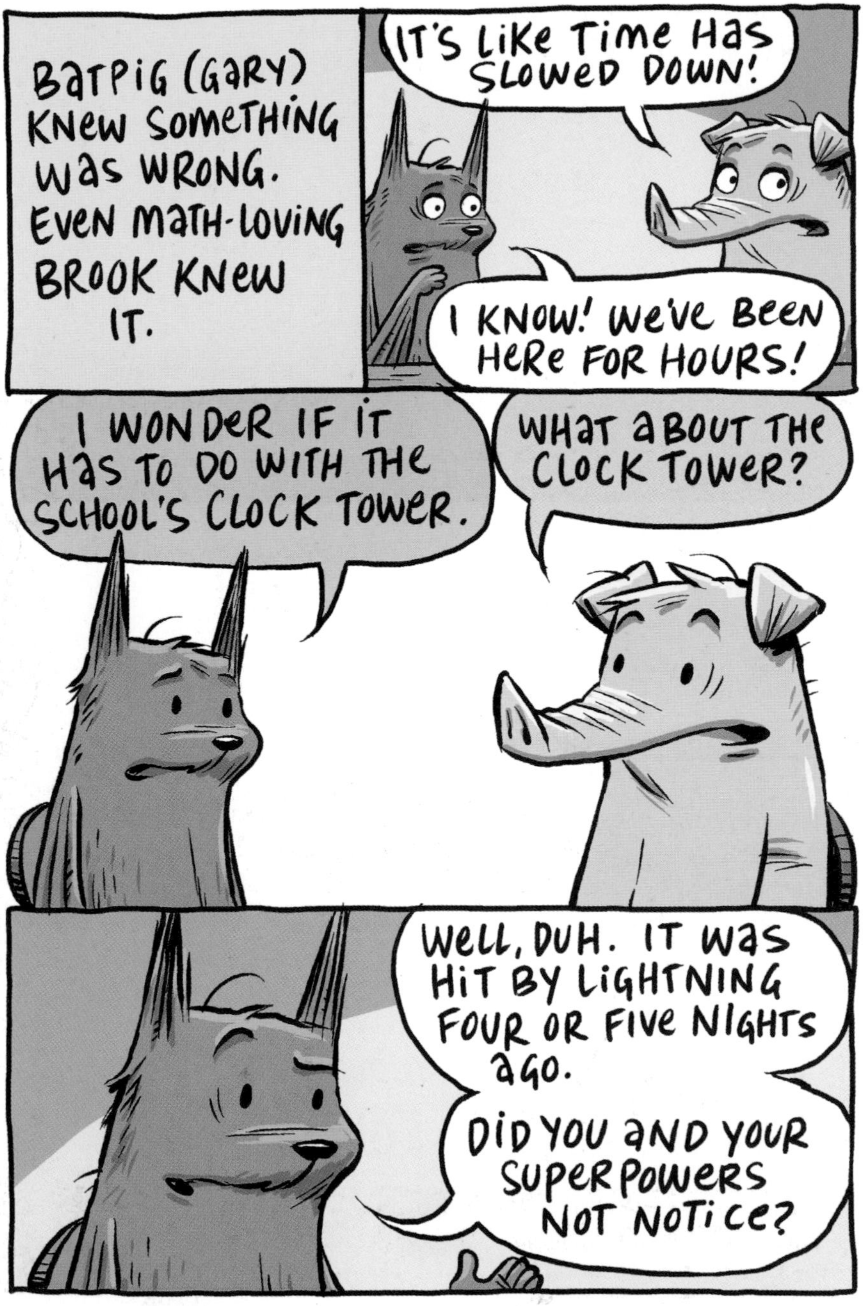
BATPIG (GARY) KNEW SOMETHING WAS WRONG. EVEN MATH-LOVING BROOK KNEW IT.
IT'S LIKE TIME HAS SLOWED DOWN!
I KNOW! WE'VE BEEN HERE FOR HOURS!
I WONDER IF IT HAS TO DO WITH THE SCHOOL'S CLOCK TOWER.
WHAT ABOUT THE CLOCK TOWER?
WELL, DUH. IT WAS HIT BY LIGHTNING FOUR OR FIVE NIGHTS AGO.
DID YOU AND YOUR SUPERPOWERS NOT NOTICE?

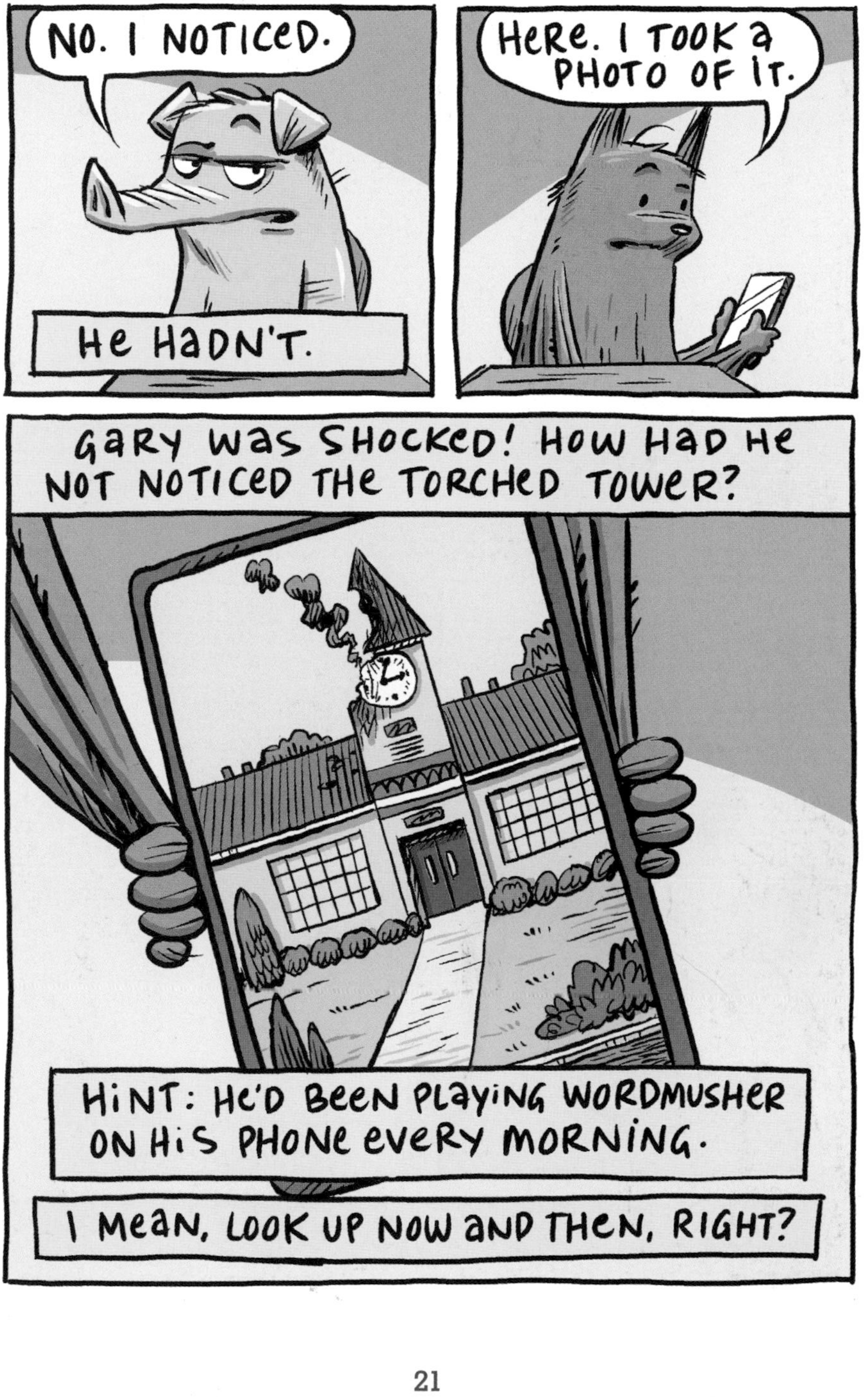

NO. I NOTICED.
HE HADN'T.
HERE. I TOOK A PHOTO OF IT.
GARY WAS SHOCKED! HOW HAD HE NOT NOTICED THE TORCHED TOWER?
HINT: HE'D BEEN PLAYING WORDMUSHER ON HIS PHONE EVERY MORNING.
I MEAN, LOOK UP NOW AND THEN, RIGHT?

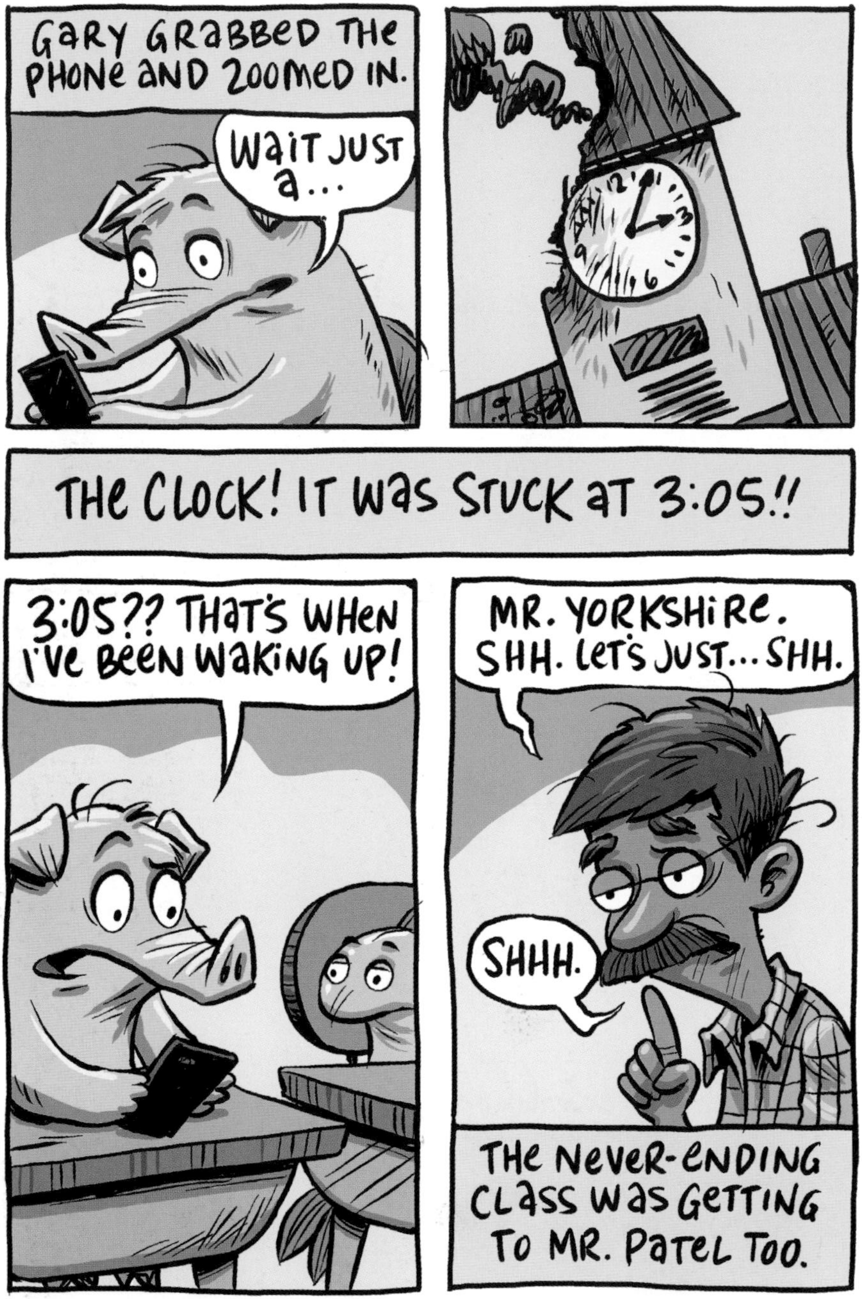
GARY GRABBED THE PHONE AND ZOOMED IN.
WAIT JUST A...
THE CLOCK! IT WAS STUCK AT 3:05!!
3:05?? THAT'S WHEN I'VE BEEN WAKING UP!
MR. YORKSHIRE. SHH. LET'S JUST... SHH.
SHHH.
THE NEVER-ENDING CLASS WAS GETTING TO MR. PATEL TOO.

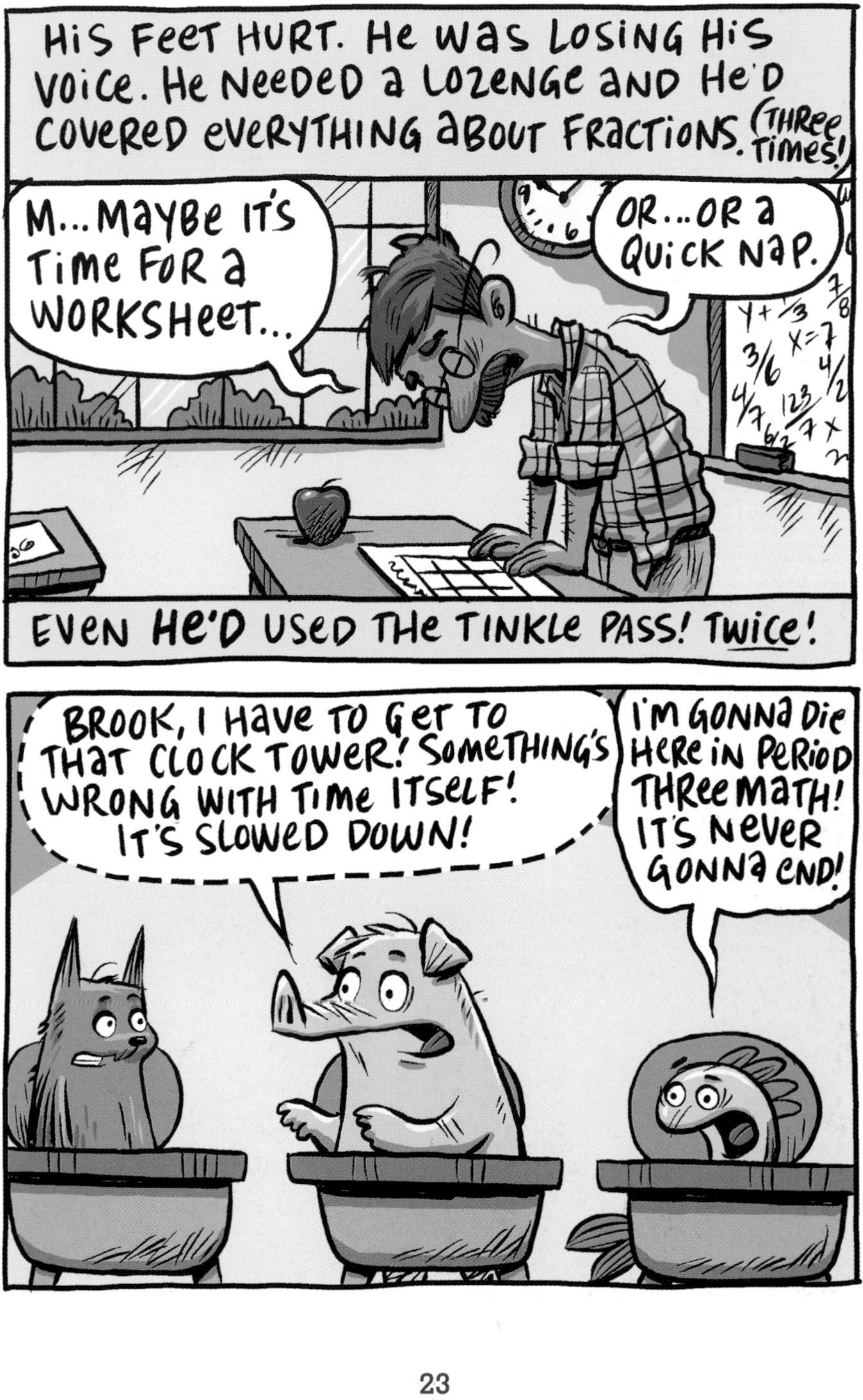
HIS FEET HURT. HE WAS LOSING HIS VOICE. HE NEEDED A LOZENGE AND HE'D COVERED EVERYTHING ABOUT FRACTIONS. (THREE TIMES!)
M... MAYBE IT'S TIME FOR A WORKSHEET...
OR... OR A QUICK NAP.
EVEN HE'D USED THE TINKLE PASS! TWICE!
BROOK, I HAVE TO GET TO THAT CLOCK TOWER! SOMETHING'S WRONG WITH TIME ITSELF! IT'S SLOWED DOWN!
I'M GONNA DIE HERE IN PERIOD THREE MATH! IT'S NEVER GONNA END!

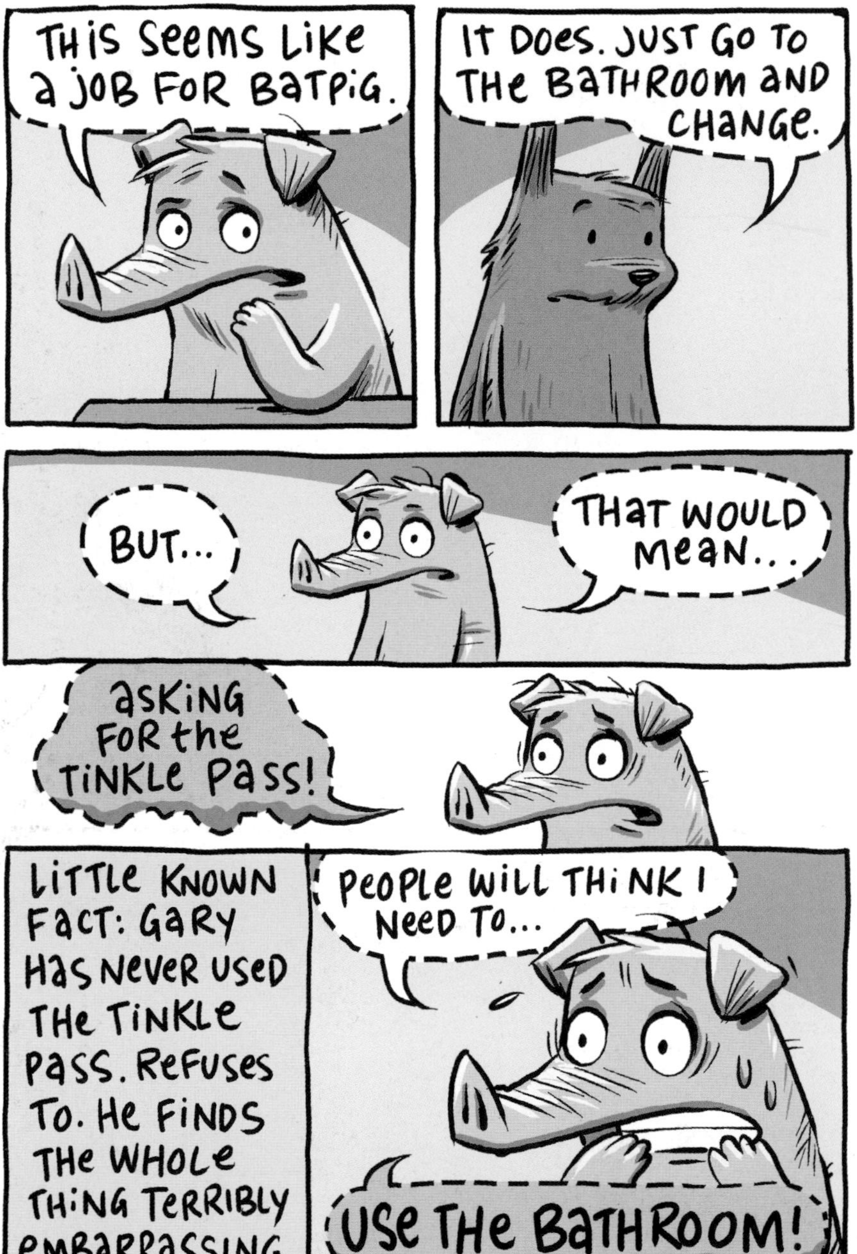
THIS SEEMS LIKE A JOB FOR BATPIG.
IT DOES. JUST GO TO THE BATHROOM AND CHANGE.
BUT...
THAT WOULD MEAN...
ASKING FOR THE TINKLE PASS!
LITTLE KNOWN FACT: GARY HAS NEVER USED THE TINKLE PASS. REFUSES TO. HE FINDS THE WHOLE THING TERRIBLY EMBARRASSING.
PEOPLE WILL THINK I NEED TO...
USE THE BATHROOM!

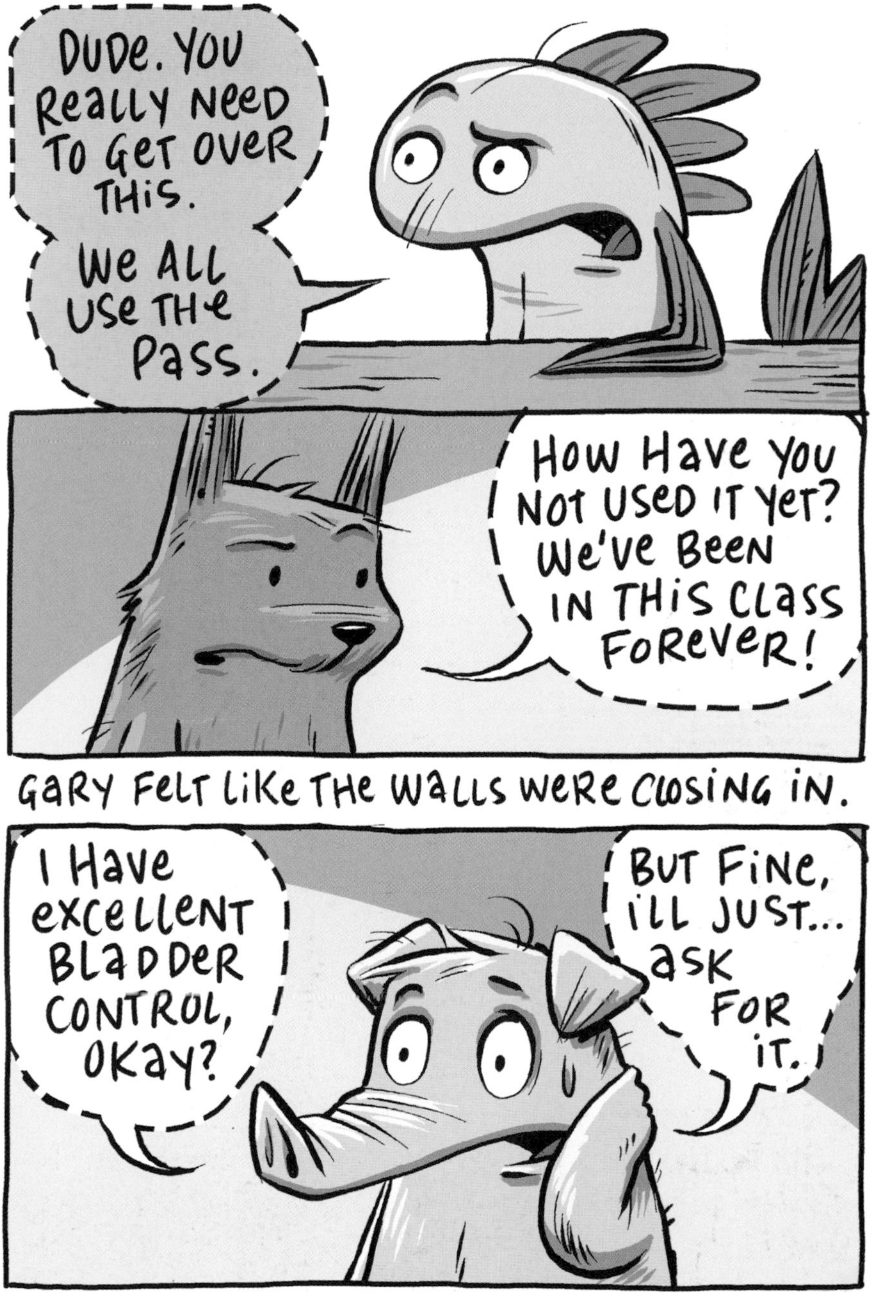
DUDE. YOU REALLY NEED TO GET OVER THIS.
WE ALL USE THE PASS.
HOW HAVE YOU NOT USED IT YET? WE'VE BEEN IN THIS CLASS FOREVER!
GARY FELT LIKE THE WALLS WERE CLOSING IN.
I HAVE EXCELLENT BLADDER CONTROL, OKAY?
BUT FINE, I'LL JUST... ASK FOR IT.

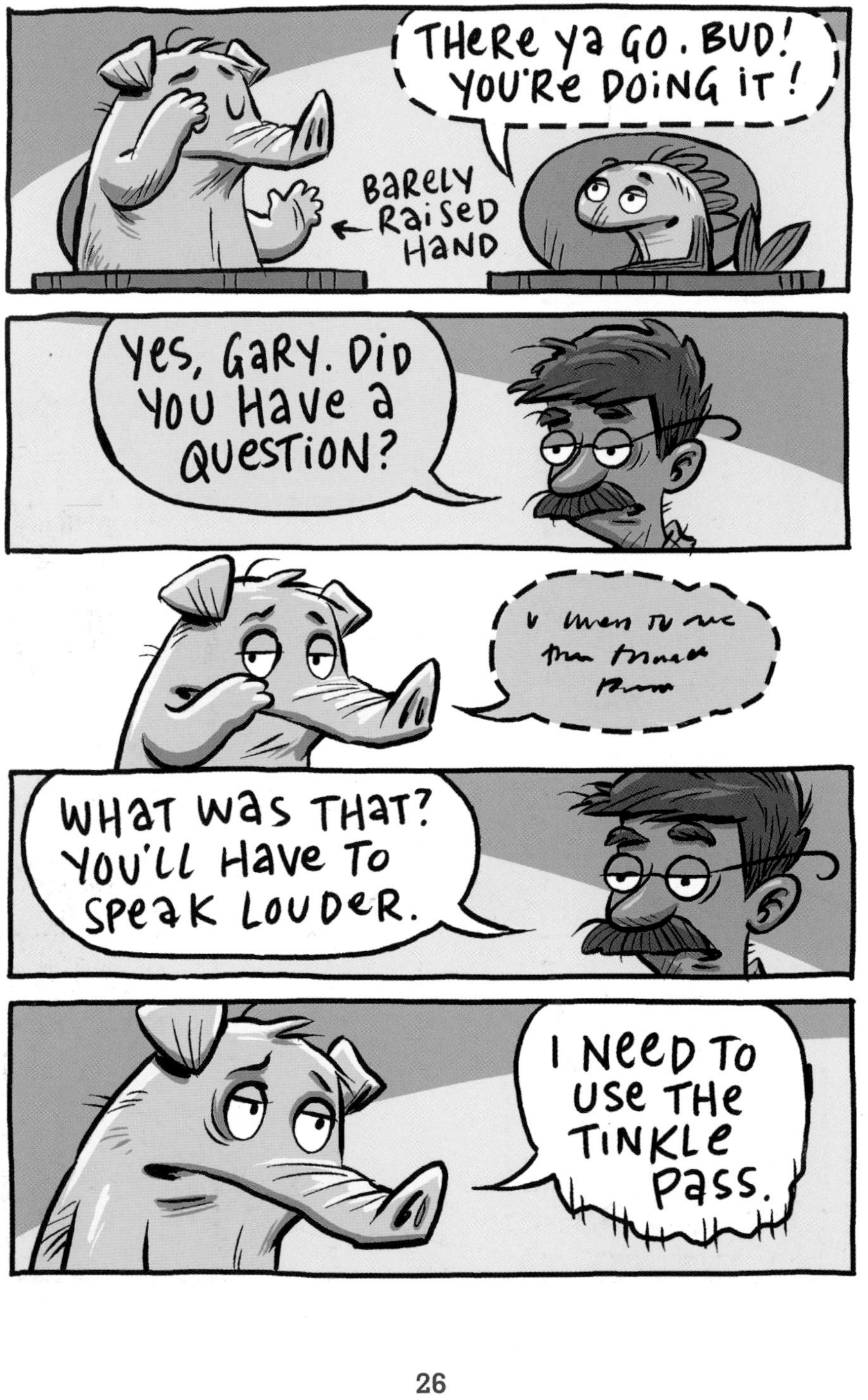
THERE YA GO, BUD! YOU'RE DOING IT!
BARELY RAISED HAND
YES, GARY. DID YOU HAVE A QUESTION?
WHAT WAS THAT? YOU'LL HAVE TO SPEAK LOUDER.
I NEED TO USE THE TINKLE PASS.

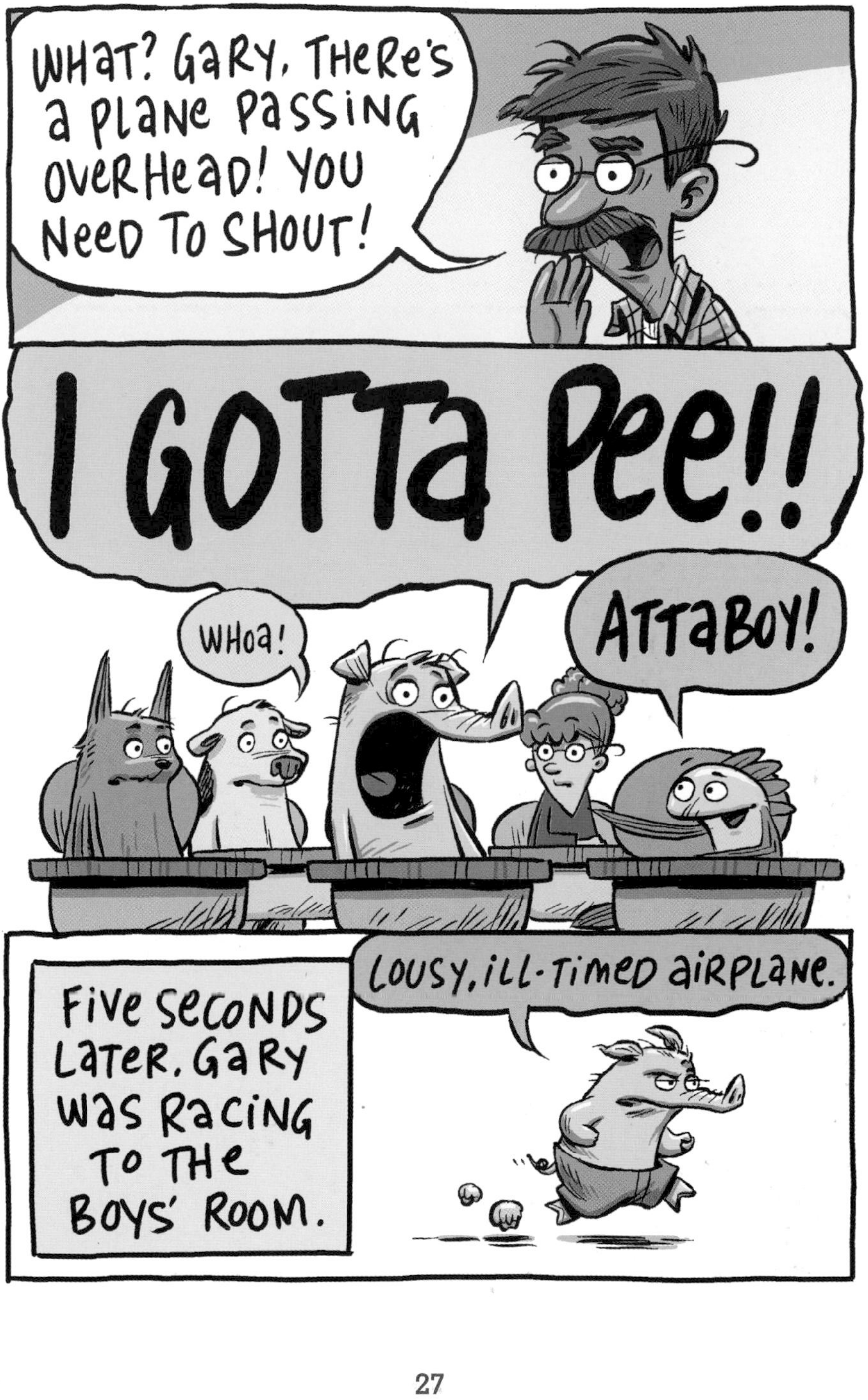
WHAT? GARY, THERE'S A PLANE PASSING OVERHEAD! YOU NEED TO SHOUT!
I GOTTA PEE!!
WHOA!
ATTABOY!
FIVE SECONDS LATER, GARY WAS RACING TO THE BOYS' ROOM.
LOUSY, ILL-TIMED AIRPLANE.

CHAPTER THREE

"TO THE TOWER!"

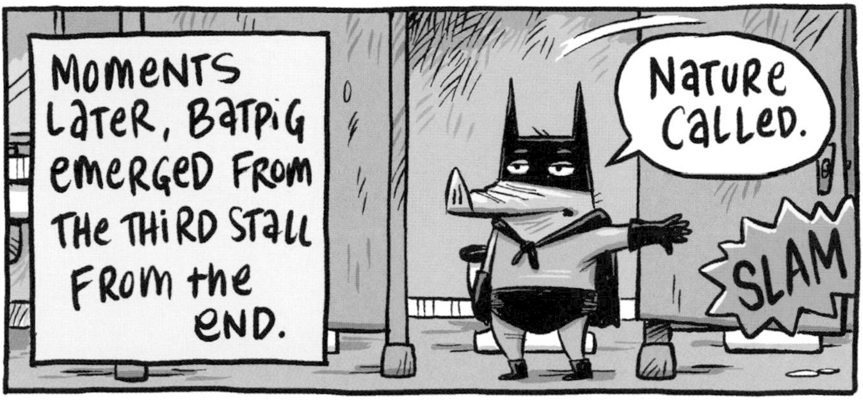
Moments later, Batpig emerged from the third stall from the end.
Nature called.
SLAM

He launched himself up the clock tower stairs.

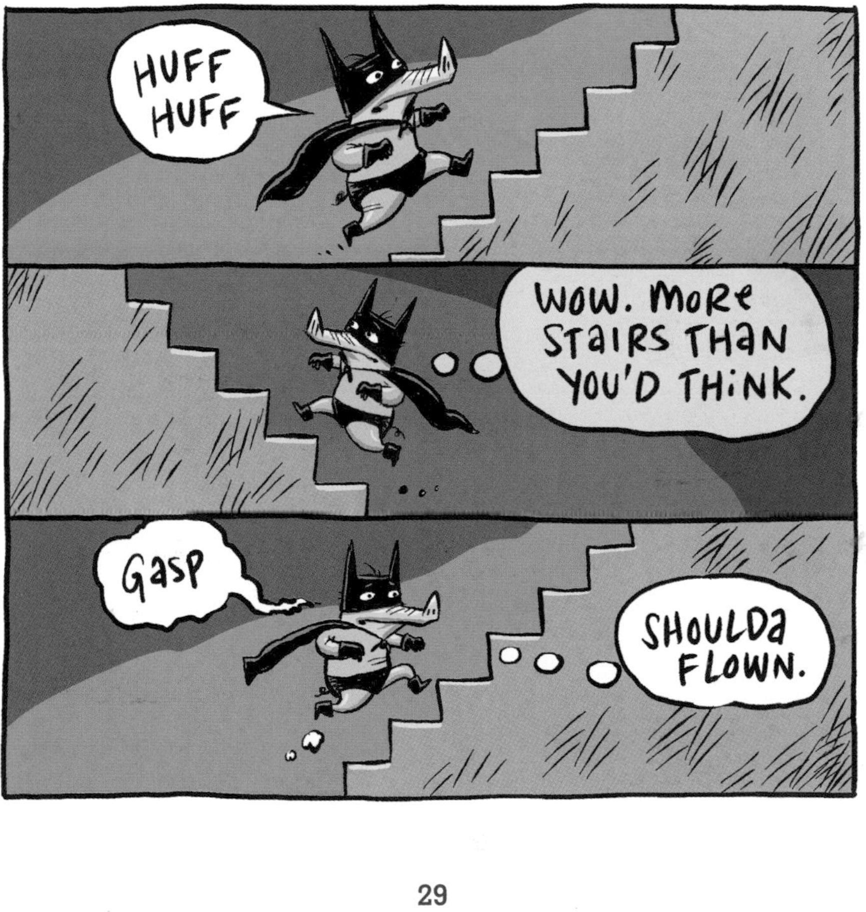
HUFF HUFF
Wow. More stairs than you'd think.
Gasp
Shoulda flown.

FINALLY (VERY WINDED), HE
REACHED THE TOP OF THE TOWER.

WHOA.

THERE WAS DAMAGE FROM THE LIGHTNING
AND FIRE EVERYWHERE. EVERYTHING
SMELLED LIKE SMOKE.

WOW. THIS PLACE
REALLY GOT ZAPPED.

JUST THEN, HE HEARD
A RUSTLING FROM
THE CORNER.

HELLO?

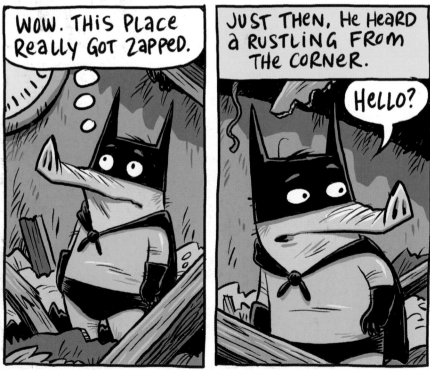

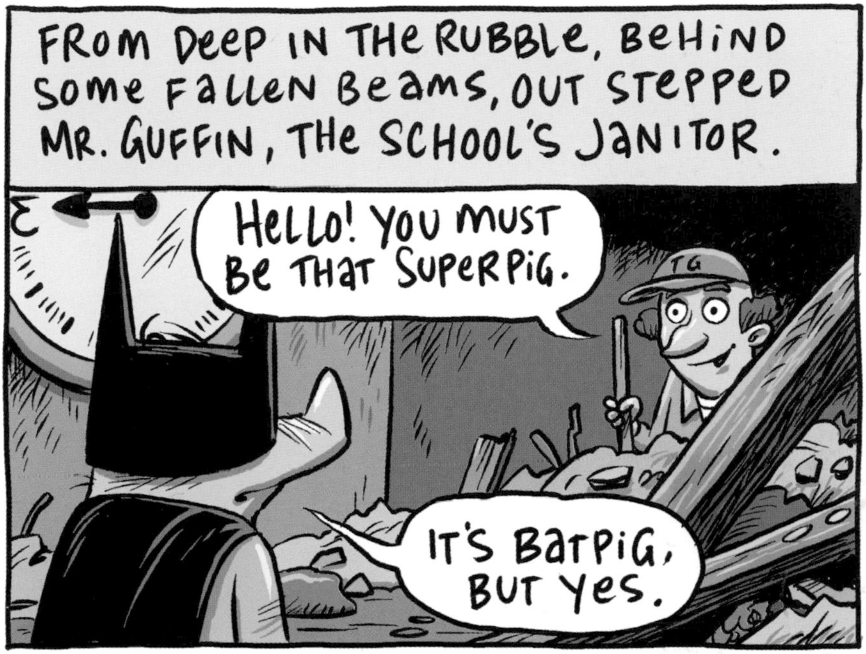
FROM DEEP IN THE RUBBLE, BEHIND SOME FALLEN BEAMS, OUT STEPPED MR. GUFFIN, THE SCHOOL'S JANITOR.
HELLO! YOU MUST BE THAT SUPERPIG.
IT'S BATPIG, BUT YES.

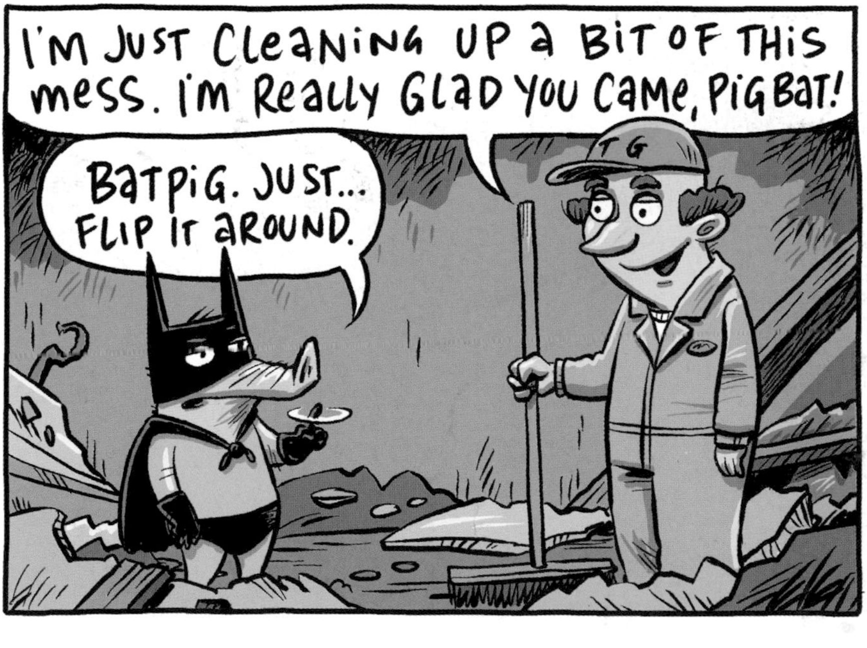
I'M JUST CLEANING UP A BIT OF THIS MESS. I'M REALLY GLAD YOU CAME, PIGBAT!
BATPIG. JUST... FLIP IT AROUND.

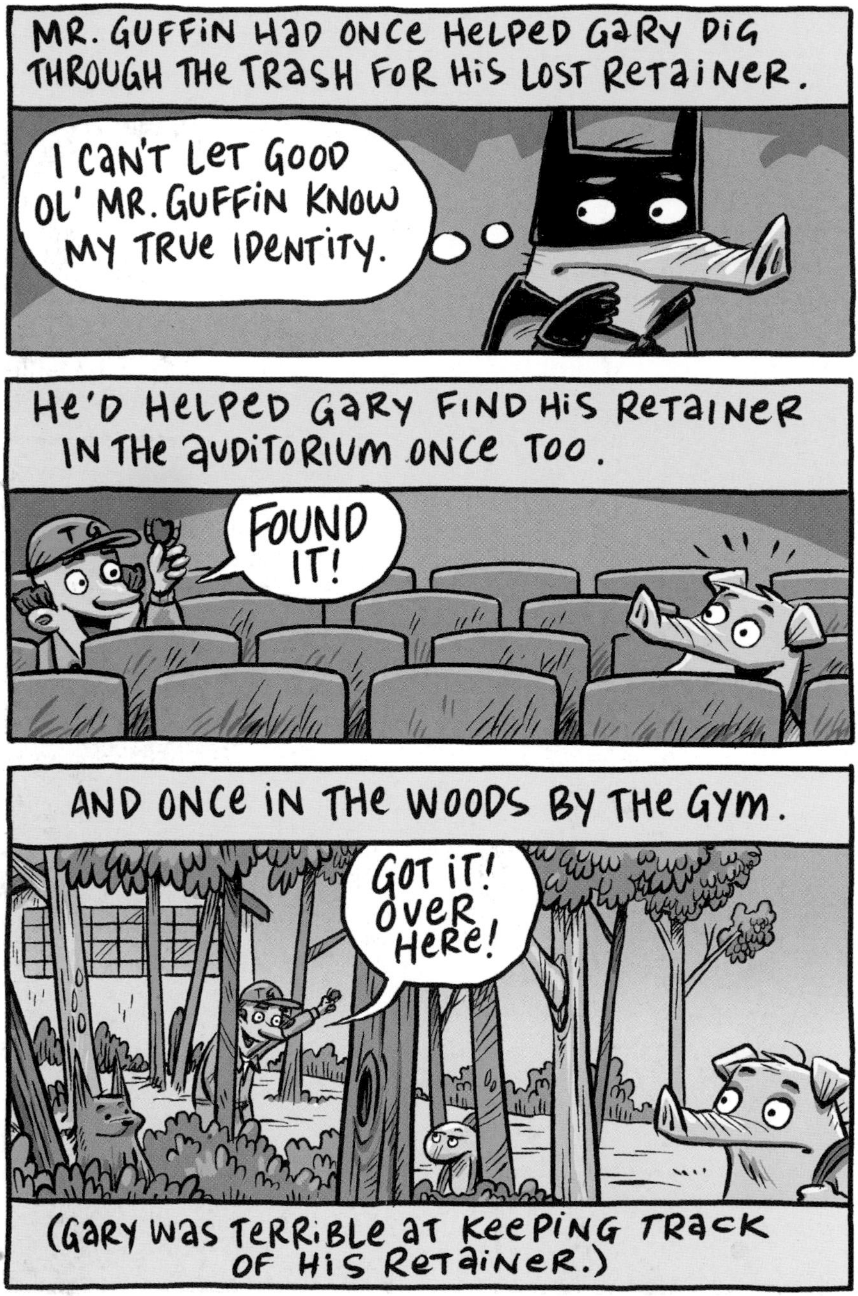
MR. GUFFIN HAD ONCE HELPED GARY DIG THROUGH THE TRASH FOR HIS LOST RETAINER.
I CAN'T LET GOOD OL' MR. GUFFIN KNOW MY TRUE IDENTITY.
HE'D HELPED GARY FIND HIS RETAINER IN THE AUDITORIUM ONCE TOO.
FOUND IT!
AND ONCE IN THE WOODS BY THE GYM.
GOT IT! OVER HERE!
(GARY WAS TERRIBLE AT KEEPING TRACK OF HIS RETAINER.)

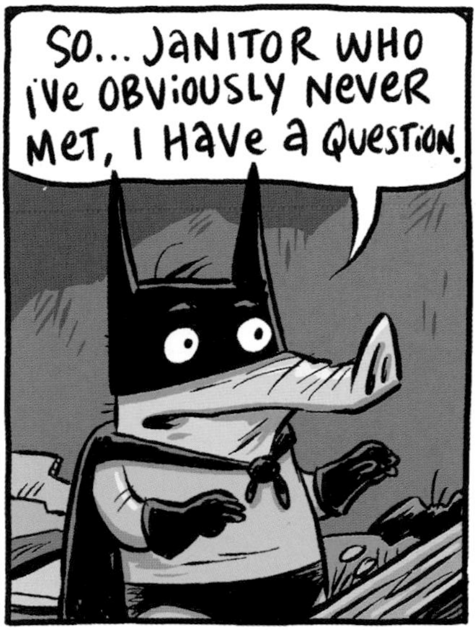
SO... JANITOR WHO I'VE OBVIOUSLY NEVER MET, I HAVE A QUESTION.

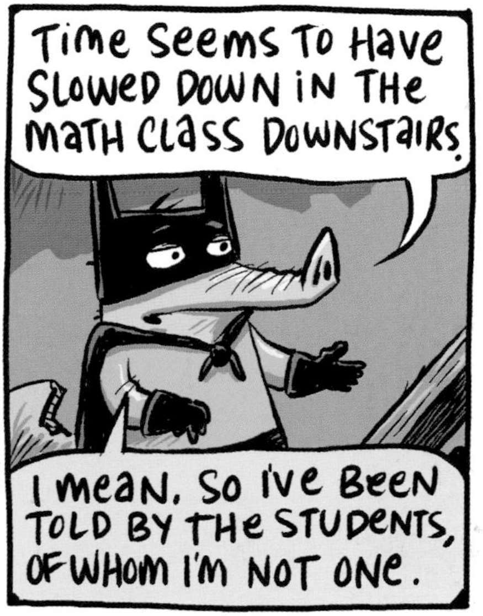
TIME SEEMS TO HAVE SLOWED DOWN IN THE MATH CLASS DOWNSTAIRS.
I MEAN, SO I'VE BEEN TOLD BY THE STUDENTS, OF WHOM I'M NOT ONE.

HE EXPLAINED THE WHOLE THING WHILE MR. GUFFIN NODDED.

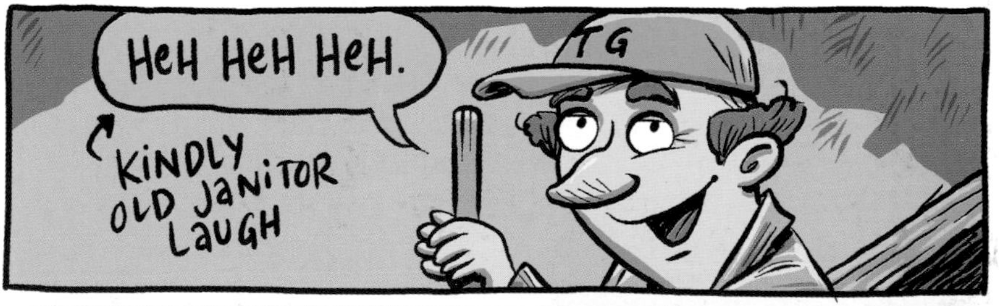
HEH HEH HEH.
KINDLY OLD JANITOR LAUGH
TG

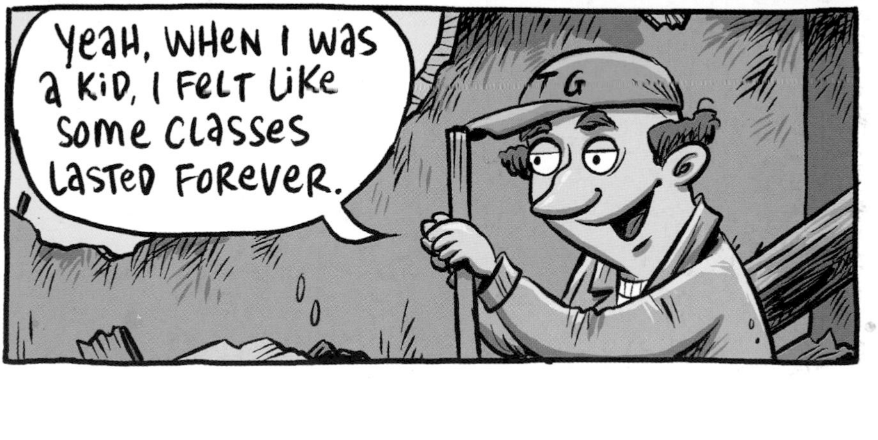
YEAH, WHEN I WAS A KID, I FELT LIKE SOME CLASSES LASTED FOREVER.
TG

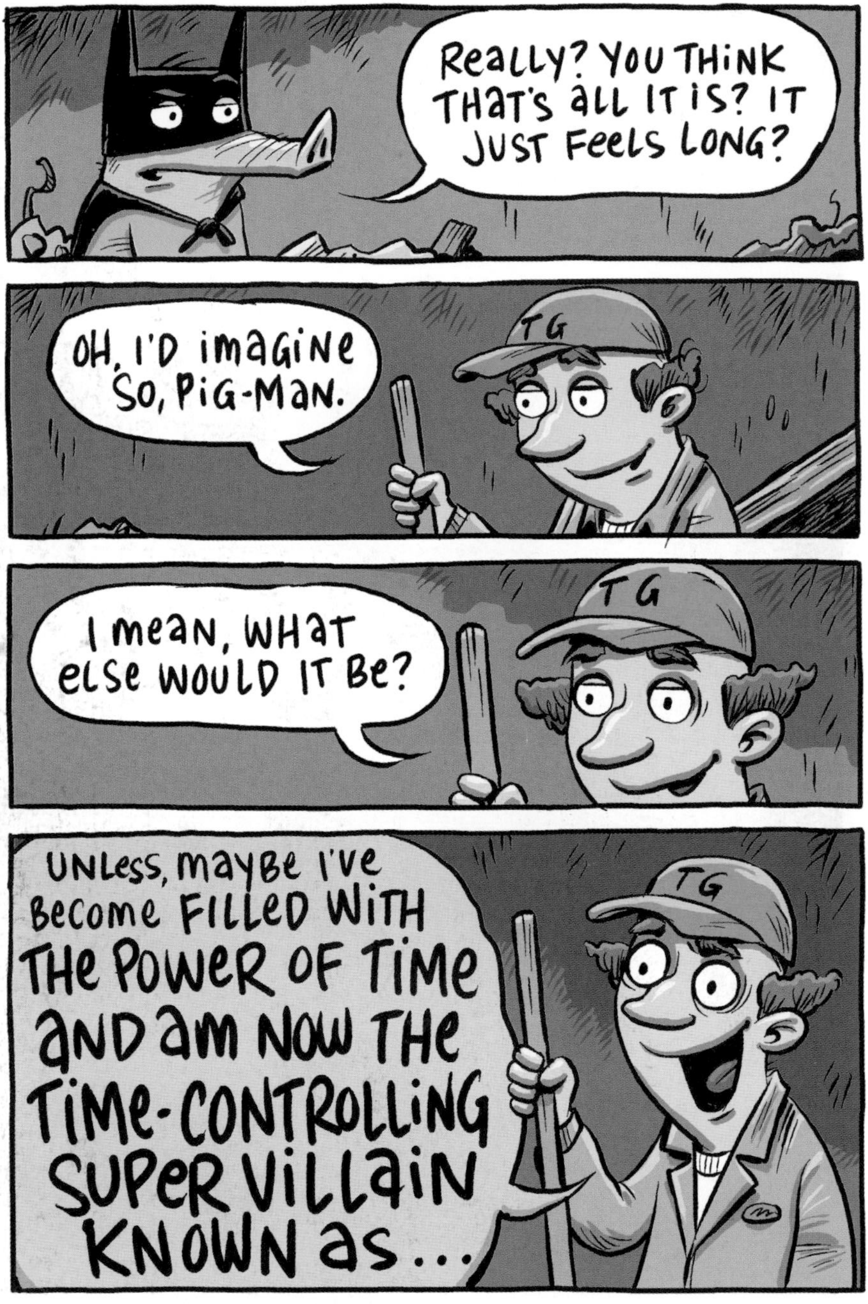
REALLY? YOU THINK THAT'S ALL IT IS? IT JUST FEELS LONG?
OH, I'D IMAGINE SO, PIG-MAN.
TG
I MEAN, WHAT ELSE WOULD IT BE?
TG
UNLESS, MAYBE I'VE BECOME FILLED WITH THE POWER OF TIME AND AM NOW THE TIME-CONTROLLING SUPER VILLAIN KNOWN AS...
TG

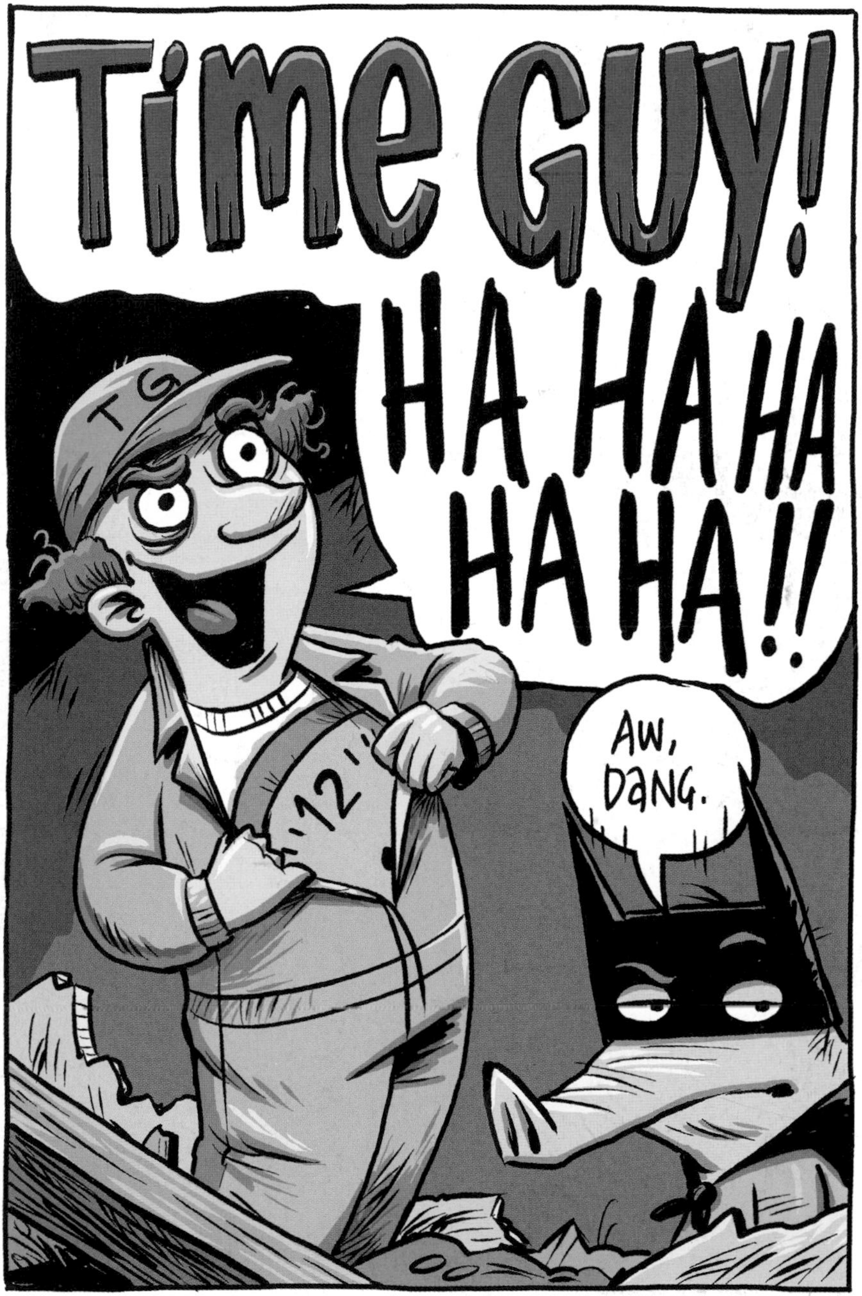
TIME GUY!
HA HA HA HA
HA HA!!
AW, DANG.

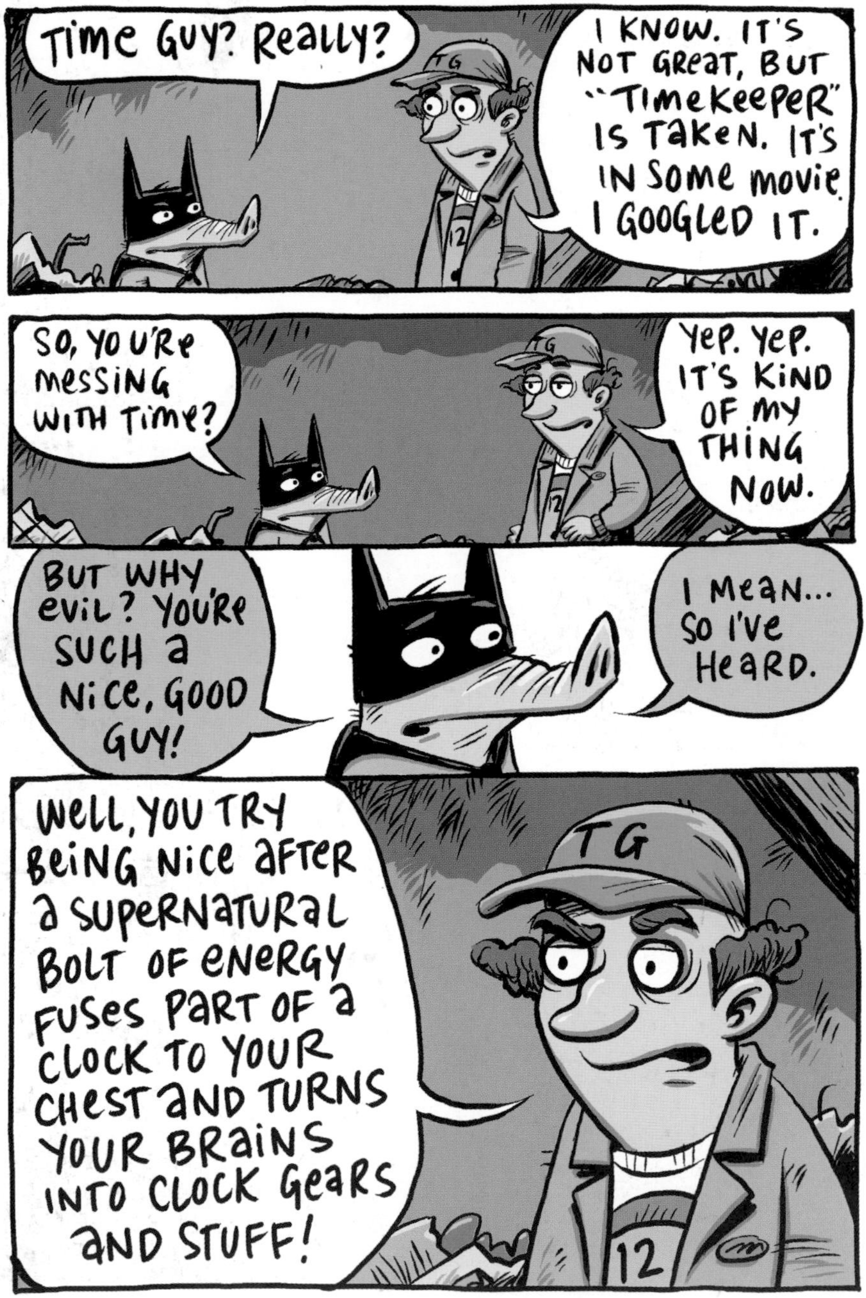
TIME GUY? REALLY?
I KNOW. IT'S NOT GREAT, BUT "TIMEKEEPER" IS TAKEN. IT'S IN SOME MOVIE. I GOOGLED IT.
TG
12
SO, YOU'RE MESSING WITH TIME?
YEP. YEP. IT'S KIND OF MY THING NOW.
BUT WHY EVIL? YOU'RE SUCH A NICE, GOOD GUY!
I MEAN... SO I'VE HEARD.
WELL, YOU TRY BEING NICE AFTER A SUPERNATURAL BOLT OF ENERGY FUSES PART OF A CLOCK TO YOUR CHEST AND TURNS YOUR BRAINS INTO CLOCK GEARS AND STUFF!

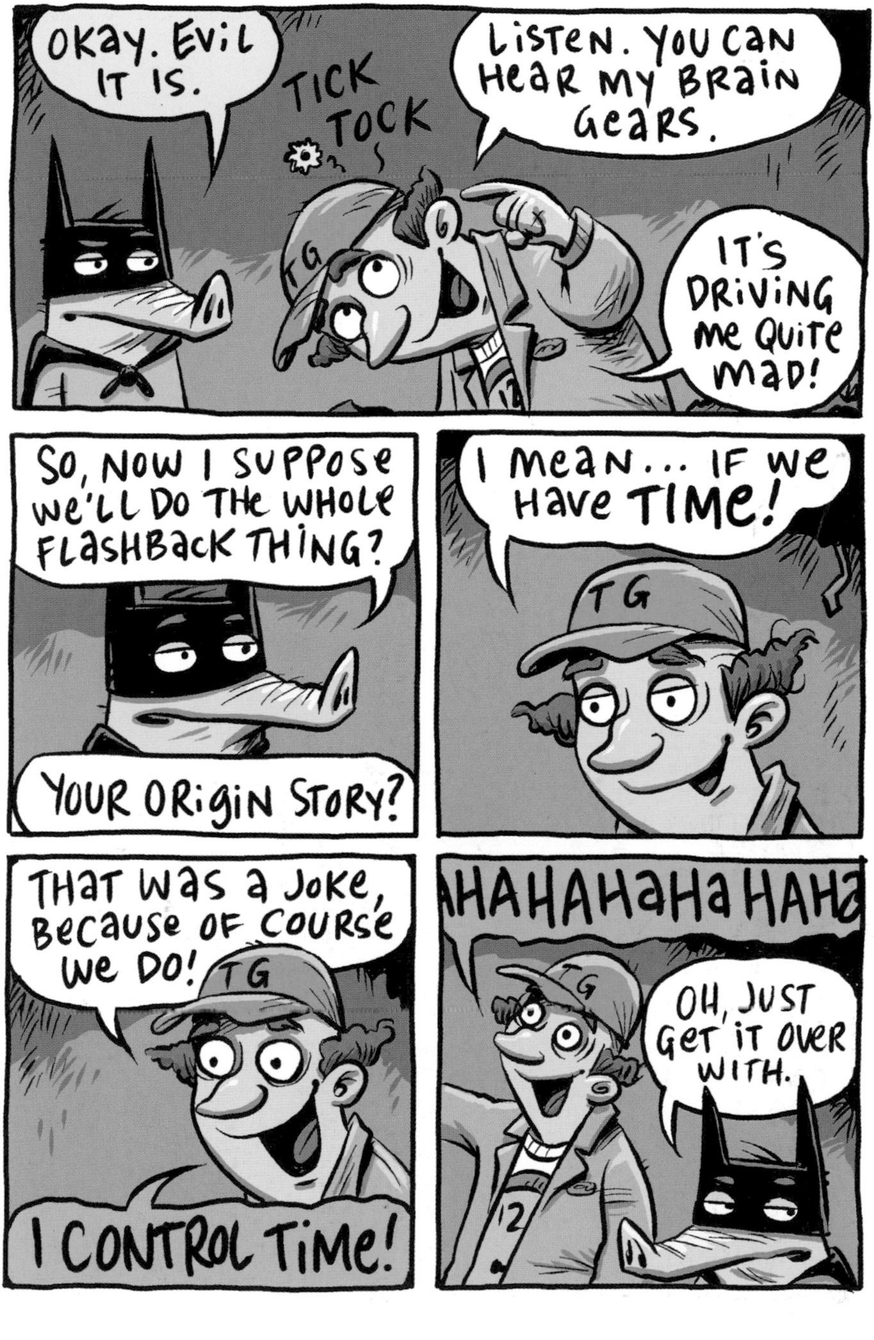
OKAY. EVIL IT IS.
TICK TOCK
LISTEN. YOU CAN HEAR MY BRAIN GEARS.
IT'S DRIVING ME QUITE MAD!
SO, NOW I SUPPOSE WE'LL DO THE WHOLE FLASHBACK THING?
YOUR ORIGIN STORY?
I MEAN... IF WE HAVE TIME!
THAT WAS A JOKE, BECAUSE OF COURSE WE DO!
I CONTROL TIME!
AHAHAHAHAHAHAHA
OH, JUST GET IT OVER WITH.

CHAPTER FOUR

"TIME ZAP"

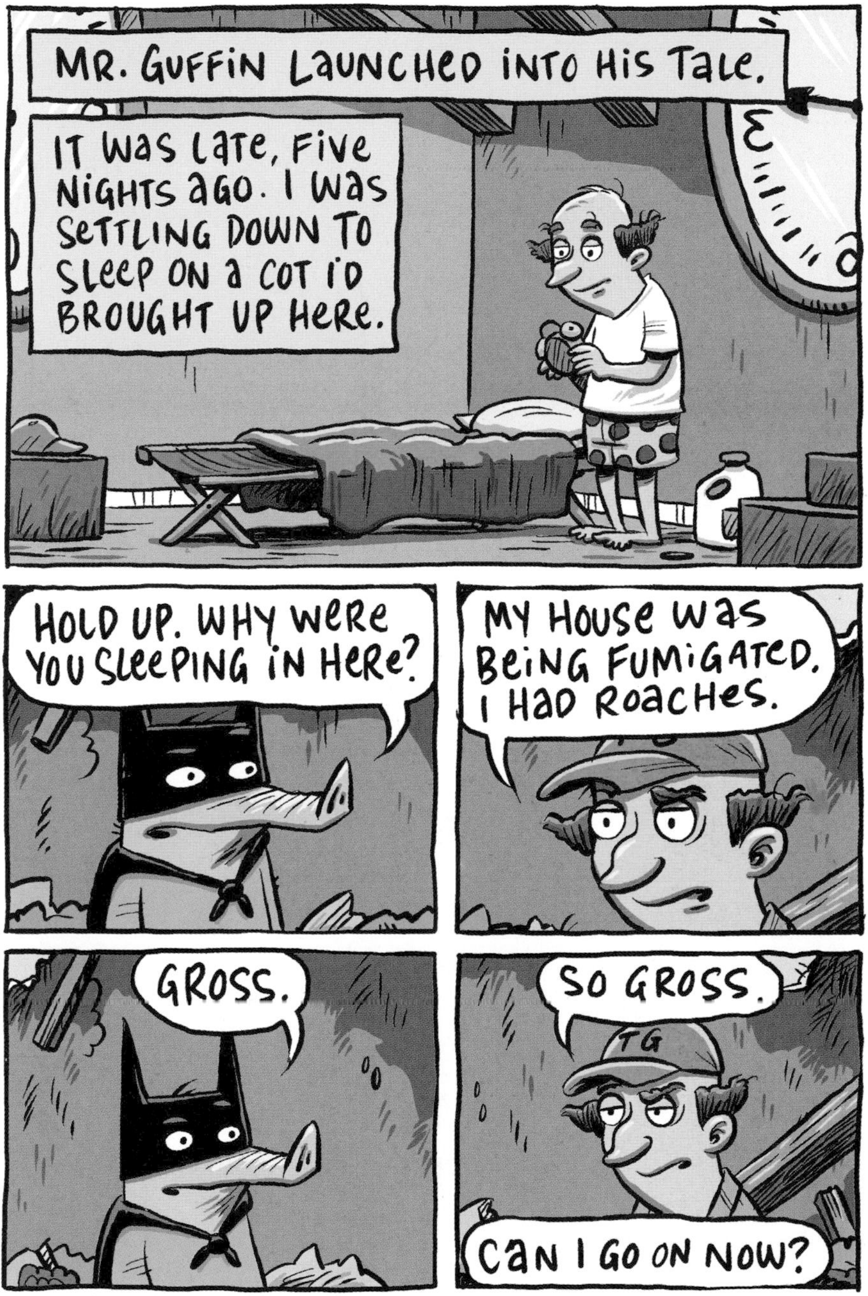
MR. GUFFIN LAUNCHED INTO HIS TALE.
IT WAS LATE, FIVE NIGHTS AGO. I WAS SETTLING DOWN TO SLEEP ON A COT I'D BROUGHT UP HERE.
HOLD UP. WHY WERE YOU SLEEPING IN HERE?
MY HOUSE WAS BEING FUMIGATED. I HAD ROACHES.
GROSS.
SO GROSS.
TG
CAN I GO ON NOW?

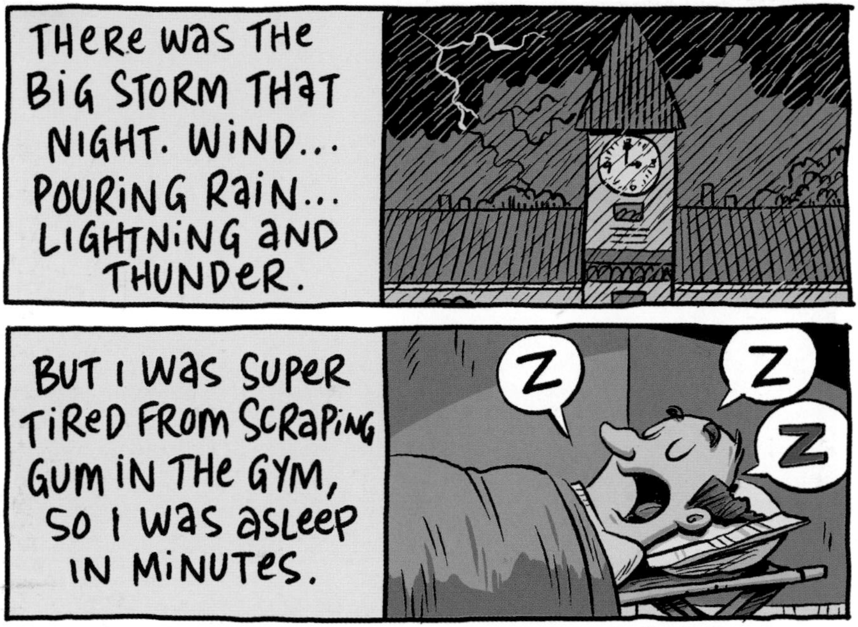
THERE WAS THE BIG STORM THAT NIGHT. WIND... POURING RAIN... LIGHTNING AND THUNDER.
BUT I WAS SUPER TIRED FROM SCRAPING GUM IN THE GYM, SO I WAS ASLEEP IN MINUTES.
Z
Z
Z

I WAS DEEP IN THE MIDDLE OF A DREAM WHERE I INVENTED AN ALL-PURPOSE BATHROOM GRAFFITI REMOVER WHEN...

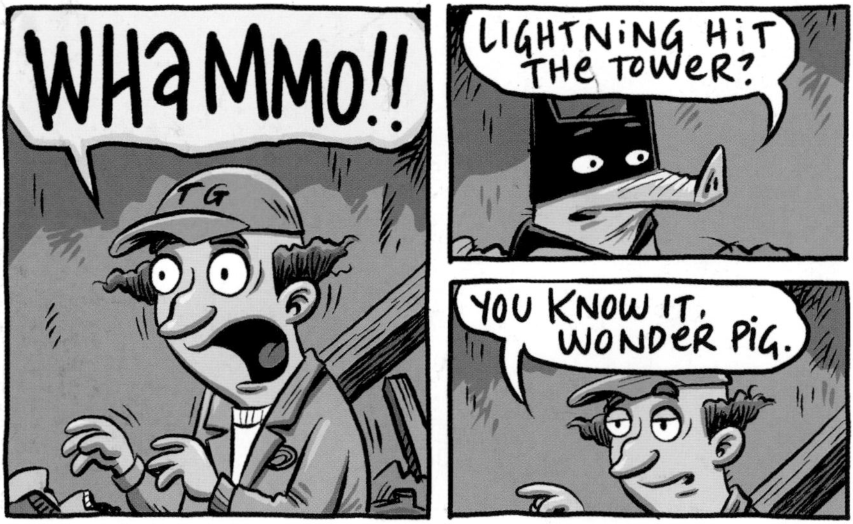
WHAMMO!!
TG
LIGHTNING HIT THE TOWER?
YOU KNOW IT, WONDER PIG.

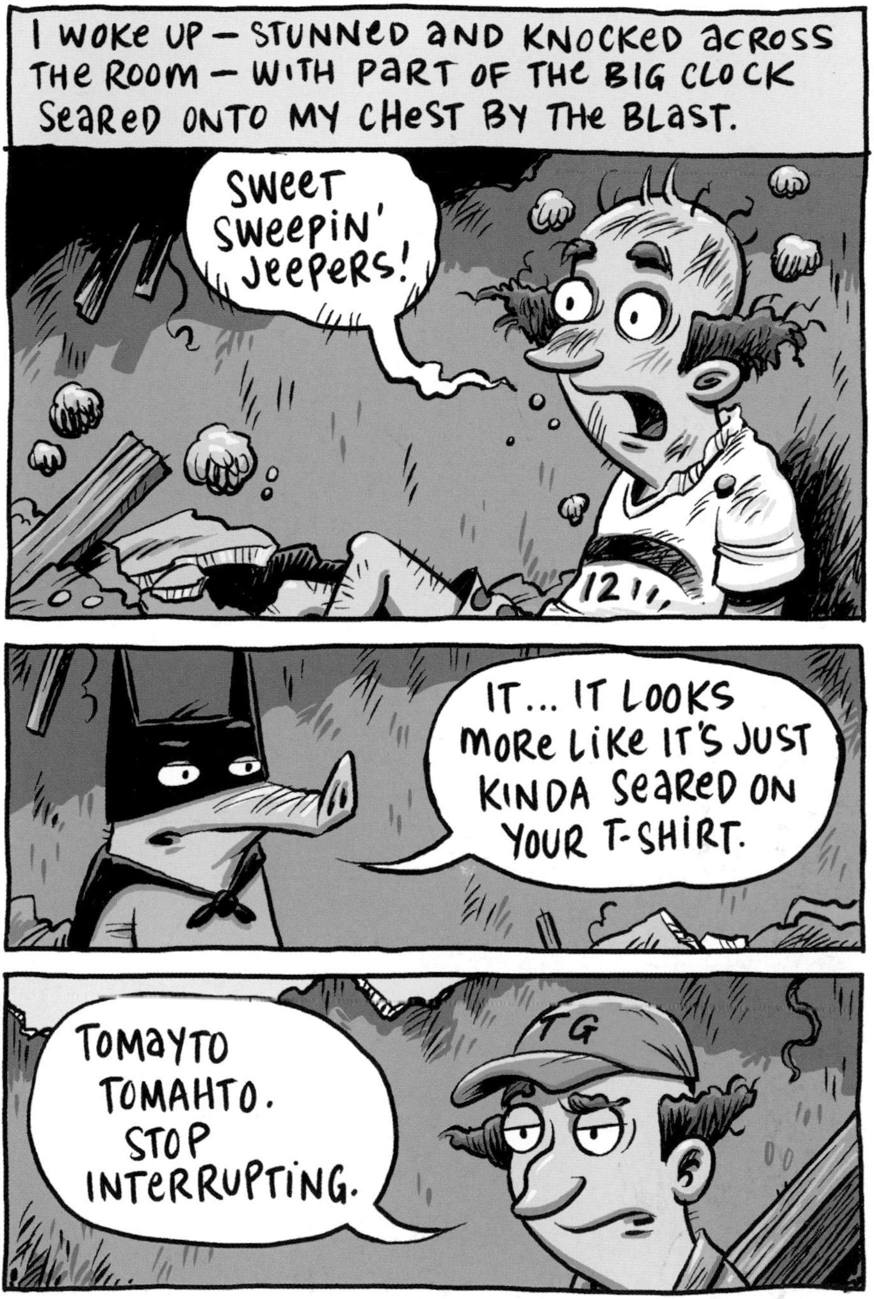
I WOKE UP — STUNNED AND KNOCKED ACROSS THE ROOM — WITH PART OF THE BIG CLOCK SEARED ONTO MY CHEST BY THE BLAST.
SWEET SWEEPIN' JEEPERS!
12
IT... IT LOOKS MORE LIKE IT'S JUST KINDA SEARED ON YOUR T-SHIRT.
TOMAYTO TOMAHTO. STOP INTERRUPTING.
TG

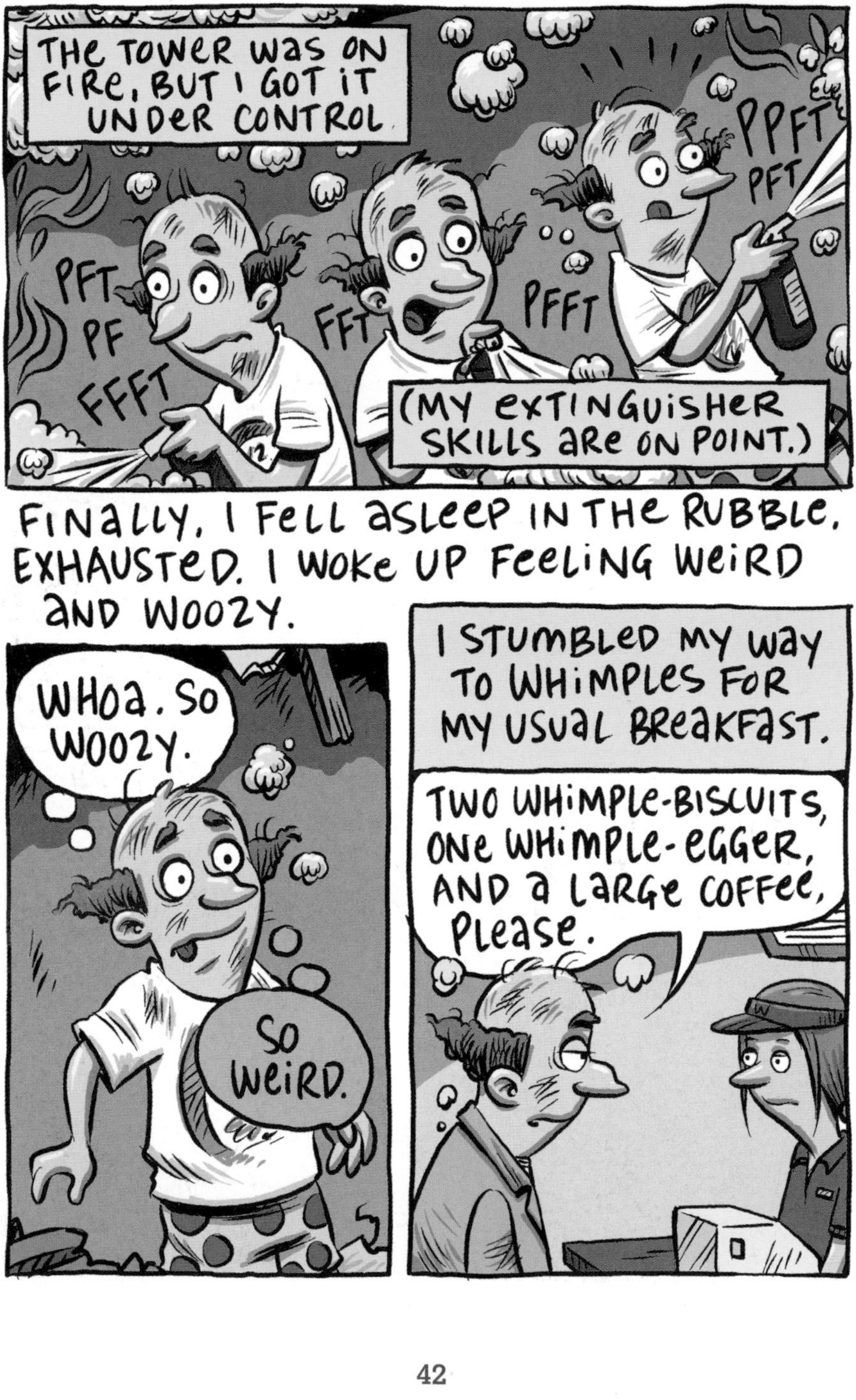
THE TOWER WAS ON FIRE, BUT I GOT IT UNDER CONTROL.
PFT PF FFFT
FFT
PFFT
PPFT PFT
(MY EXTINGUISHER SKILLS ARE ON POINT.)
FINALLY, I FELL ASLEEP IN THE RUBBLE, EXHAUSTED. I WOKE UP FEELING WEIRD AND WOOZY.
WHOA. SO WOOZY.
SO WEIRD.
I STUMBLED MY WAY TO WHIMPLES FOR MY USUAL BREAKFAST.
TWO WHIMPLE-BISCUITS, ONE WHIMPLE-EGGER, AND A LARGE COFFEE, PLEASE.

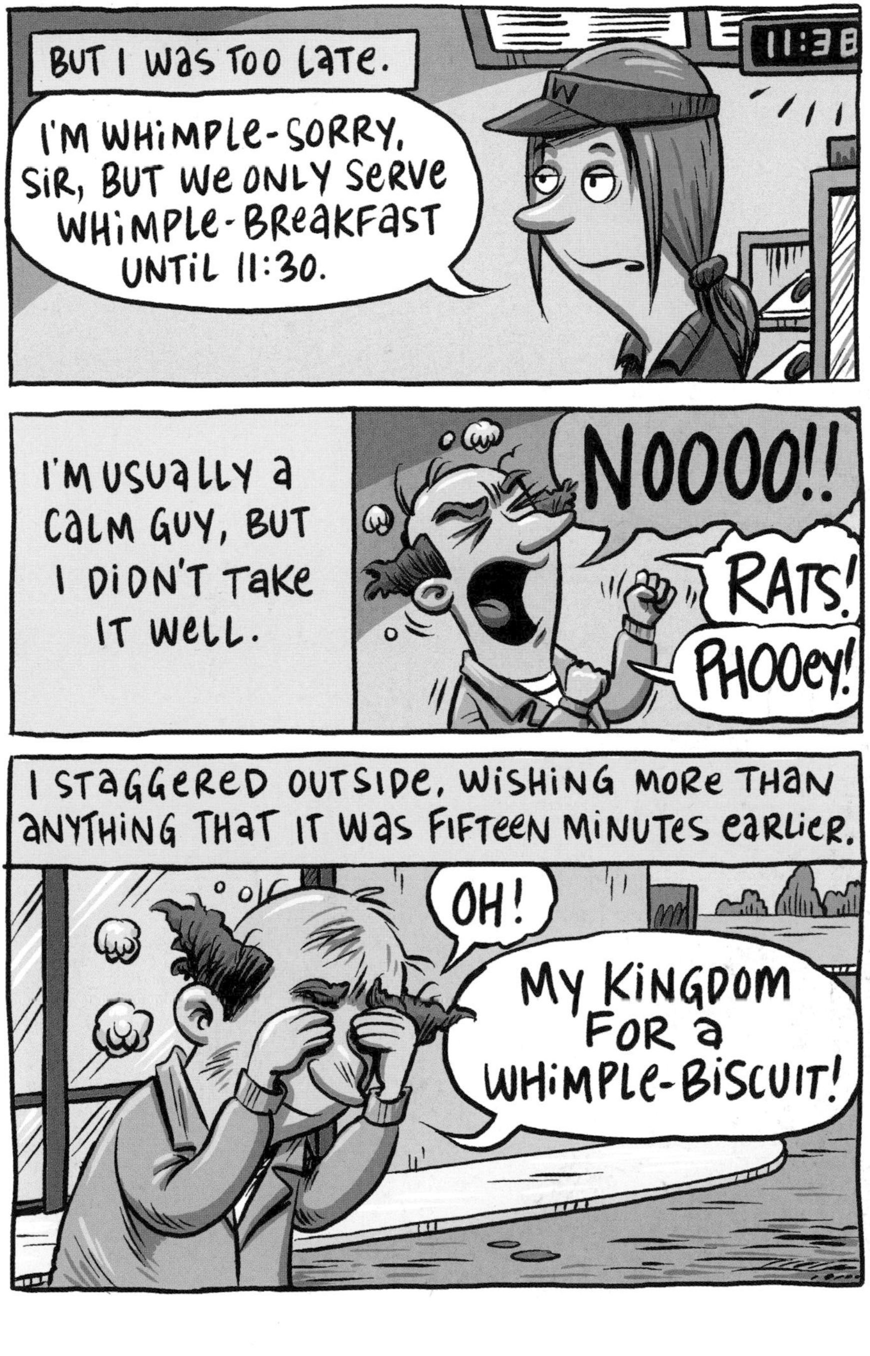
BUT I WAS TOO LATE.
I'M WHIMPLE-SORRY, SIR, BUT WE ONLY SERVE WHIMPLE-BREAKFAST UNTIL 11:30.
I'M USUALLY A CALM GUY, BUT I DIDN'T TAKE IT WELL.
NOOOO!!
RATS!
PHOOEY!
I STAGGERED OUTSIDE, WISHING MORE THAN ANYTHING THAT IT WAS FIFTEEN MINUTES EARLIER.
OH!
MY KINGDOM FOR A WHIMPLE-BISCUIT!

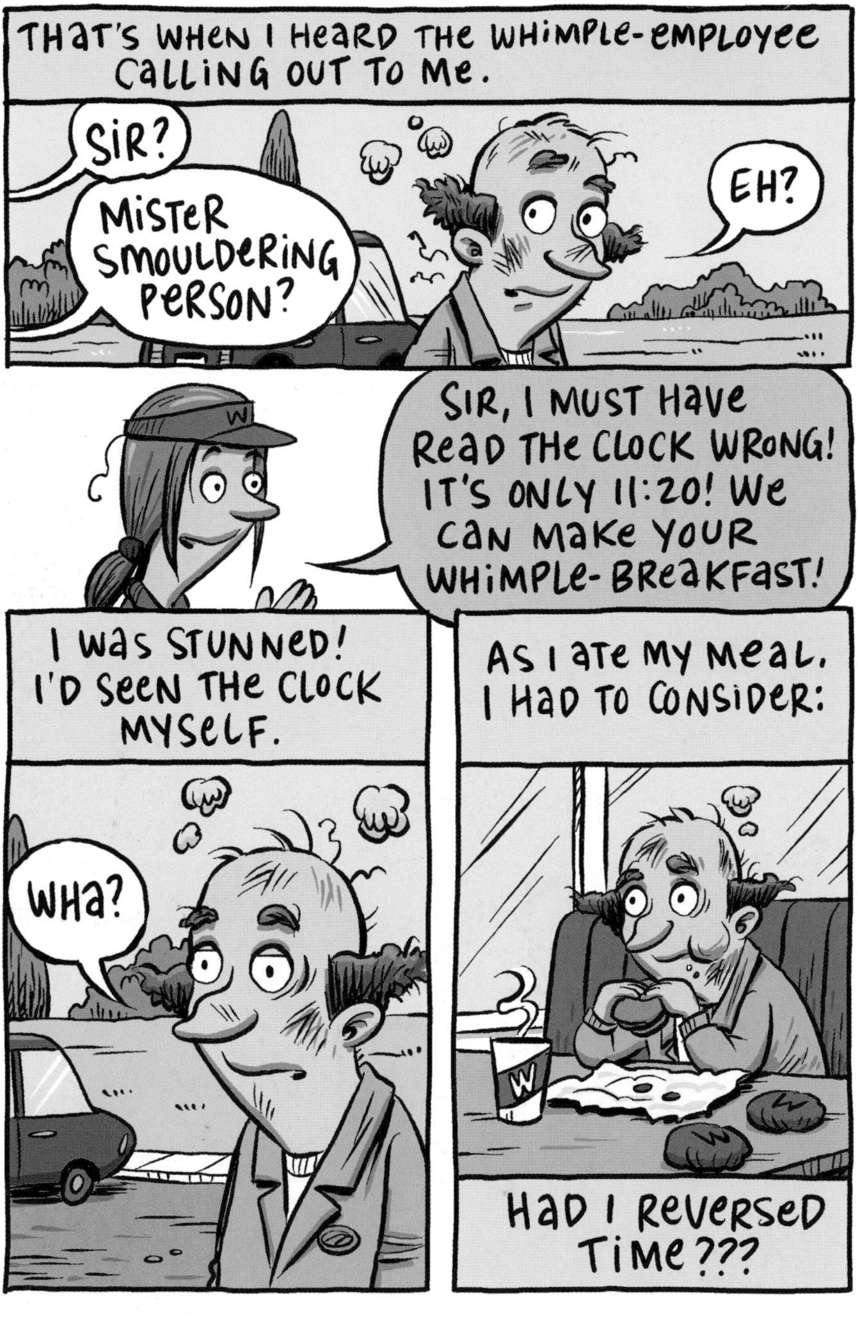
THAT'S WHEN I HEARD THE WHIMPLE-EMPLOYEE CALLING OUT TO ME.
SIR?
MISTER SMOULDERING PERSON?
EH?
SIR, I MUST HAVE READ THE CLOCK WRONG! IT'S ONLY 11:20! WE CAN MAKE YOUR WHIMPLE-BREAKFAST!
I WAS STUNNED! I'D SEEN THE CLOCK MYSELF.
WHA?
AS I ATE MY MEAL, I HAD TO CONSIDER:
HAD I REVERSED TIME???

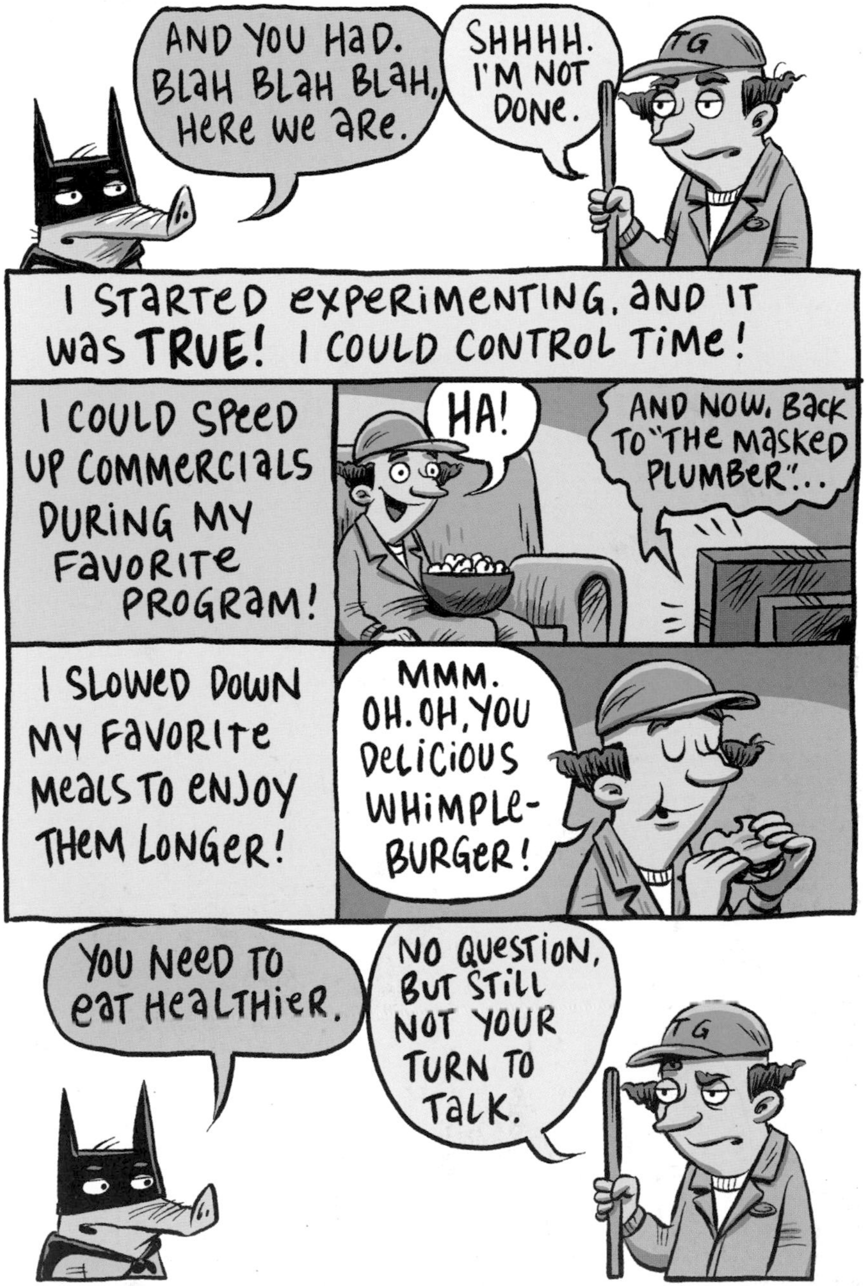
AND YOU HAD. BLAH BLAH BLAH, HERE WE ARE.
SHHHH. I'M NOT DONE.
I STARTED EXPERIMENTING. AND IT WAS TRUE! I COULD CONTROL TIME!
I COULD SPEED UP COMMERCIALS DURING MY FAVORITE PROGRAM!
HA!
AND NOW, BACK TO "THE MASKED PLUMBER"...
I SLOWED DOWN MY FAVORITE MEALS TO ENJOY THEM LONGER!
MMM. OH. OH, YOU DELICIOUS WHIMPLE-BURGER!
YOU NEED TO EAT HEALTHIER.
NO QUESTION, BUT STILL NOT YOUR TURN TO TALK.

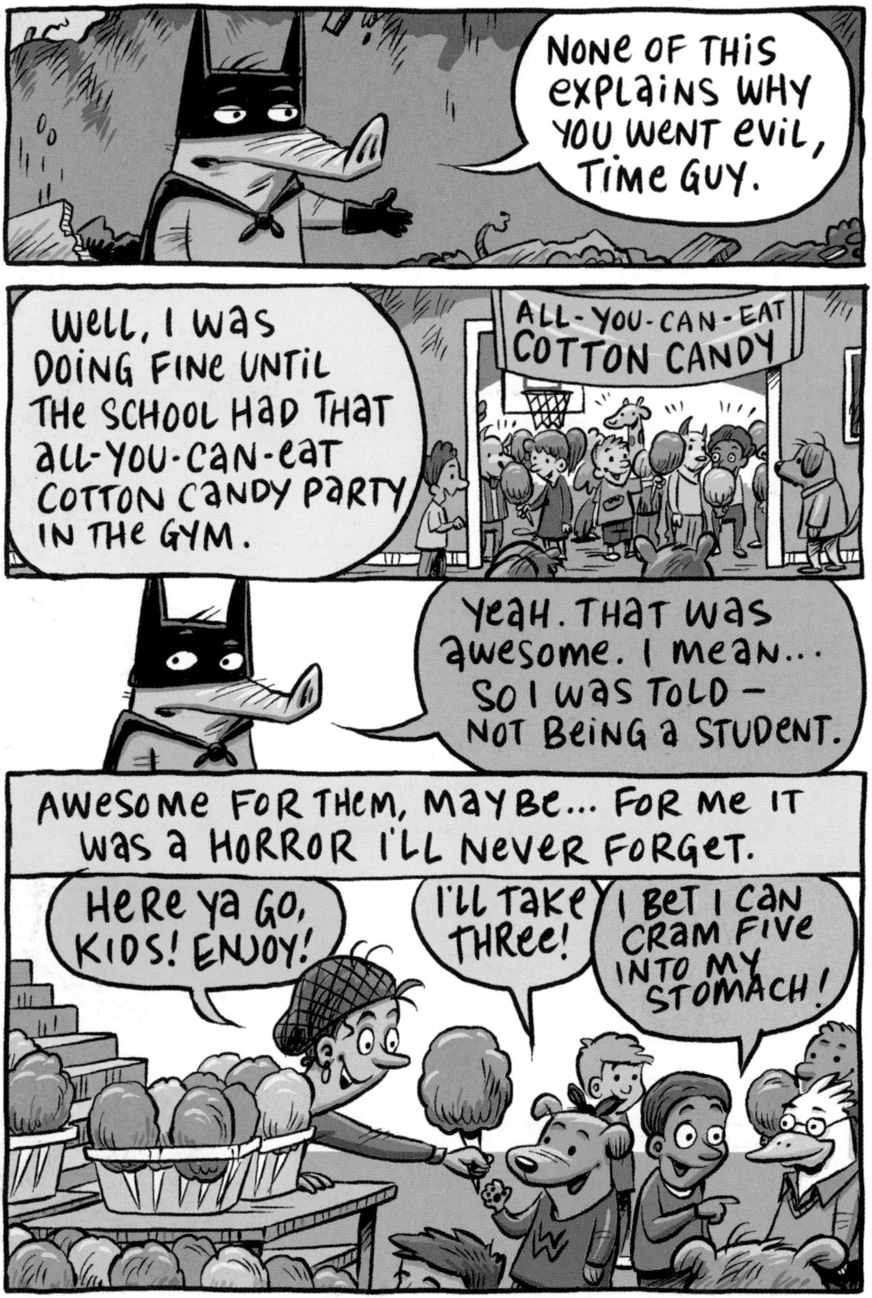
None of this explains why you went evil, Time Guy.
Well, I was doing fine until the school had that all-you-can-eat cotton candy party in the gym.
ALL-YOU-CAN-EAT COTTON CANDY
Yeah. That was awesome. I mean... So I was told — not being a student.
Awesome for them, maybe... For me it was a horror I'll never forget.
Here ya go, kids! Enjoy!
I'll take three!
I bet I can cram five into my stomach!

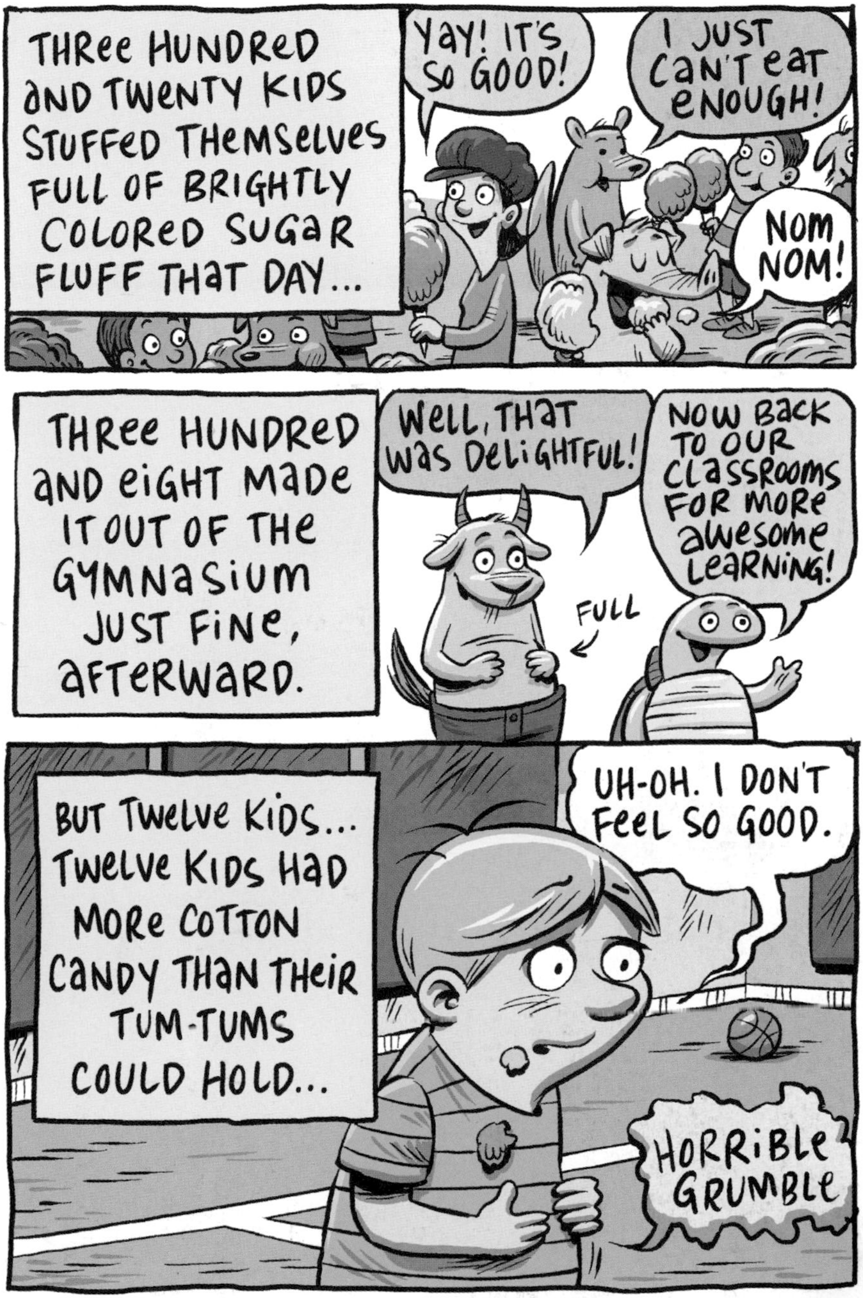
THREE HUNDRED AND TWENTY KIDS STUFFED THEMSELVES FULL OF BRIGHTLY COLORED SUGAR FLUFF THAT DAY...
YAY! IT'S SO GOOD!
I JUST CAN'T EAT ENOUGH!
NOM NOM!
THREE HUNDRED AND EIGHT MADE IT OUT OF THE GYMNASIUM JUST FINE, AFTERWARD.
WELL, THAT WAS DELIGHTFUL!
NOW BACK TO OUR CLASSROOMS FOR MORE AWESOME LEARNING!
FULL
BUT TWELVE KIDS... TWELVE KIDS HAD MORE COTTON CANDY THAN THEIR TUM-TUMS COULD HOLD...
UH-OH. I DON'T FEEL SO GOOD.
HORRIBLE GRUMBLE

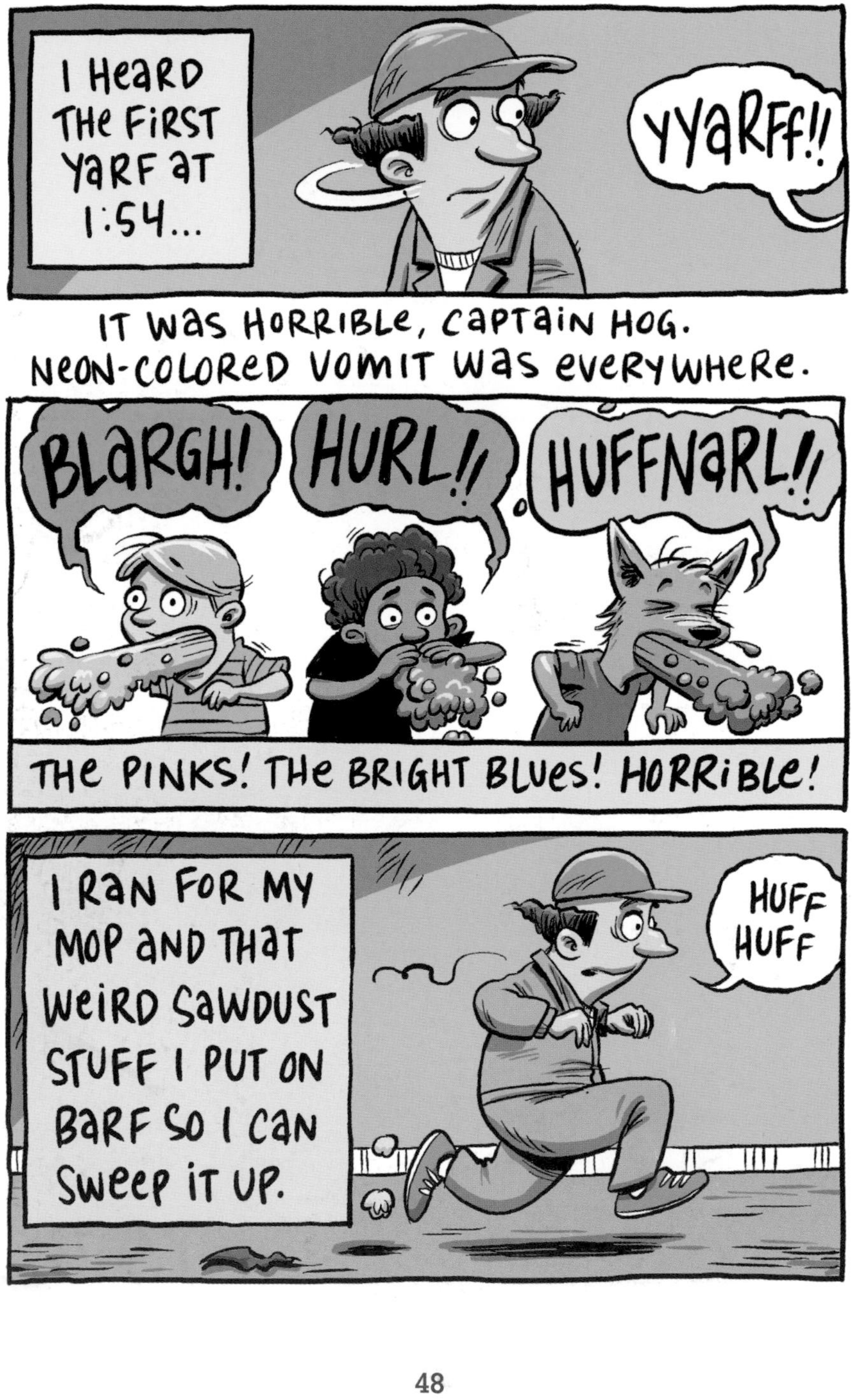
I HEARD THE FIRST YARF AT 1:54...
YYARFF!!
IT WAS HORRIBLE, CAPTAIN HOG.
NEON-COLORED VOMIT WAS EVERYWHERE.
BLARGH!
HURL!!
HUFFNARL!!
THE PINKS! THE BRIGHT BLUES! HORRIBLE!
I RAN FOR MY MOP AND THAT WEIRD SAWDUST STUFF I PUT ON BARF SO I CAN SWEEP IT UP.
HUFF HUFF

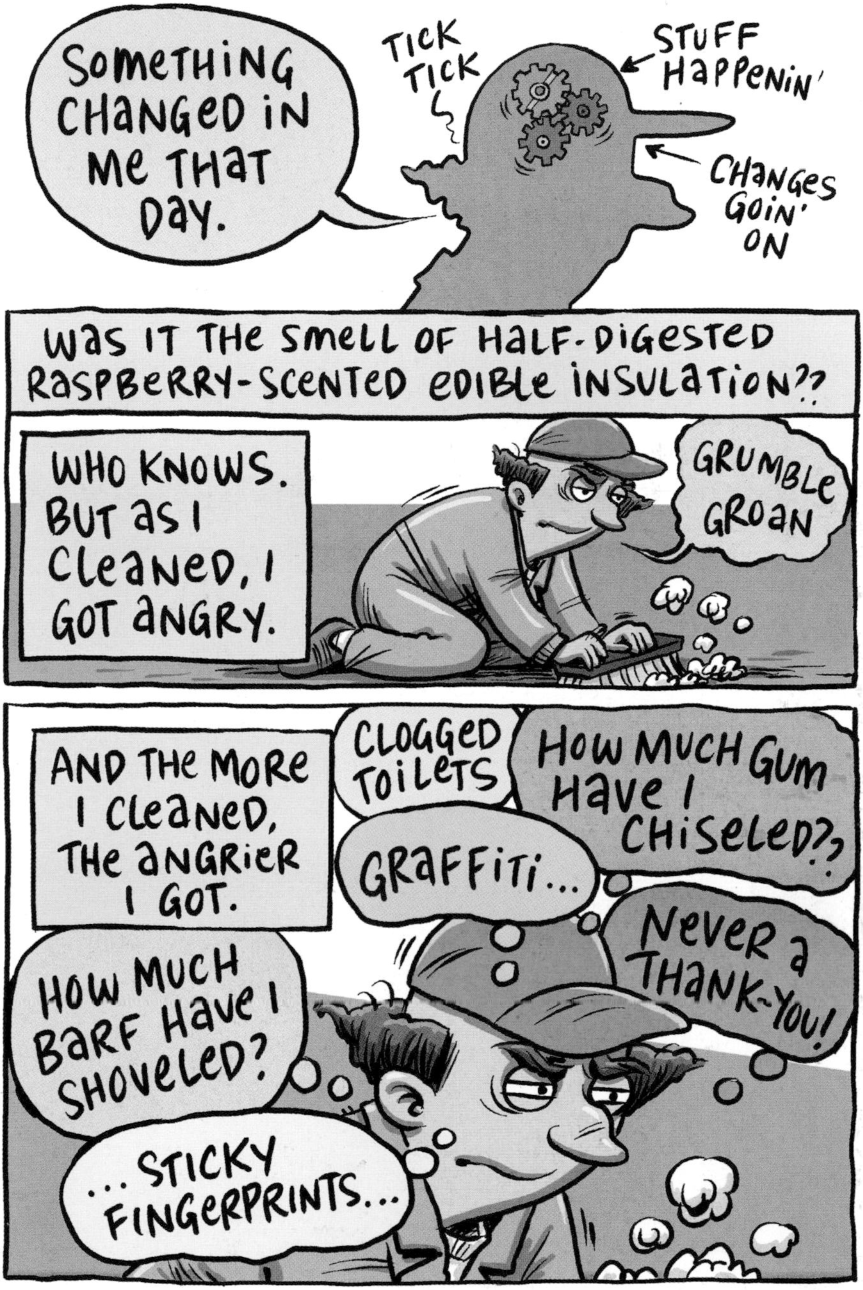
SomeTHING CHANGeD IN Me THaT Day.
TICK TICK
STUFF HaPPeNIN'
CHaNGeS GOIN' ON
Was IT THe SmeLL OF HaLF-DIGeSTeD RaSPBeRRY-SCeNTeD eDIBLe INSULaTION??
WHO KNOWS. BUT aS I CLeaNeD, I GOT aNGRY.
GRUMBLe GROaN
AND THe MORe I CLeaNeD, THe aNGRIeR I GOT.
CLOGGeD TOILeTS
HOW MUCH GUm Have I CHISeLeD??
GRaFFITI...
HOW MUCH BaRF Have I SHOVeLeD?
NeVeR a THaNK-YOU!
...STICKY FINGeRPRINTS...

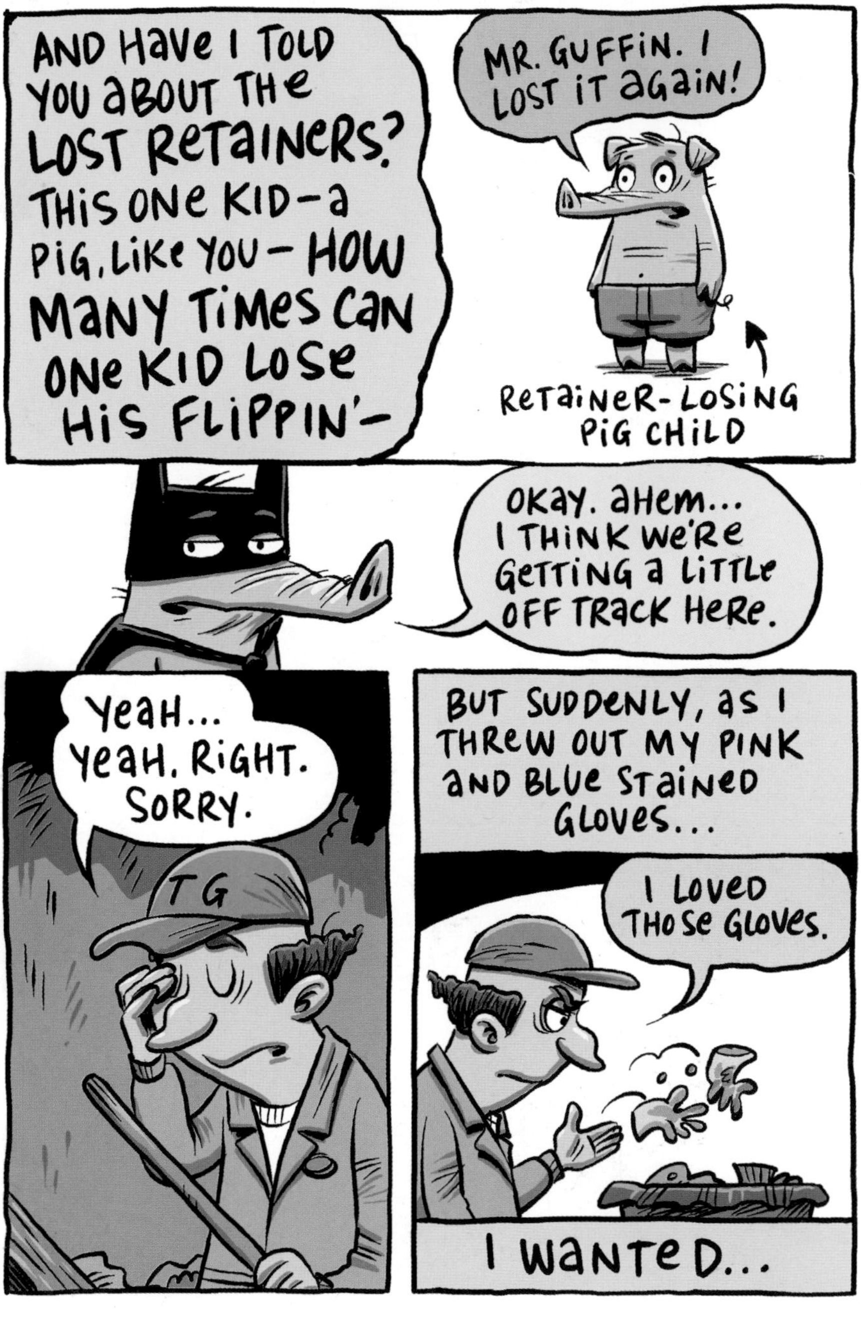
AND HAVE I TOLD YOU ABOUT THE LOST RETAINERS? THIS ONE KID—A PIG, LIKE YOU—HOW MANY TIMES CAN ONE KID LOSE HIS FLIPPIN'—
MR. GUFFIN. I LOST IT AGAIN!
RETAINER-LOSING PIG CHILD
OKAY. AHEM... I THINK WE'RE GETTING A LITTLE OFF TRACK HERE.
YEAH... YEAH. RIGHT. SORRY.
TG
BUT SUDDENLY, AS I THREW OUT MY PINK AND BLUE STAINED GLOVES...
I LOVED THOSE GLOVES.
I WANTED...

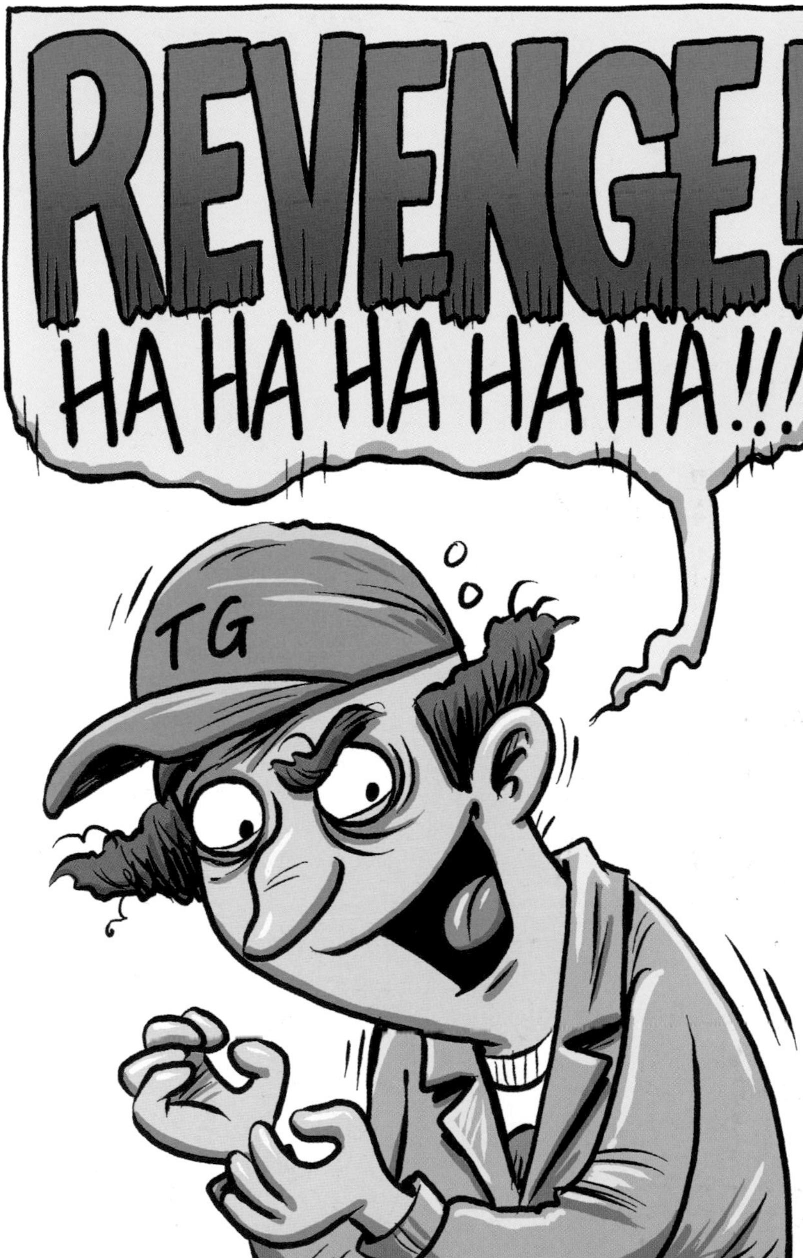
REVENGE!
HA HA HA HA HA HA!!!
TG

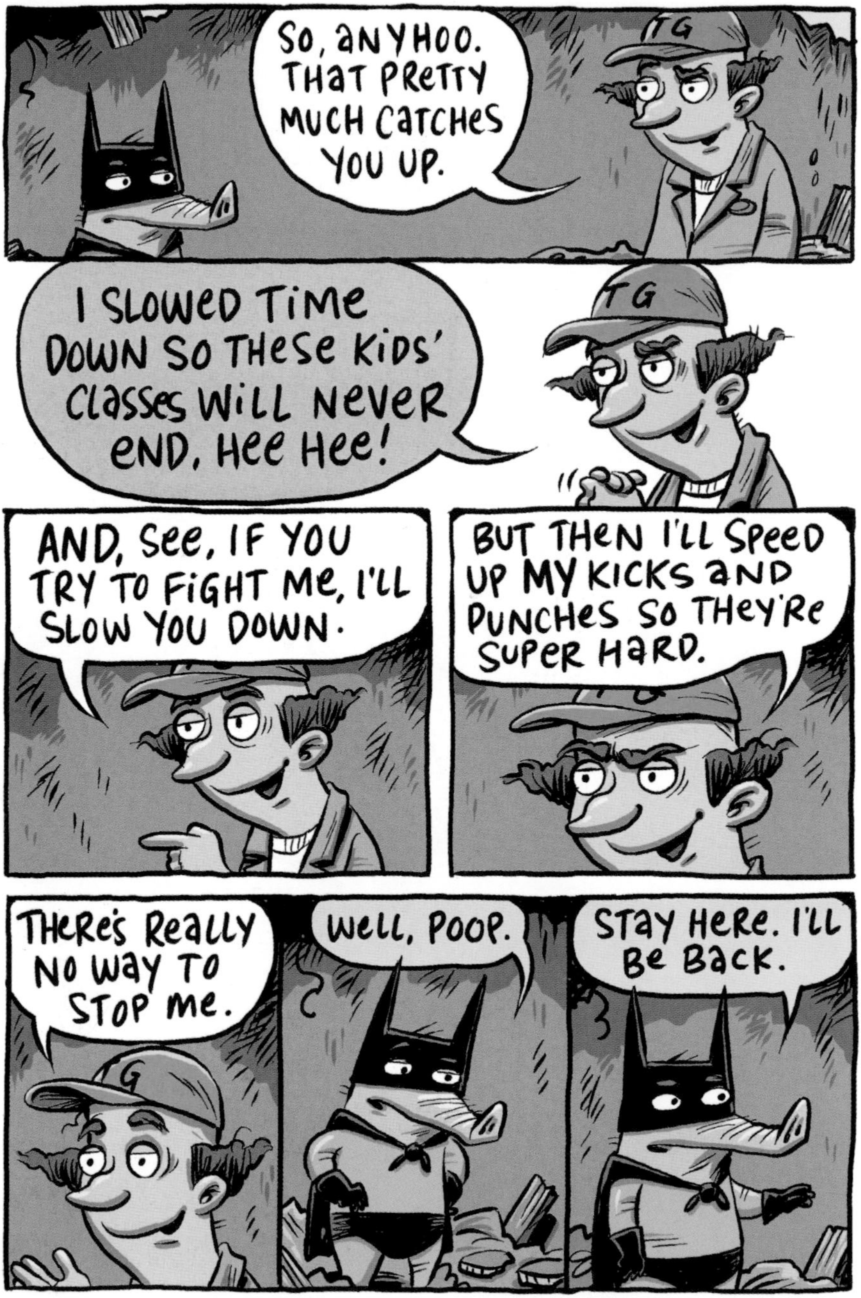
So, anyhoo. That pretty much catches you up.
I slowed time down so these kids' classes will never end, hee hee!
And, see, if you try to fight me, I'll slow you down.
But then I'll speed up my kicks and punches so they're super hard.
There's really no way to stop me.
Well, poop.
Stay here. I'll be back.

CHAPTER FIVE

"TIME TO REGROUP"

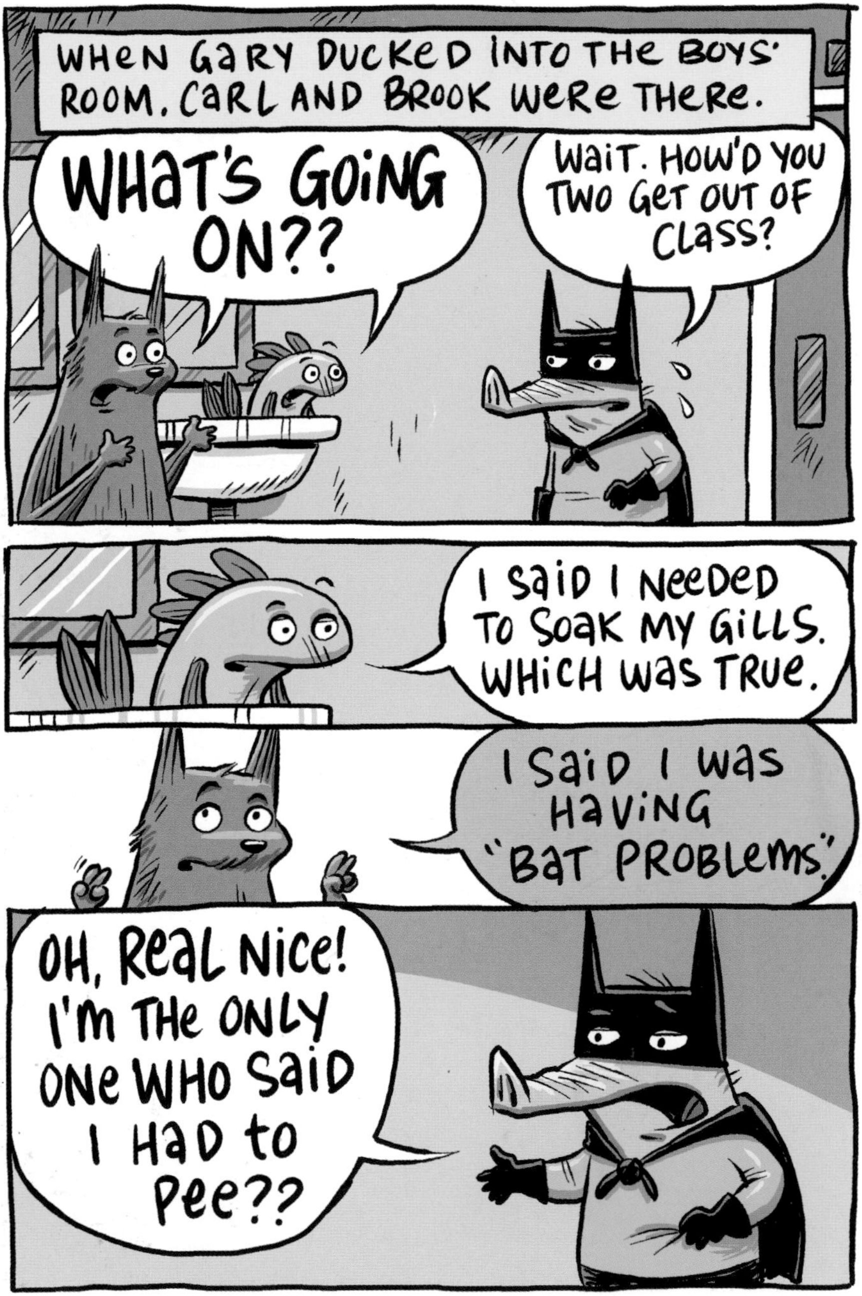
WHEN GARY DUCKED INTO THE BOYS' ROOM, CARL AND BROOK WERE THERE.
WHAT'S GOING ON??
WAIT. HOW'D YOU TWO GET OUT OF CLASS?
I SAID I NEEDED TO SOAK MY GILLS. WHICH WAS TRUE.
I SAID I WAS HAVING "BAT PROBLEMS."
OH, REAL NICE! I'M THE ONLY ONE WHO SAID I HAD TO PEE??

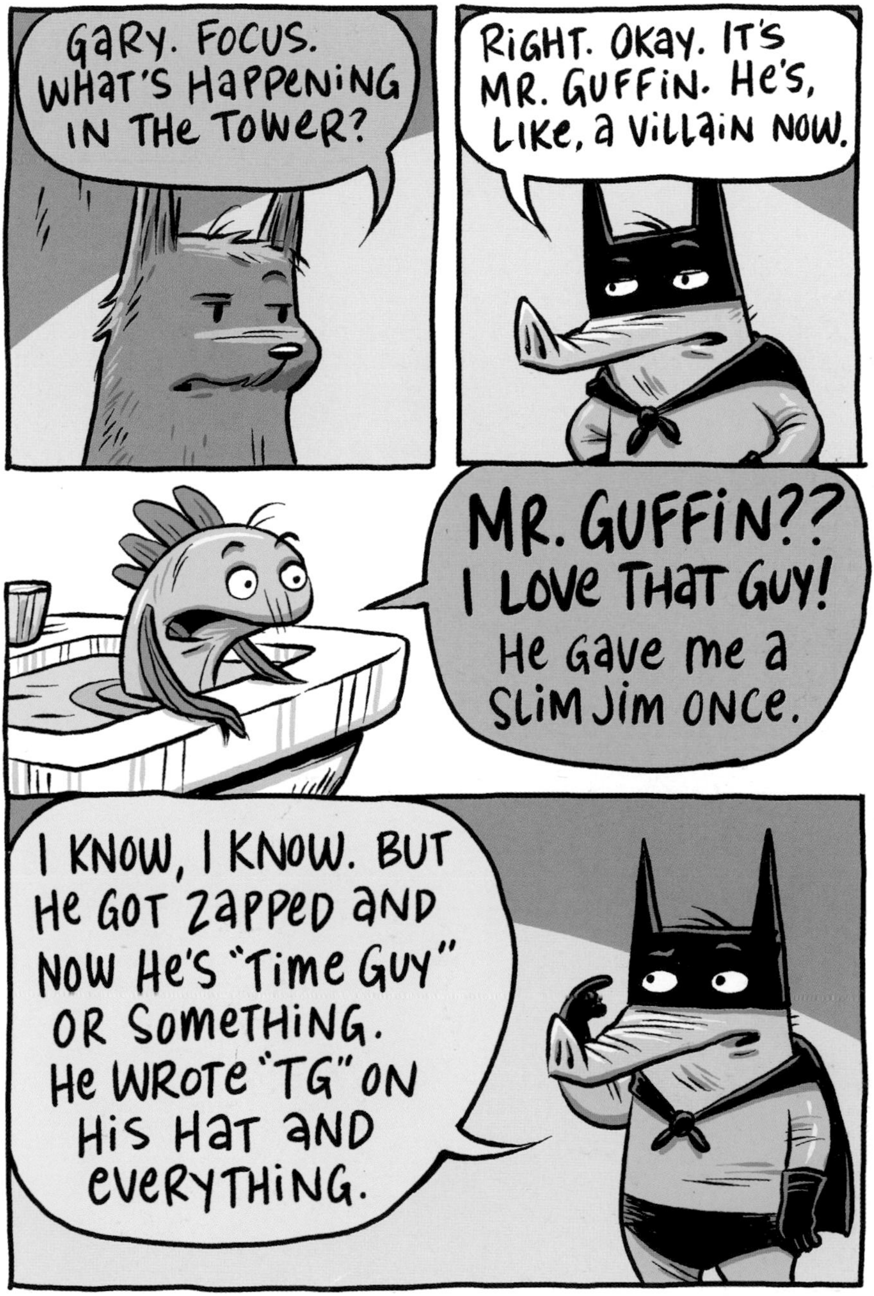
GARY. FOCUS. WHAT'S HAPPENING IN THE TOWER?
RIGHT. OKAY. IT'S MR. GUFFIN. HE'S, LIKE, A VILLAIN NOW.
MR. GUFFIN?? I LOVE THAT GUY! HE GAVE ME A SLIM JIM ONCE.
I KNOW, I KNOW. BUT HE GOT ZAPPED AND NOW HE'S "TIME GUY" OR SOMETHING. HE WROTE "TG" ON HIS HAT AND EVERYTHING.

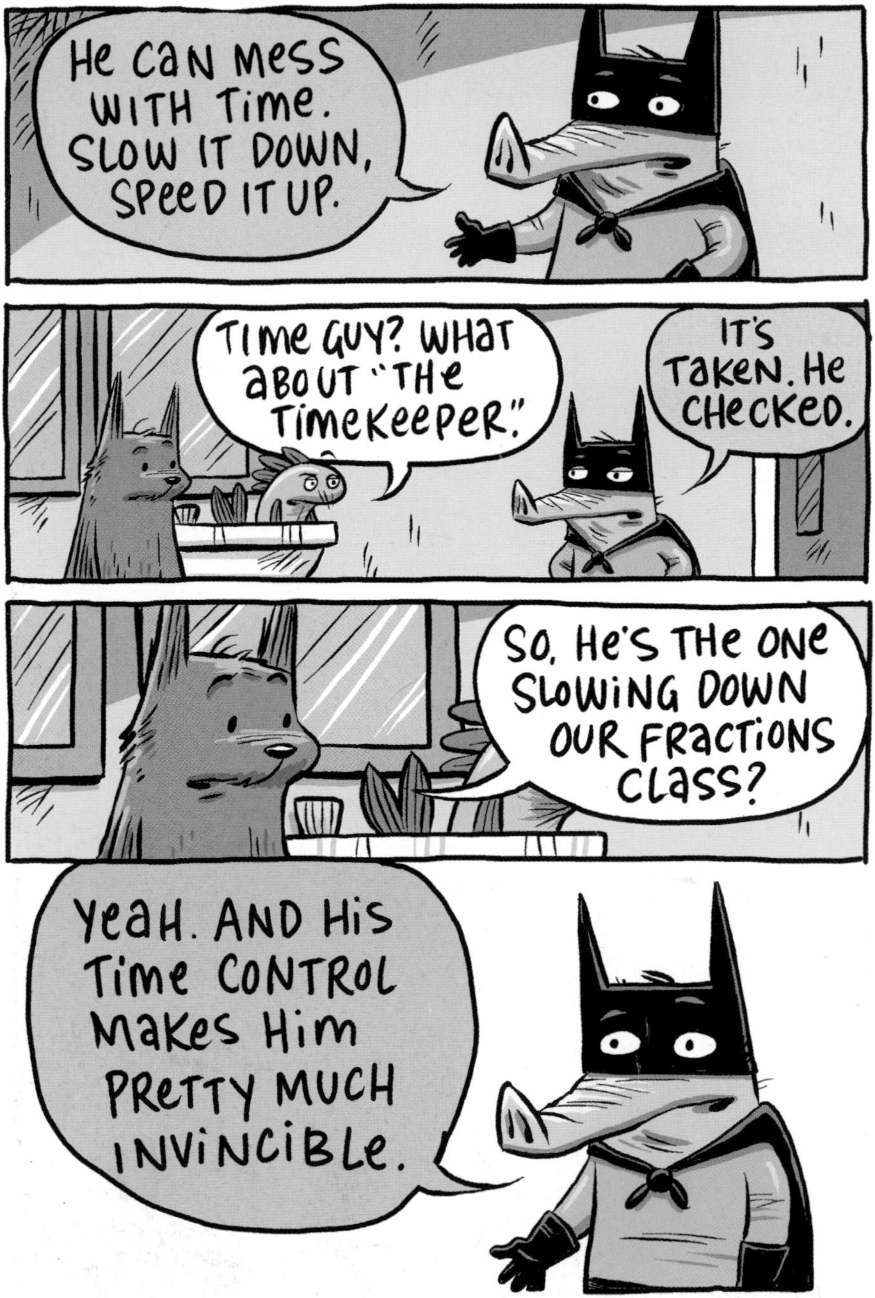
HE CAN MESS WITH TIME. SLOW IT DOWN, SPEED IT UP.
TIME GUY? WHAT ABOUT "THE TIMEKEEPER."
IT'S TAKEN. HE CHECKED.
SO, HE'S THE ONE SLOWING DOWN OUR FRACTIONS CLASS?
YEAH. AND HIS TIME CONTROL MAKES HIM PRETTY MUCH INVINCIBLE.

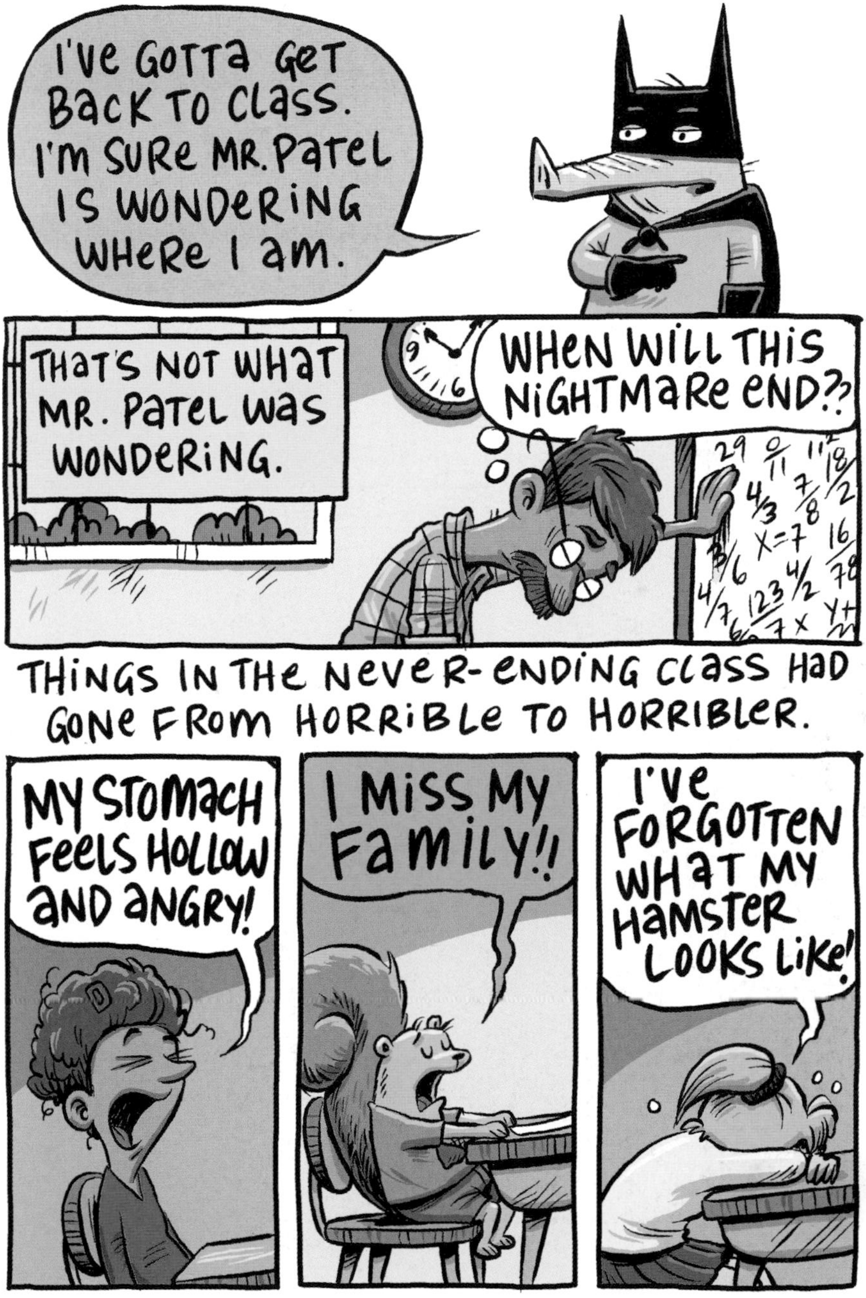
I've gotta get back to class. I'm sure Mr. Patel is wondering where I am.
That's not what Mr. Patel was wondering.
When will this nightmare end??
Things in the never-ending class had gone from horrible to horribler.
My stomach feels hollow and angry!
I miss my family!!
I've forgotten what my hamster looks like!

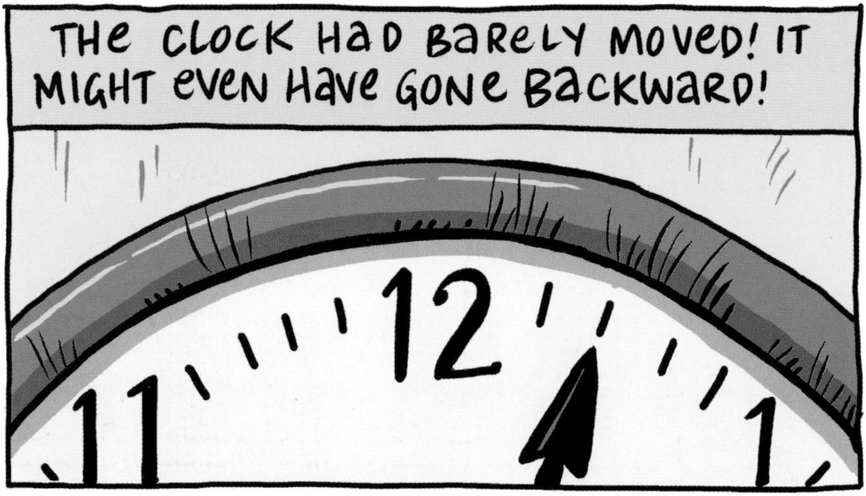
THE CLOCK HAD BARELY MOVED! IT MIGHT EVEN HAVE GONE BACKWARD!
12
11
1

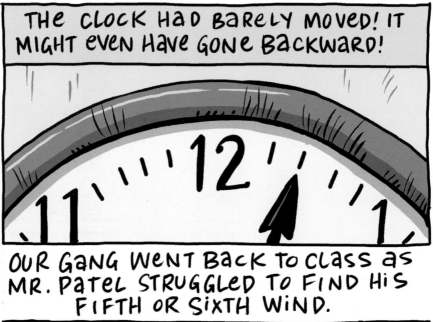

OUR GANG WENT BACK TO CLASS AS MR. PATEL STRUGGLED TO FIND HIS FIFTH OR SIXTH WIND.

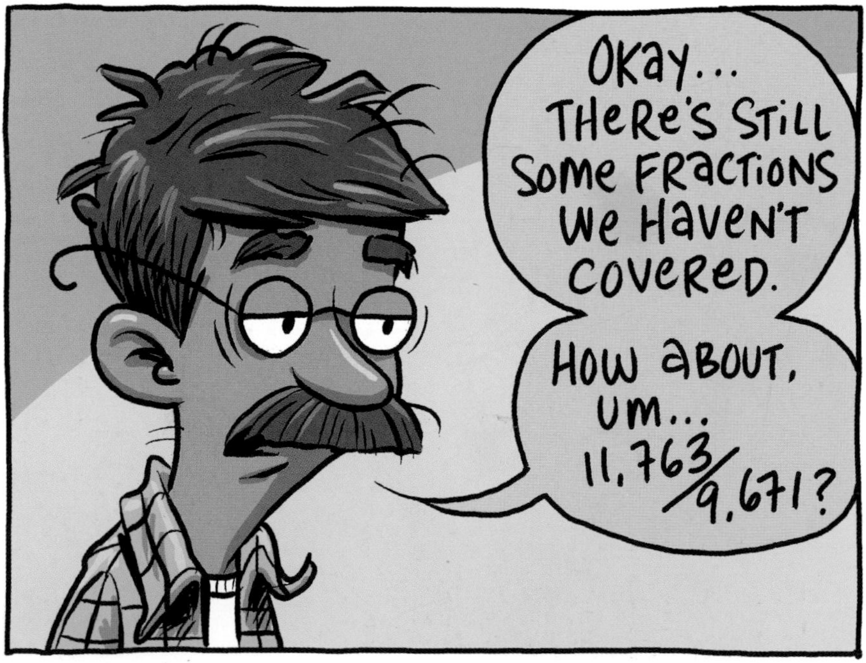
OKAY... THERE'S STILL SOME FRACTIONS WE HAVEN'T COVERED.
HOW ABOUT, UM... 11,763/9,671?

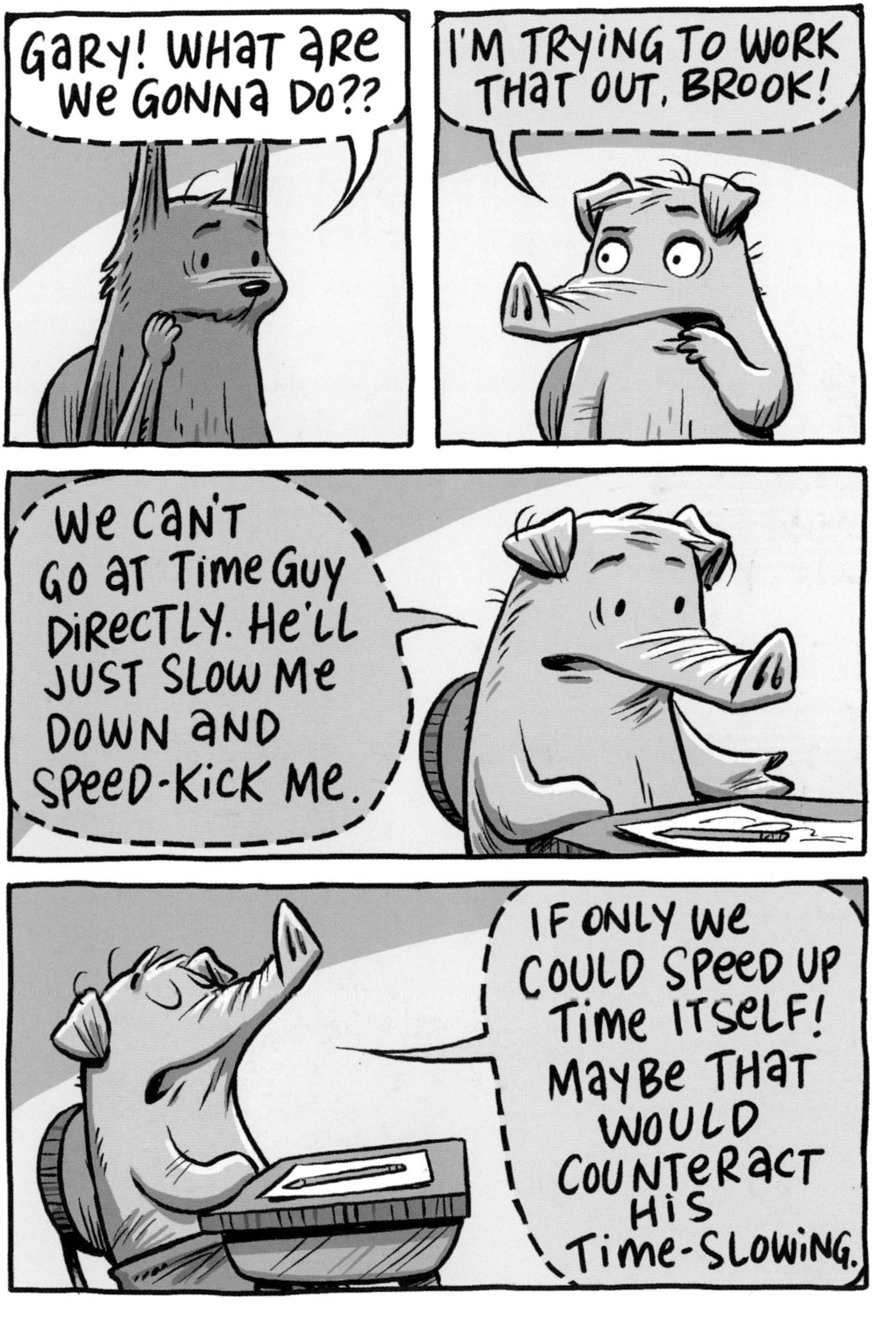
GARY! WHAT ARE WE GONNA DO??
I'M TRYING TO WORK THAT OUT, BROOK!
WE CAN'T GO AT TIME GUY DIRECTLY. HE'LL JUST SLOW ME DOWN AND SPEED-KICK ME.
IF ONLY WE COULD SPEED UP TIME ITSELF! MAYBE THAT WOULD COUNTERACT HIS TIME-SLOWING.

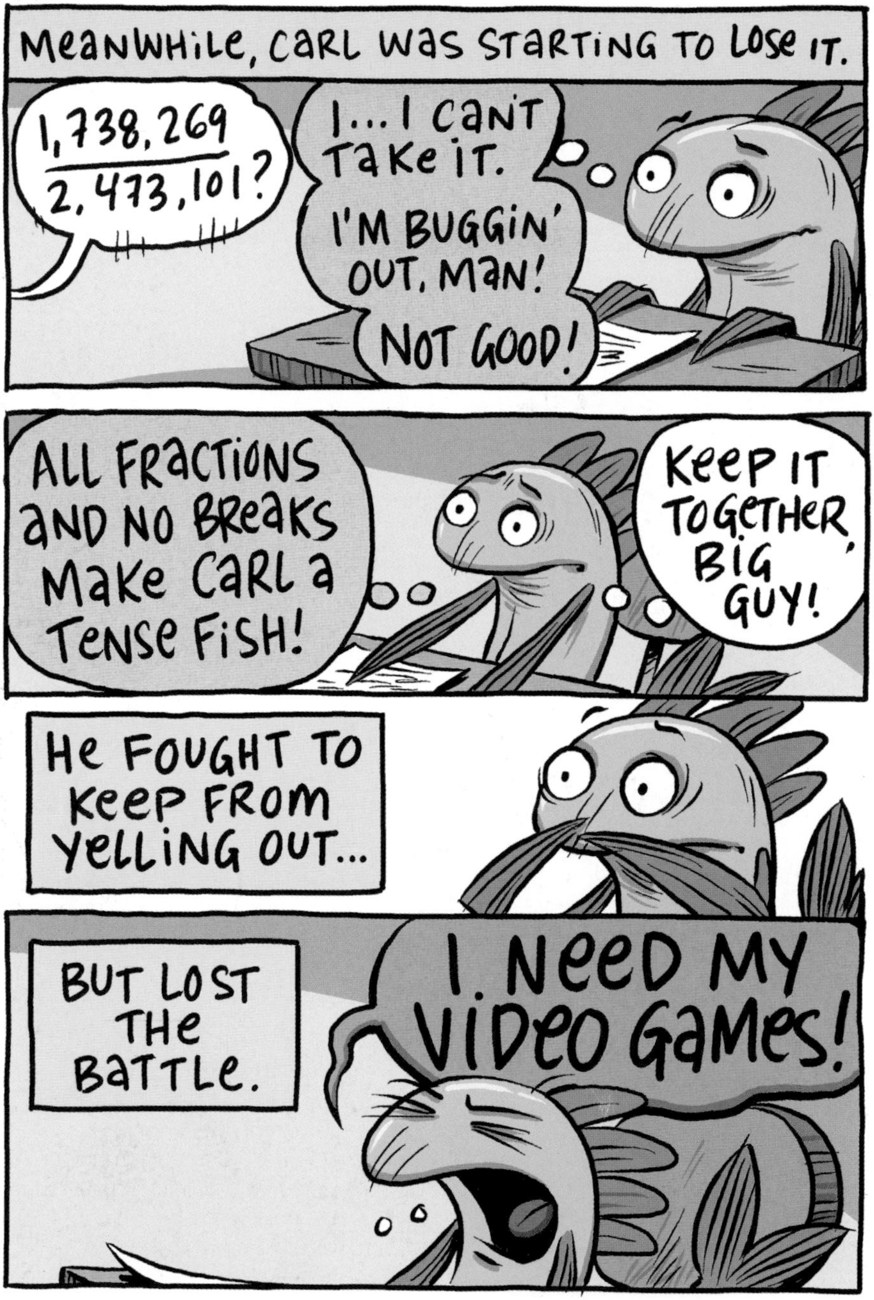
MEANWHILE, CARL WAS STARTING TO LOSE IT.
1,738,269 / 2,473,101?
I... I CAN'T TAKE IT.
I'M BUGGIN' OUT, MAN!
NOT GOOD!
ALL FRACTIONS AND NO BREAKS MAKE CARL A TENSE FISH!
KEEP IT TOGETHER, BIG GUY!
HE FOUGHT TO KEEP FROM YELLING OUT...
BUT LOST THE BATTLE.
I NEED MY VIDEO GAMES!

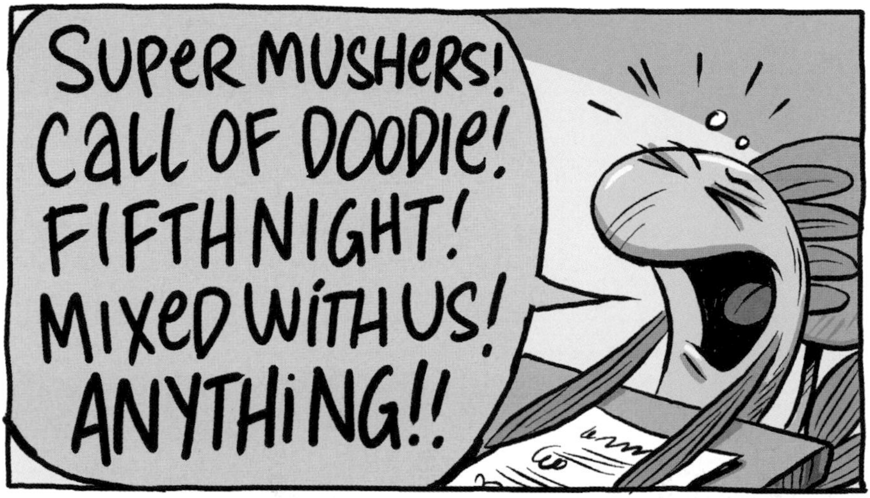
SUPER MUSHERS! CALL OF DOODIE! FIFTH NIGHT! MIXED WITH US! ANYTHING!!

SUDDENLY, HE WAS ON HIS DESK.

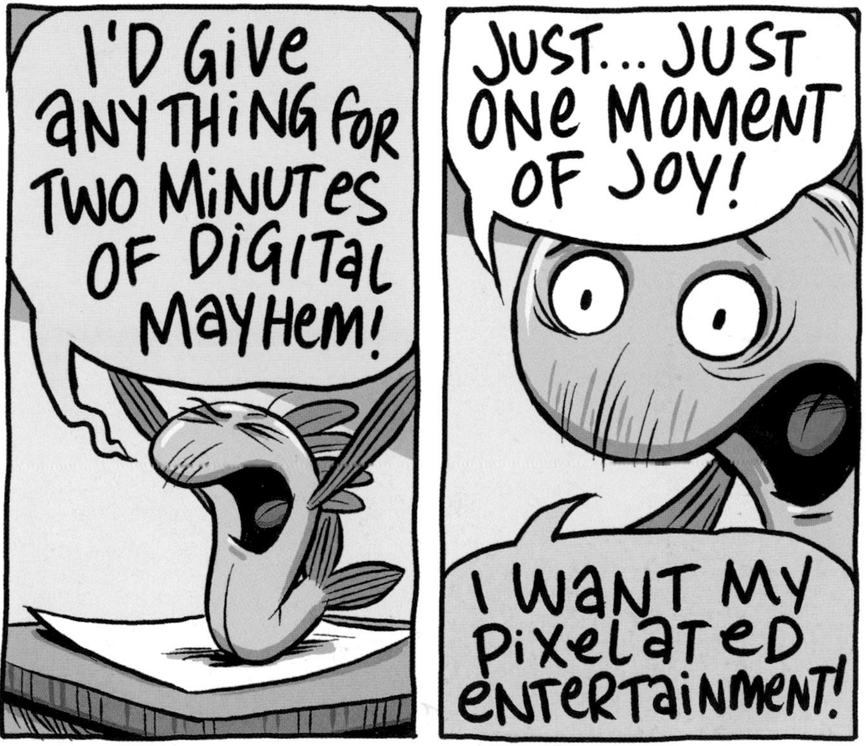
I'D GIVE ANYTHING FOR TWO MINUTES OF DIGITAL MAYHEM!
JUST... JUST ONE MOMENT OF JOY!
I WANT MY PIXELATED ENTERTAINMENT!

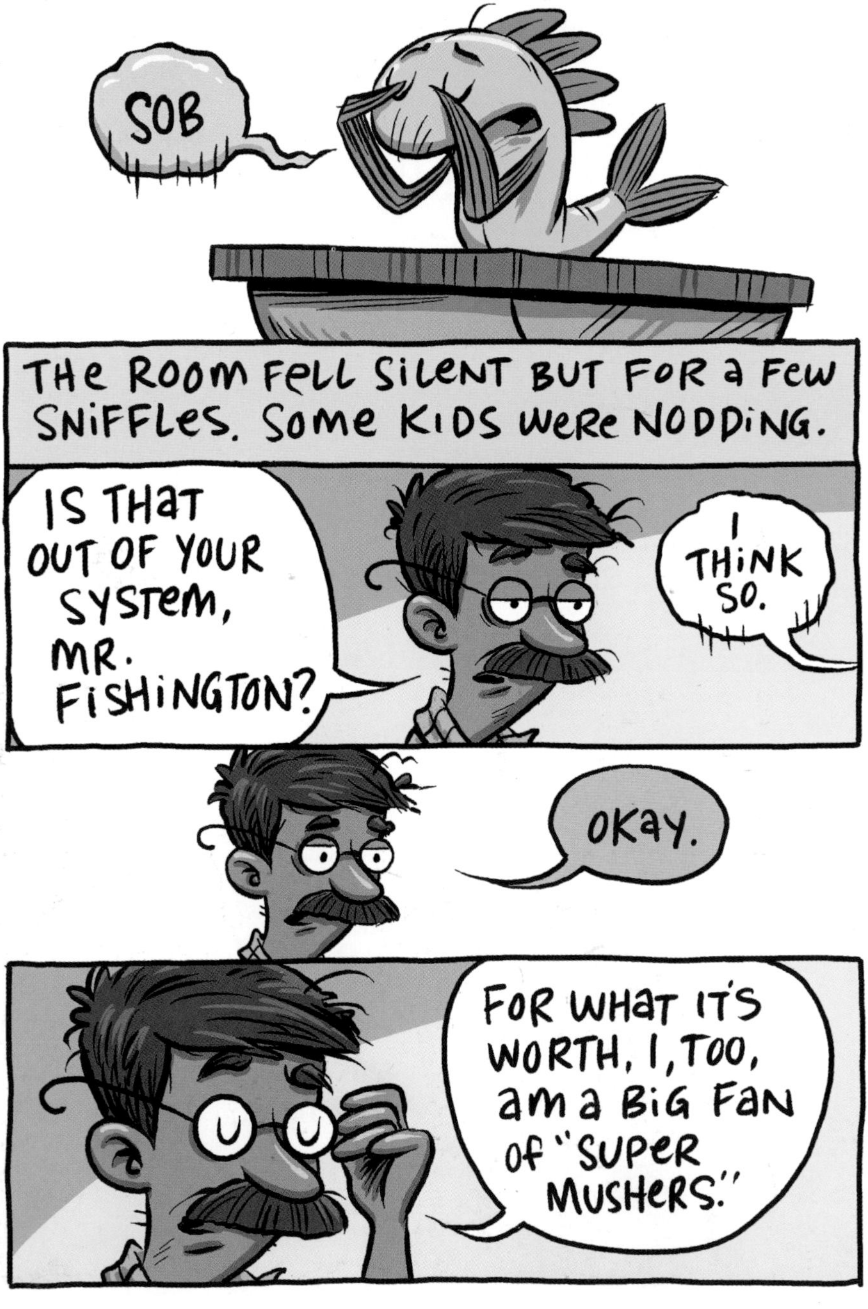
SOB
THE ROOM FELL SILENT BUT FOR A FEW SNIFFLES. SOME KIDS WERE NODDING.
IS THAT OUT OF YOUR SYSTEM, MR. FISHINGTON?
I THINK SO.
OKAY.
FOR WHAT IT'S WORTH, I, TOO, AM A BIG FAN OF "SUPER MUSHERS."

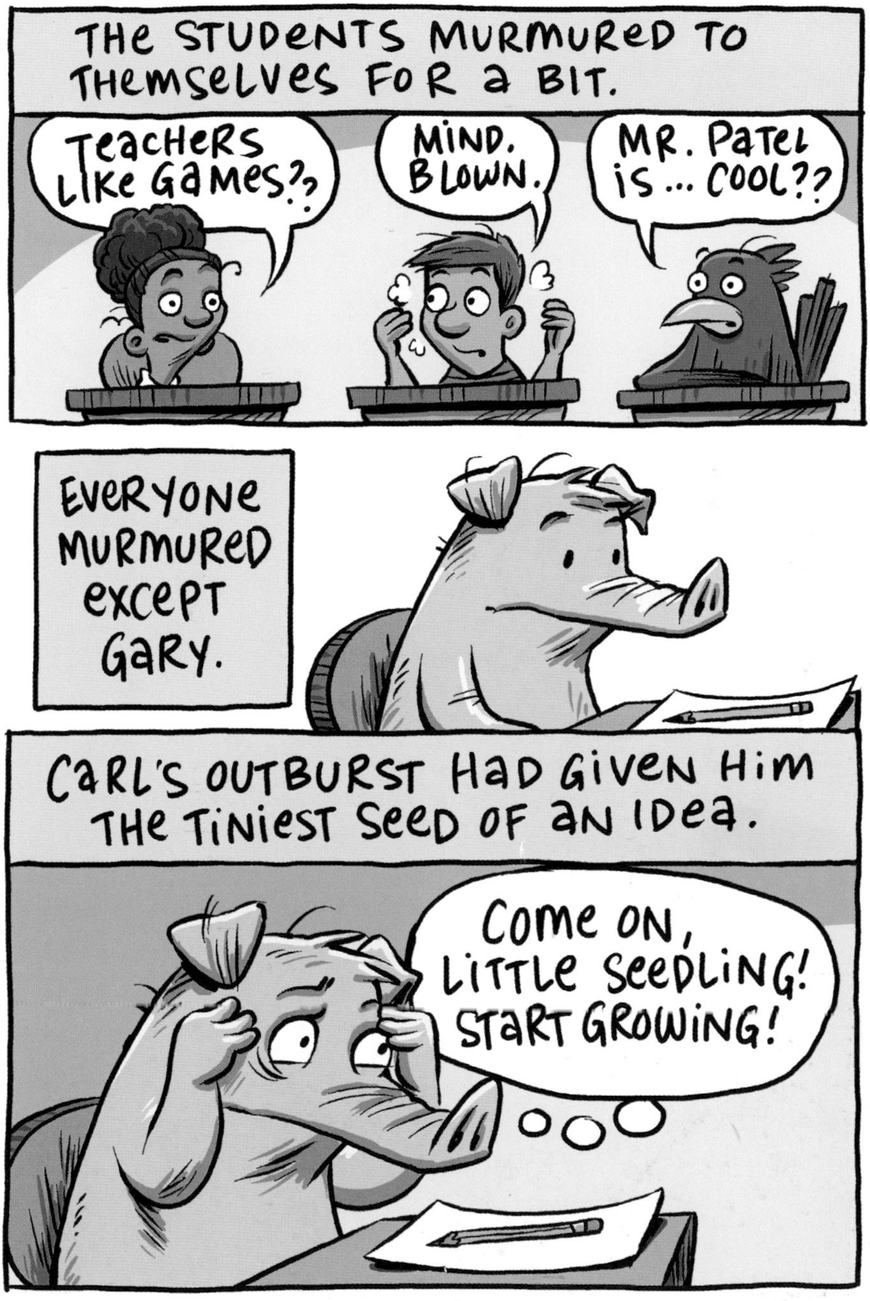
THE STUDENTS MURMURED TO THEMSELVES FOR A BIT.
TEACHERS LIKE GAMES??
MIND. BLOWN.
MR. PATEL IS... COOL??
EVERYONE MURMURED EXCEPT GARY.
CARL'S OUTBURST HAD GIVEN HIM THE TINIEST SEED OF AN IDEA.
COME ON, LITTLE SEEDLING! START GROWING!

CHAPTER SIX

"AN IDEA SPROUTS"

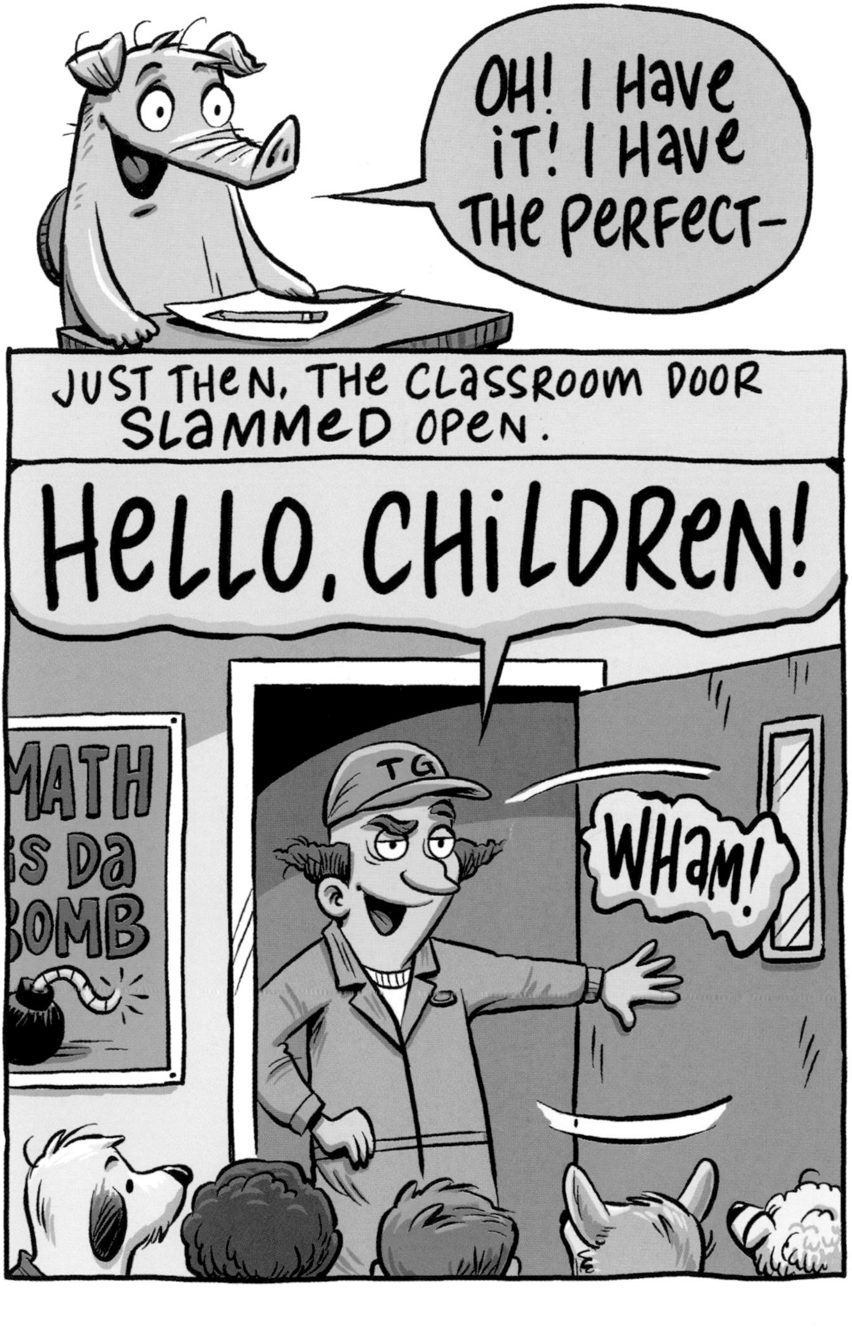
OH! I HAVE IT! I HAVE THE PERFECT-
JUST THEN, THE CLASSROOM DOOR SLAMMED OPEN.
HELLO, CHILDREN!
MATH IS DA BOMB
TG
WHAM!

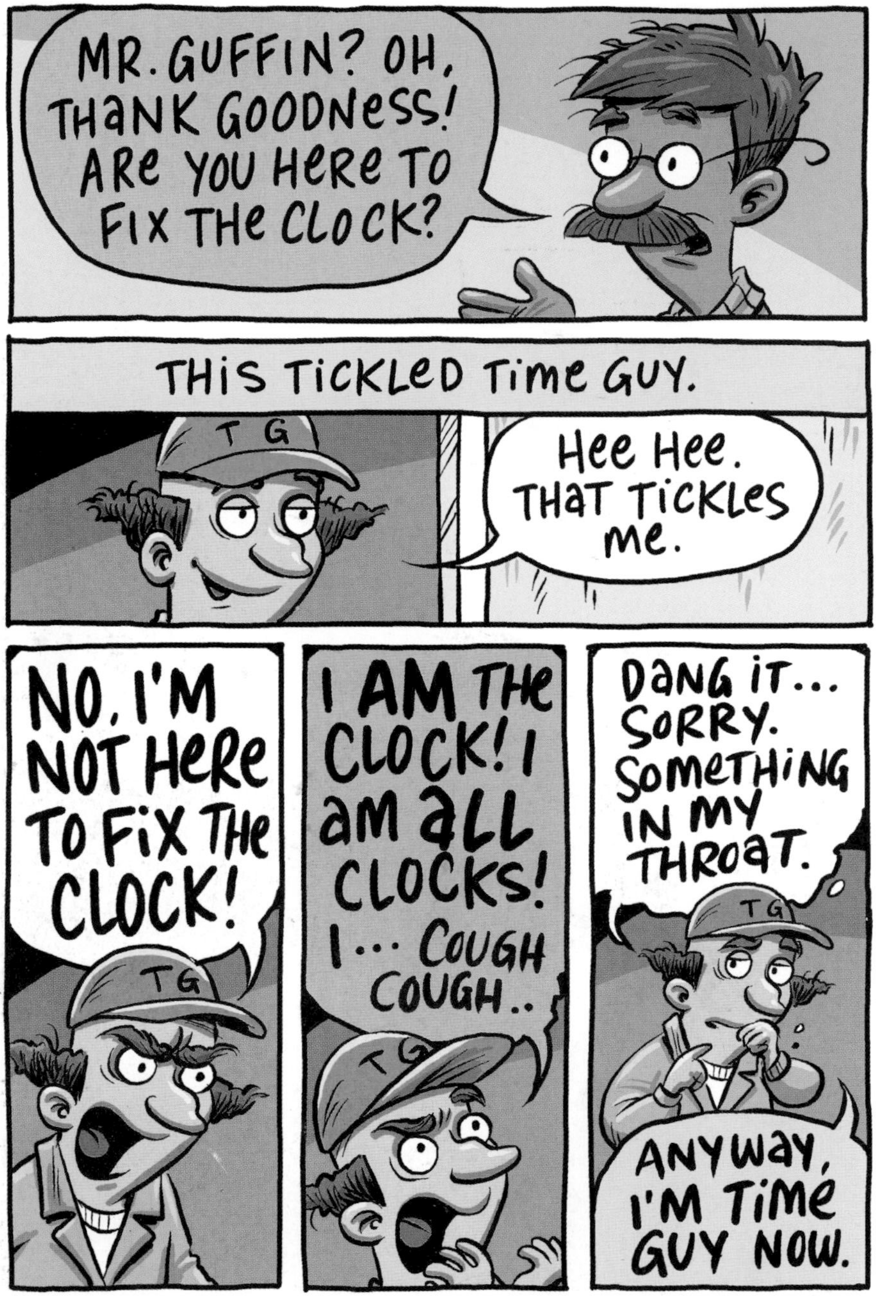
MR. GUFFIN? OH, THANK GOODNESS! ARE YOU HERE TO FIX THE CLOCK?
THIS TICKLED TIME GUY.
HEE HEE. THAT TICKLES ME.
NO, I'M NOT HERE TO FIX THE CLOCK!
I AM THE CLOCK! I AM ALL CLOCKS! I... COUGH COUGH..
DANG IT... SORRY. SOMETHING IN MY THROAT.
ANYWAY, I'M TIME GUY NOW.

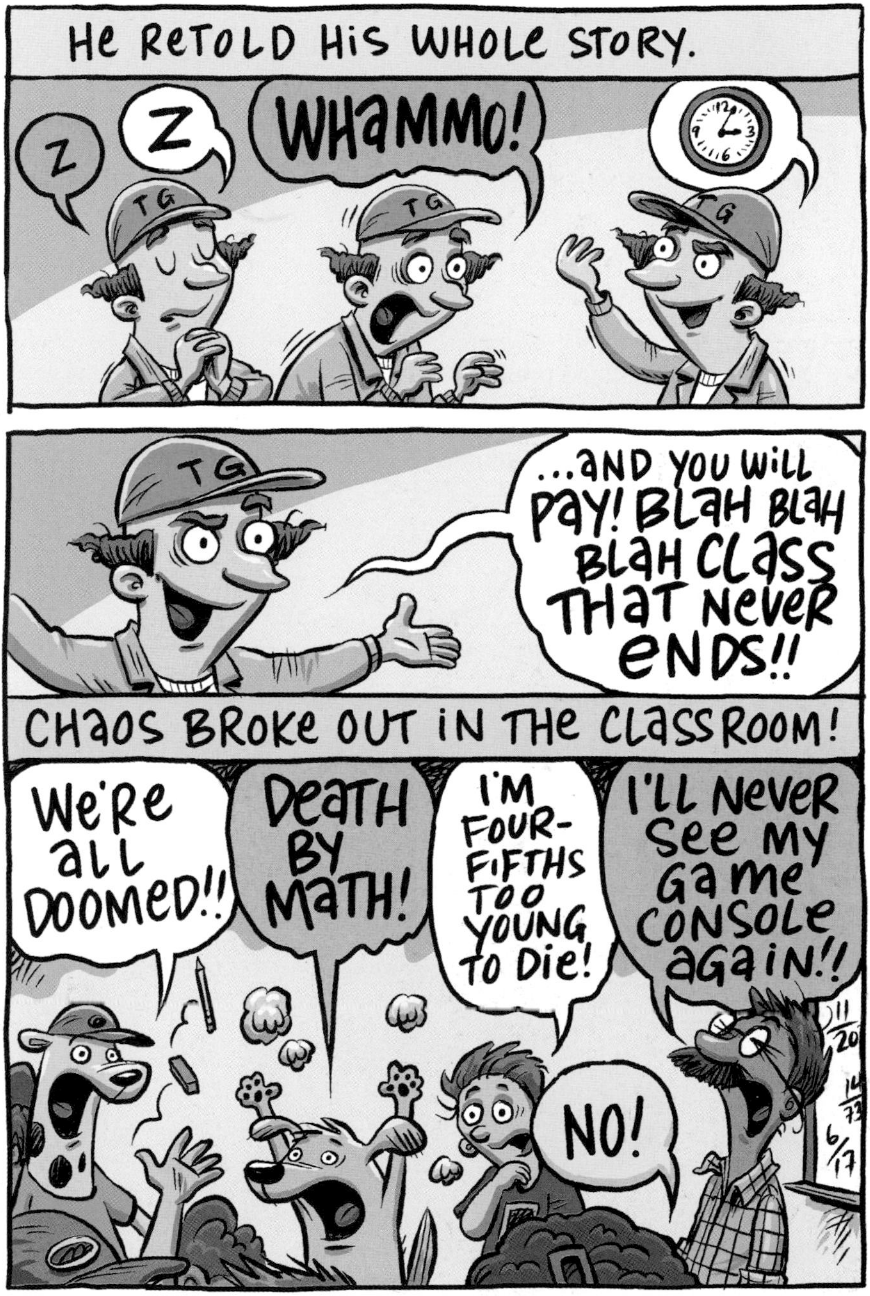
He retold his whole story.
Z
Z
WHAMMO!
...and you will pay! Blah blah blah class that never ends!!
Chaos broke out in the classroom!
We're all doomed!!
Death by math!
I'm four-fifths too young to die!
I'll never see my game console again!!
NO!

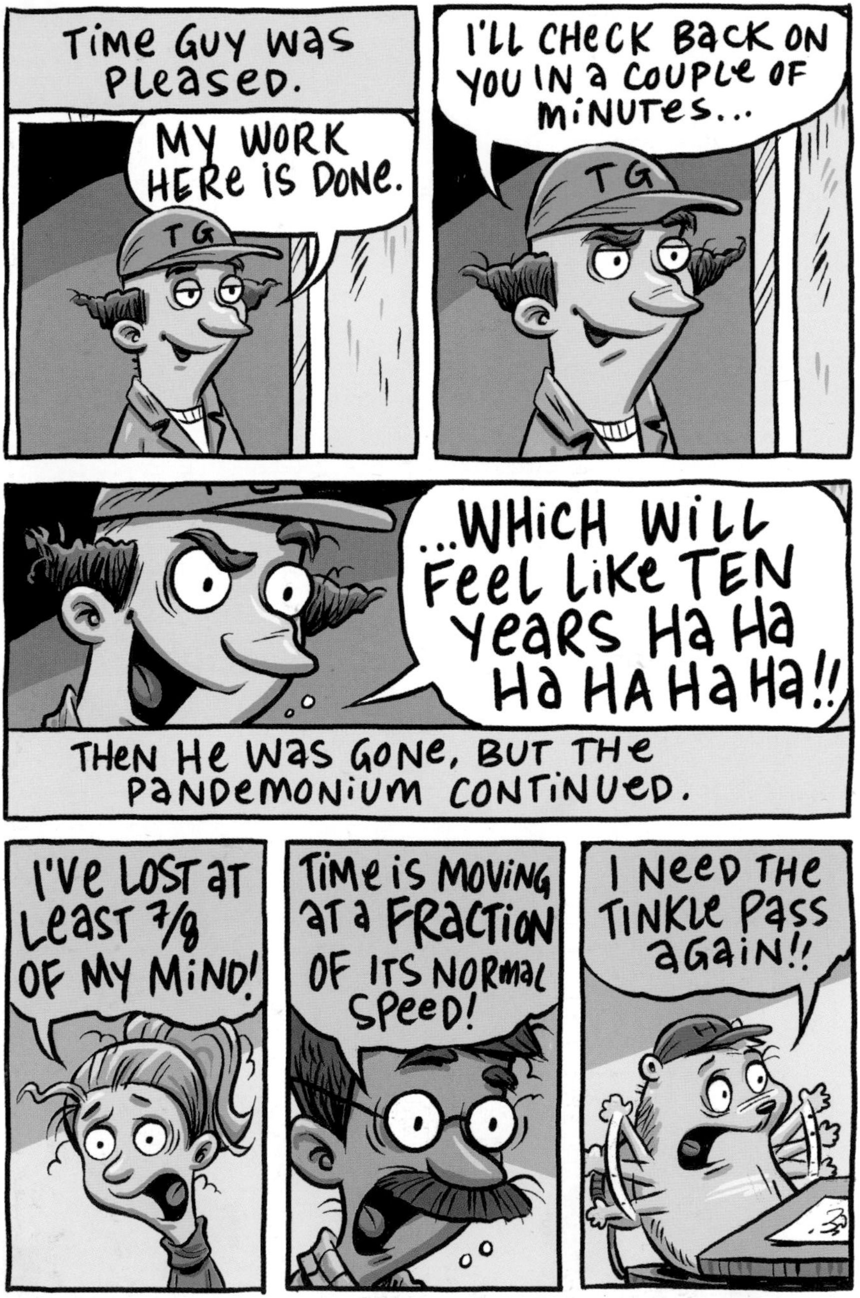
TIME GUY WAS PLEASED.
MY WORK HERE IS DONE.
I'LL CHECK BACK ON YOU IN A COUPLE OF MINUTES...
...WHICH WILL FEEL LIKE TEN YEARS HA HA HA HA HA HA!!
THEN HE WAS GONE, BUT THE PANDEMONIUM CONTINUED.
I'VE LOST AT LEAST 7/8 OF MY MIND!
TIME IS MOVING AT A FRACTION OF ITS NORMAL SPEED!
I NEED THE TINKLE PASS AGAIN!!

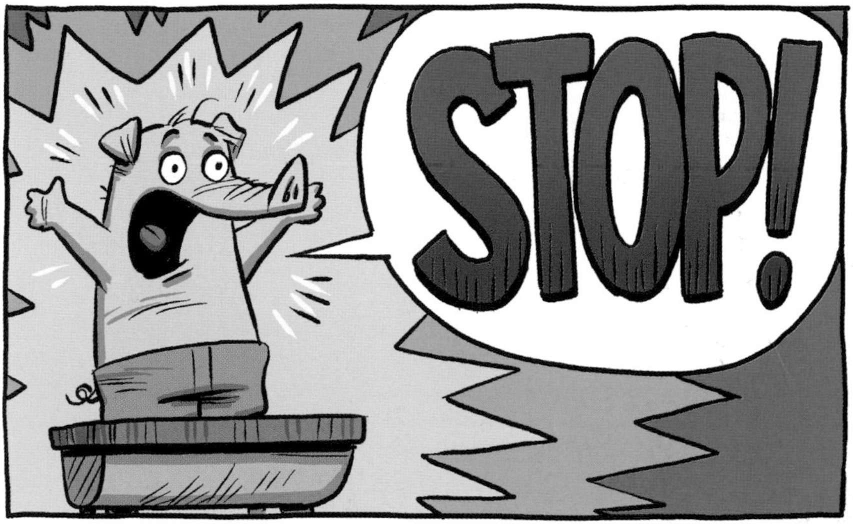
STOP!

EVERYONE FROZE.

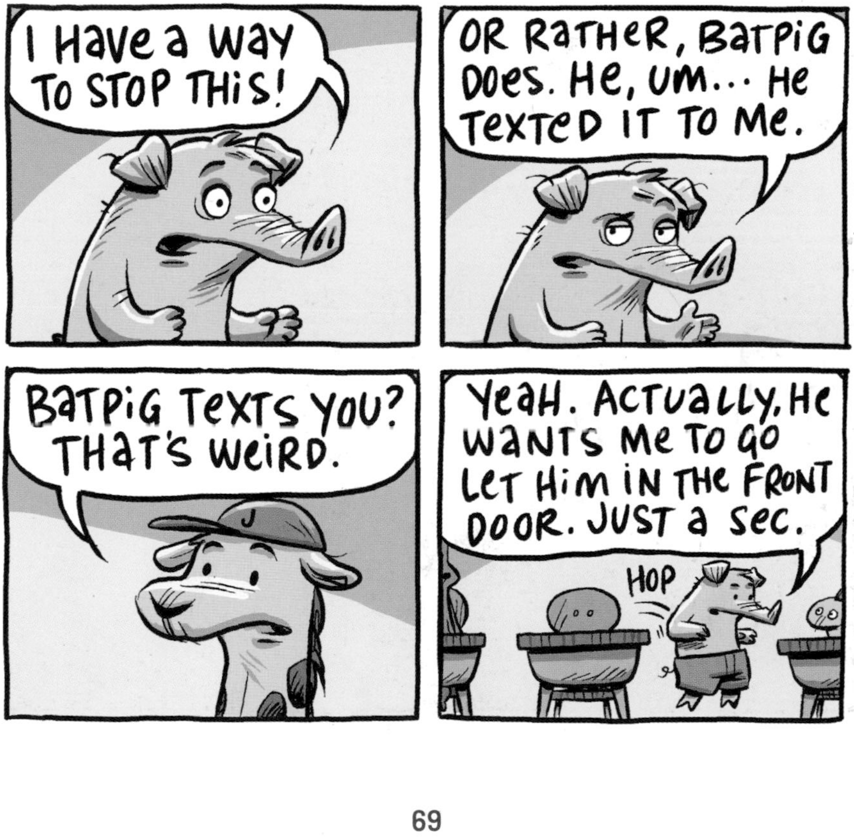
I HAVE A WAY TO STOP THIS!
OR RATHER, BATPIG DOES. HE, UM... HE TEXTED IT TO ME.
BATPIG TEXTS YOU? THAT'S WEIRD.
YEAH. ACTUALLY, HE WANTS ME TO GO LET HIM IN THE FRONT DOOR. JUST A SEC.
HOP

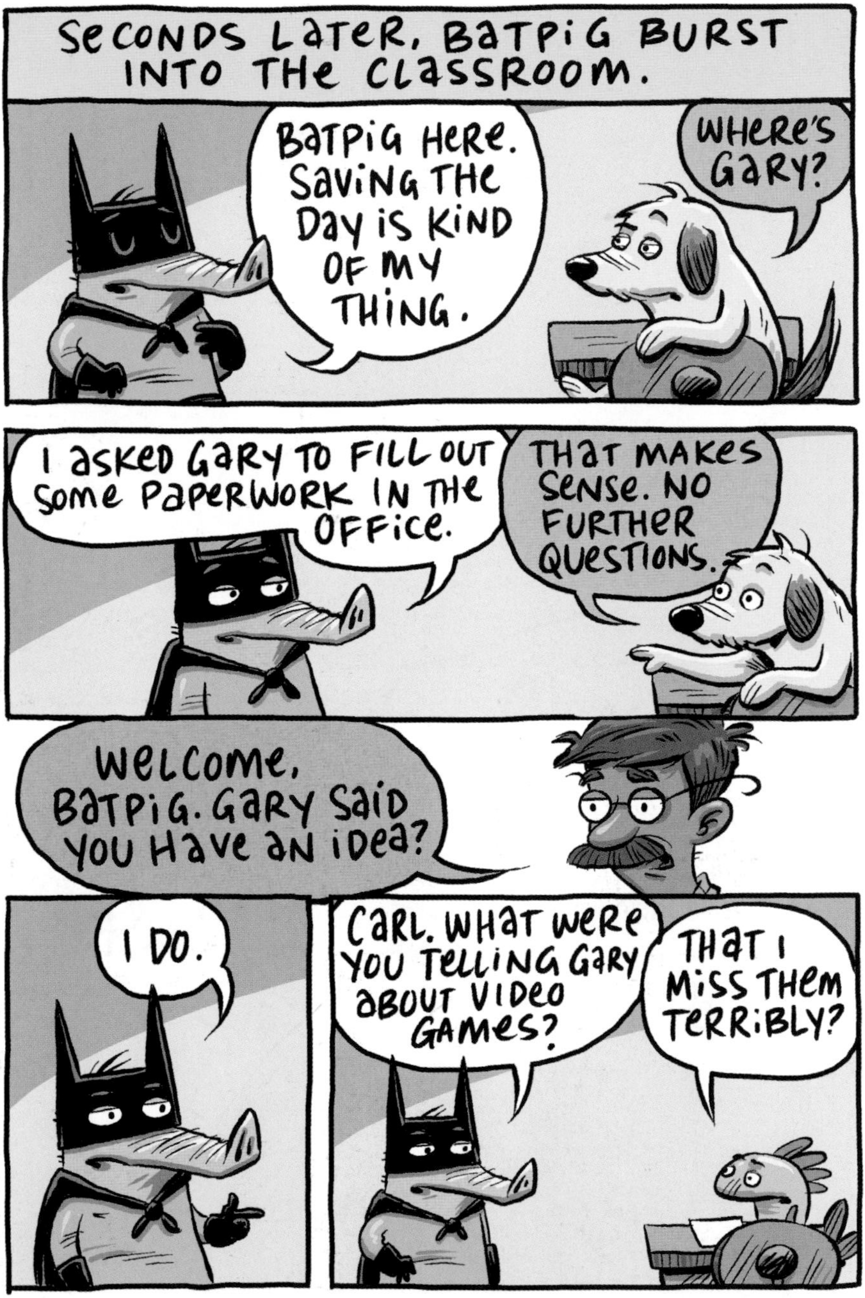
SECONDS LATER, BATPIG BURST INTO THE CLASSROOM.
BATPIG HERE. SAVING THE DAY IS KIND OF MY THING.
WHERE'S GARY?
I ASKED GARY TO FILL OUT SOME PAPERWORK IN THE OFFICE.
THAT MAKES SENSE. NO FURTHER QUESTIONS.
WELCOME, BATPIG. GARY SAID YOU HAVE AN IDEA?
I DO.
CARL. WHAT WERE YOU TELLING GARY ABOUT VIDEO GAMES?
THAT I MISS THEM TERRIBLY?

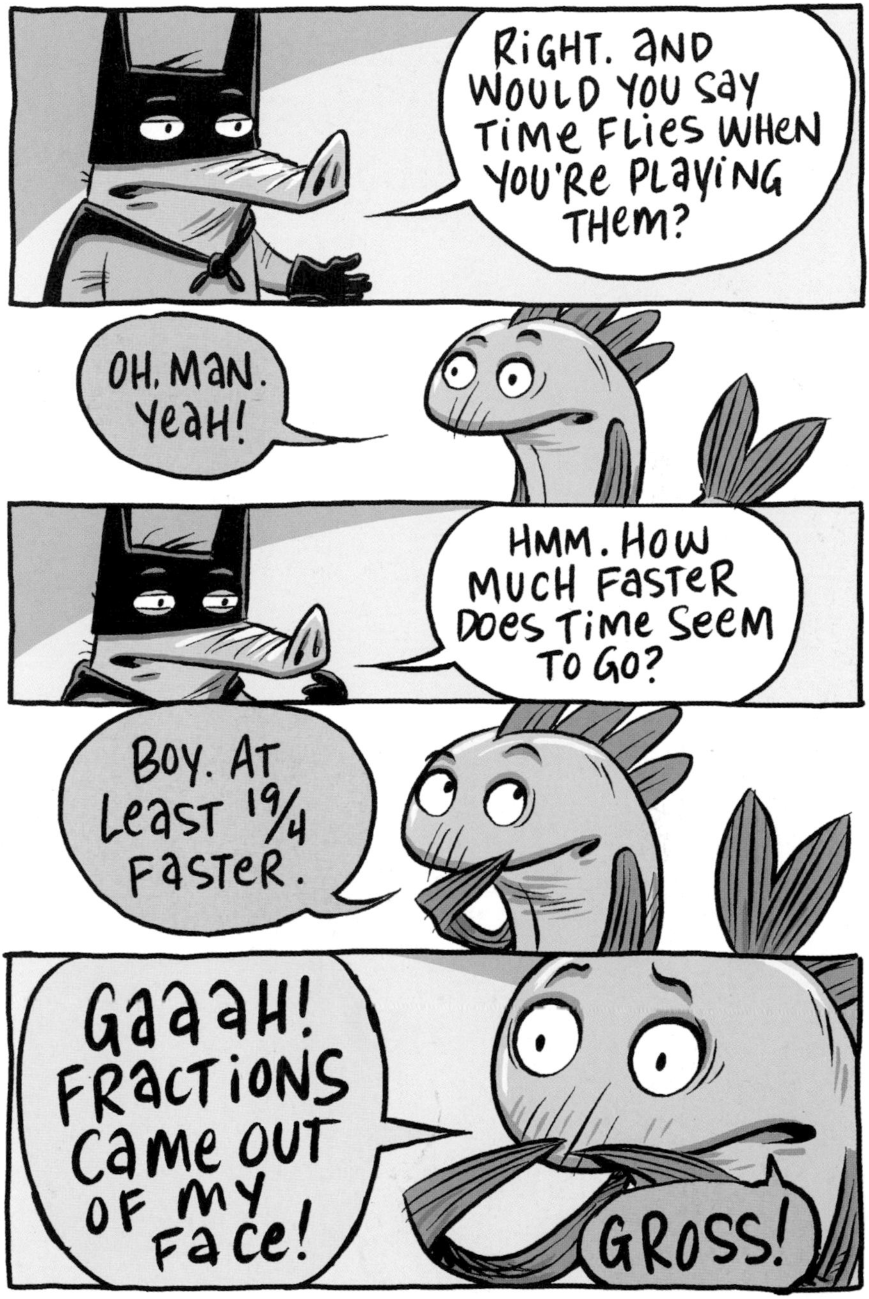
RIGHT. AND WOULD YOU SAY TIME FLIES WHEN YOU'RE PLAYING THEM?
OH, MAN. YEAH!
HMM. HOW MUCH FASTER DOES TIME SEEM TO GO?
BOY. AT LEAST 19/4 FASTER.
GAAAH! FRACTIONS CAME OUT OF MY FACE!
GROSS!

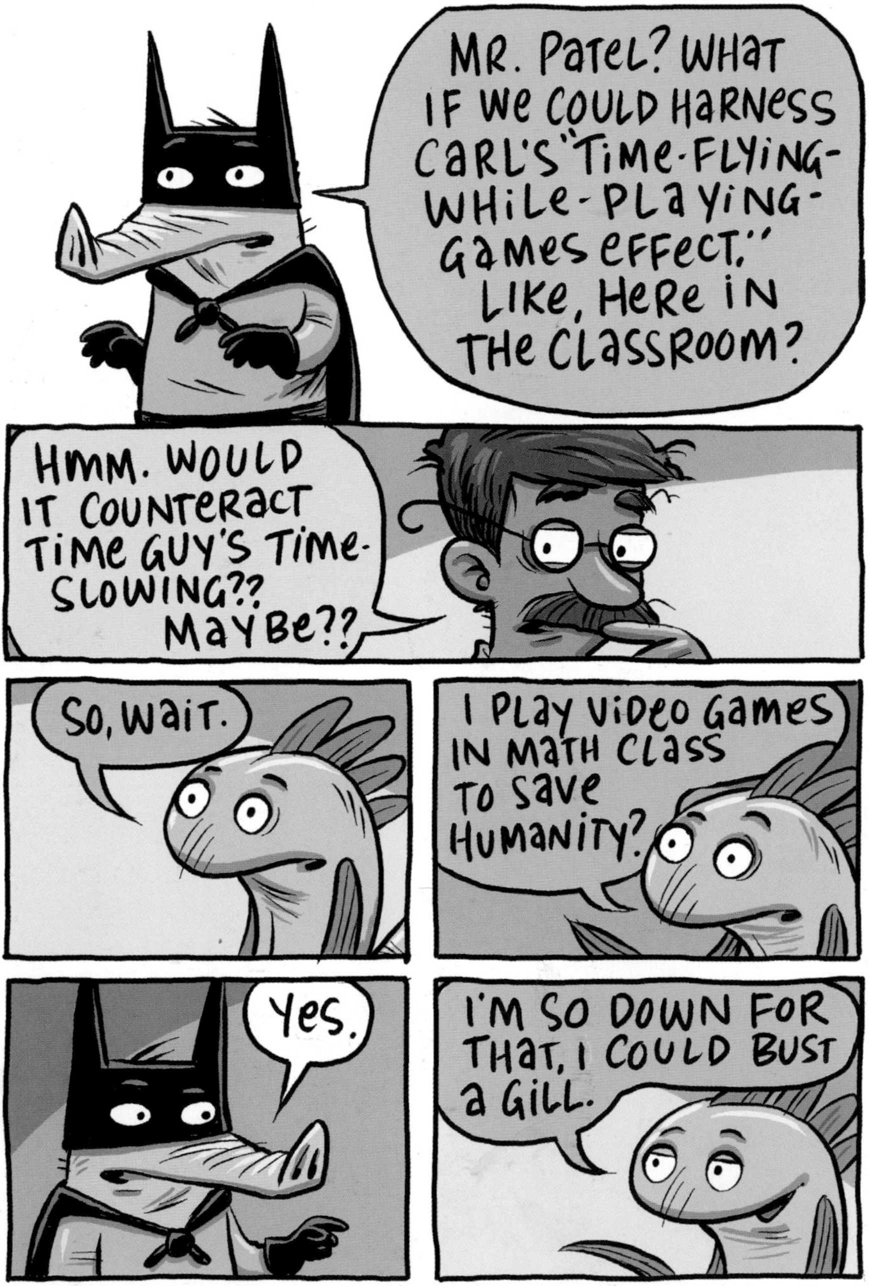
MR. PATEL? WHAT IF WE COULD HARNESS CARL'S "TIME-FLYING-WHILE-PLAYING-GAMES EFFECT." LIKE, HERE IN THE CLASSROOM?
HMM. WOULD IT COUNTERACT TIME GUY'S TIME-SLOWING?? MAYBE??
SO, WAIT.
I PLAY VIDEO GAMES IN MATH CLASS TO SAVE HUMANITY?
YES.
I'M SO DOWN FOR THAT, I COULD BUST A GILL.

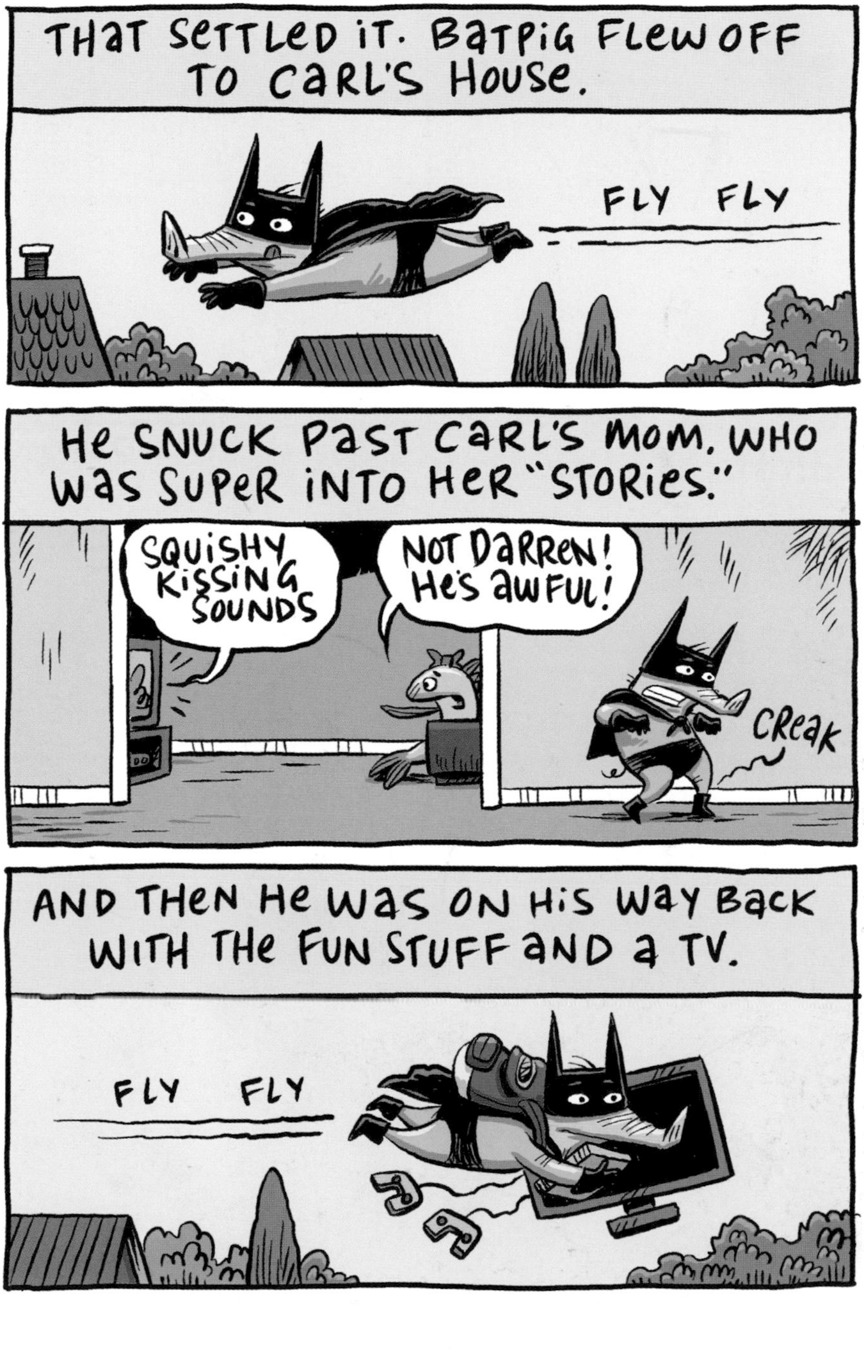
THAT SETTLED IT. BATPIG FLEW OFF TO CARL'S HOUSE.
FLY FLY
HE SNUCK PAST CARL'S MOM, WHO WAS SUPER INTO HER "STORIES."
SQUISHY KISSING SOUNDS
NOT DARREN! HE'S AWFUL!
CREAK
AND THEN HE WAS ON HIS WAY BACK WITH THE FUN STUFF AND A TV.
FLY FLY

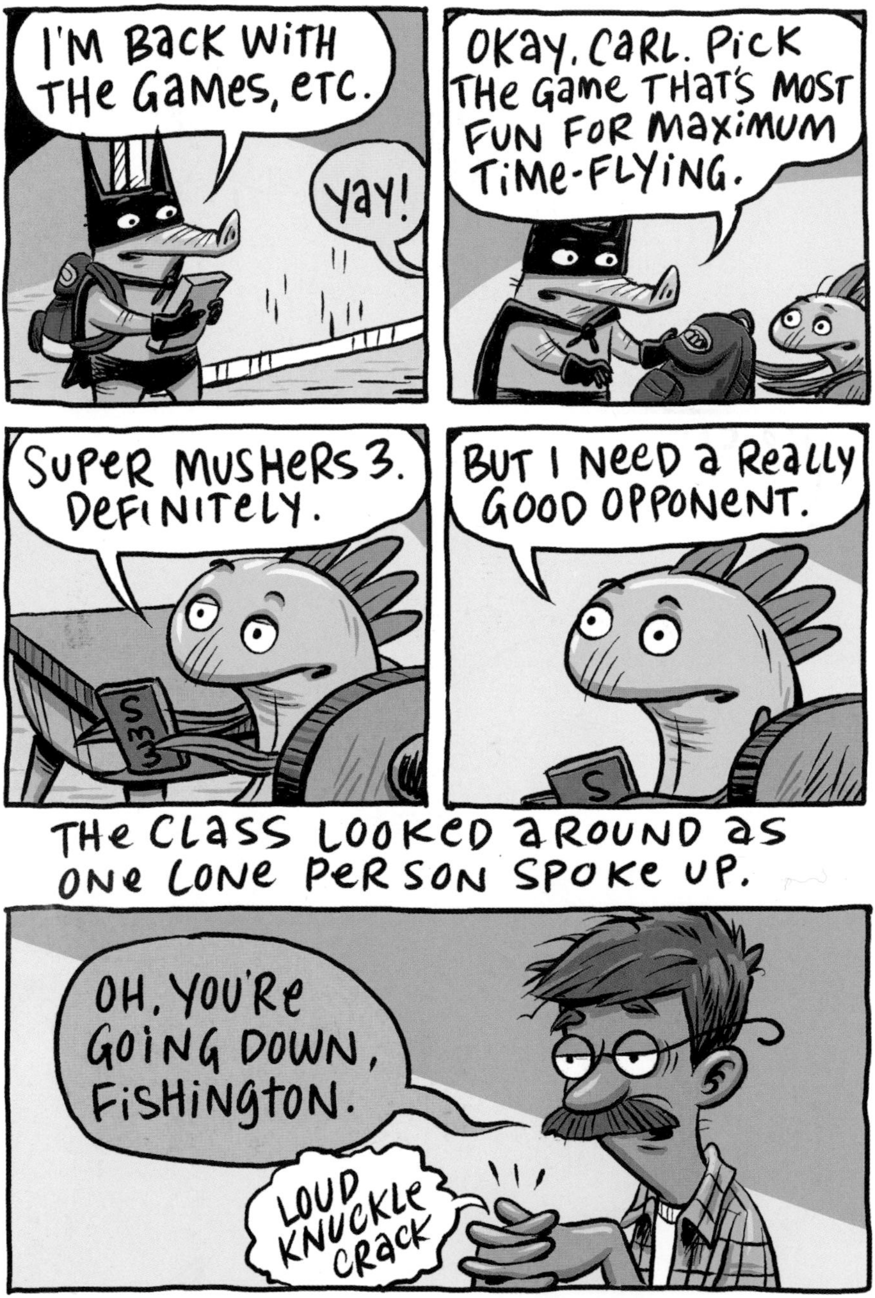
I'M BACK WITH THE GAMES, ETC.
YAY!
OKAY, CARL. PICK THE GAME THAT'S MOST FUN FOR MAXIMUM TIME-FLYING.
SUPER MUSHERS 3. DEFINITELY.
SM3
BUT I NEED A REALLY GOOD OPPONENT.
S
THE CLASS LOOKED AROUND AS ONE LONE PERSON SPOKE UP.
OH, YOU'RE GOING DOWN, FISHINGTON.
LOUD KNUCKLE CRACK

CHAPTER SEVEN

"LET'S GET READY TO MUSH!"

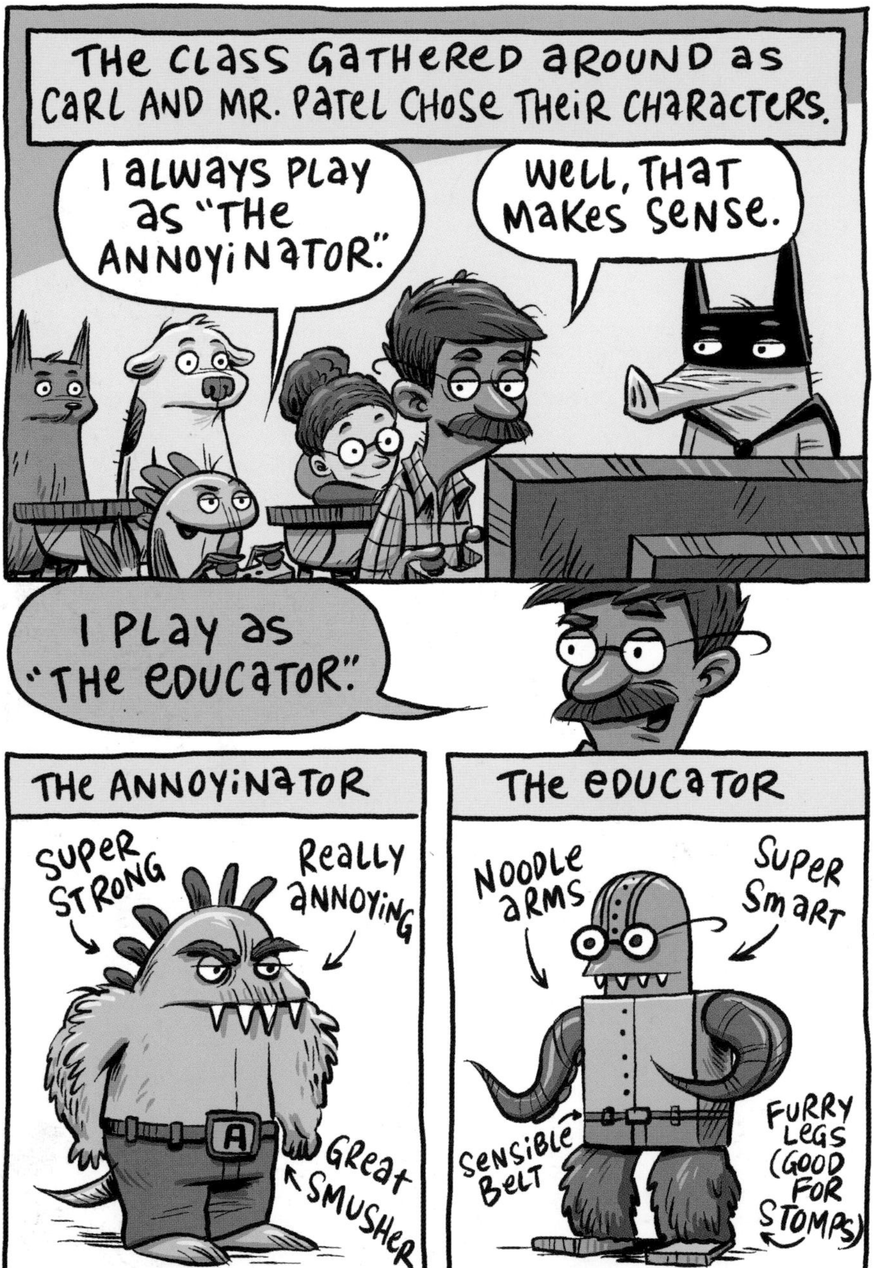
THE CLASS GATHERED AROUND AS CARL AND MR. PATEL CHOSE THEIR CHARACTERS.
I ALWAYS PLAY AS "THE ANNOYINATOR."
WELL, THAT MAKES SENSE.
I PLAY AS "THE EDUCATOR."
THE ANNOYINATOR
SUPER STRONG
REALLY ANNOYING
GREAT SMUSHER
THE EDUCATOR
NOODLE ARMS
SUPER SMART
SENSIBLE BELT
FURRY LEGS (GOOD FOR STOMPS)

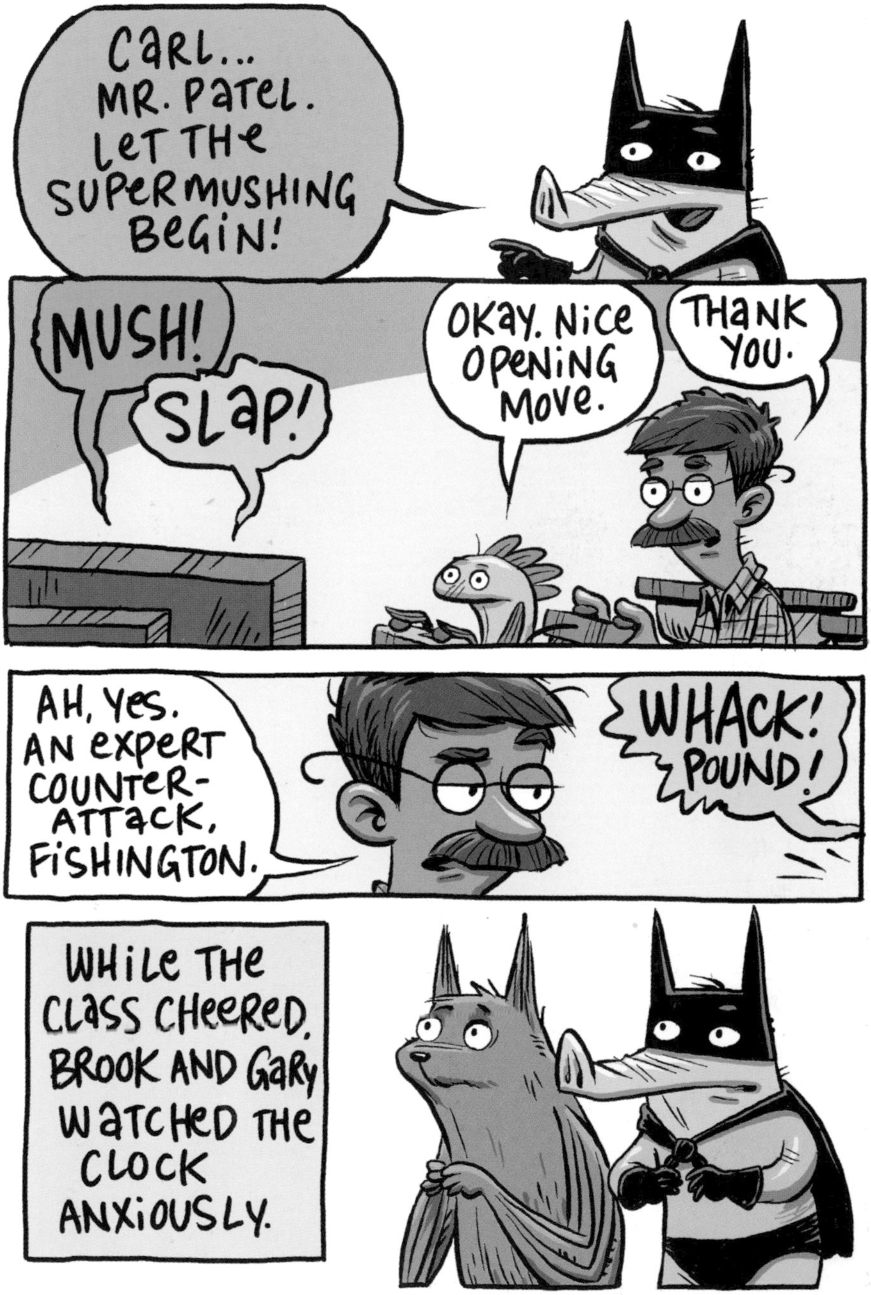
CARL... MR. PATEL. LET THE SUPERMUSHING BEGIN!
MUSH!
SLAP!
OKAY. NICE OPENING MOVE.
THANK YOU.
AH, YES. AN EXPERT COUNTER-ATTACK, FISHINGTON.
WHACK! POUND!
WHILE THE CLASS CHEERED, BROOK AND GARY WATCHED THE CLOCK ANXIOUSLY.

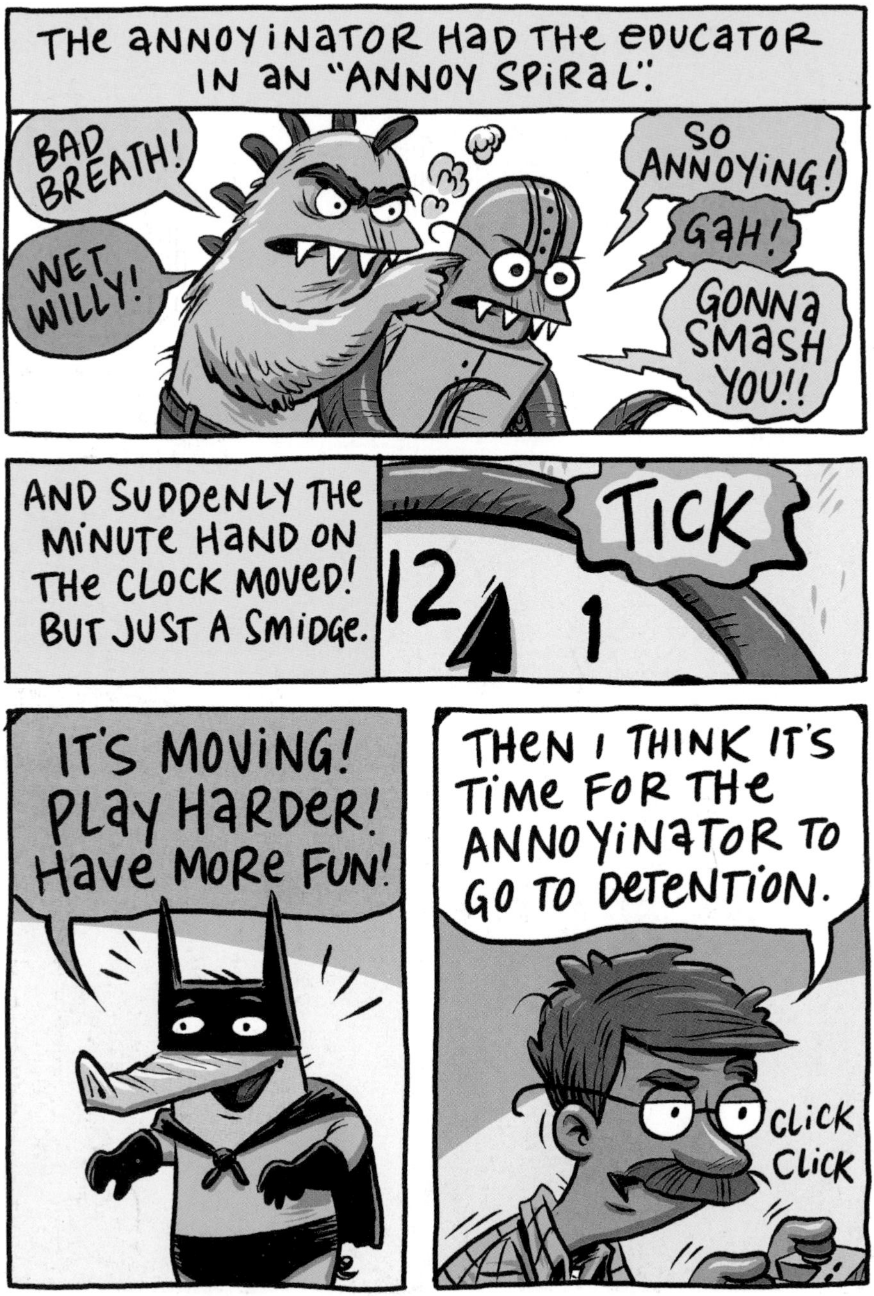
THE ANNOYINATOR HAD THE EDUCATOR IN AN "ANNOY SPIRAL".
BAD BREATH!
WET WILLY!
SO ANNOYING!
GAH!
GONNA SMASH YOU!!
AND SUDDENLY THE MINUTE HAND ON THE CLOCK MOVED! BUT JUST A SMIDGE.
TICK
12
1
IT'S MOVING! PLAY HARDER! HAVE MORE FUN!
THEN I THINK IT'S TIME FOR THE ANNOYINATOR TO GO TO DETENTION.
CLICK CLICK

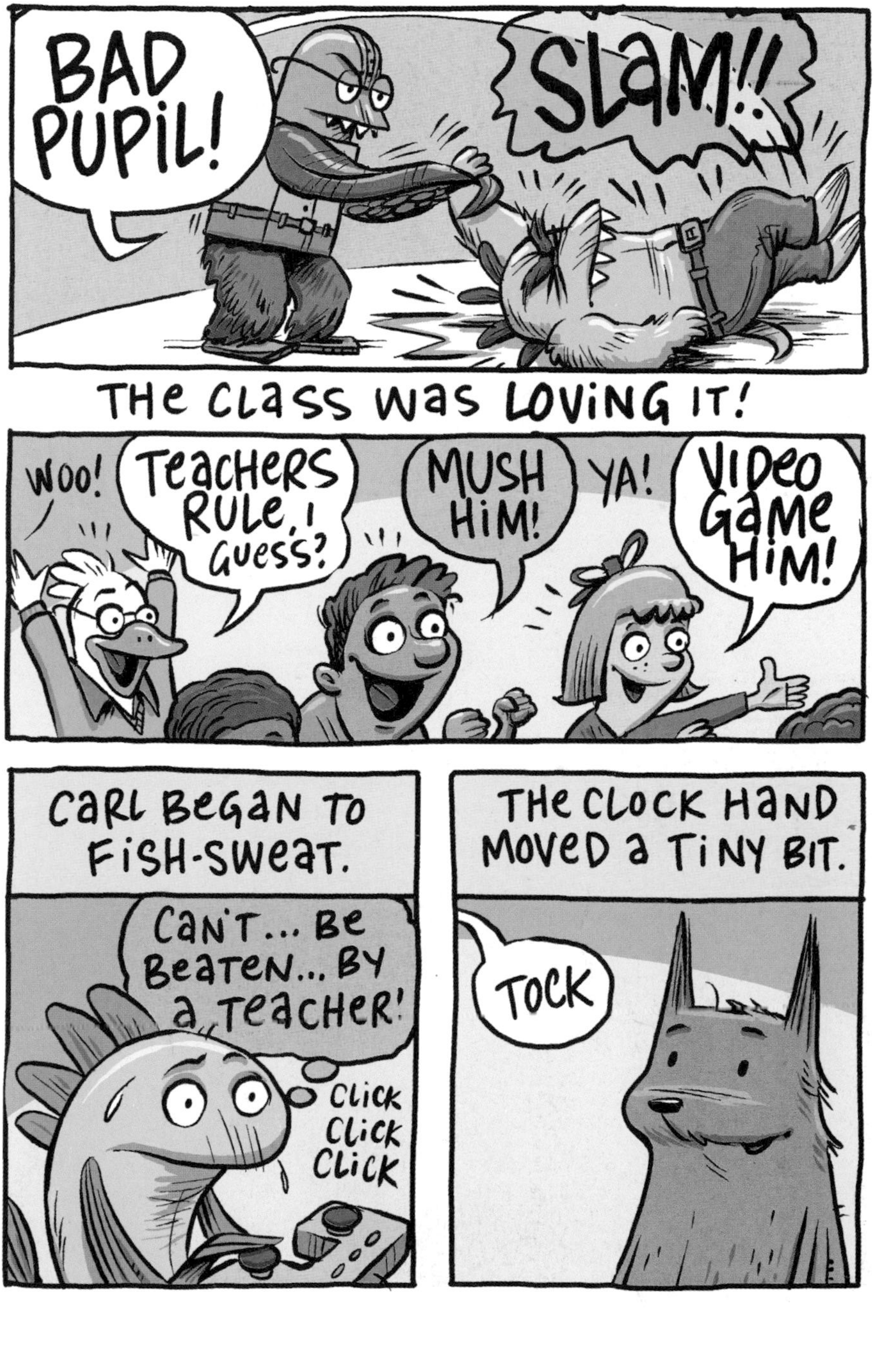
BAD PUPIL!
SLAM!!
THE CLASS WAS LOVING IT!
WOO!
TEACHERS RULE, I GUESS?
MUSH HIM!
YA!
VIDEO GAME HIM!
CARL BEGAN TO FISH-SWEAT.
CAN'T... BE BEATEN... BY A TEACHER!
CLICK CLICK CLICK
THE CLOCK HAND MOVED A TINY BIT.
TOCK

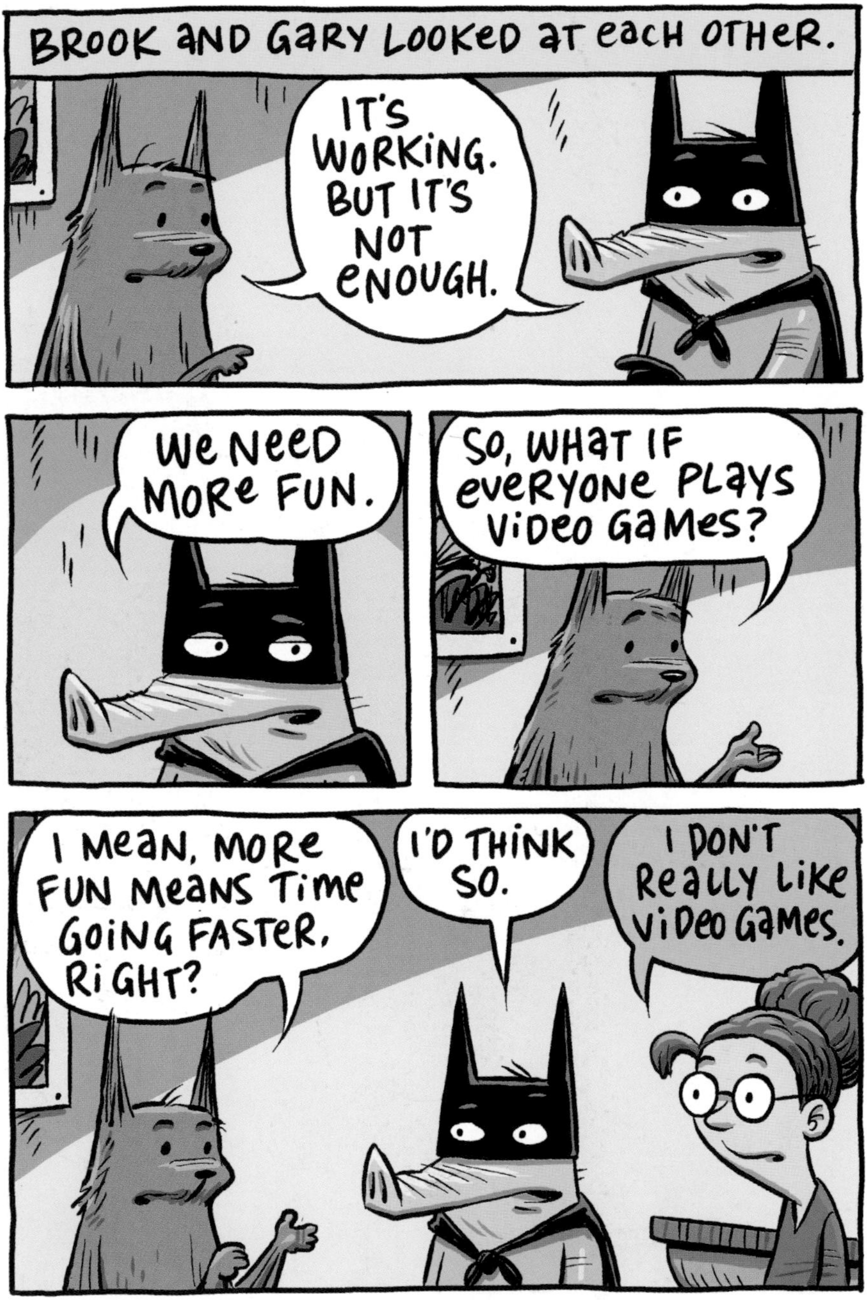
BROOK AND GARY LOOKED AT EACH OTHER.
IT'S WORKING. BUT IT'S NOT ENOUGH.
WE NEED MORE FUN.
SO, WHAT IF EVERYONE PLAYS VIDEO GAMES?
I MEAN, MORE FUN MEANS TIME GOING FASTER, RIGHT?
I'D THINK SO.
I DON'T REALLY LIKE VIDEO GAMES.

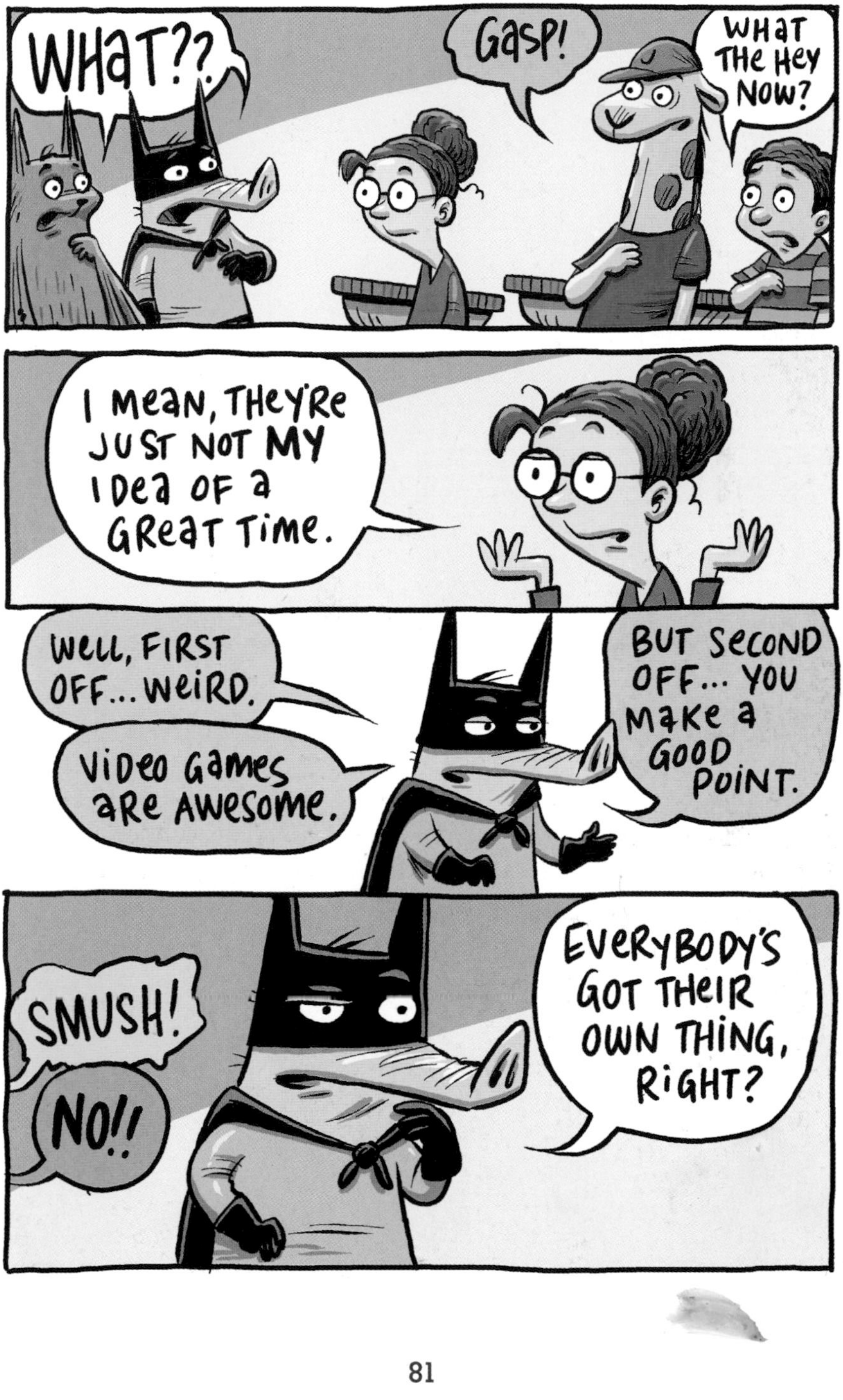
WHAT??
GASP!
WHAT THE HEY NOW?
I MEAN, THEY'RE JUST NOT MY IDEA OF A GREAT TIME.
WELL, FIRST OFF... WEIRD.
VIDEO GAMES ARE AWESOME.
BUT SECOND OFF... YOU MAKE A GOOD POINT.
EVERYBODY'S GOT THEIR OWN THING, RIGHT?
SMUSH!
NO!!

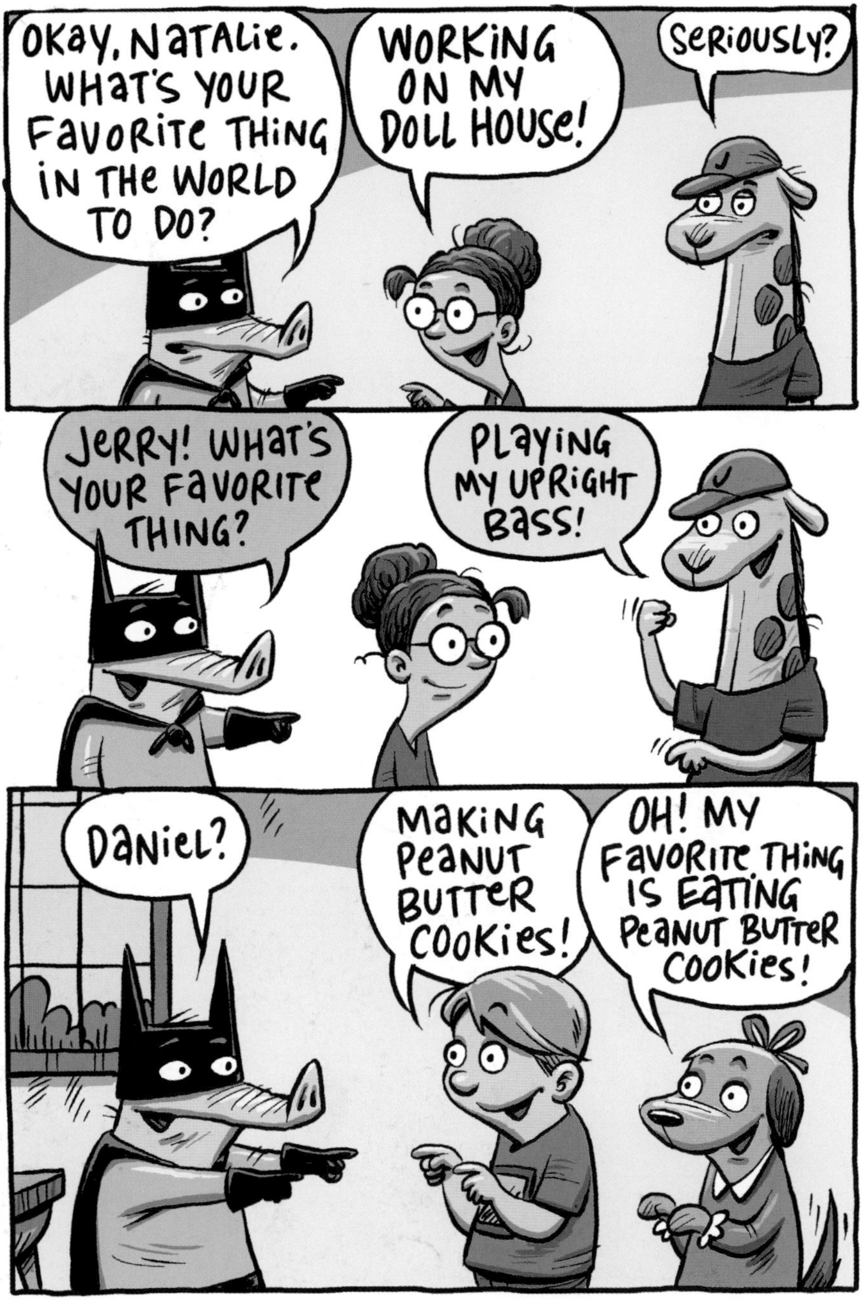
OKAY, NATALIE. WHAT'S YOUR FAVORITE THING IN THE WORLD TO DO?
WORKING ON MY DOLL HOUSE!
SERIOUSLY?
JERRY! WHAT'S YOUR FAVORITE THING?
PLAYING MY UPRIGHT BASS!
DANIEL?
MAKING PEANUT BUTTER COOKIES!
OH! MY FAVORITE THING IS EATING PEANUT BUTTER COOKIES!

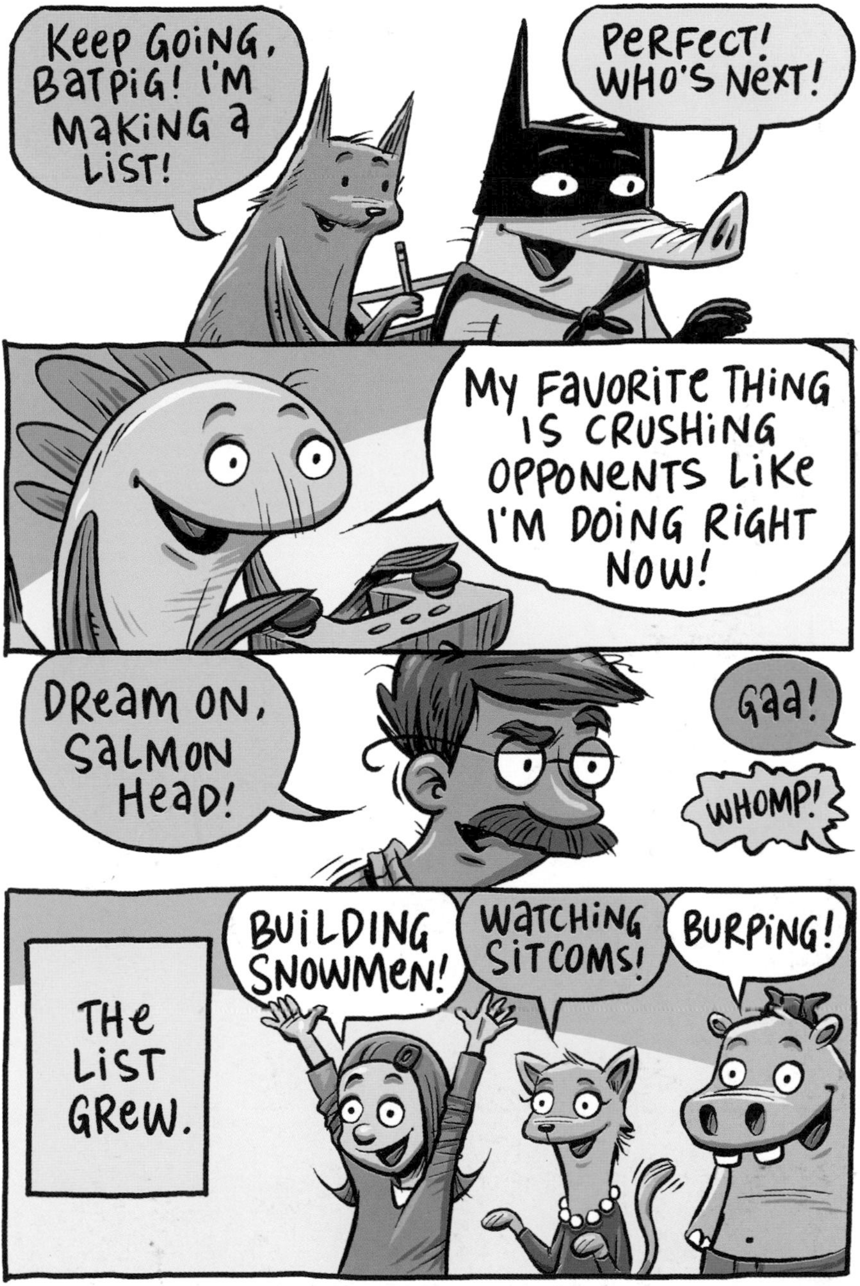
Keep Going, Batpig! I'm making a list!
Perfect! Who's next!
My favorite thing is crushing opponents like I'm doing right now!
Dream on, Salmon Head!
Gaa!
WHOMP!
The list grew.
Building snowmen!
Watching sitcoms!
Burping!

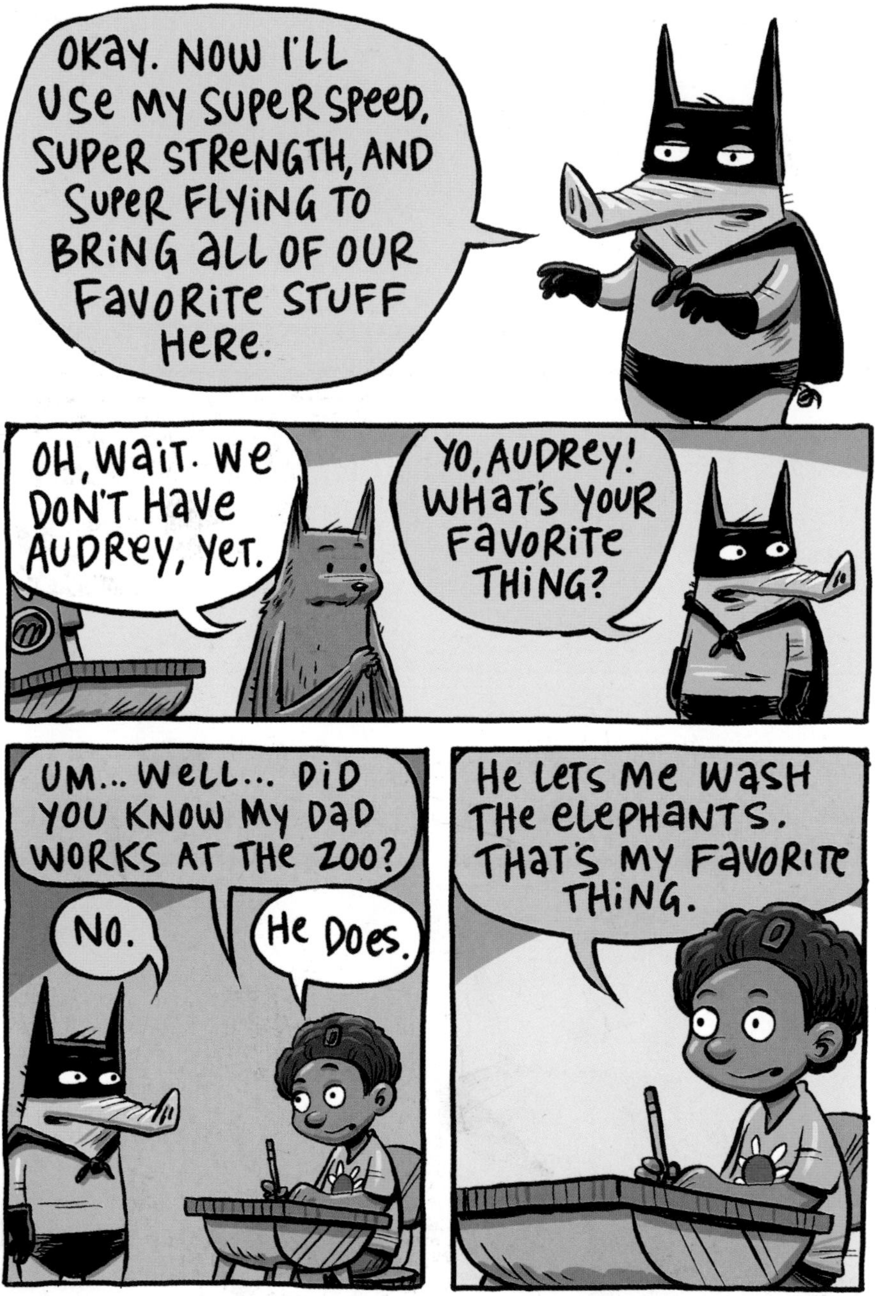
OKAY. NOW I'LL USE MY SUPER SPEED, SUPER STRENGTH, AND SUPER FLYING TO BRING ALL OF OUR FAVORITE STUFF HERE.
OH, WAIT. WE DON'T HAVE AUDREY, YET.
YO, AUDREY! WHAT'S YOUR FAVORITE THING?
UM... WELL... DID YOU KNOW MY DAD WORKS AT THE ZOO?
NO.
HE DOES.
HE LETS ME WASH THE ELEPHANTS. THAT'S MY FAVORITE THING.

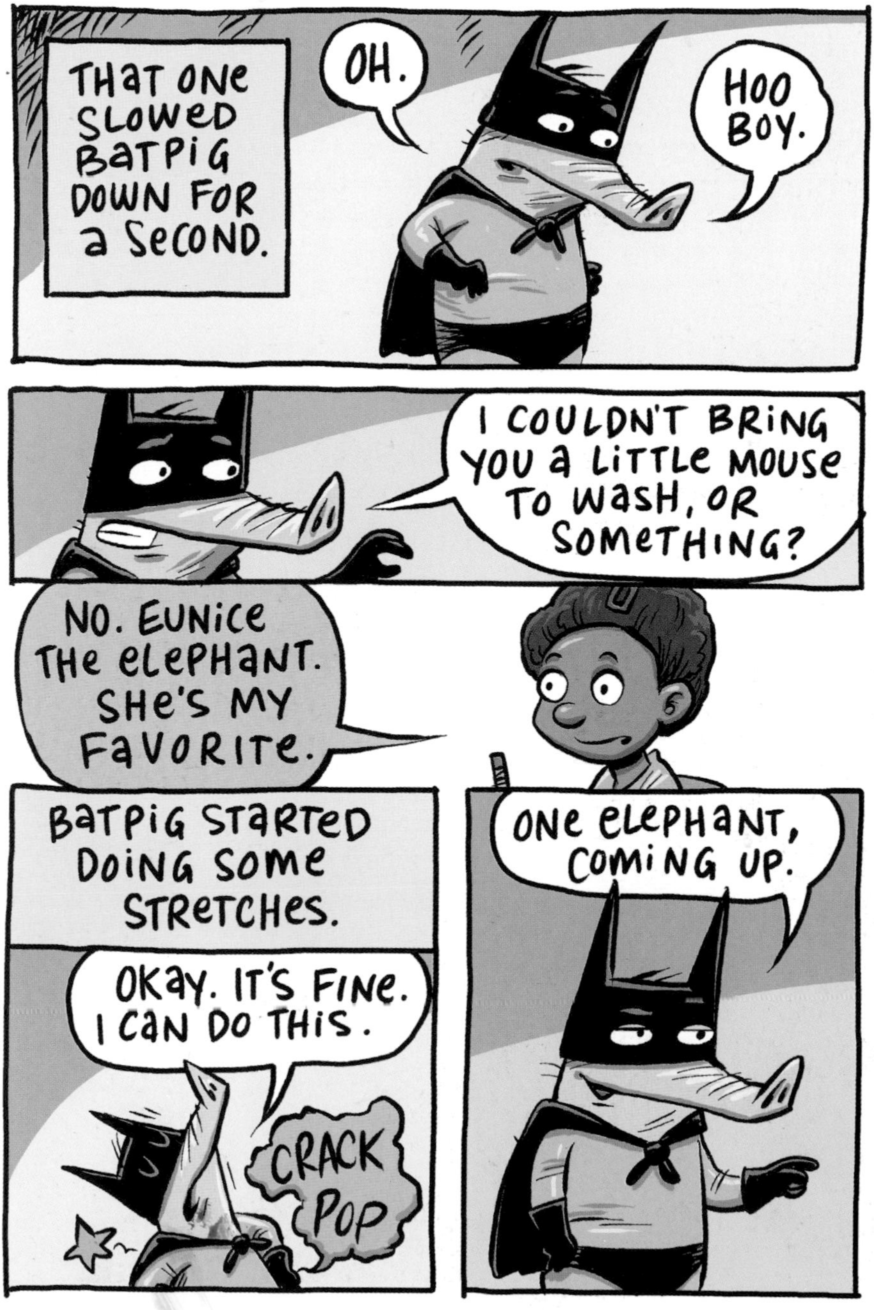
THAT ONE SLOWED BATPIG DOWN FOR A SECOND.
OH.
HOO BOY.
I COULDN'T BRING YOU A LITTLE MOUSE TO WASH, OR SOMETHING?
NO. EUNICE THE ELEPHANT. SHE'S MY FAVORITE.
BATPIG STARTED DOING SOME STRETCHES.
OKAY. IT'S FINE. I CAN DO THIS.
CRACK
POP
ONE ELEPHANT, COMING UP.

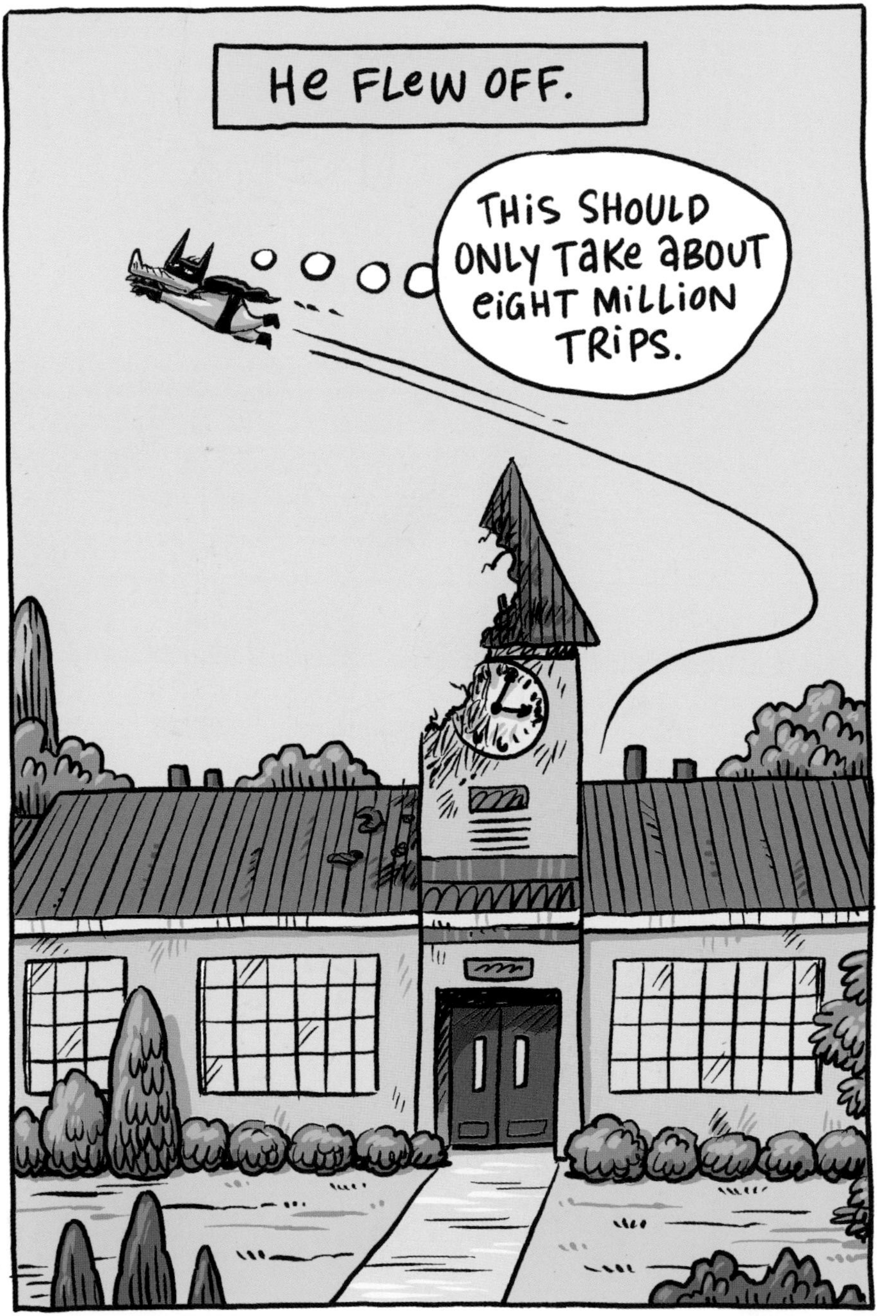
HE FLEW OFF.
THIS SHOULD ONLY TAKE ABOUT EIGHT MILLION TRIPS.

CHAPTER EIGHT

"THESE ARE A FEW OF OUR FAVORITE THINGS"

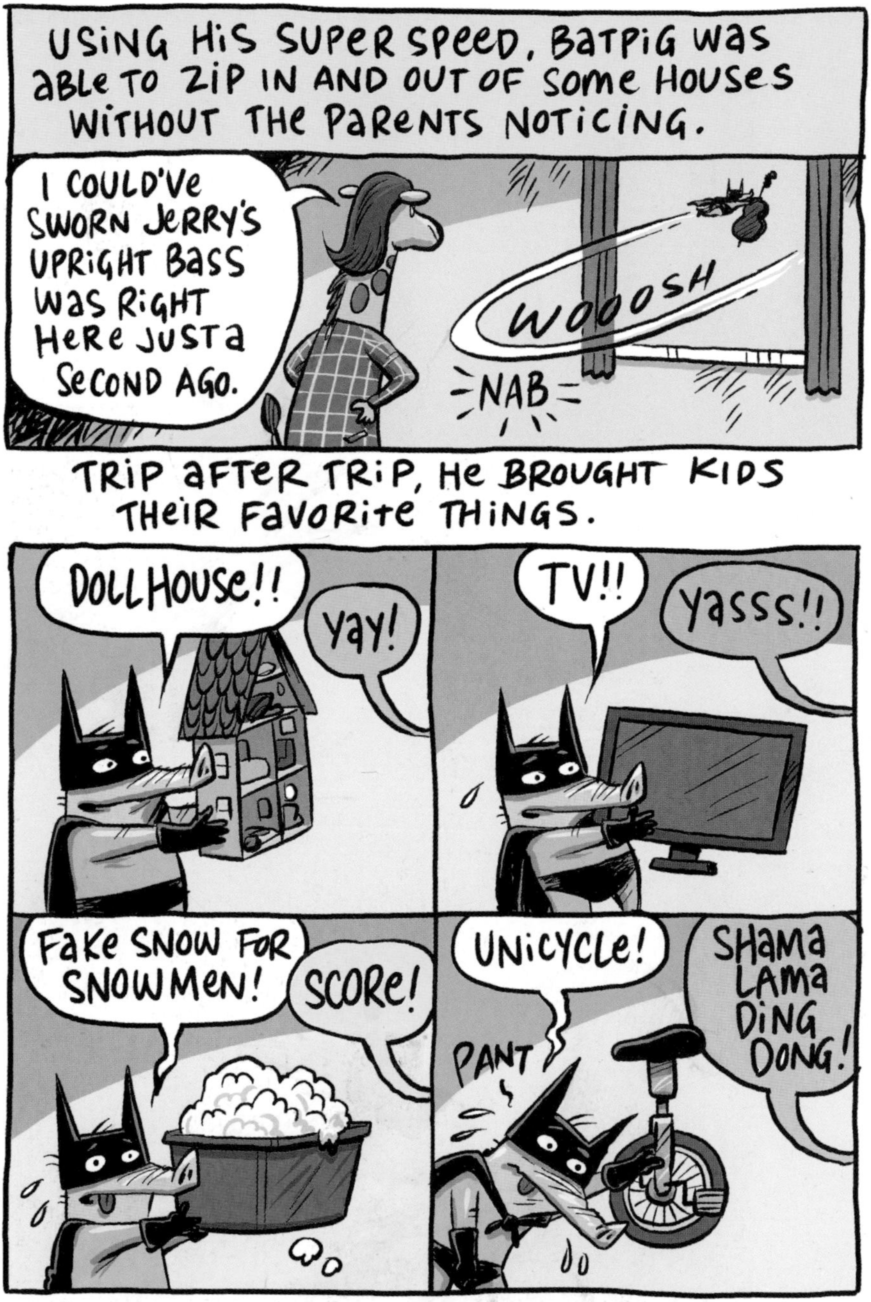
USING HIS SUPER SPEED, BATPIG WAS ABLE TO ZIP IN AND OUT OF SOME HOUSES WITHOUT THE PARENTS NOTICING.
I COULD'VE SWORN JERRY'S UPRIGHT BASS WAS RIGHT HERE JUST A SECOND AGO.
WOOOOSH
NAB
TRIP AFTER TRIP, HE BROUGHT KIDS THEIR FAVORITE THINGS.
DOLLHOUSE!!
YAY!
TV!!
YASSS!!
FAKE SNOW FOR SNOWMEN!
SCORE!
UNICYCLE!
SHAMA LAMA DING DONG!
PANT

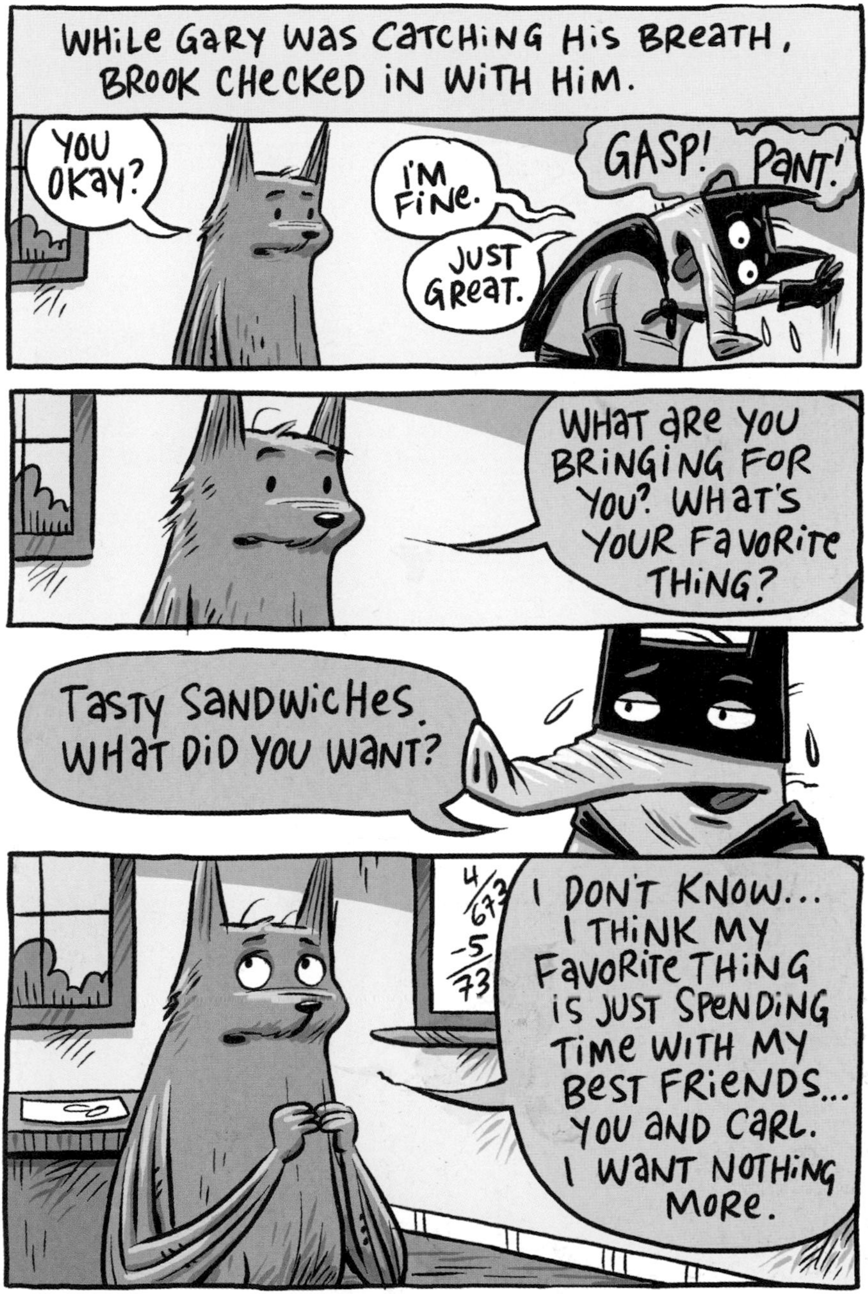
WHILE GARY WAS CATCHING HIS BREATH, BROOK CHECKED IN WITH HIM.
YOU OKAY?
I'M FINE.
JUST GREAT.
GASP! PANT!
WHAT ARE YOU BRINGING FOR YOU? WHAT'S YOUR FAVORITE THING?
TASTY SANDWICHES. WHAT DID YOU WANT?
I DON'T KNOW... I THINK MY FAVORITE THING IS JUST SPENDING TIME WITH MY BEST FRIENDS... YOU AND CARL. I WANT NOTHING MORE.

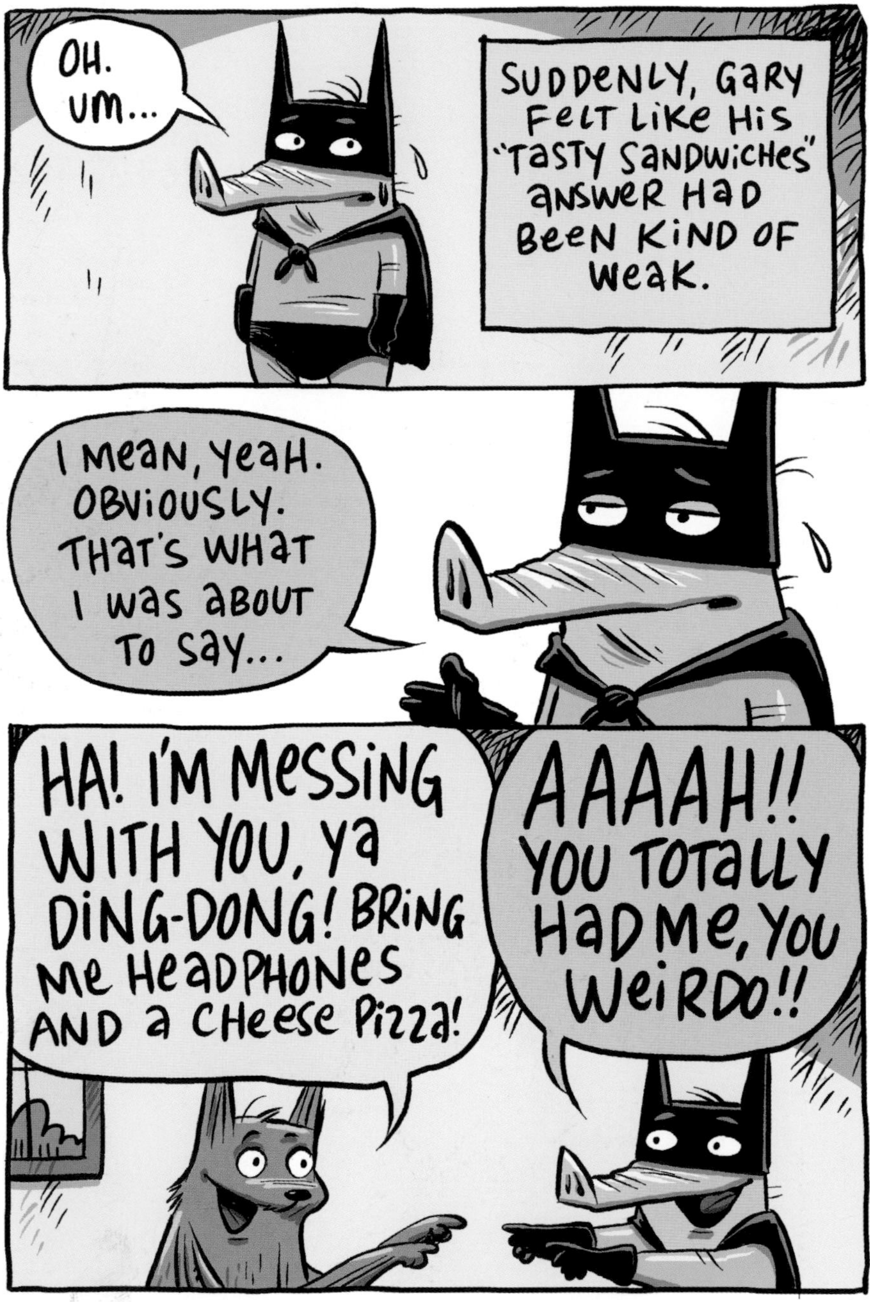
OH. UM...
SUDDENLY, GARY FELT LIKE HIS "TASTY SANDWICHES" ANSWER HAD BEEN KIND OF WEAK.
I MEAN, YEAH. OBVIOUSLY. THAT'S WHAT I WAS ABOUT TO SAY...
HA! I'M MESSING WITH YOU, YA DING-DONG! BRING ME HEADPHONES AND A CHEESE PIZZA!
AAAAH!! YOU TOTALLY HAD ME, YOU WEIRDO!!

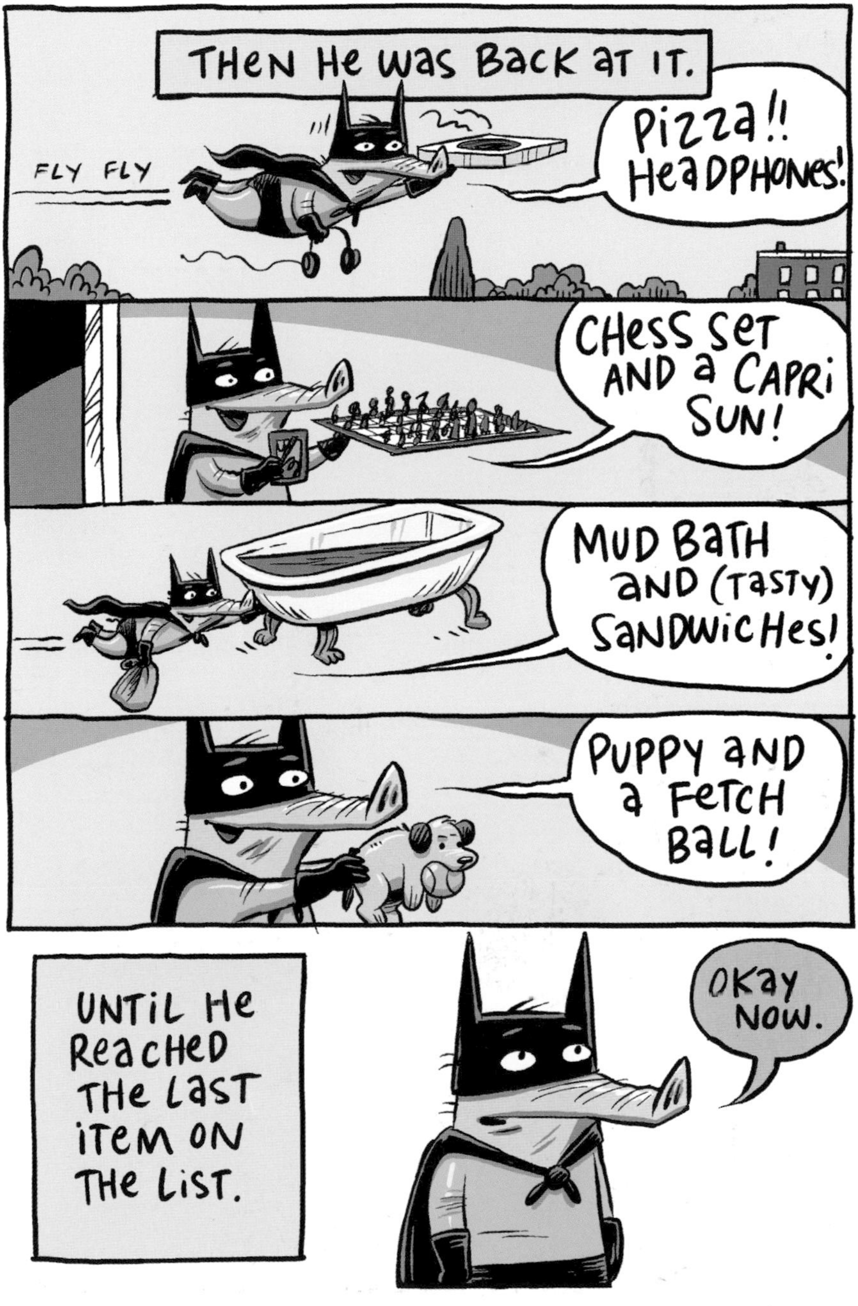
THEN HE WAS BACK AT IT.
FLY FLY
PIZZA!! HEADPHONES!
CHESS SET AND A CAPRI SUN!
MUD BATH AND (TASTY) SANDWICHES!
PUPPY AND A FETCH BALL!
UNTIL HE REACHED THE LAST ITEM ON THE LIST.
OKAY NOW.

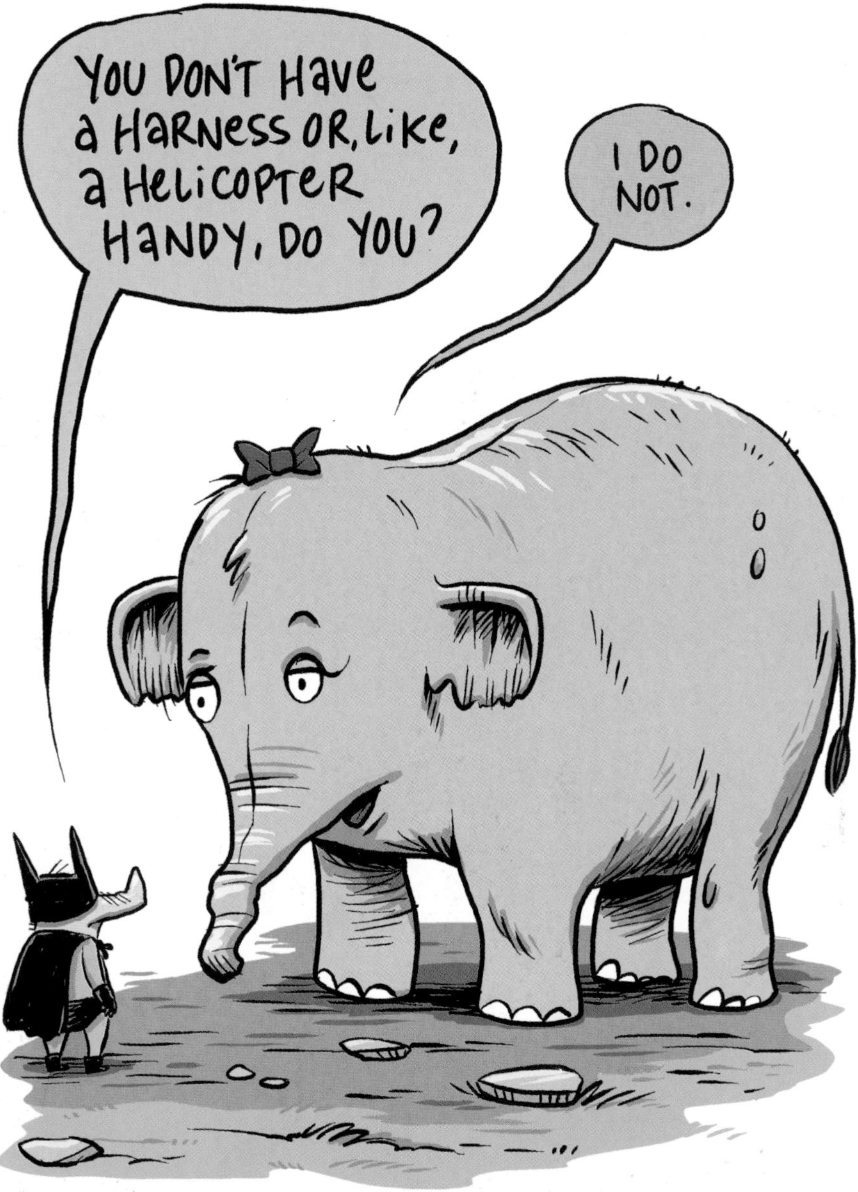
YOU DON'T HAVE a HARNESS OR, LIKE, a HELICOPTER HANDY, DO YOU?
I DO NOT.

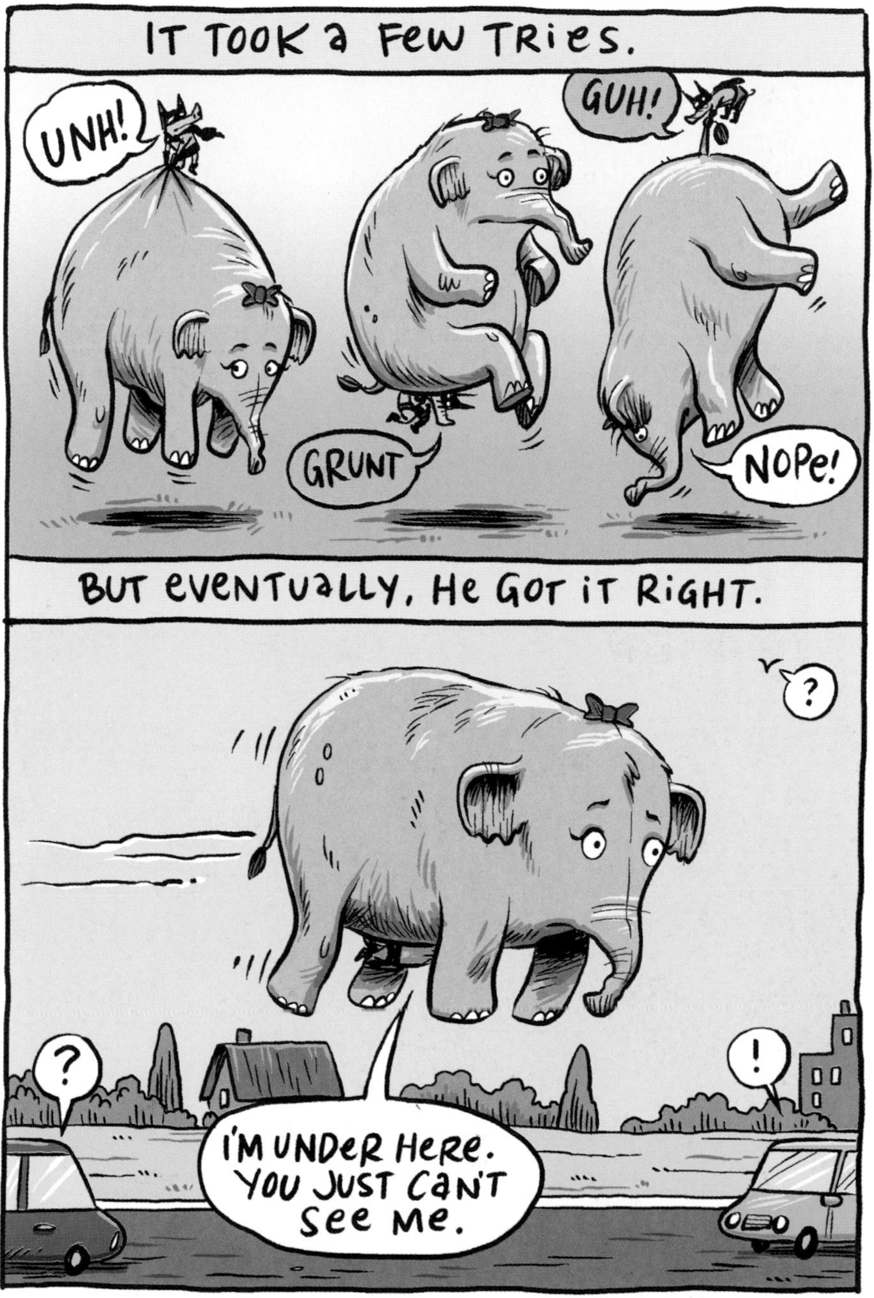
IT TOOK a Few TRies.
UNH!
GUH!
GRUNT
NOPe!
BUT eventually, He GOT iT RiGHT.
?
?
!
I'M UNDER HeRe. YOU JUST CaN'T See Me.

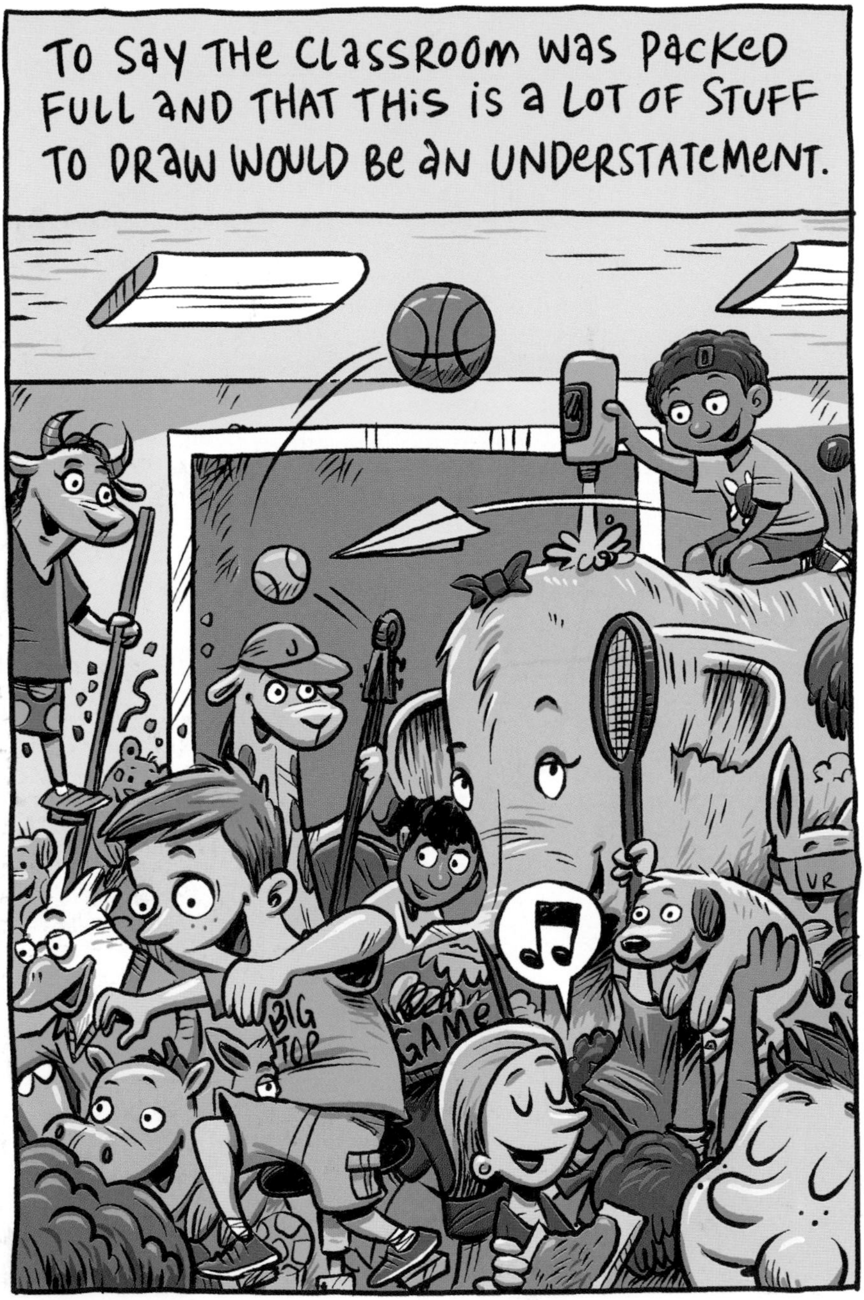
TO SAY THE CLASSROOM WAS PACKED FULL AND THAT THIS IS A LOT OF STUFF TO DRAW WOULD BE AN UNDERSTATEMENT.
BIG TOP
GAME
VR

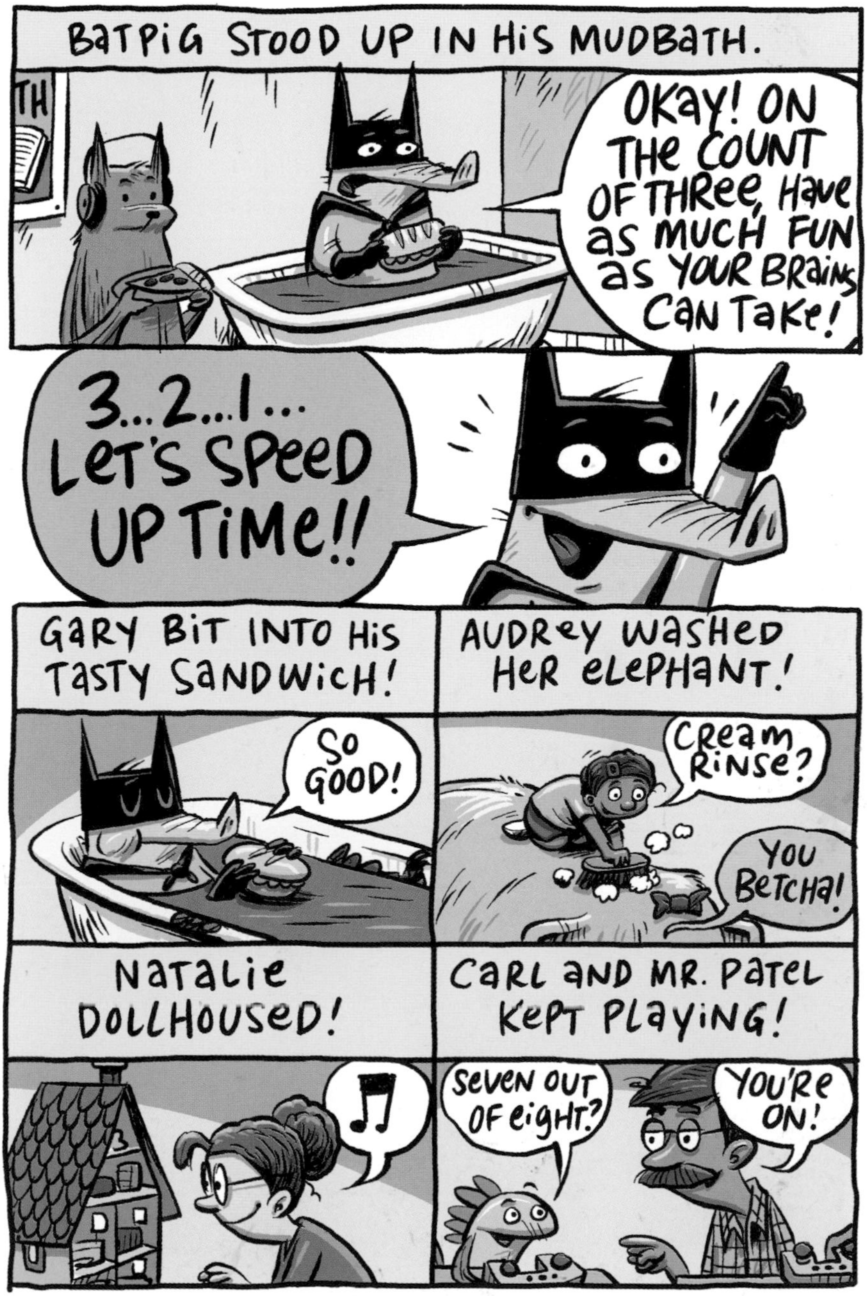
BATPIG STOOD UP IN HIS MUDBATH.
OKAY! ON THE COUNT OF THREE, HAVE AS MUCH FUN AS YOUR BRAINS CAN TAKE!
3...2...1... LET'S SPEED UP TIME!!
GARY BIT INTO HIS TASTY SANDWICH!
SO GOOD!
AUDREY WASHED HER ELEPHANT!
CREAM RINSE?
YOU BETCHA!
NATALIE DOLLHOUSED!
♫
CARL AND MR. PATEL KEPT PLAYING!
SEVEN OUT OF EIGHT?
YOU'RE ON!

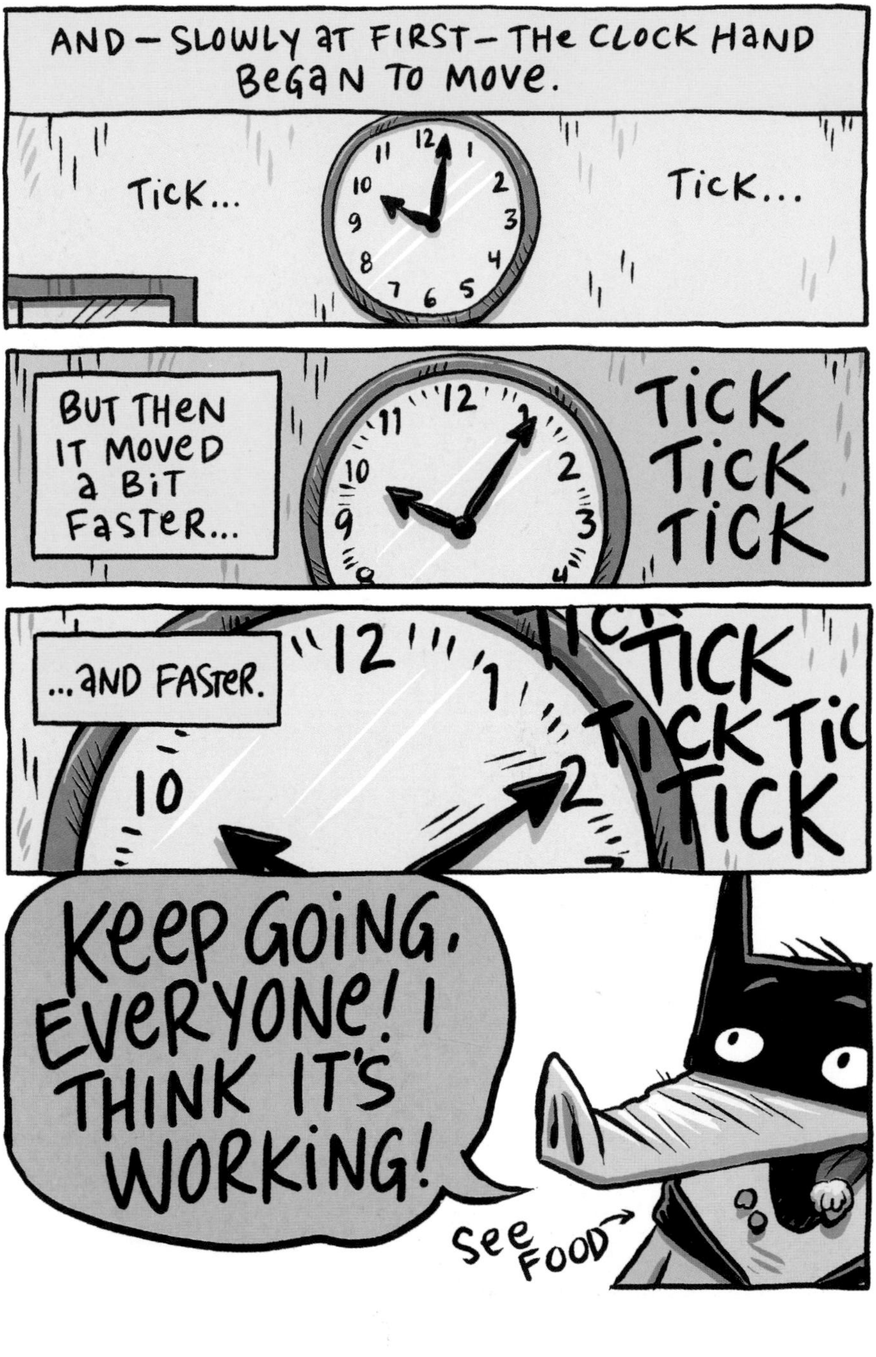
AND—SLOWLY AT FIRST—THE CLOCK HAND BEGAN TO MOVE.
TICK...
TICK...
BUT THEN IT MOVED A BIT FASTER...
TICK
TICK
TICK
...AND FASTER.
TICK
TICK TIC
TICK
KEEP GOING, EVERYONE! I THINK IT'S WORKING!
SEE FOOD

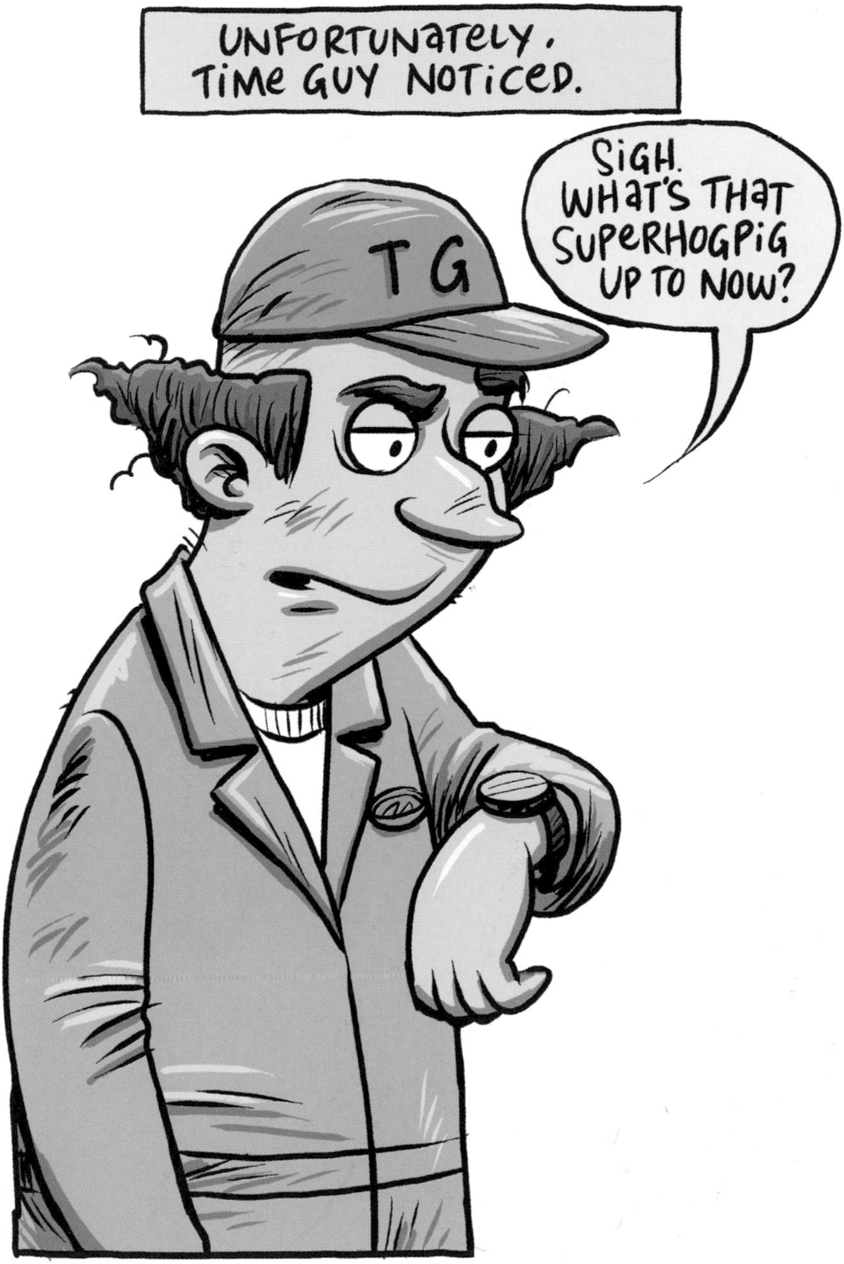
UNFORTUNATELY, TIME GUY NOTICED.
SIGH. WHAT'S THAT SUPERHOGPIG UP TO NOW?
TG

CHAPTER NINE

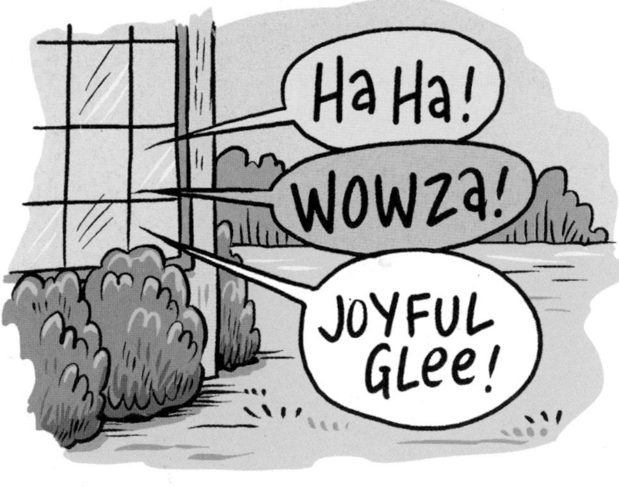
Ha Ha!
WOWZA!
JOYFUL GLEE!

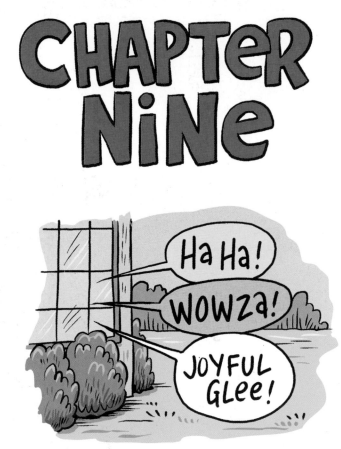

"FUN HARDER"

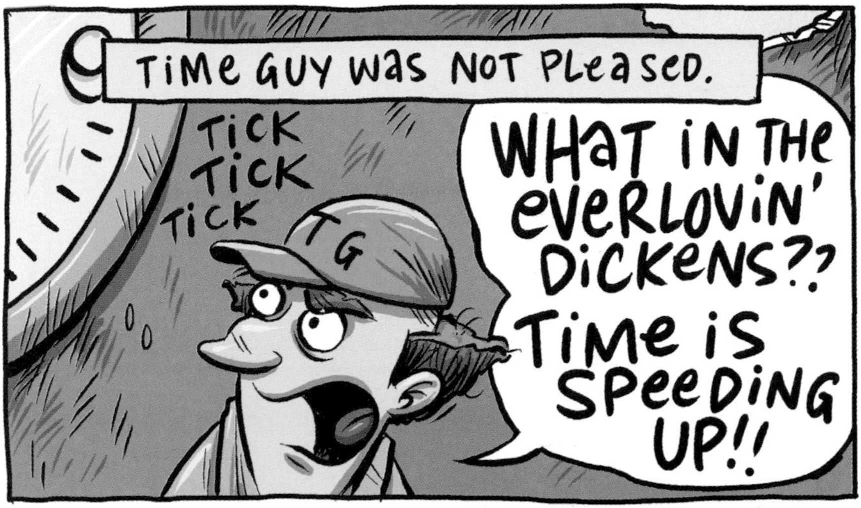
TIME GUY WAS NOT PLEASED.
TICK
TICK
TICK
TG
WHAT IN THE EVERLOVIN' DICKENS?? TIME IS SPEEDING UP!!

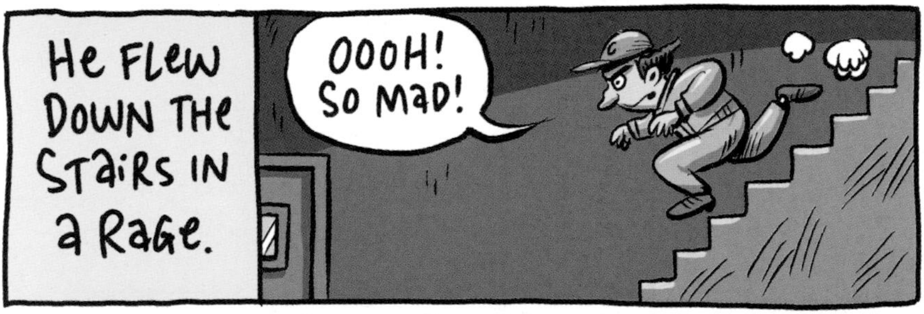
HE FLEW DOWN THE STAIRS IN A RAGE.
OOOH! SO MAD!

IN THE HALL HE STOPPED, LISTENING.

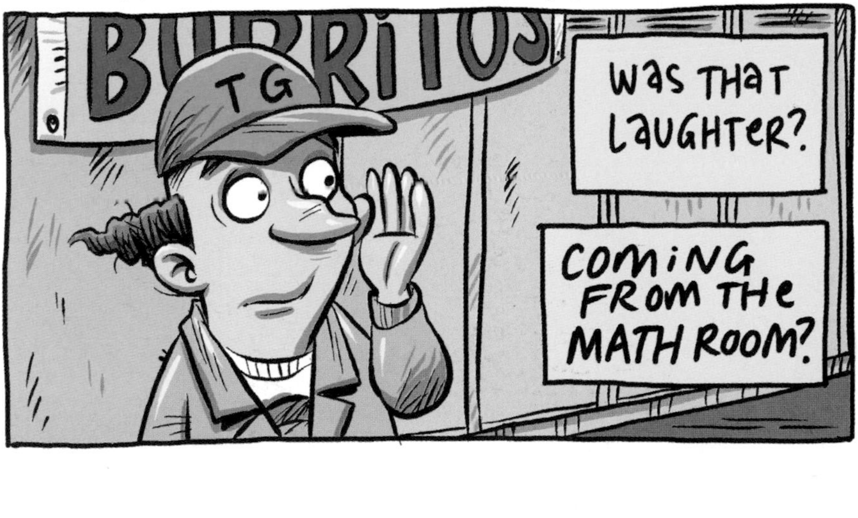
BURRITOS
TG
WAS THAT LAUGHTER?
COMING FROM THE MATH ROOM?

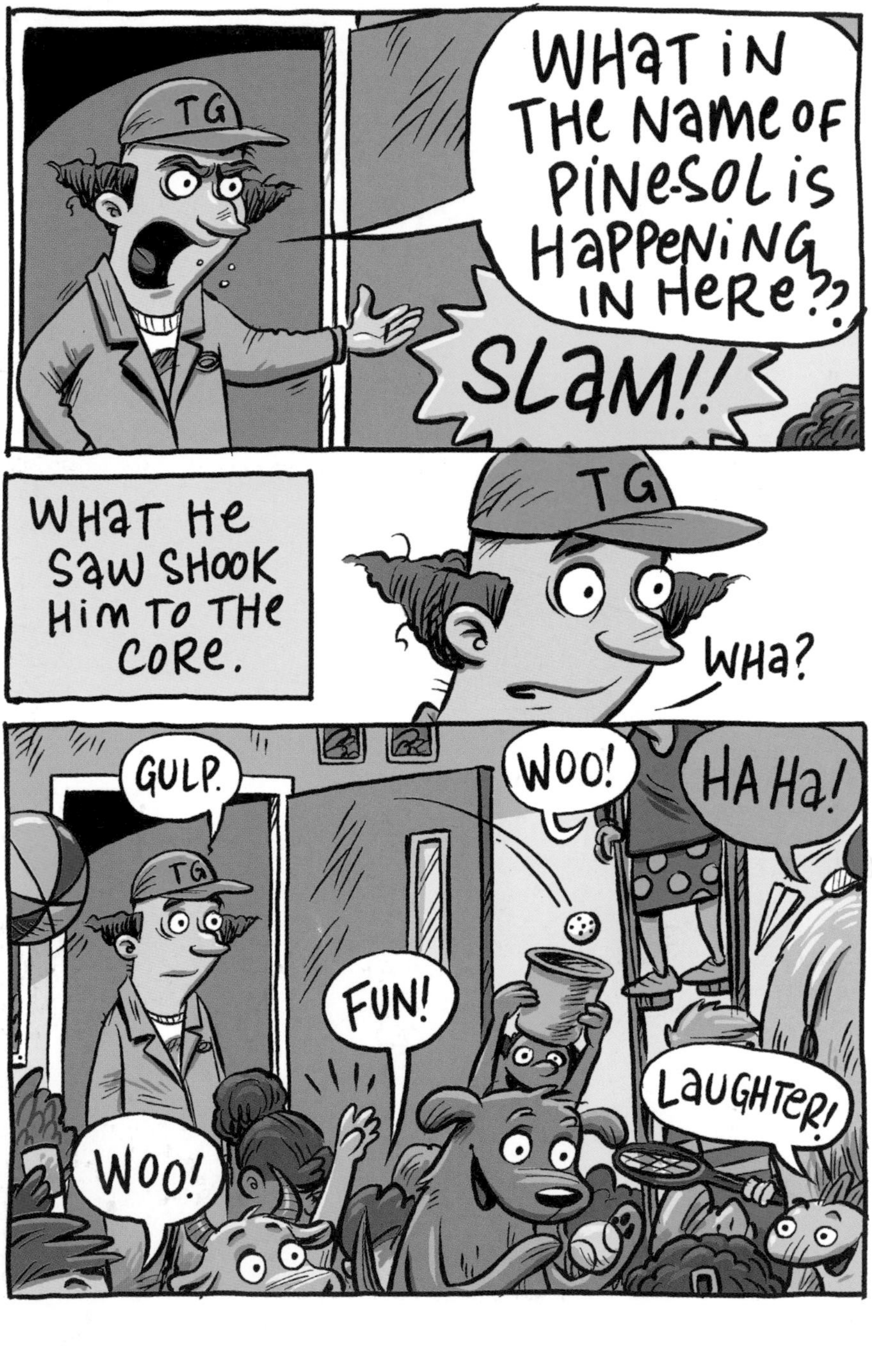
WHAT IN THE NAME OF PINE-SOL IS HAPPENING IN HERE??
SLAM!!
WHAT HE SAW SHOOK HIM TO THE CORE.
WHA?
GULP.
WOO!
HA HA!
FUN!
LAUGHTER!
WOO!

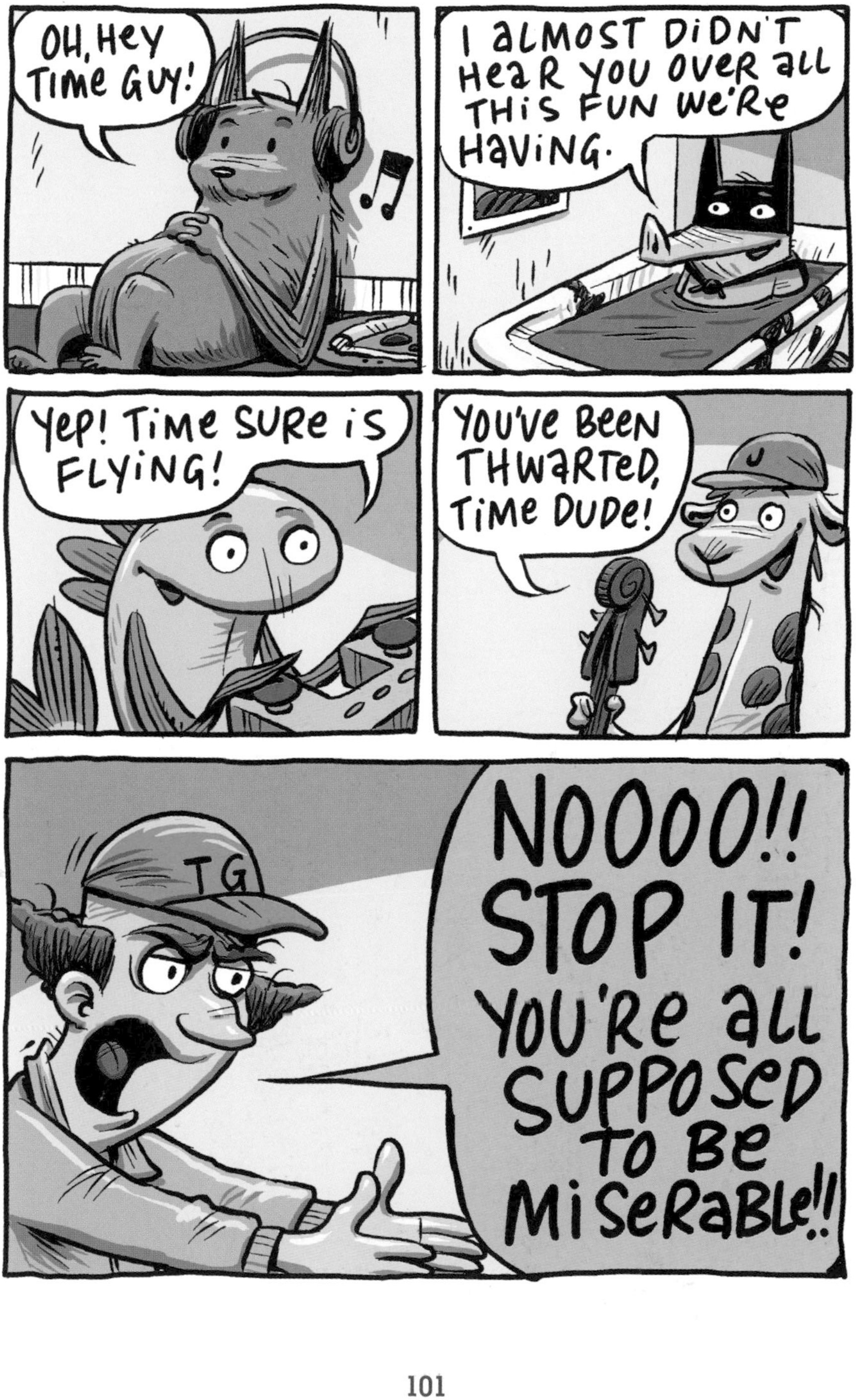
OH, HEY TIME GUY!
I ALMOST DIDN'T HEAR YOU OVER ALL THIS FUN WE'RE HAVING.
YEP! TIME SURE IS FLYING!
YOU'VE BEEN THWARTED, TIME DUDE!
TG
NOOOO!! STOP IT! YOU'RE ALL SUPPOSED TO BE MISERABLE!!

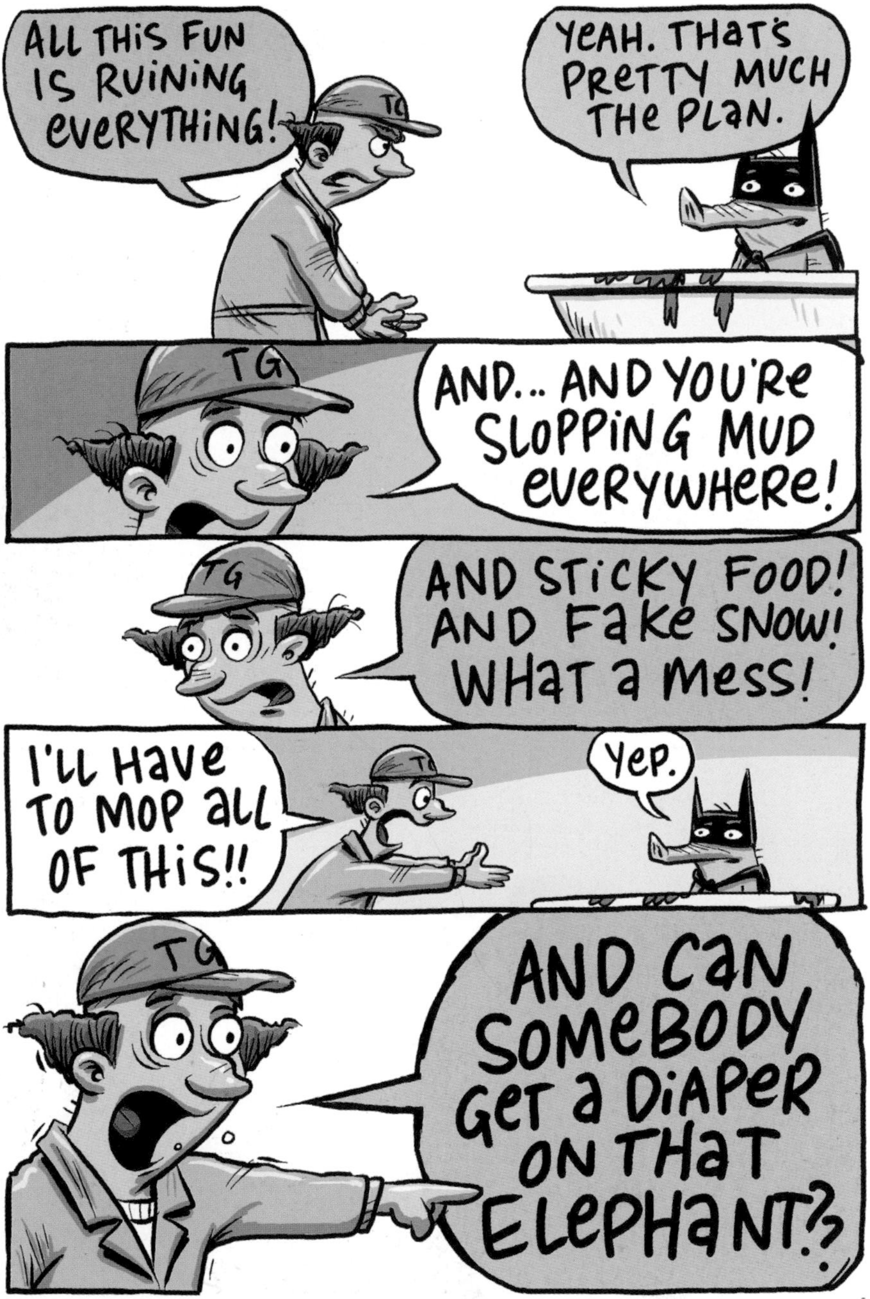
ALL THIS FUN IS RUINING EVERYTHING!
YEAH. THAT'S PRETTY MUCH THE PLAN.
TG
AND... AND YOU'RE SLOPPING MUD EVERYWHERE!
AND STICKY FOOD! AND FAKE SNOW! WHAT A MESS!
I'LL HAVE TO MOP ALL OF THIS!!
YEP.
AND CAN SOMEBODY GET A DIAPER ON THAT ELEPHANT?

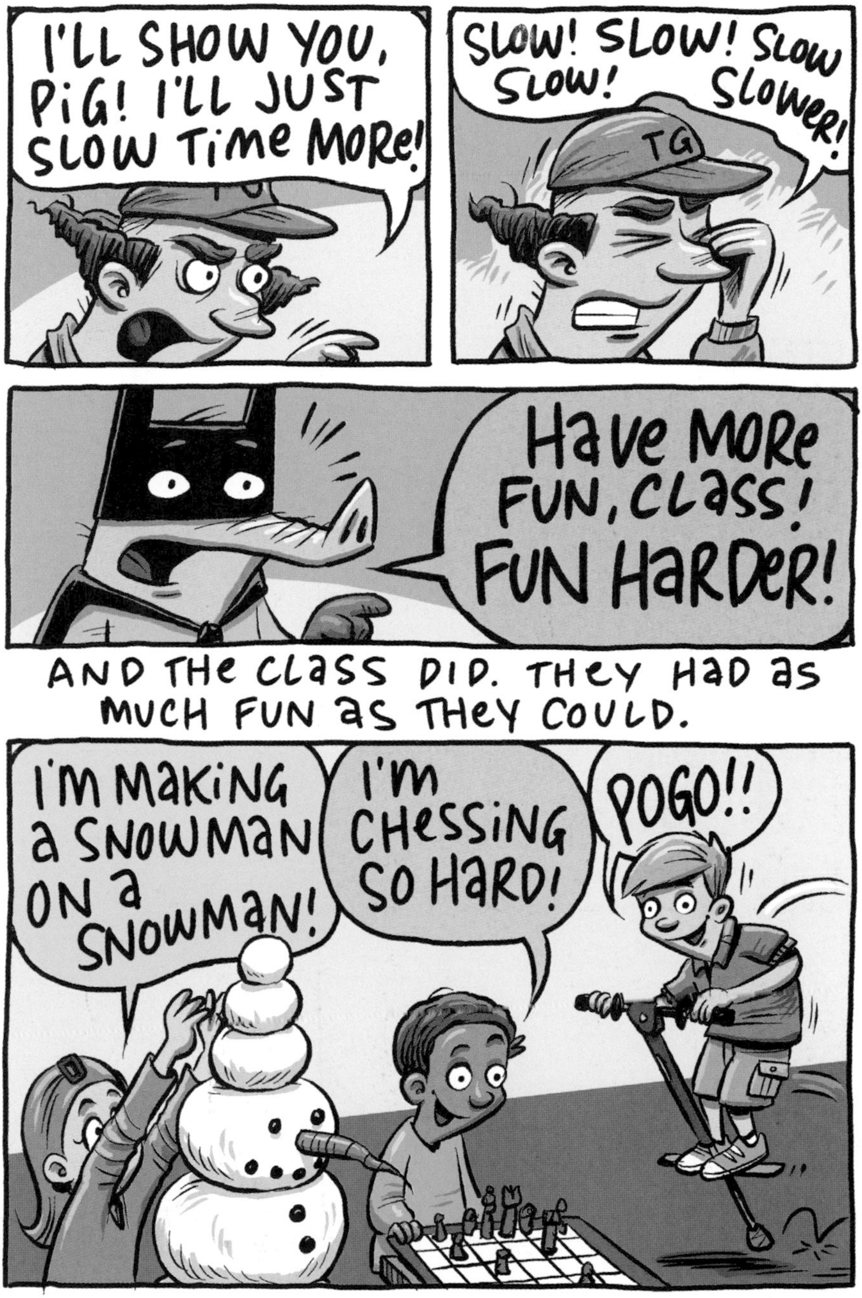
I'LL SHOW YOU, PIG! I'LL JUST SLOW TIME MORE!
SLOW! SLOW! SLOW SLOW! SLOWER!
TG
Have MORE FUN, CLASS! FUN HARDER!
AND THE CLASS DID. THEY HAD AS MUCH FUN AS THEY COULD.
I'M MAKING A SNOWMAN ON A SNOWMAN!
I'M CHESSING SO HARD!
POGO!!

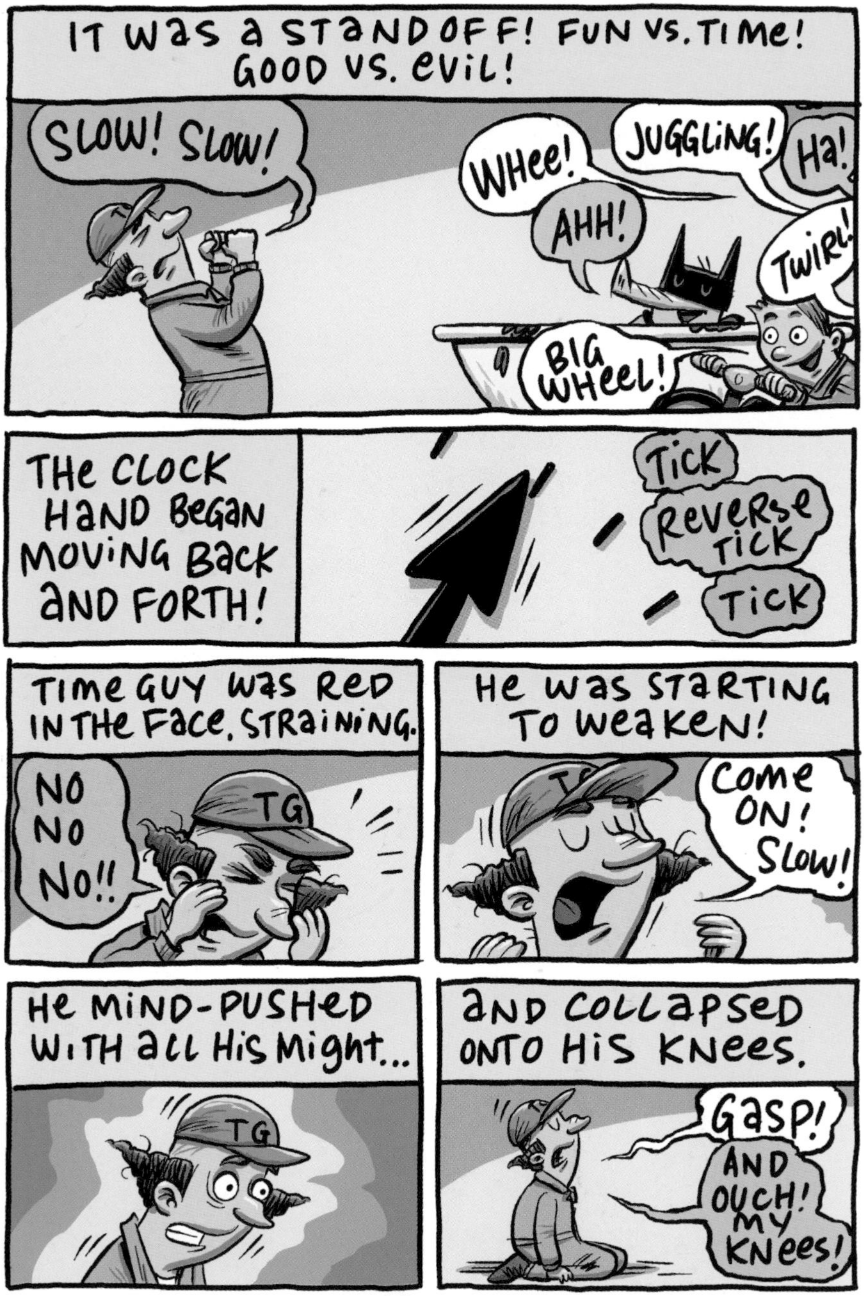
IT WAS A STANDOFF! FUN VS. TIME! GOOD VS. EVIL!
SLOW! SLOW!
WHEE!
JUGGLING!
HA!
AHH!
TWIRL!
BIG WHEEL!
THE CLOCK HAND BEGAN MOVING BACK AND FORTH!
TICK
REVERSE TICK
TICK
TIME GUY WAS RED IN THE FACE, STRAINING.
NO NO NO!!
TG
HE WAS STARTING TO WEAKEN!
COME ON! SLOW!
HE MIND-PUSHED WITH ALL HIS MIGHT...
TG
AND COLLAPSED ONTO HIS KNEES.
GASP!
AND OUCH! MY KNEES!

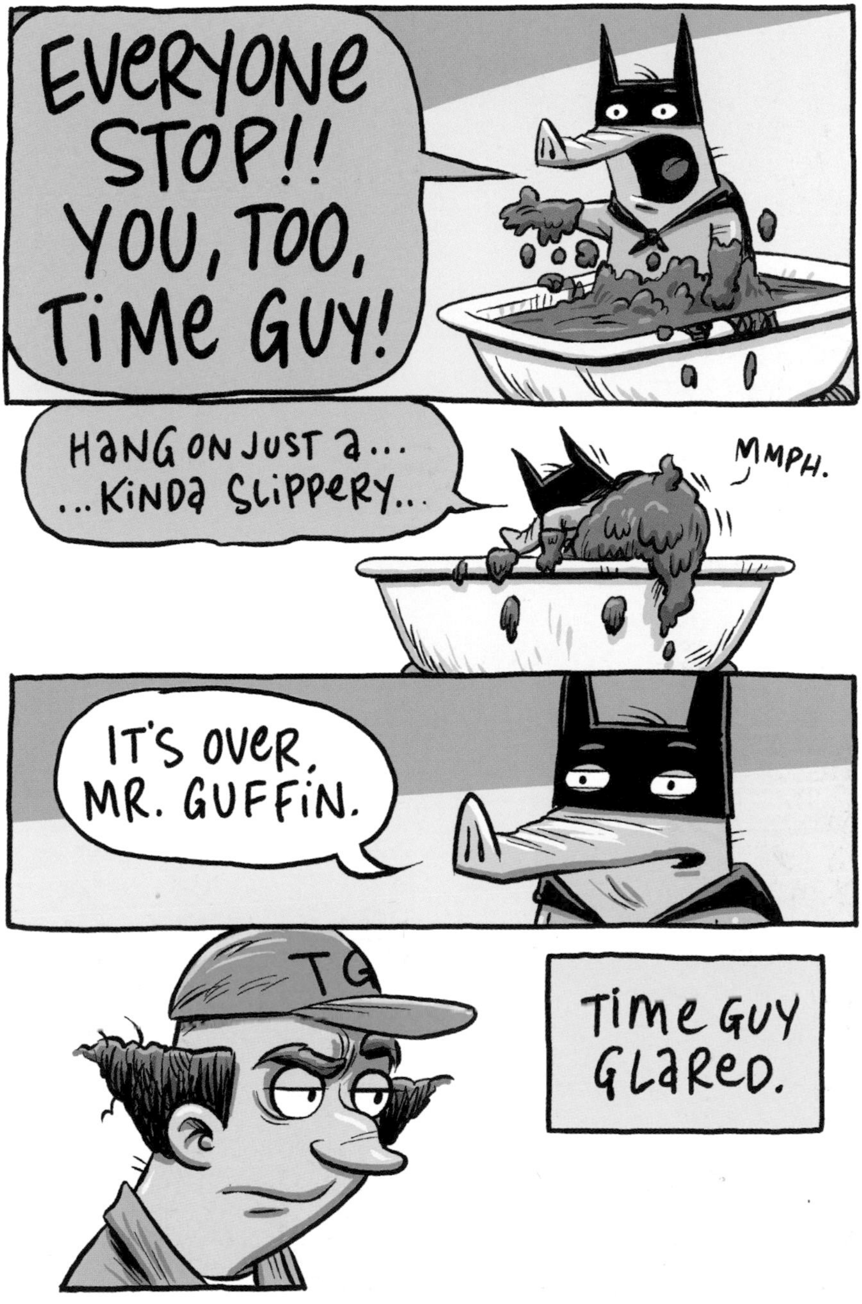
EVERYONE STOP!! YOU, TOO, TIME GUY!
HANG ON JUST A... ...KINDA SLIPPERY...
MMPH.
IT'S OVER, MR. GUFFIN.
TIME GUY GLARED.

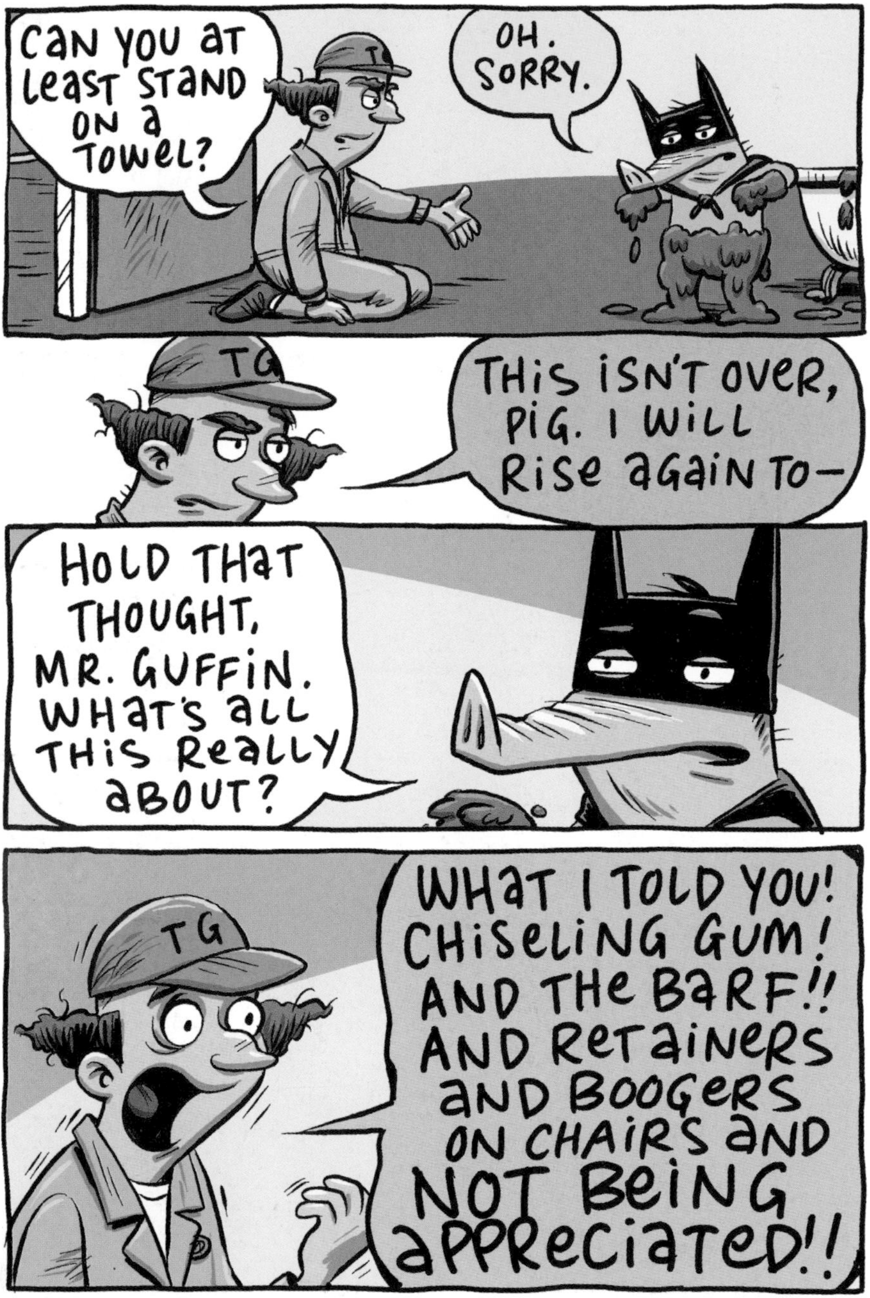
CAN YOU AT LEAST STAND ON A TOWEL?
OH. SORRY.
THIS ISN'T OVER, PIG. I WILL RISE AGAIN TO—
HOLD THAT THOUGHT, MR. GUFFIN. WHAT'S ALL THIS REALLY ABOUT?
WHAT I TOLD YOU! CHISELING GUM! AND THE BARF!! AND RETAINERS AND BOOGERS ON CHAIRS AND NOT BEING APPRECIATED!!

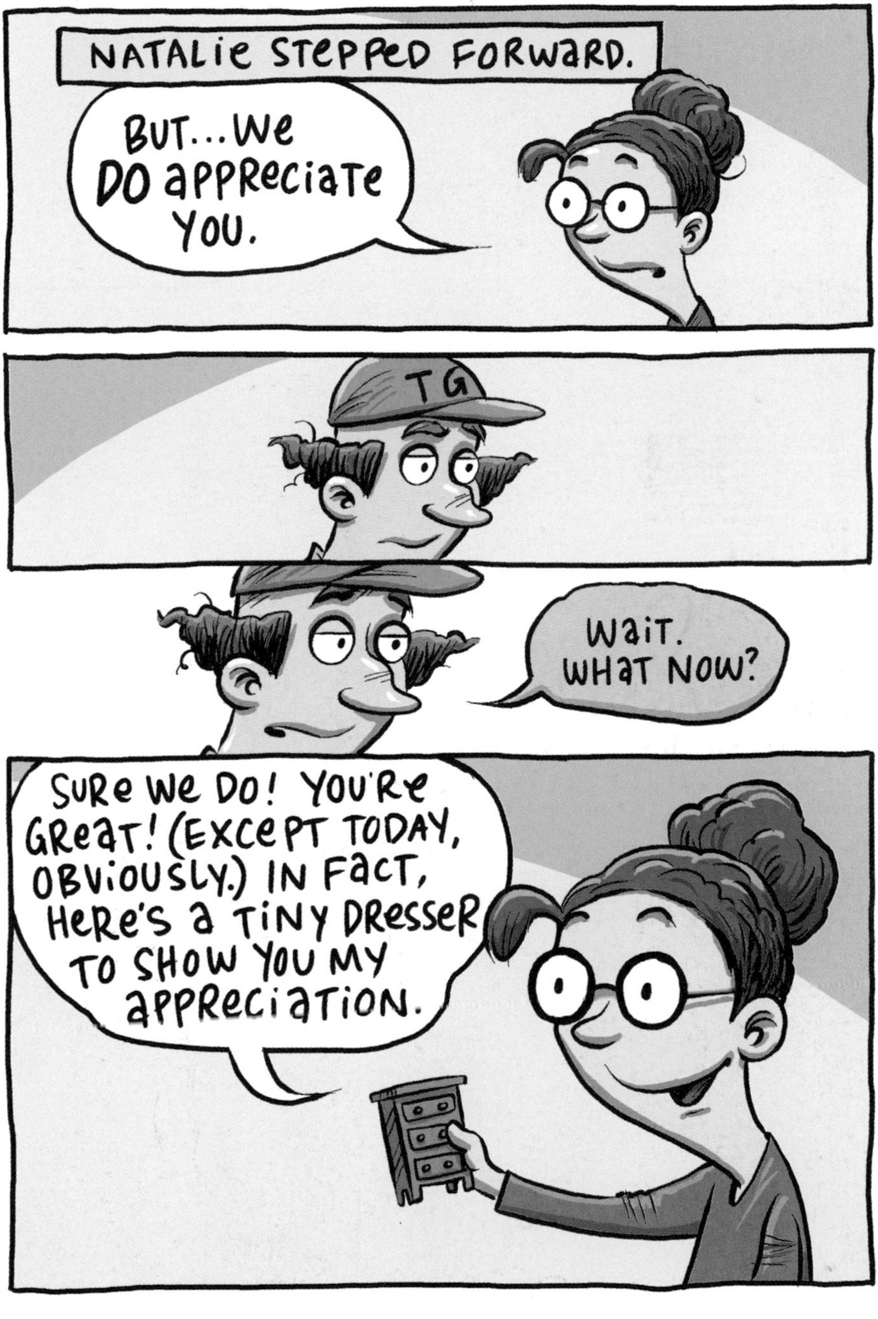
NATALIE STEPPED FORWARD.
BUT... WE DO APPRECIATE YOU.
WAIT. WHAT NOW?
SURE WE DO! YOU'RE GREAT! (EXCEPT TODAY, OBVIOUSLY.) IN FACT, HERE'S A TINY DRESSER TO SHOW YOU MY APPRECIATION.

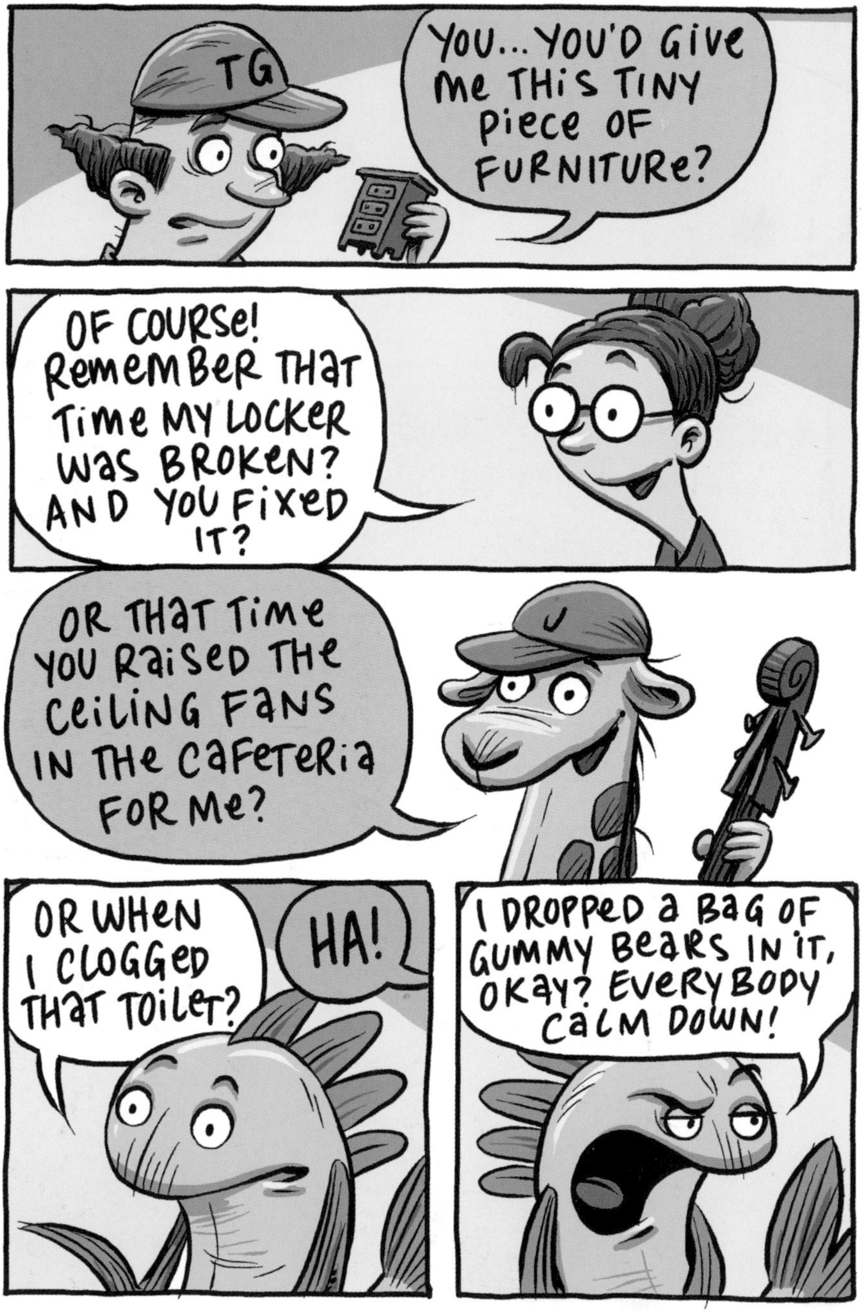
YOU... YOU'D GIVE ME THIS TINY PIECE OF FURNITURE?
OF COURSE! REMEMBER THAT TIME MY LOCKER WAS BROKEN? AND YOU FIXED IT?
OR THAT TIME YOU RAISED THE CEILING FANS IN THE CAFETERIA FOR ME?
OR WHEN I CLOGGED THAT TOILET?
HA!
I DROPPED A BAG OF GUMMY BEARS IN IT, OKAY? EVERYBODY CALM DOWN!

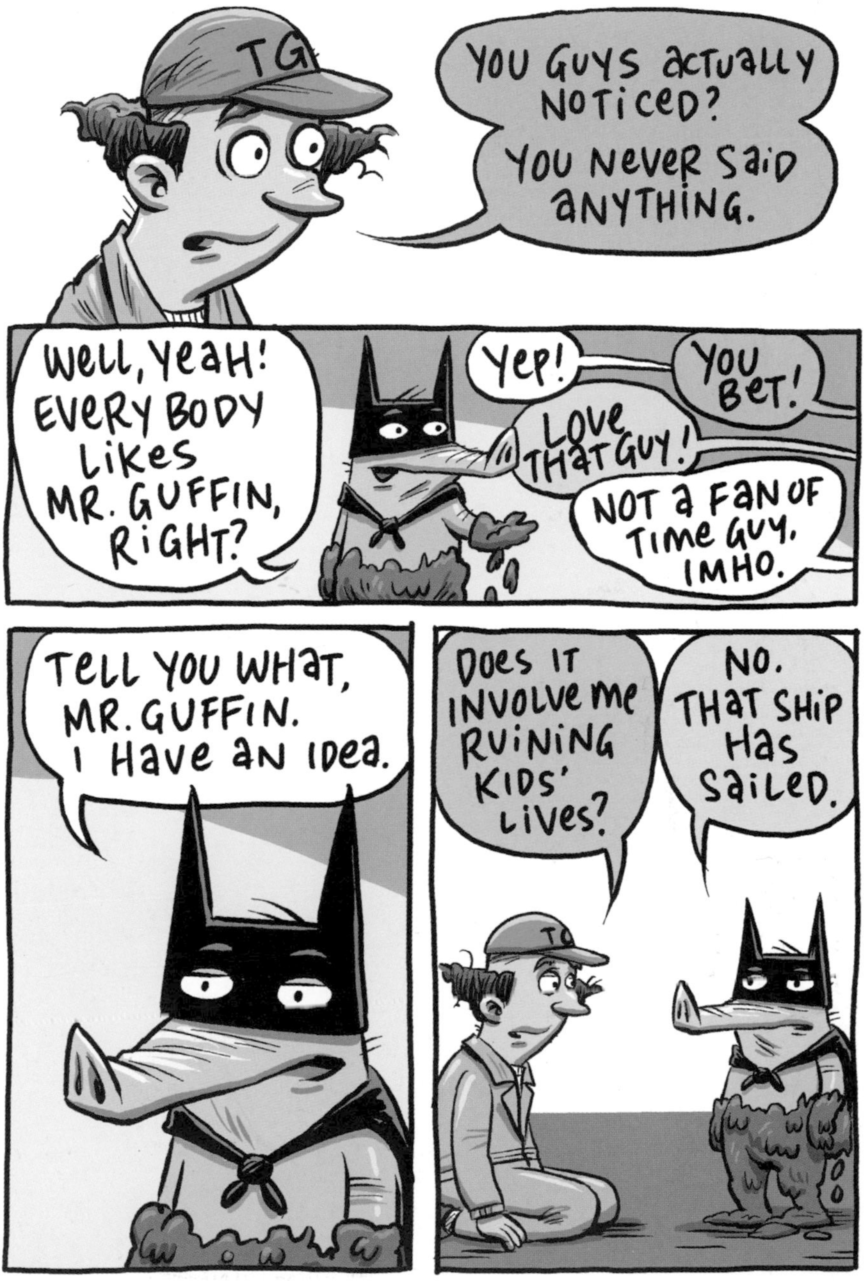
YOU GUYS ACTUALLY NOTICED?
YOU NEVER SAID ANYTHING.
WELL, YEAH! EVERYBODY LIKES MR. GUFFIN, RIGHT?
YEP!
YOU BET!
LOVE THAT GUY!
NOT A FAN OF TIME GUY, IMHO.
TELL YOU WHAT, MR. GUFFIN. I HAVE AN IDEA.
DOES IT INVOLVE ME RUINING KIDS' LIVES?
NO. THAT SHIP HAS SAILED.

CHAPTER TEN

TG
!

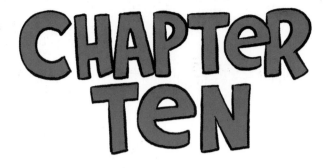

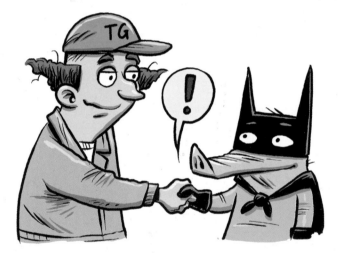

"TRUCE!"

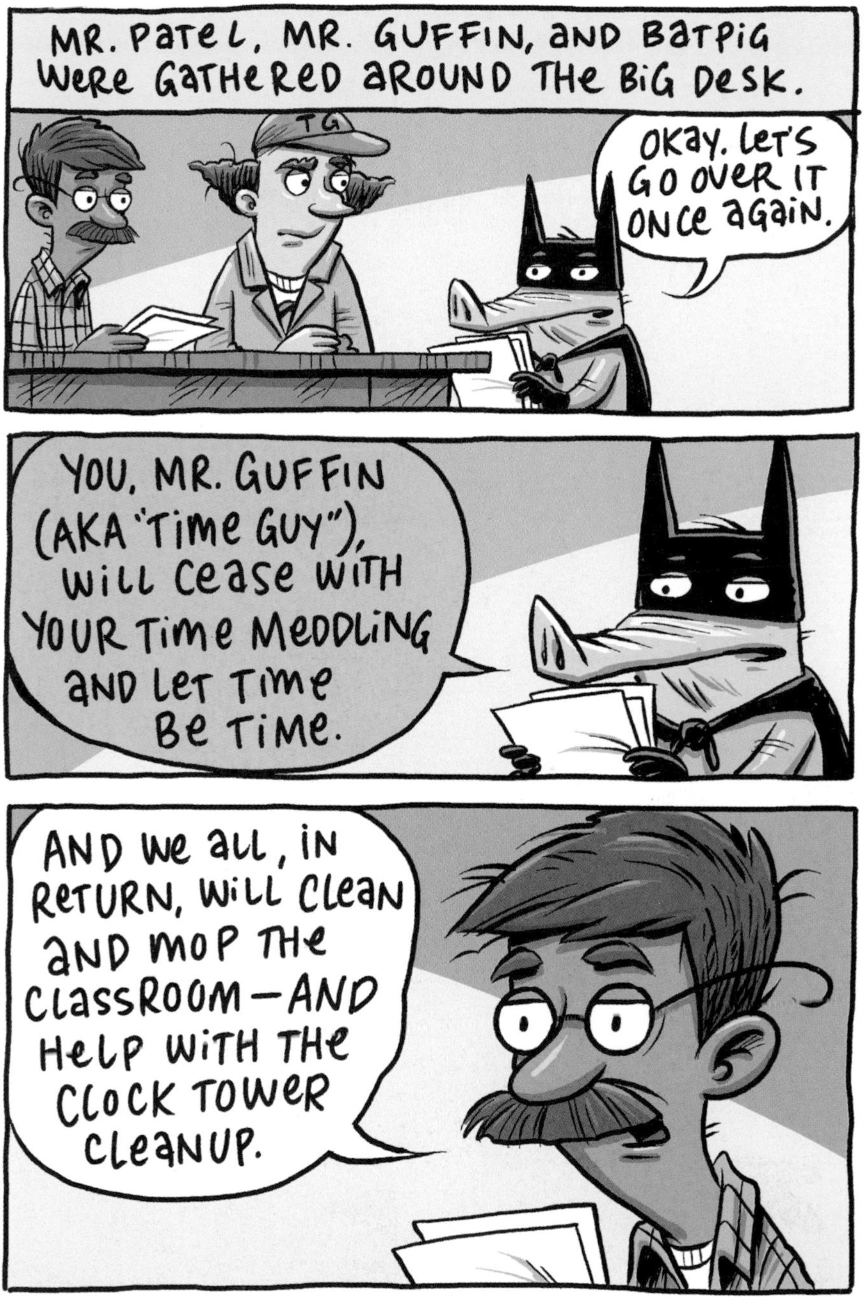
MR. PATEL, MR. GUFFIN, AND BATPIG WERE GATHERED AROUND THE BIG DESK.
TG
OKAY. LET'S GO OVER IT ONCE AGAIN.
YOU, MR. GUFFIN (AKA "TIME GUY"), WILL CEASE WITH YOUR TIME MEDDLING AND LET TIME BE TIME.
AND WE ALL, IN RETURN, WILL CLEAN AND MOP THE CLASSROOM—AND HELP WITH THE CLOCK TOWER CLEANUP.

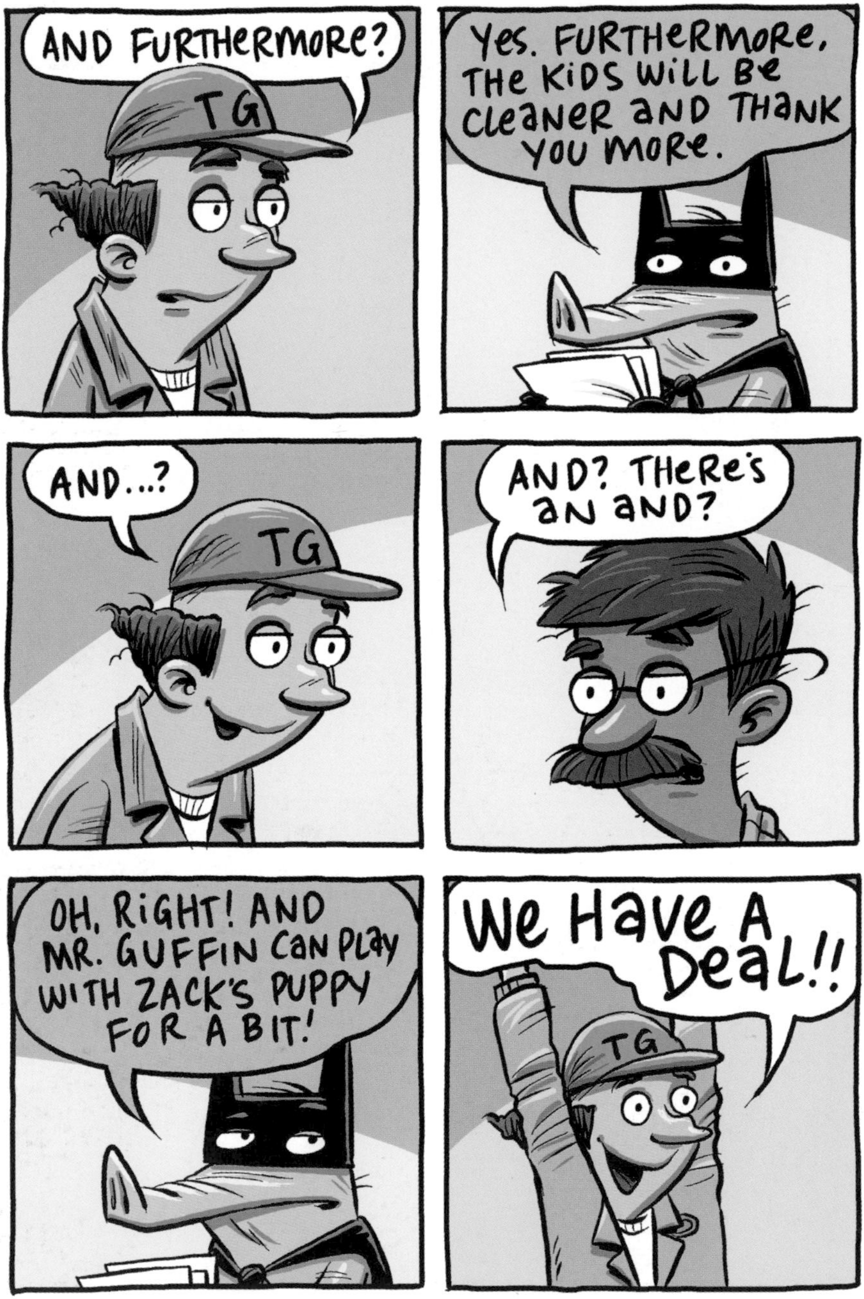
AND FURTHERMORE?
TG
YES. FURTHERMORE, THE KIDS WILL BE CLEANER AND THANK YOU MORE.
AND...?
TG
AND? THERE'S AN AND?
OH, RIGHT! AND MR. GUFFIN CAN PLAY WITH ZACK'S PUPPY FOR A BIT!
WE HAVE A DEAL!!
TG

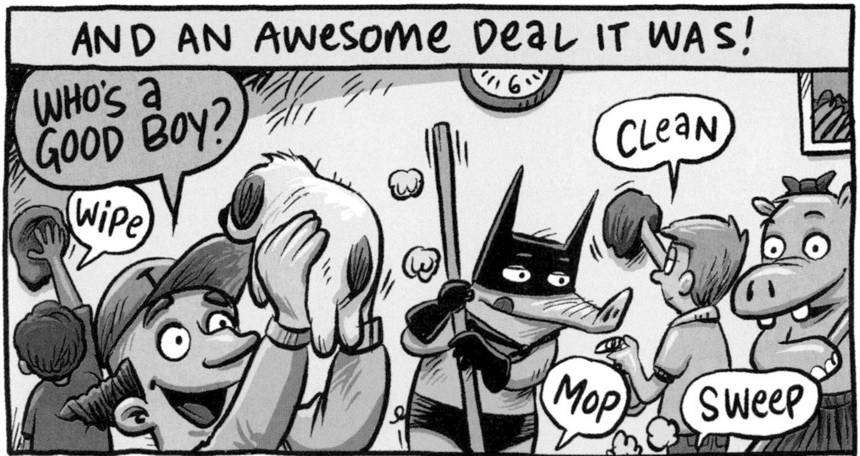
AND AN AWESOME DEAL IT WAS!
WHO'S a GOOD BOY?
Wipe
CLean
Mop
SWeep

IN NO TIME, THEY HaD THE CLASSROOM SPaRKLING aGAIN.

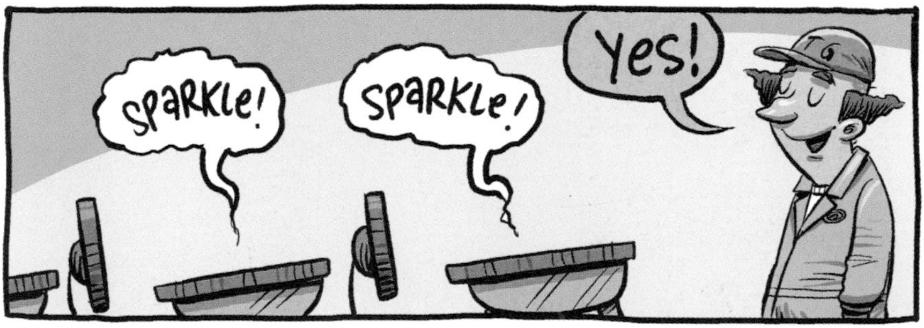
SPaRKLe!
SPaRKLe!
Yes!

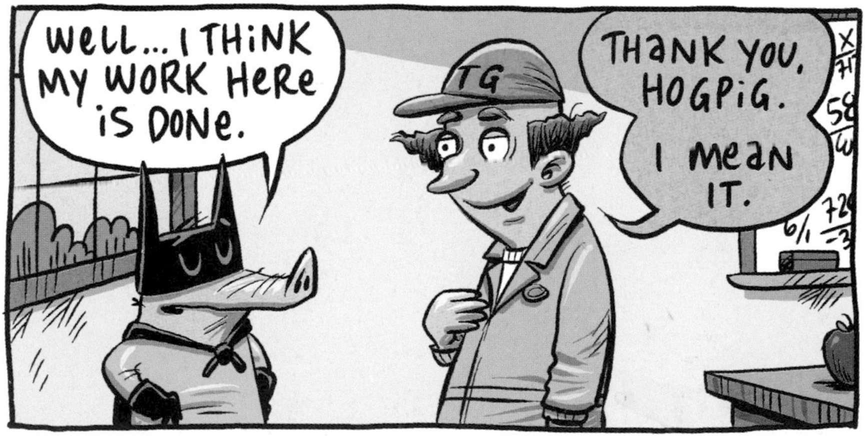
WeLL... I THINK MY WORK HeRe iS DONe.
THaNK YOU, HOGPiG.
I meaN IT.
TG

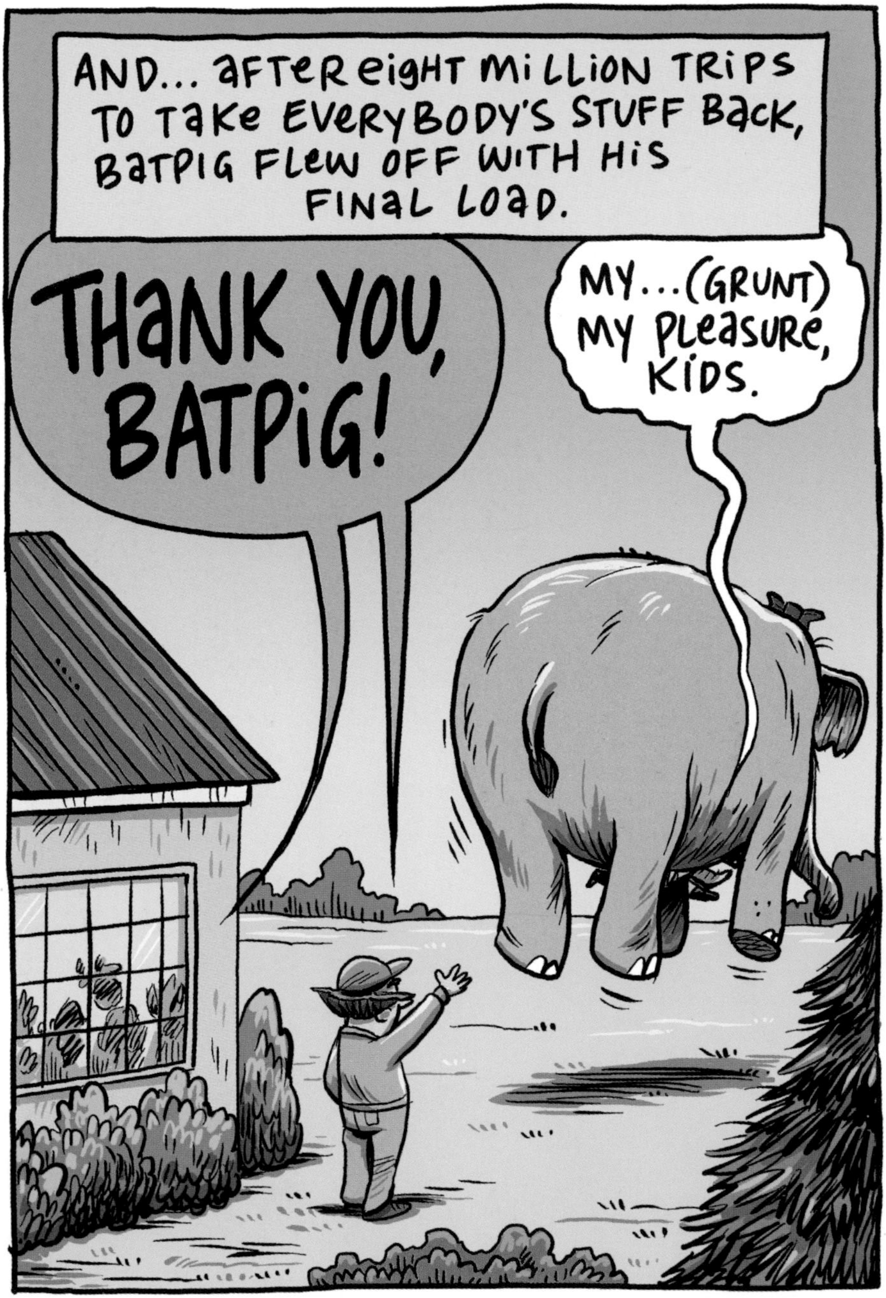
AND... AFTER EIGHT MILLION TRIPS TO TAKE EVERYBODY'S STUFF BACK, BATPIG FLEW OFF WITH HIS FINAL LOAD.
THANK YOU, BATPIG!
MY...(GRUNT) MY PLEASURE, KIDS.

CHAPTER ELEVEN

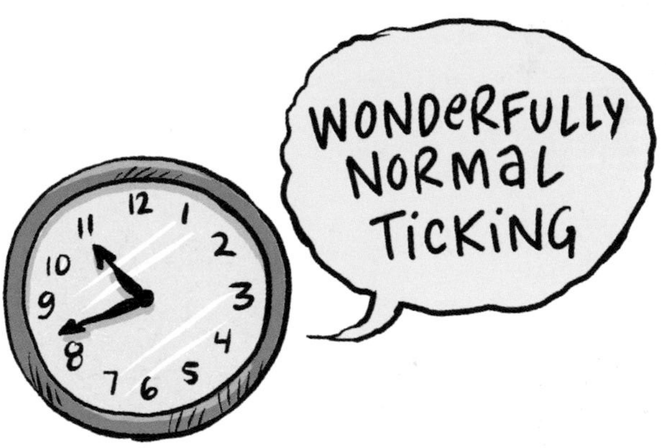
WONDERFULLY NORMAL TICKING

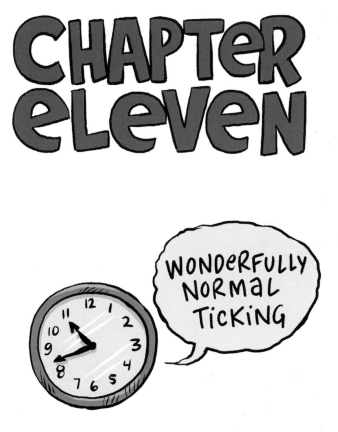

"SAVED BY THE BELL"

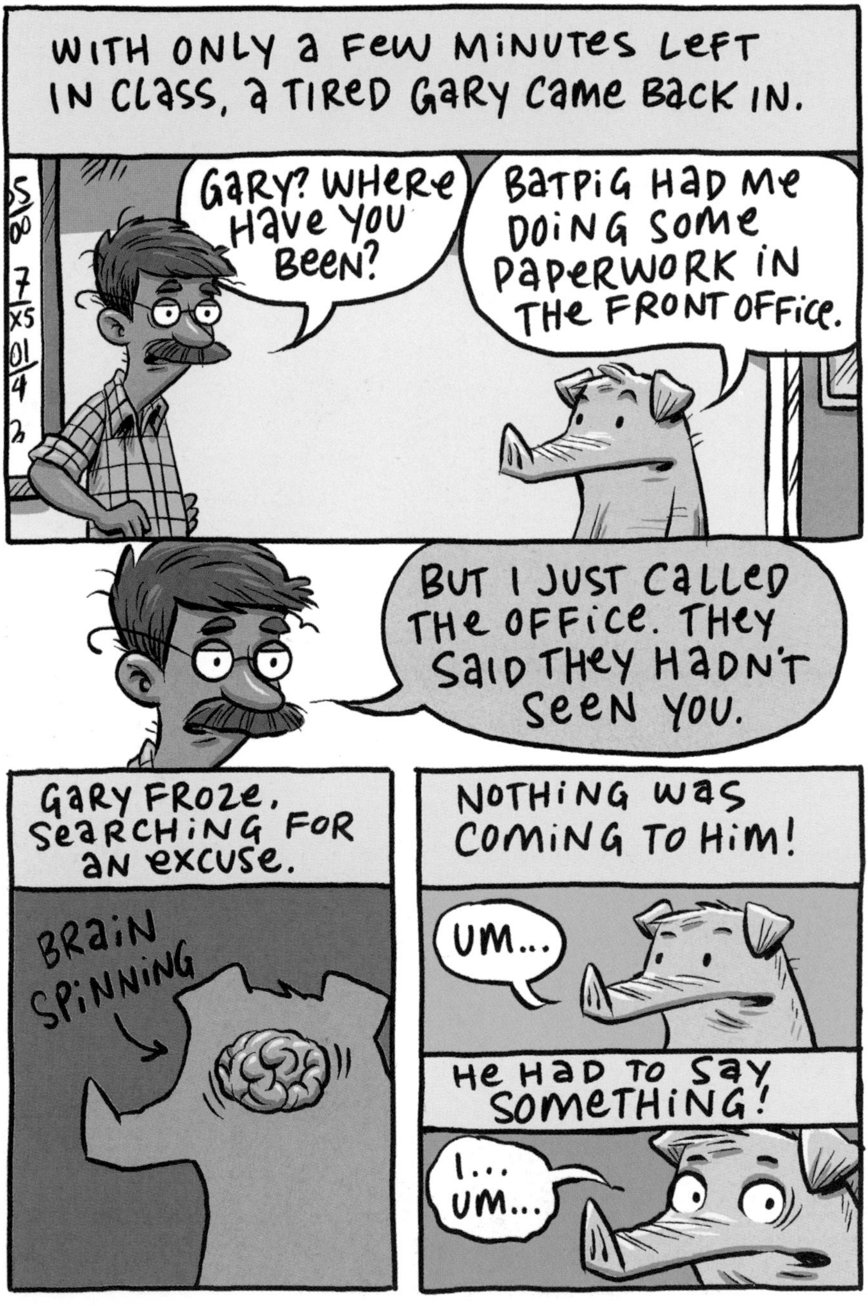
WITH ONLY A FEW MINUTES LEFT IN CLASS, A TIRED GARY CAME BACK IN.
GARY? WHERE HAVE YOU BEEN?
BATPIG HAD ME DOING SOME PAPERWORK IN THE FRONT OFFICE.
BUT I JUST CALLED THE OFFICE. THEY SAID THEY HADN'T SEEN YOU.
GARY FROZE, SEARCHING FOR AN EXCUSE.
BRAIN SPINNING
NOTHING WAS COMING TO HIM!
UM...
HE HAD TO SAY SOMETHING!
I... UM...

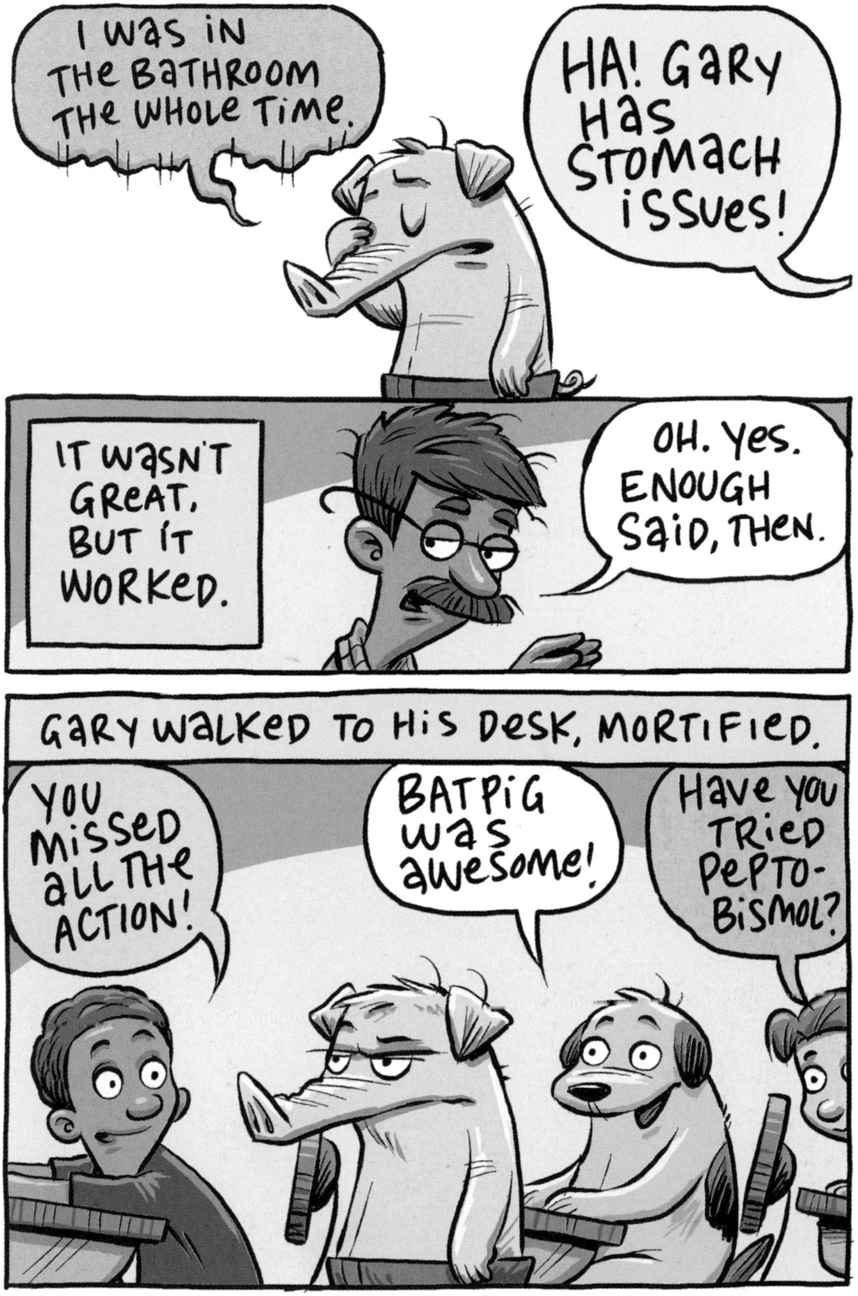
I was in the bathroom the whole time.
HA! Gary has stomach issues!
It wasn't great, but it worked.
Oh. Yes. Enough said, then.
Gary walked to his desk, mortified.
You missed all the action!
Batpig was awesome!
Have you tried Pepto-Bismol?

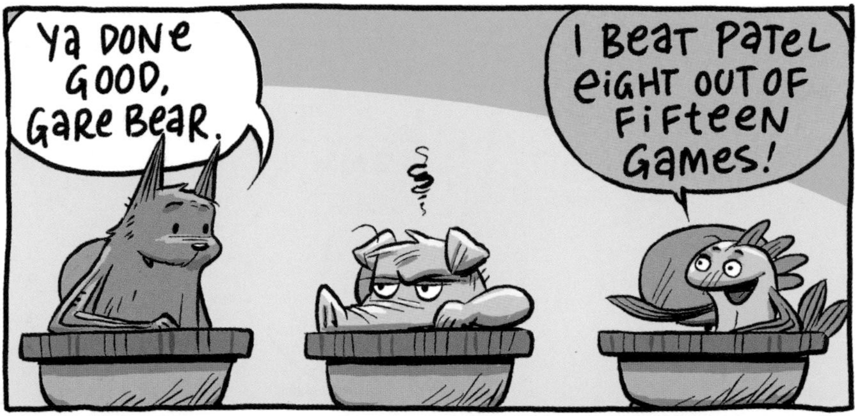
YA DONE GOOD, GARE BEAR.
I BEAT PATEL EIGHT OUT OF FIFTEEN GAMES!

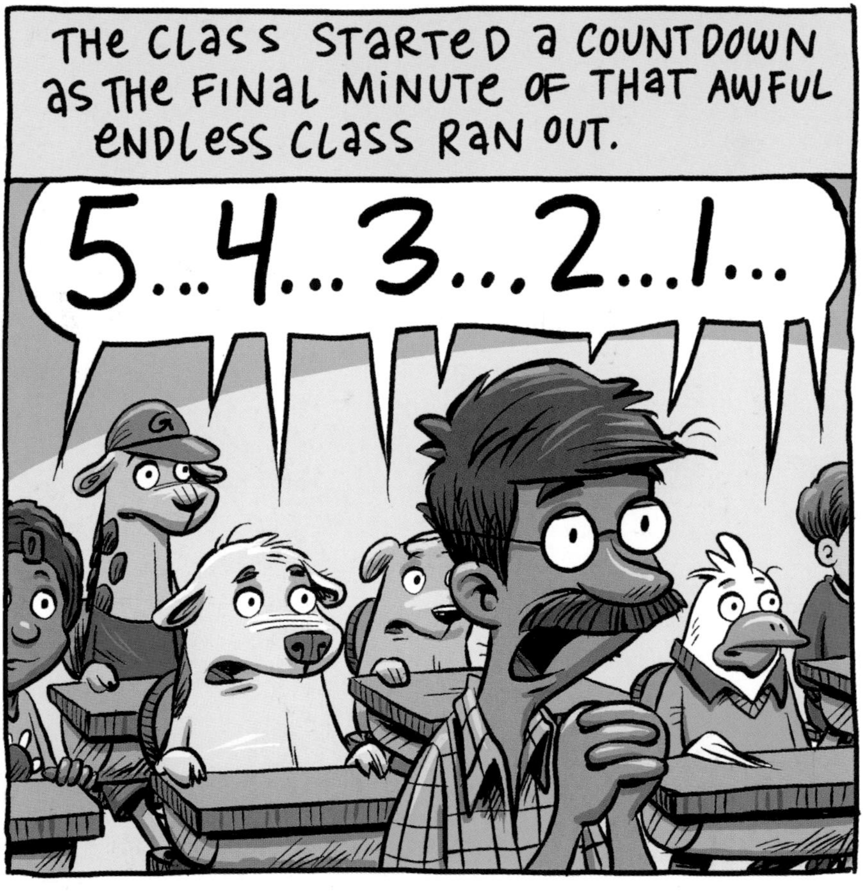
THE CLASS STARTED A COUNTDOWN AS THE FINAL MINUTE OF THAT AWFUL ENDLESS CLASS RAN OUT.
5...4...3...2...1...

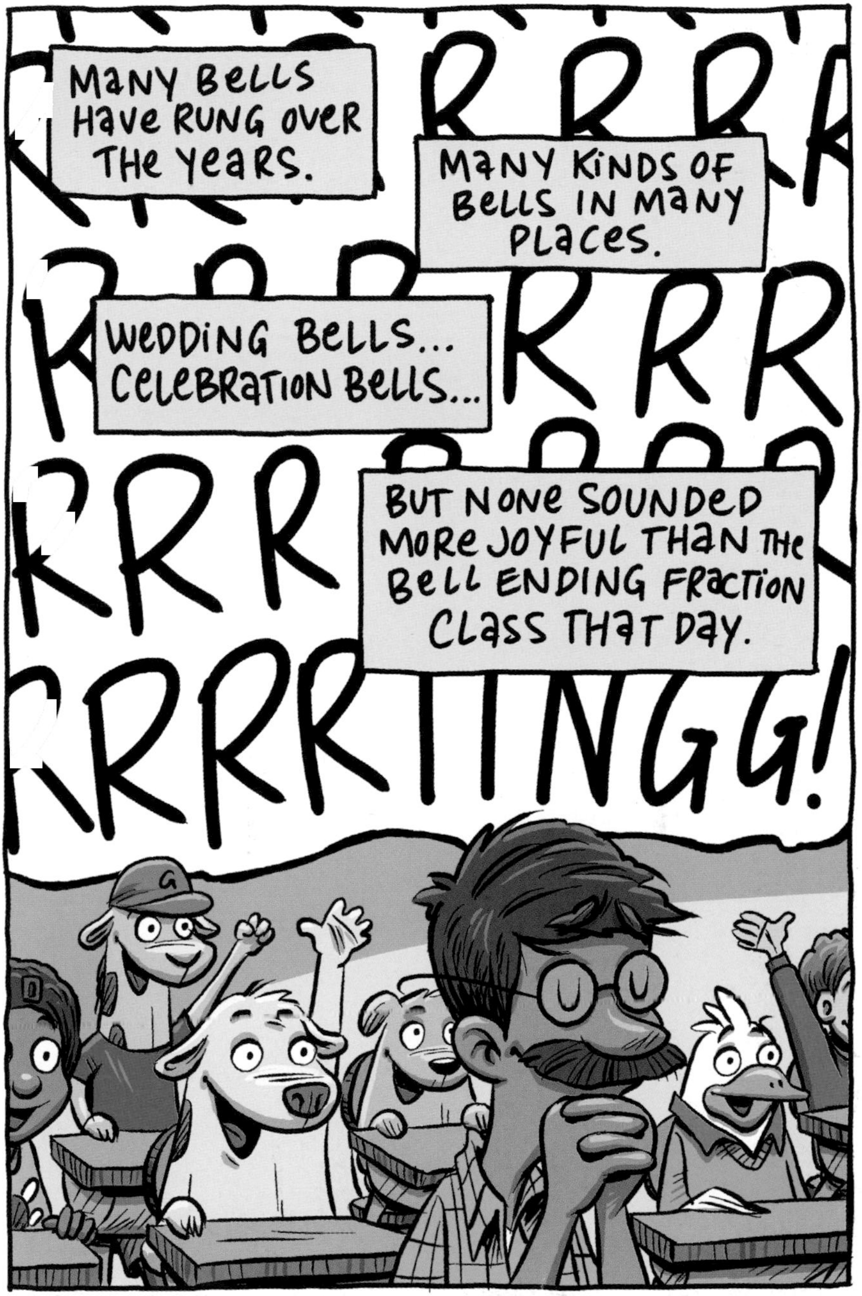
MANY BELLS HAVE RUNG OVER THE YEARS.
MANY KINDS OF BELLS IN MANY PLACES.
WEDDING BELLS... CELEBRATION BELLS...
BUT NONE SOUNDED MORE JOYFUL THAN THE BELL ENDING FRACTION CLASS THAT DAY.
RRRRRRRRRRRRRRRRRRRRRRRRRRRRRIINGG!

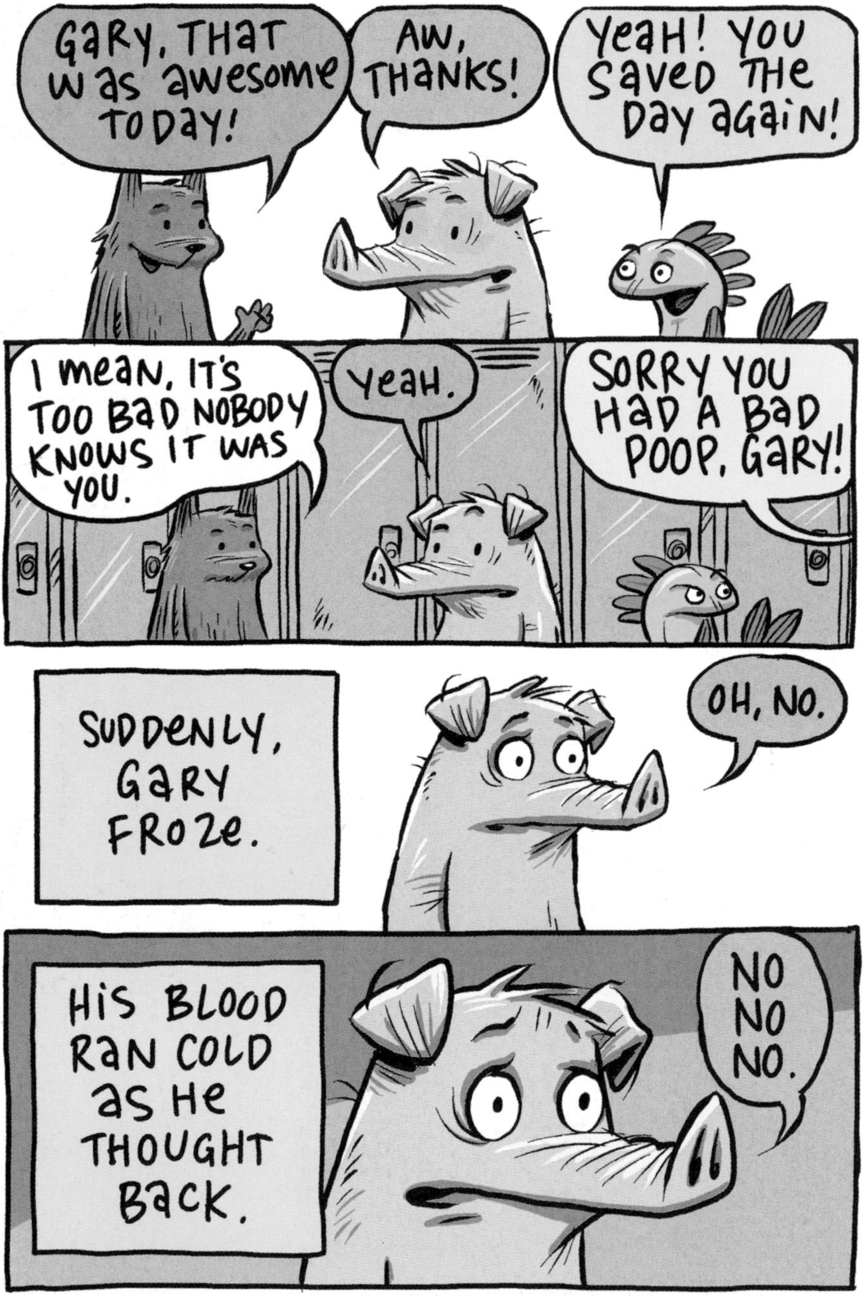
GARY, THAT WAS AWESOME TODAY!
AW, THANKS!
YEAH! YOU SAVED THE DAY AGAIN!
I MEAN, IT'S TOO BAD NOBODY KNOWS IT WAS YOU.
YEAH.
SORRY YOU HAD A BAD POOP, GARY!
SUDDENLY, GARY FROZE.
OH, NO.
HIS BLOOD RAN COLD AS HE THOUGHT BACK.
NO NO NO.

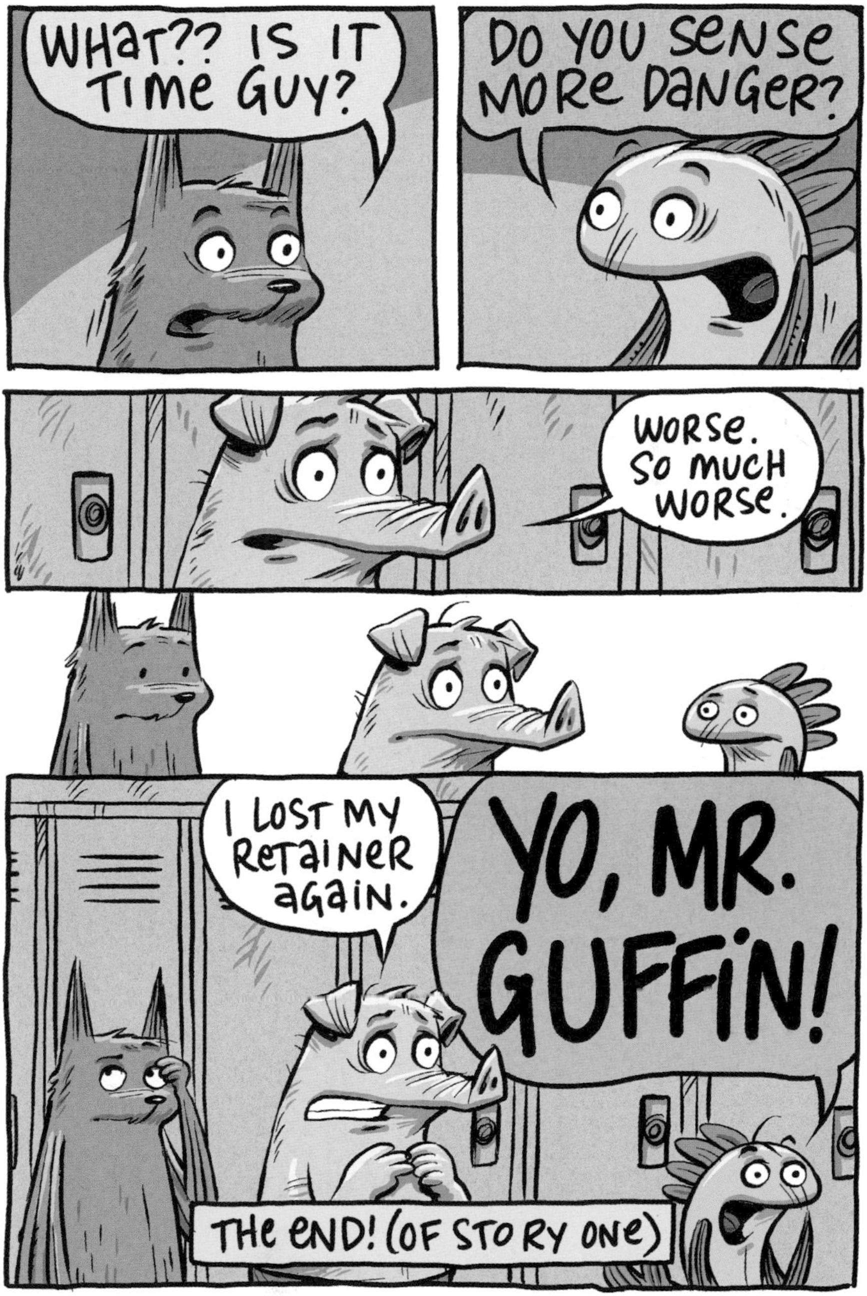
WHAT?? IS IT TIME GUY?
DO YOU SENSE MORE DANGER?
WORSE. SO MUCH WORSE.
I LOST MY RETAINER AGAIN.
YO, MR. GUFFIN!
THE END! (OF STORY ONE)

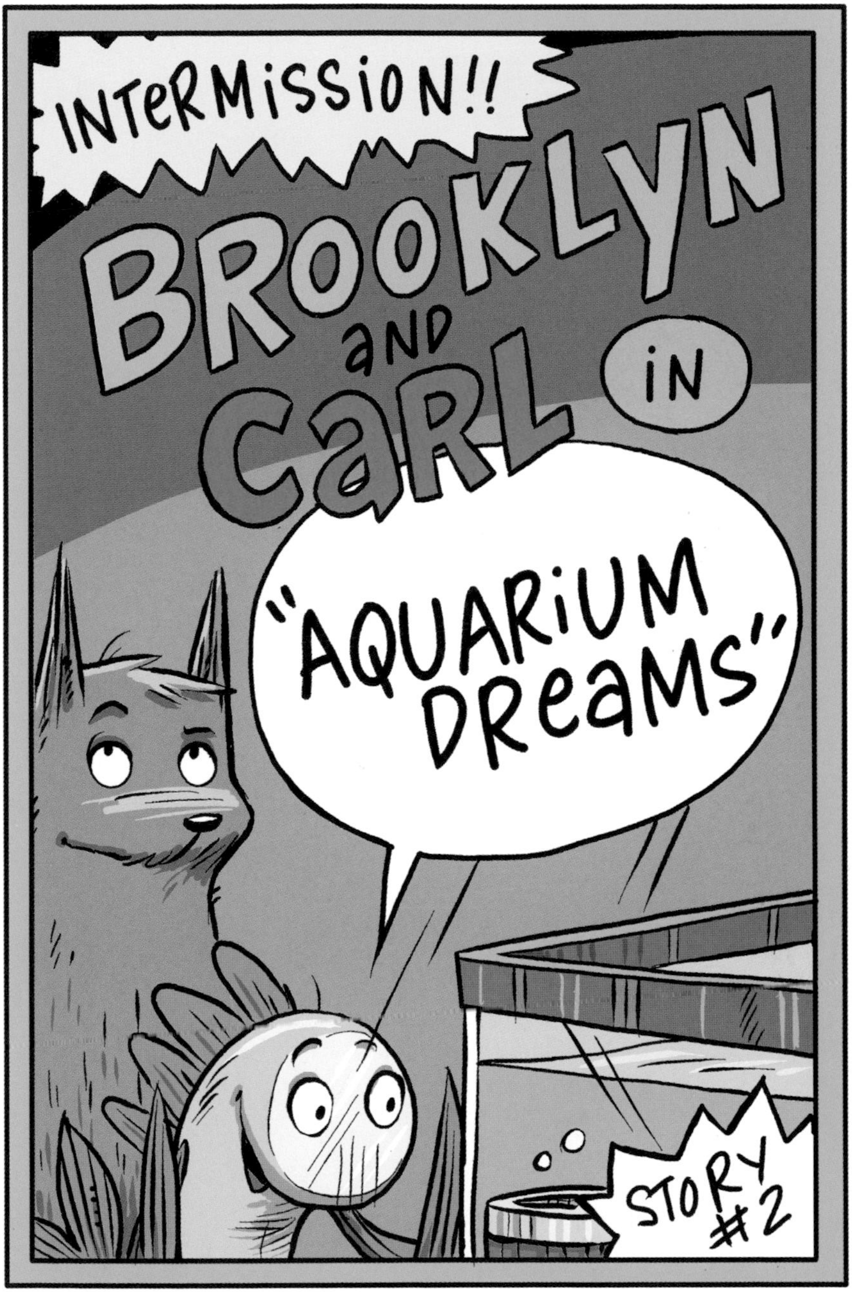
INTERMISSION!!
BROOKLYN
and
CARL
in
"AQUARIUM DREAMS"
STORY #2

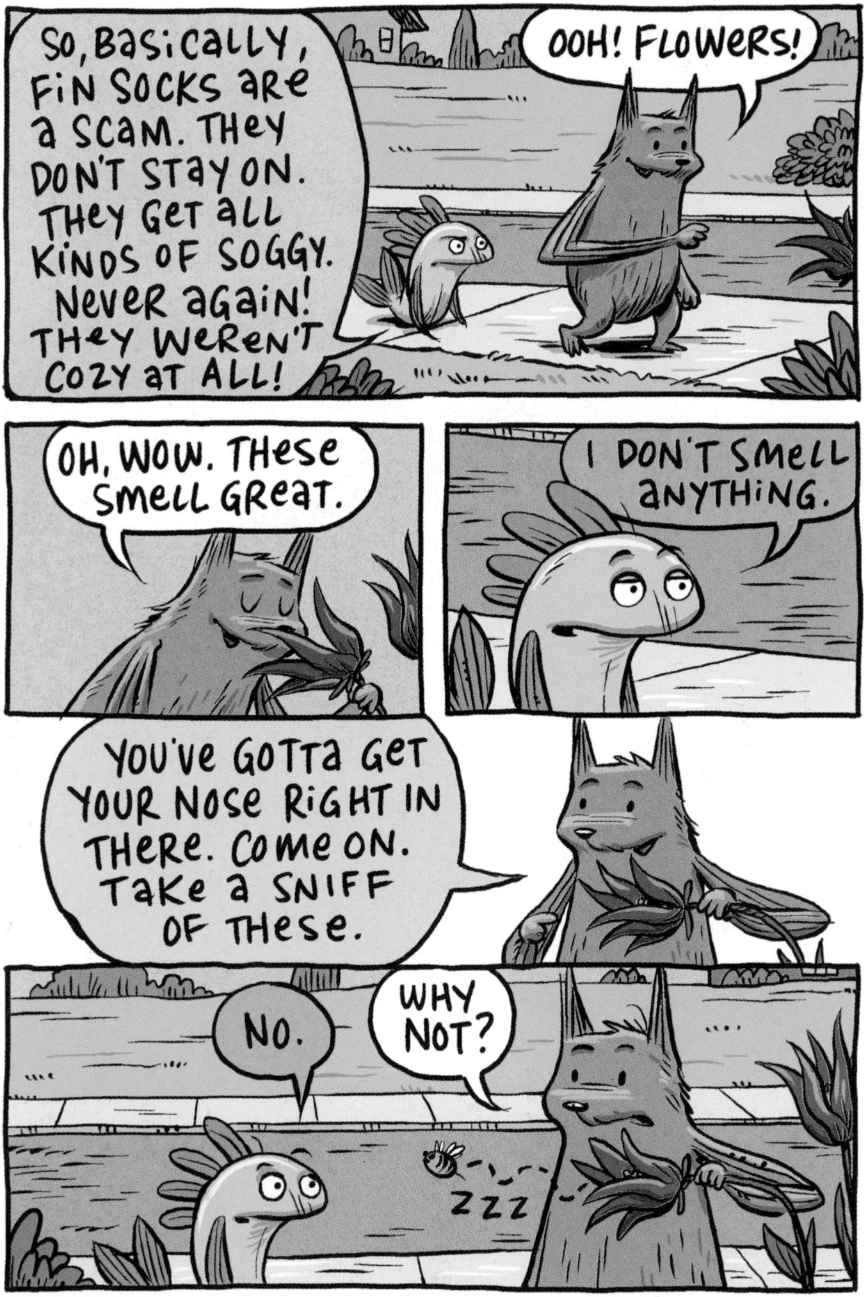
So, basically, fin socks are a scam. They don't stay on. They get all kinds of soggy. Never again! They weren't cozy at all!
Ooh! Flowers!
Oh, wow. These smell great.
I don't smell anything.
You've gotta get your nose right in there. Come on. Take a sniff of these.
No.
Why not?
zzz

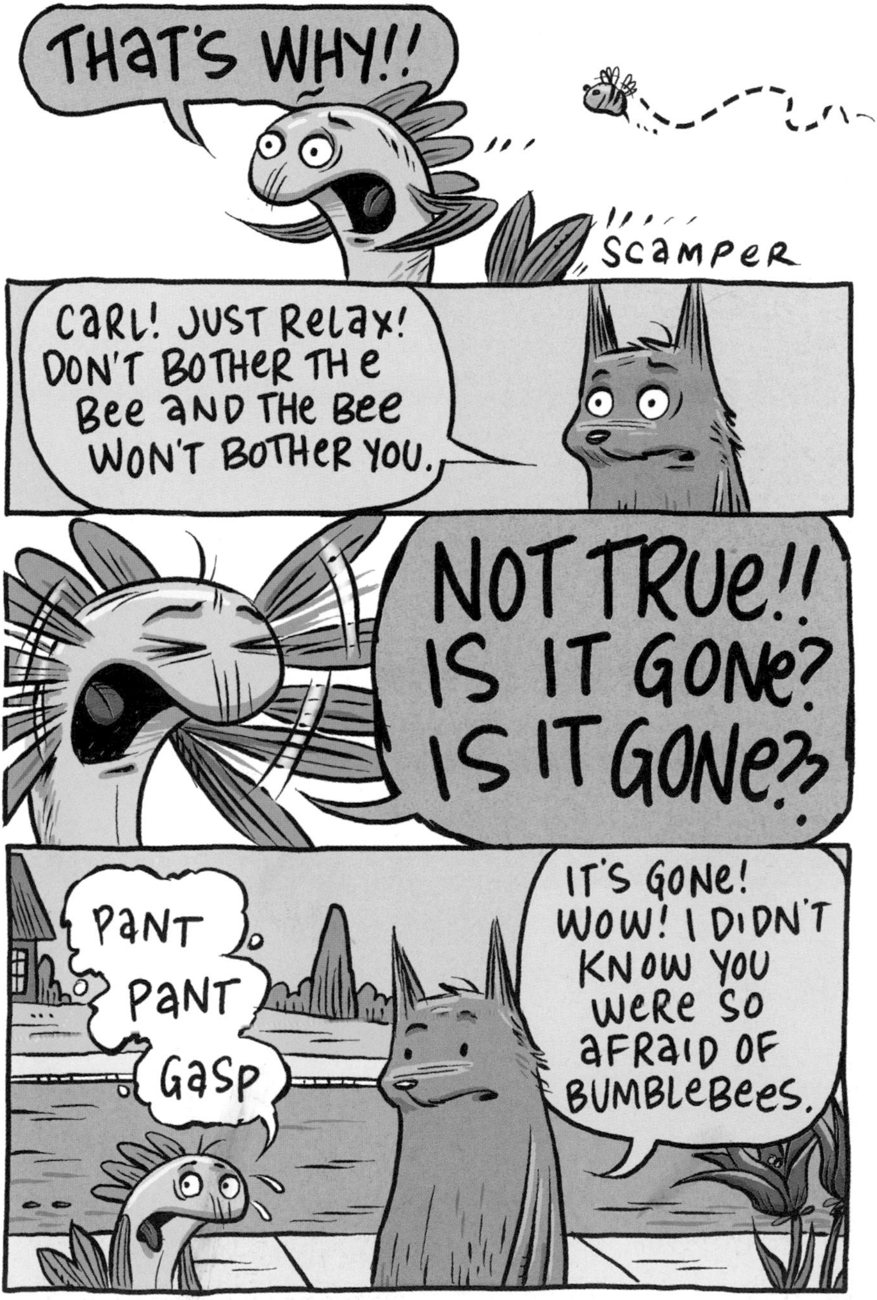
THAT'S WHY!!
SCAMPER
CARL! JUST RELAX! DON'T BOTHER THE BEE AND THE BEE WON'T BOTHER YOU.
NOT TRUE!! IS IT GONE? IS IT GONE??
PANT
PANT
GASP
IT'S GONE! WOW! I DIDN'T KNOW YOU WERE SO AFRAID OF BUMBLEBEES.

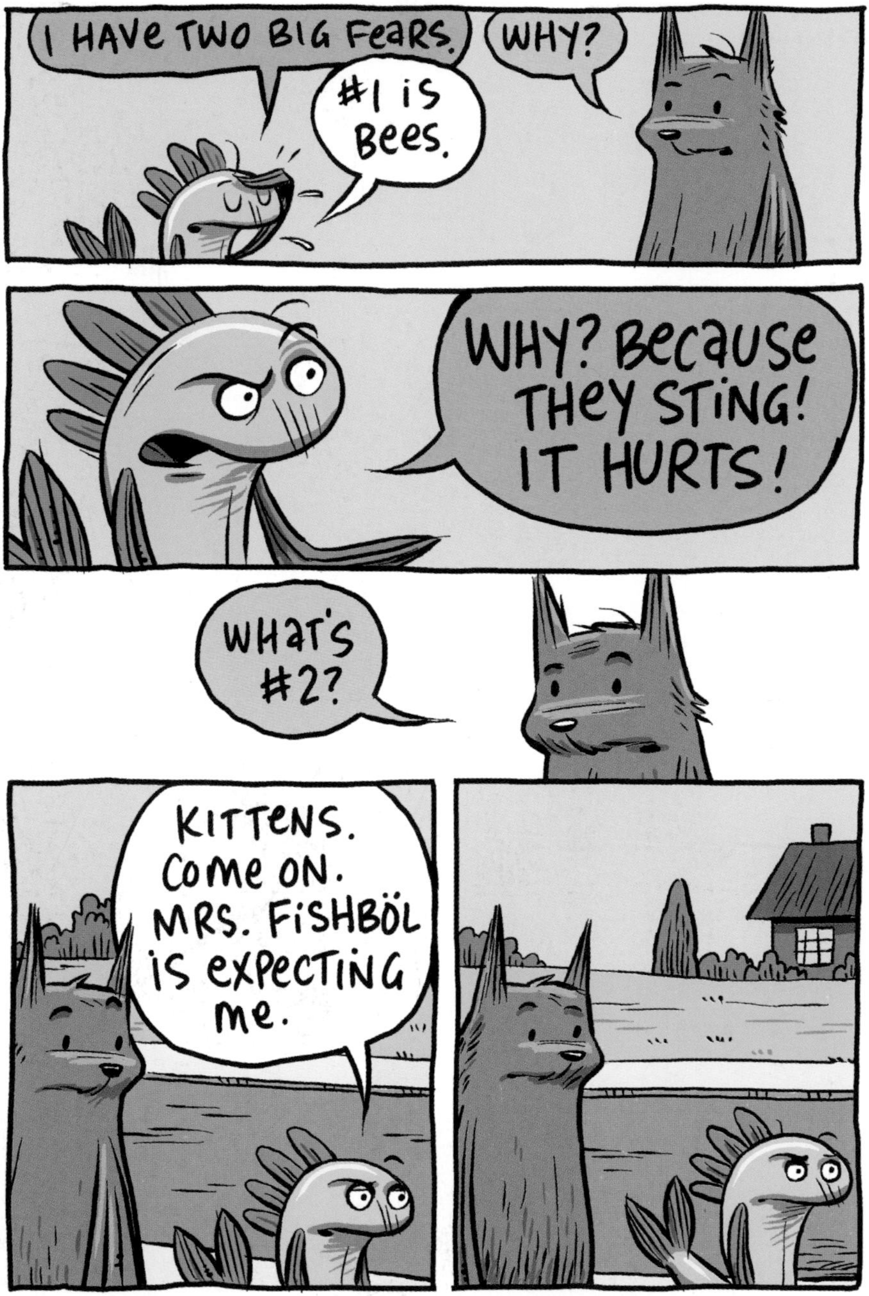
I HAVE TWO BIG FEARS.
WHY?
#1 IS BEES.
WHY? BECAUSE THEY STING! IT HURTS!
WHAT'S #2?
KITTENS. COME ON. MRS. FISHBÖL IS EXPECTING ME.

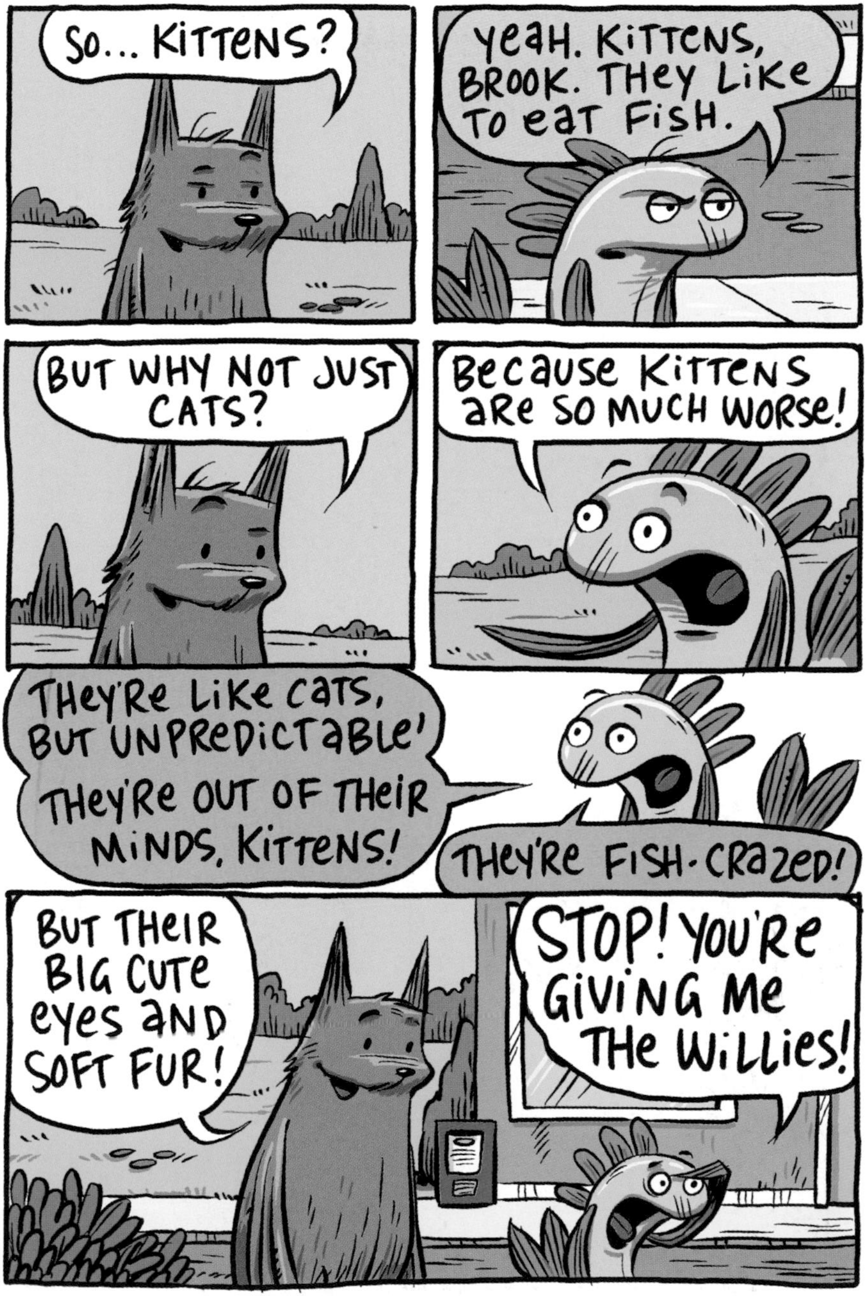
SO... KITTENS?
YEAH. KITTENS, BROOK. THEY LIKE TO EAT FISH.
BUT WHY NOT JUST CATS?
BECAUSE KITTENS ARE SO MUCH WORSE!
THEY'RE LIKE CATS, BUT UNPREDICTABLE'
THEY'RE OUT OF THEIR MINDS, KITTENS!
THEY'RE FISH-CRAZED!
BUT THEIR BIG CUTE EYES AND SOFT FUR!
STOP! YOU'RE GIVING ME THE WILLIES!

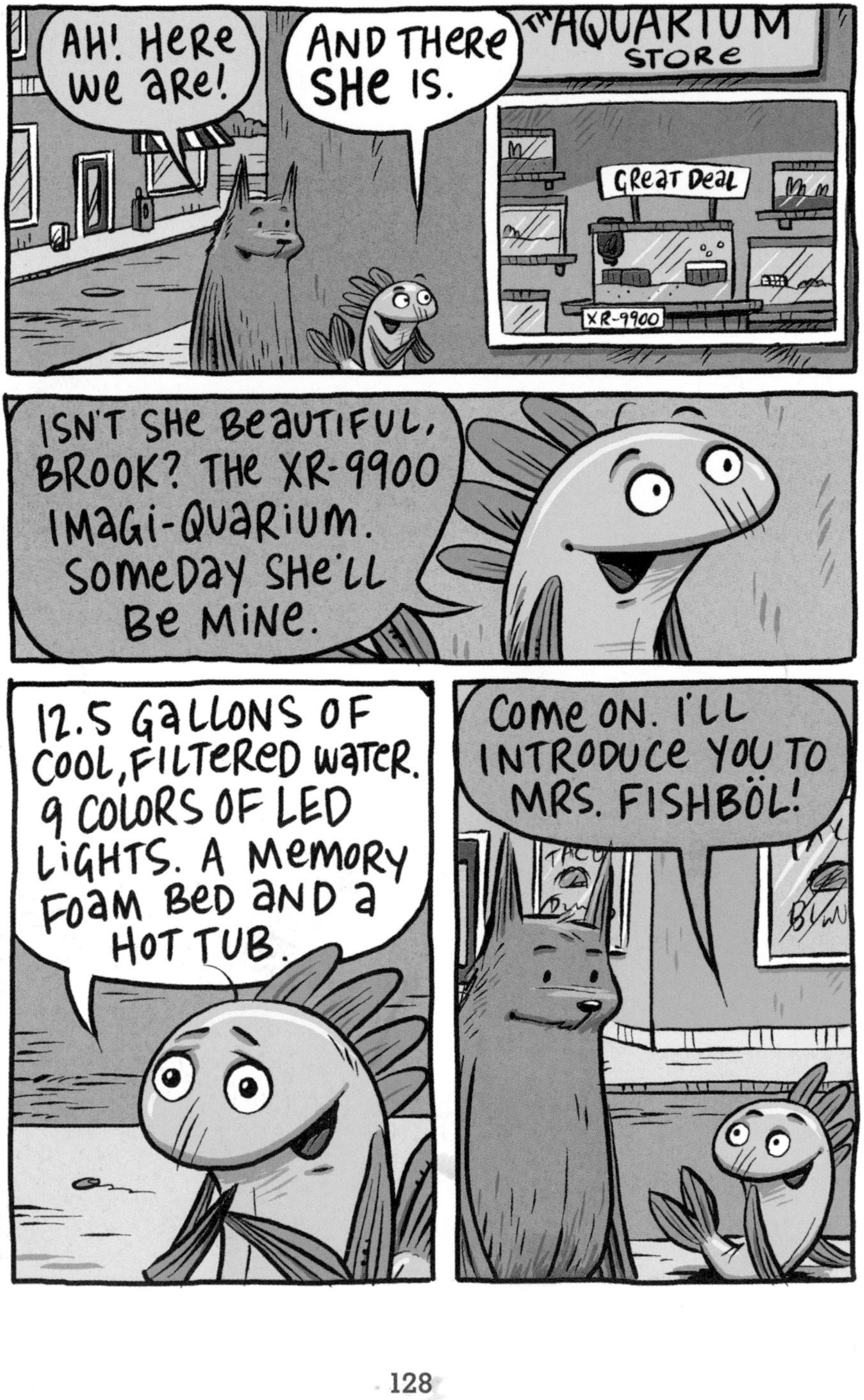
AH! HERE WE ARE!
AND THERE SHE IS.
THE AQUARIUM STORE
GREAT DEAL
XR-9900
ISN'T SHE BEAUTIFUL, BROOK? THE XR-9900 IMAGI-QUARIUM. SOMEDAY SHE'LL BE MINE.
12.5 GALLONS OF COOL, FILTERED WATER. 9 COLORS OF LED LIGHTS. A MEMORY FOAM BED AND A HOT TUB.
COME ON. I'LL INTRODUCE YOU TO MRS. FISHBÖL!

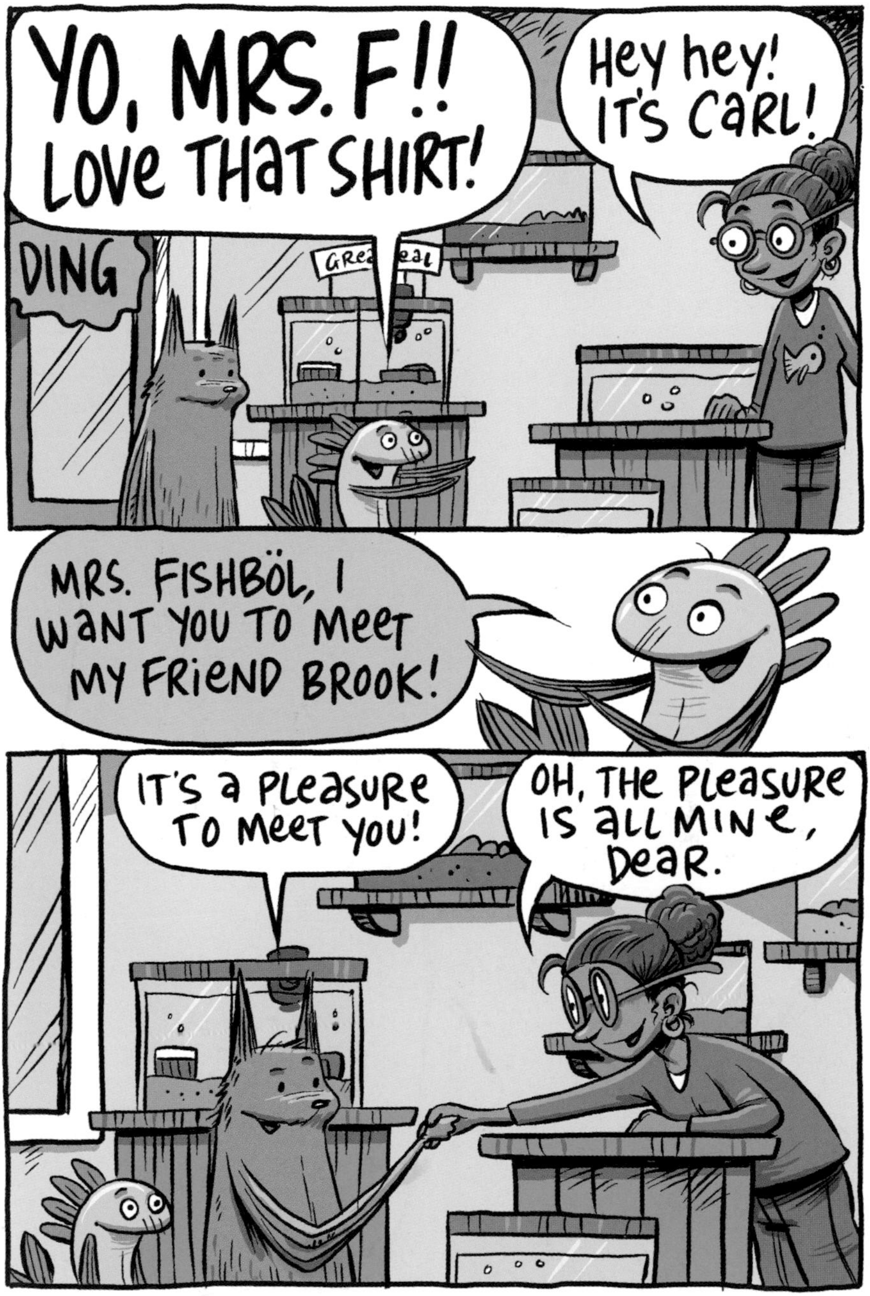
YO, MRS. F!! LOVE THAT SHIRT!
Hey hey! IT'S CARL!
DING
MRS. FISHBÖL, I WANT YOU TO MEET MY FRIEND BROOK!
IT'S a PLEASURE TO MEET YOU!
OH, THE PLEASURE IS ALL MINE, DEAR.

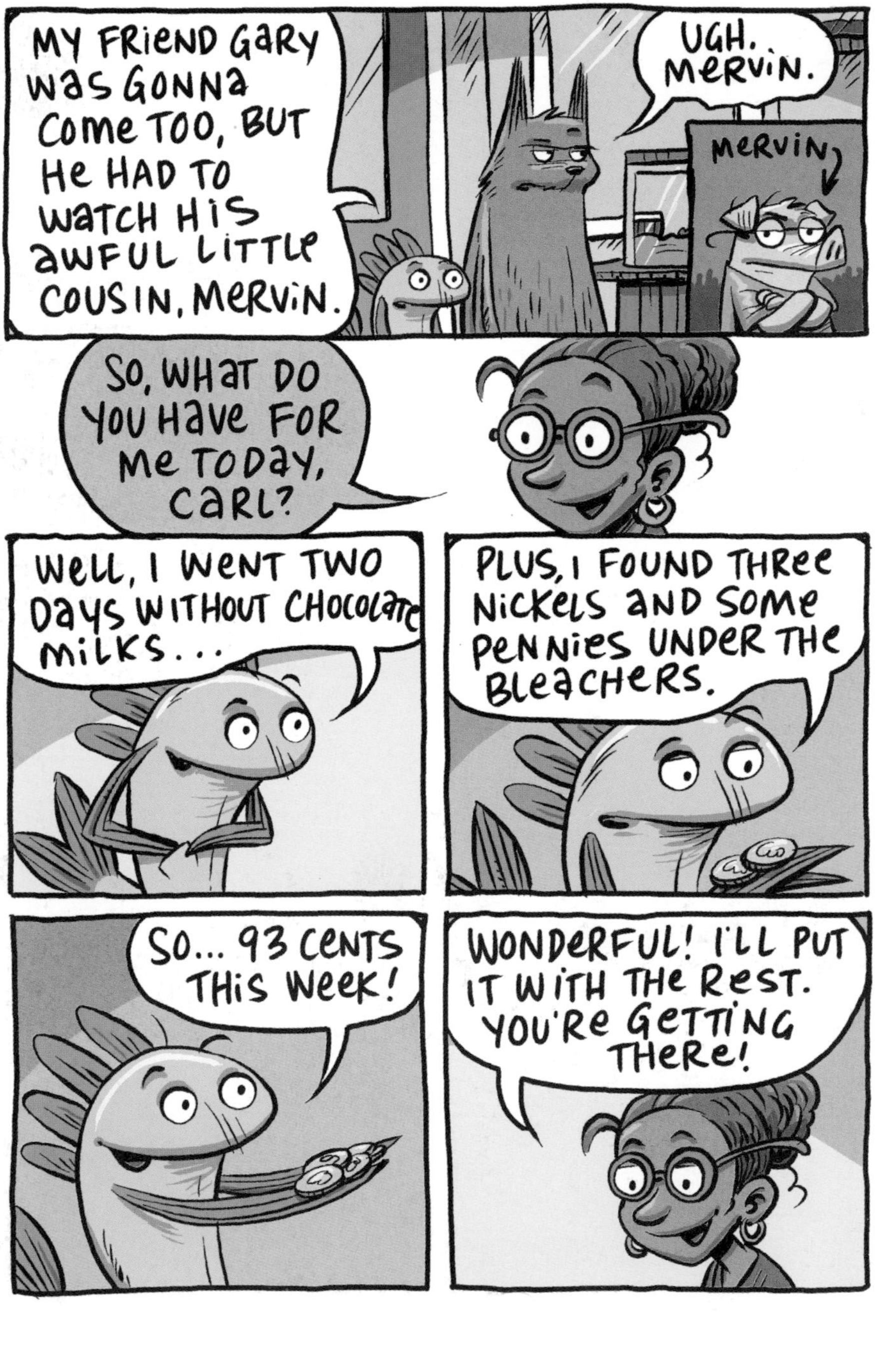
MY FRIEND GARY WAS GONNA COME TOO, BUT HE HAD TO WATCH HIS AWFUL LITTLE COUSIN, MERVIN.
UGH. MERVIN.
MERVIN
SO, WHAT DO YOU HAVE FOR ME TODAY, CARL?
WELL, I WENT TWO DAYS WITHOUT CHOCOLATE MILKS...
PLUS, I FOUND THREE NICKELS AND SOME PENNIES UNDER THE BLEACHERS.
SO... 93 CENTS THIS WEEK!
WONDERFUL! I'LL PUT IT WITH THE REST. YOU'RE GETTING THERE!

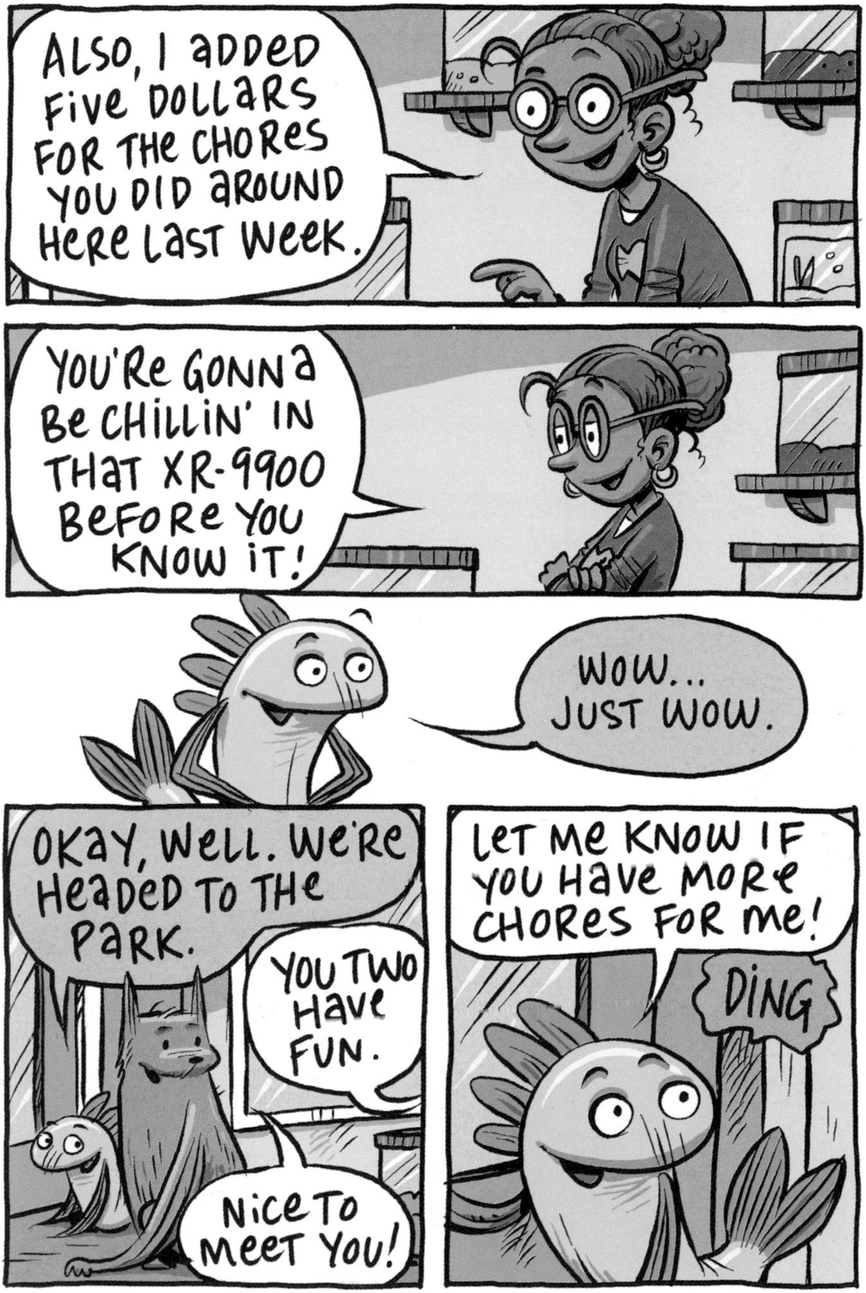

ALSO, I ADDED FIVE DOLLARS FOR THE CHORES YOU DID AROUND HERE LAST WEEK.
YOU'RE GONNA BE CHILLIN' IN THAT XR-9900 BEFORE YOU KNOW IT!
WOW... JUST WOW.
OKAY, WELL. WE'RE HEADED TO THE PARK.
YOU TWO HAVE FUN.
NICE TO MEET YOU!
LET ME KNOW IF YOU HAVE MORE CHORES FOR ME!
DING

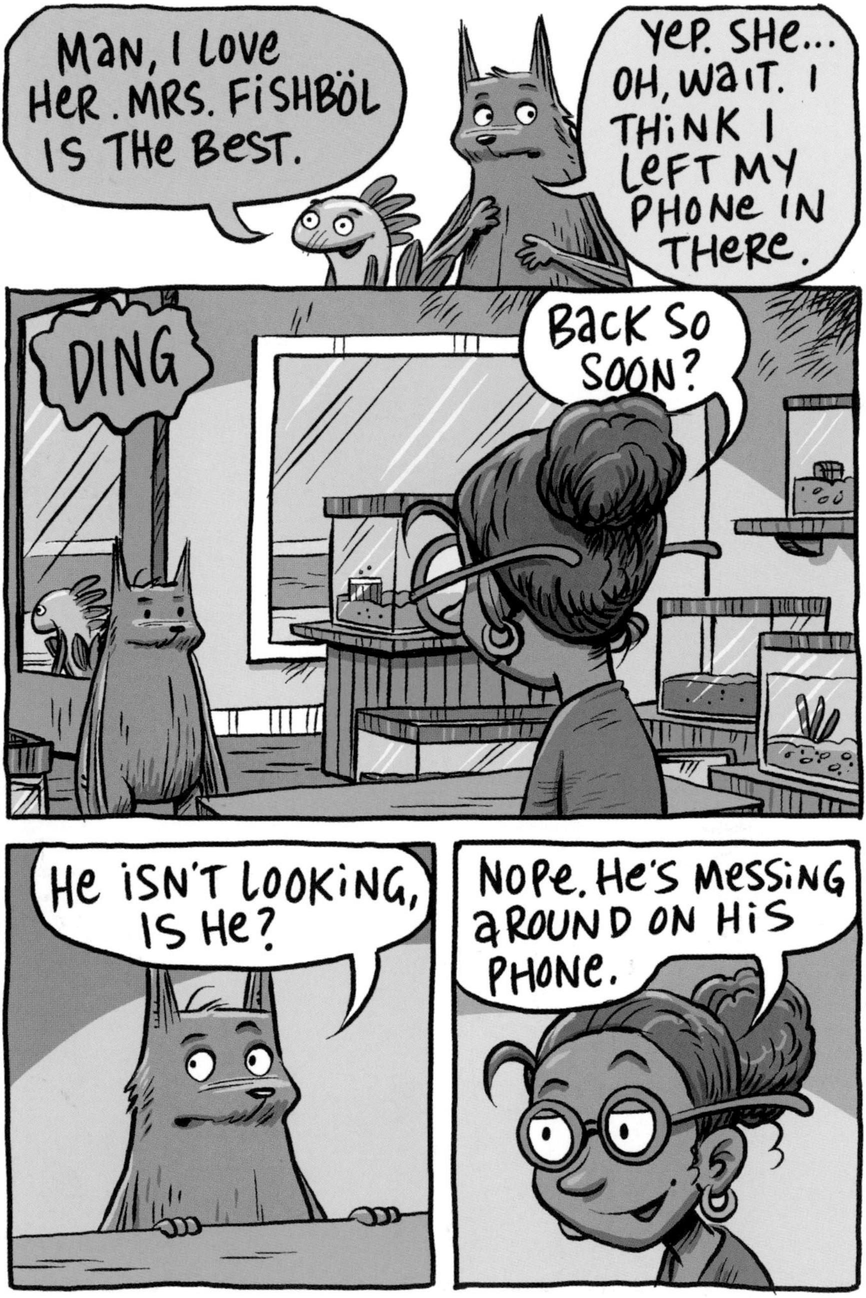
MAN, I LOVE HER. MRS. FISHBÖL IS THE BEST.
YEP. SHE... OH, WAIT. I THINK I LEFT MY PHONE IN THERE.
DING
BACK SO SOON?
HE ISN'T LOOKING, IS HE?
NOPE. HE'S MESSING AROUND ON HIS PHONE.

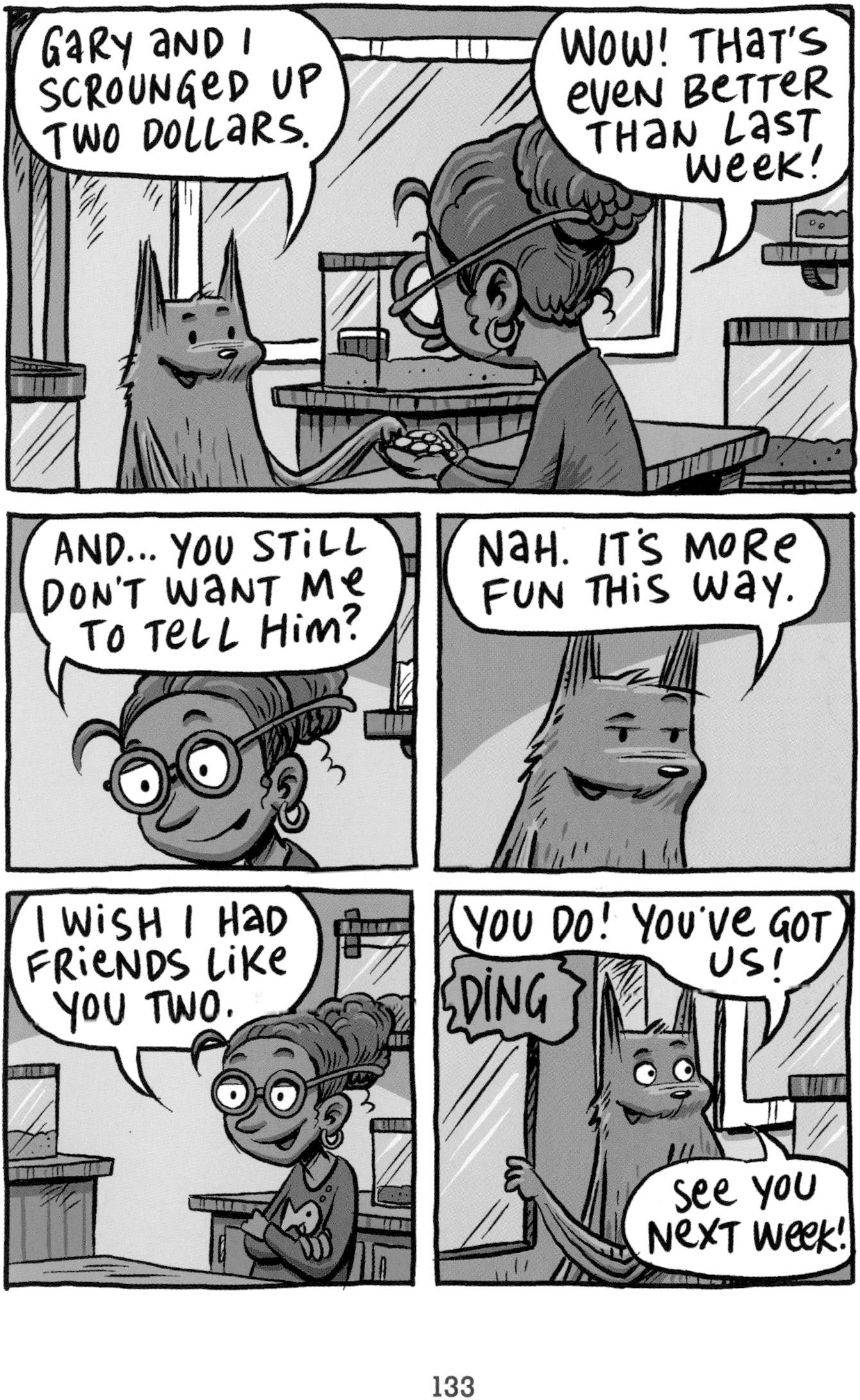
GARY AND I SCROUNGED UP TWO DOLLARS.
WOW! THAT'S EVEN BETTER THAN LAST WEEK!
AND... YOU STILL DON'T WANT ME TO TELL HIM?
NAH. IT'S MORE FUN THIS WAY.
I WISH I HAD FRIENDS LIKE YOU TWO.
YOU DO! YOU'VE GOT US!
DING
SEE YOU NEXT WEEK!

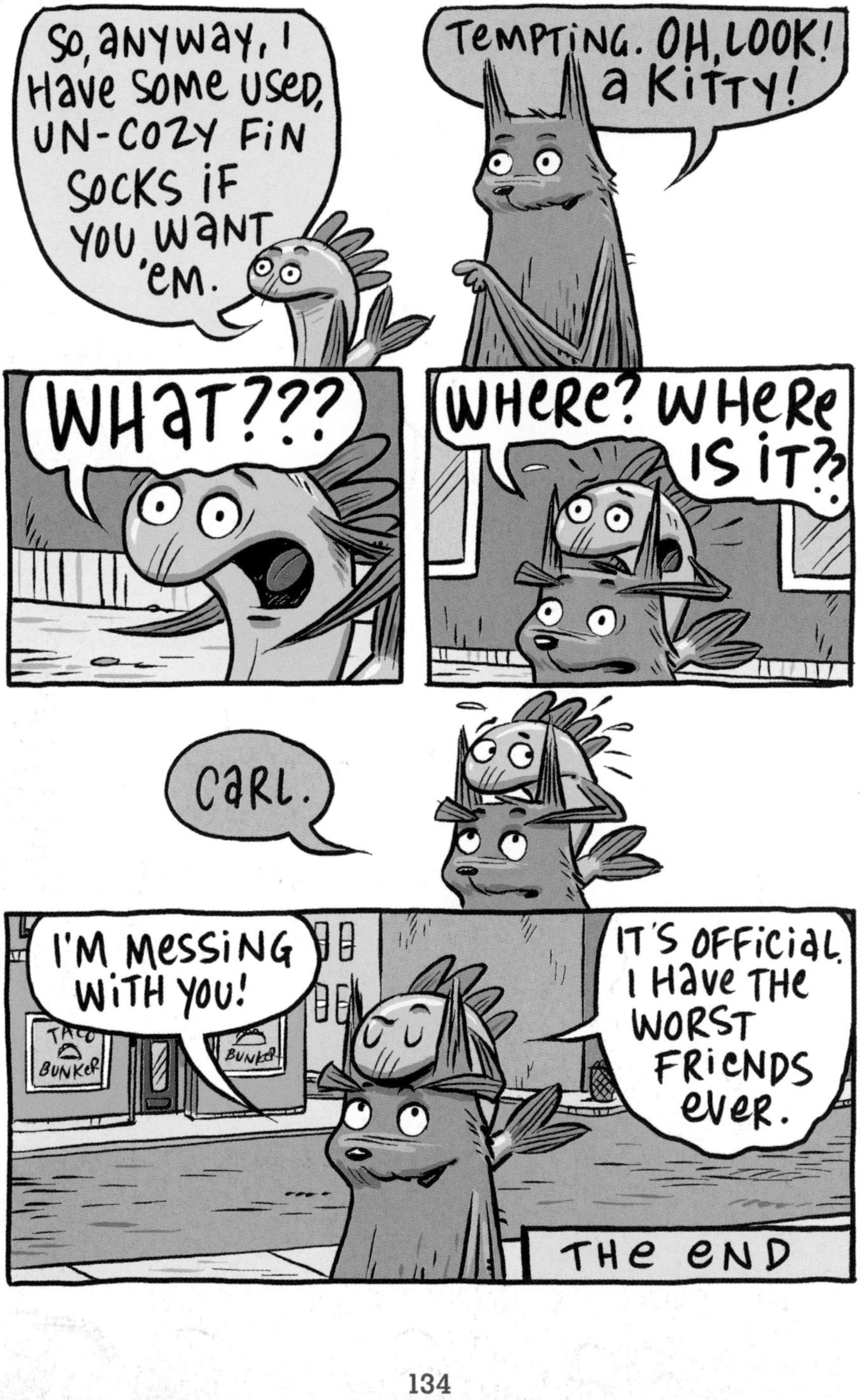
So, anyway, I have some used, un-cozy fin socks if you want 'em.
Tempting. Oh, look! a kitty!
WHAT???
Where? Where is it??
Carl.
I'M MESSING WITH YOU!
IT'S OFFICIAL. I HAVE THE WORST FRIENDS EVER.
TACO BUNKER
BUNKER
THE END

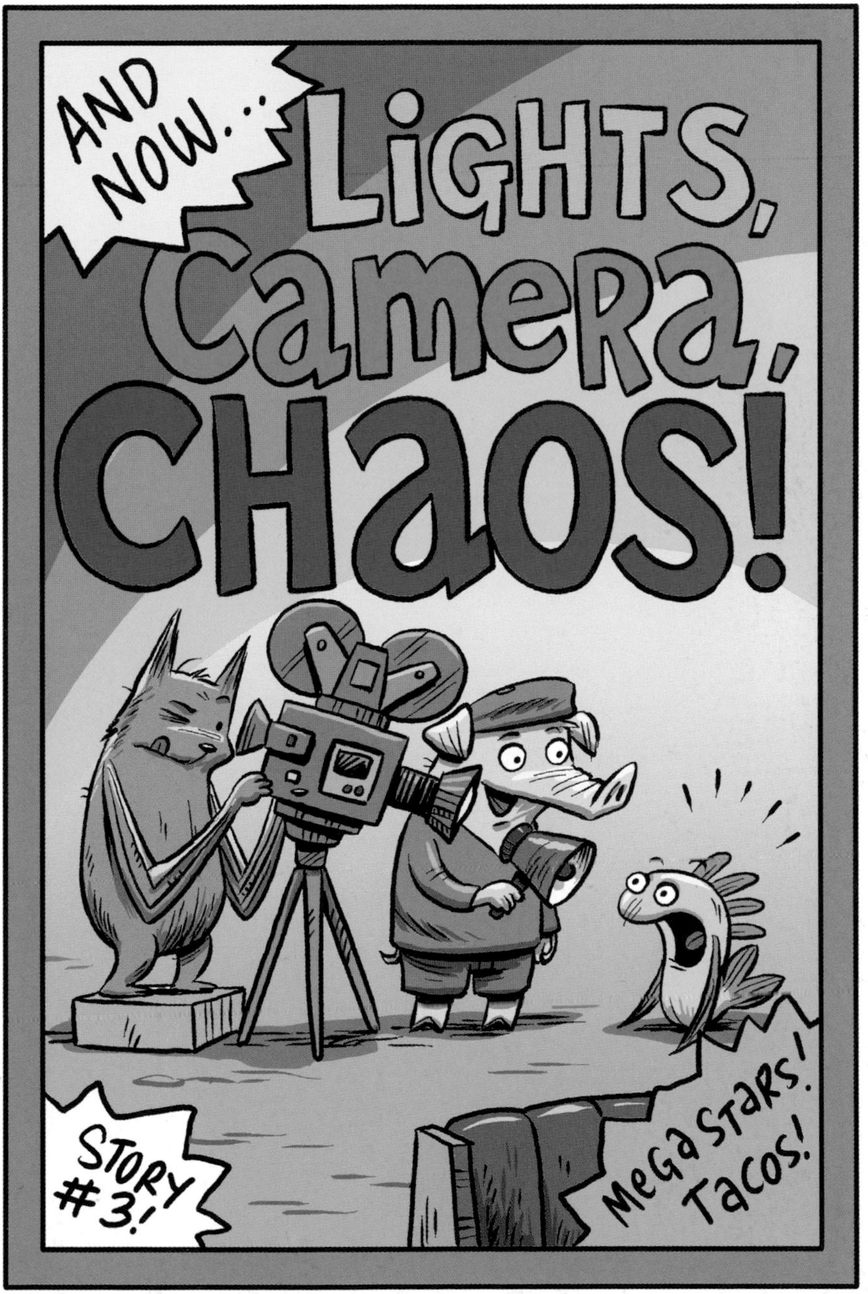
AND NOW...
LIGHTS, CAMERA, CHAOS!
STORY #3!
MEGASTARS! TACOS!

CHAPTER ONE

"FAR OUT"

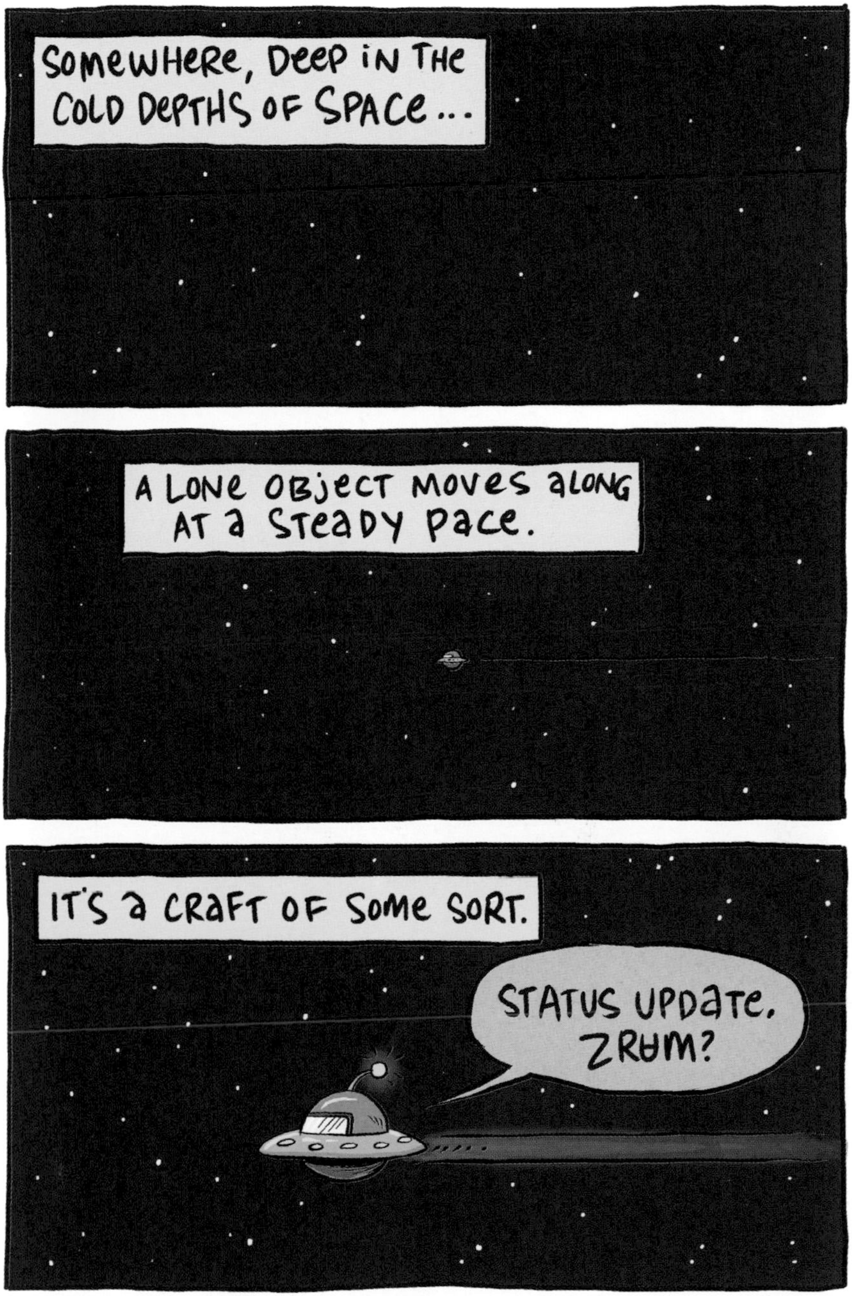
SOMEWHERE, DEEP IN THE COLD DEPTHS OF SPACE...
A LONE OBJECT MOVES ALONG AT A STEADY PACE.
IT'S A CRAFT OF SOME SORT.
STATUS UPDATE, ZRUM?

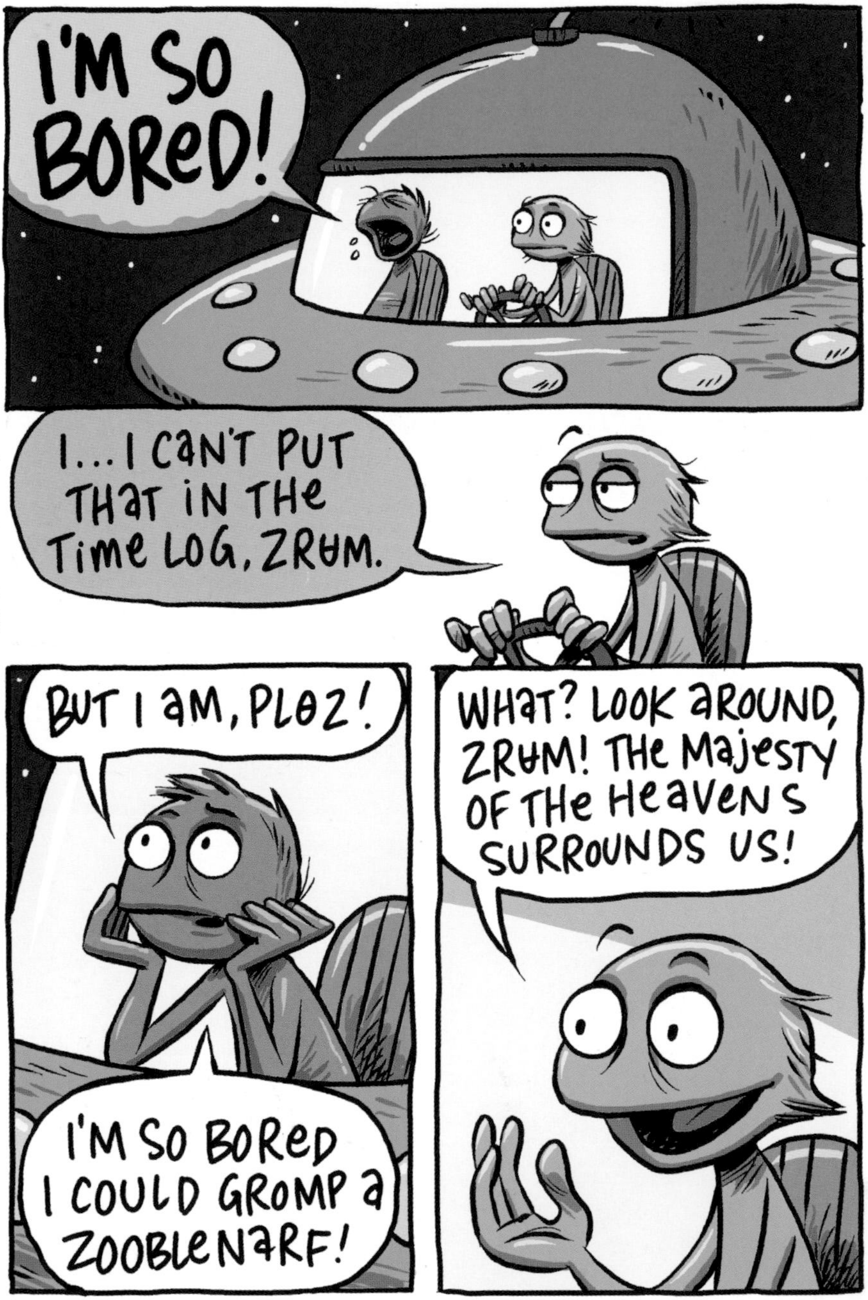
I'M SO BORED!
I... I CAN'T PUT THAT IN THE TIME LOG, ZRUM.
BUT I AM, PLOZ!
I'M SO BORED I COULD GROMP A ZOOBLENARF!
WHAT? LOOK AROUND, ZRUM! THE MAJESTY OF THE HEAVENS SURROUNDS US!

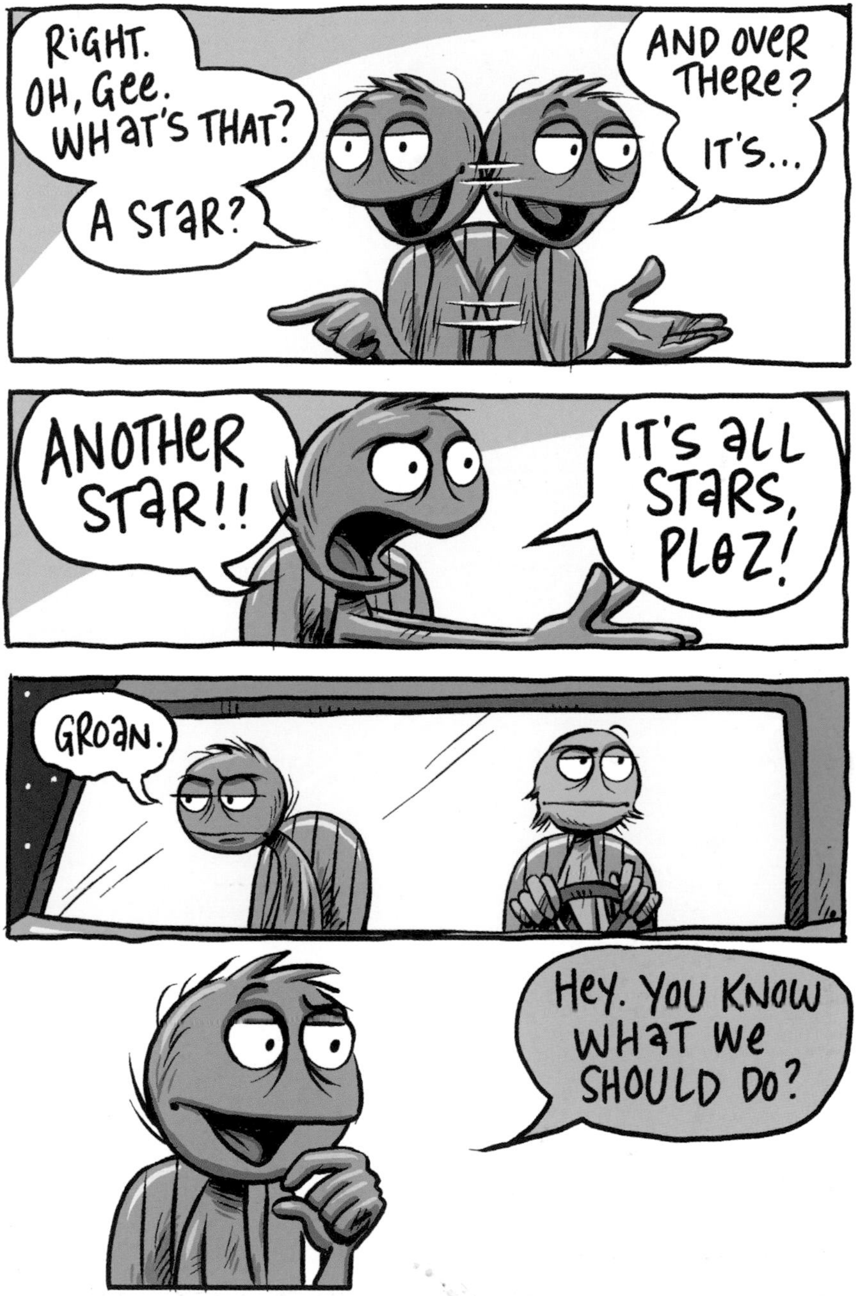
RIGHT. OH, GEE. WHAT'S THAT?
A STAR?
AND OVER THERE?
IT'S...
ANOTHER STAR!!
IT'S ALL STARS, PLOZ!
GROAN.
HEY. YOU KNOW WHAT WE SHOULD DO?

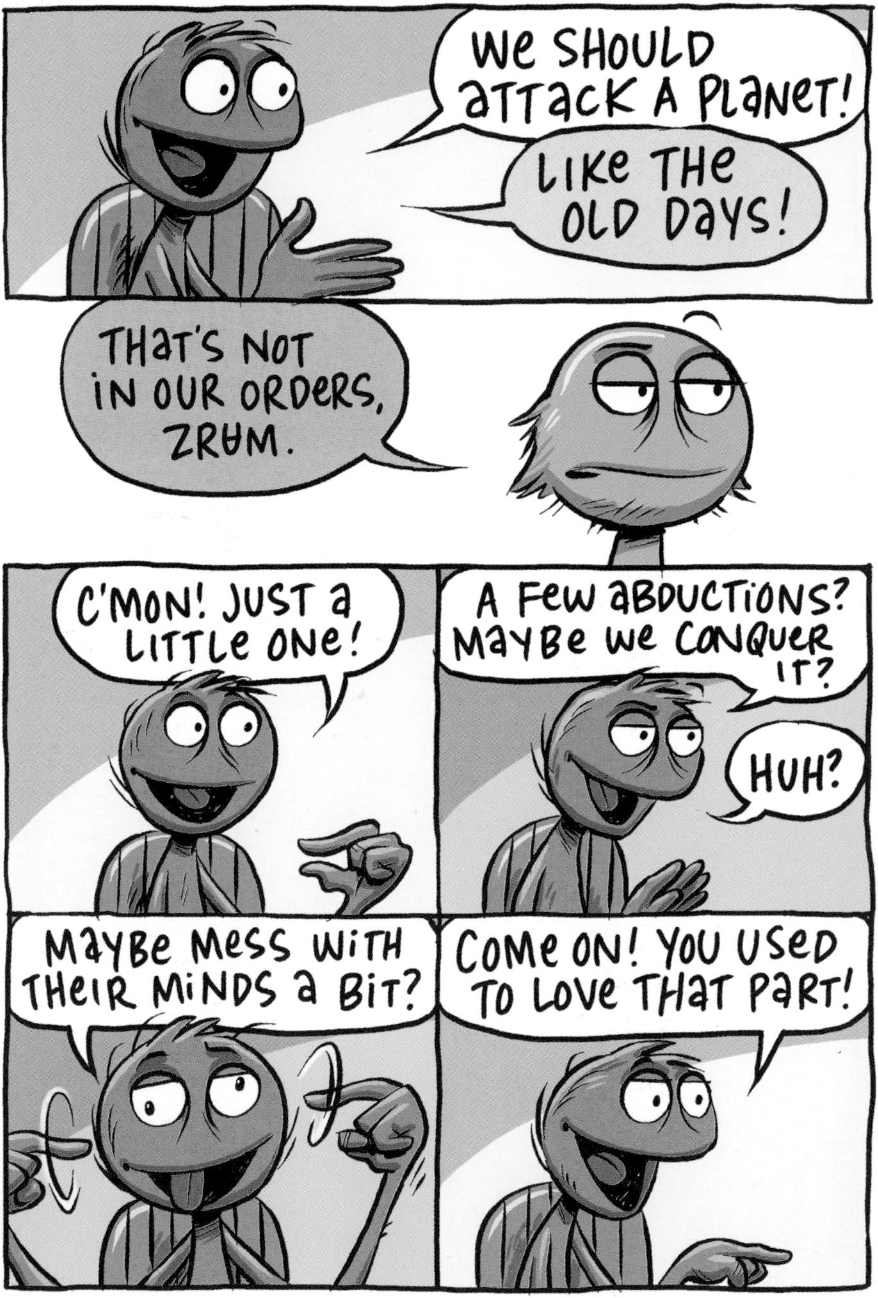
WE SHOULD ATTACK A PLANET!
LIKE THE OLD DAYS!
THAT'S NOT IN OUR ORDERS, ZRUM.
C'MON! JUST A LITTLE ONE!
A FEW ABDUCTIONS? MAYBE WE CONQUER IT?
HUH?
MAYBE MESS WITH THEIR MINDS A BIT?
COME ON! YOU USED TO LOVE THAT PART!

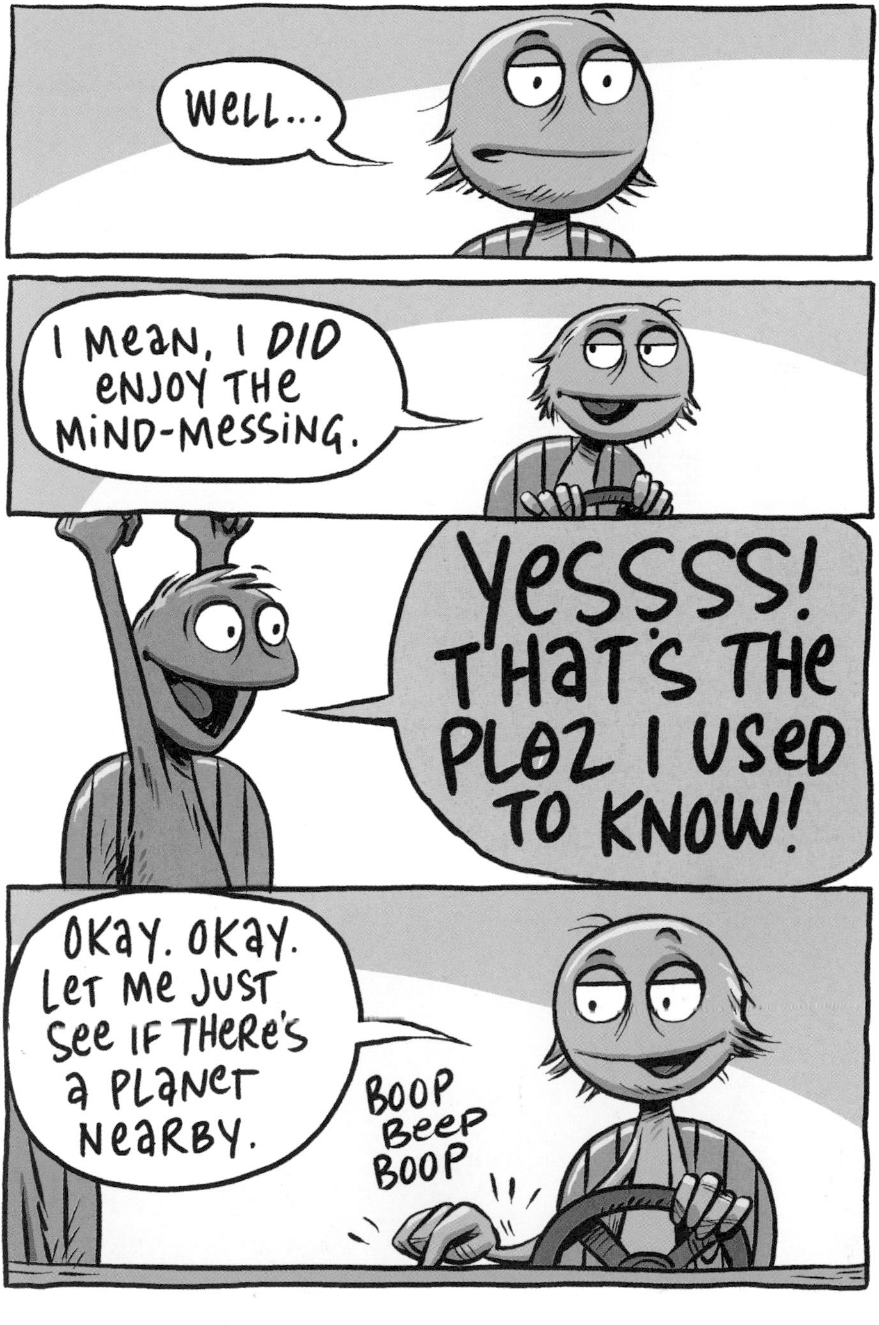
WELL...
I MEAN, I DID ENJOY THE MIND-MESSING.
YESSSS! THAT'S THE PLOZ I USED TO KNOW!
OKAY. OKAY. LET ME JUST SEE IF THERE'S A PLANET NEARBY.
BOOP BEEP BOOP

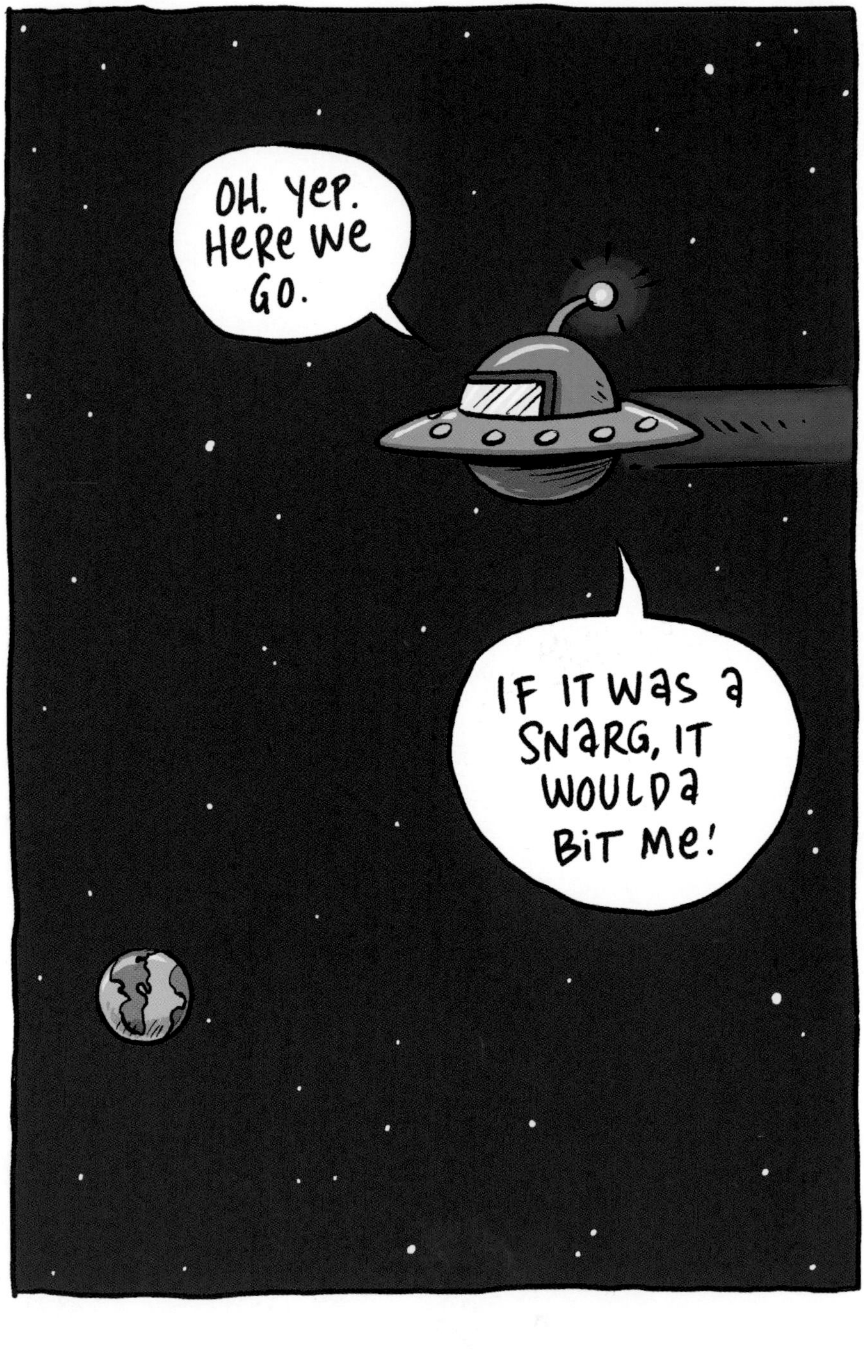
OH. YEP. HERE WE GO.
IF IT WAS A SNARG, IT WOULDA BIT ME!

CHAPTER TWO

"CARDS ON THE TABLE"

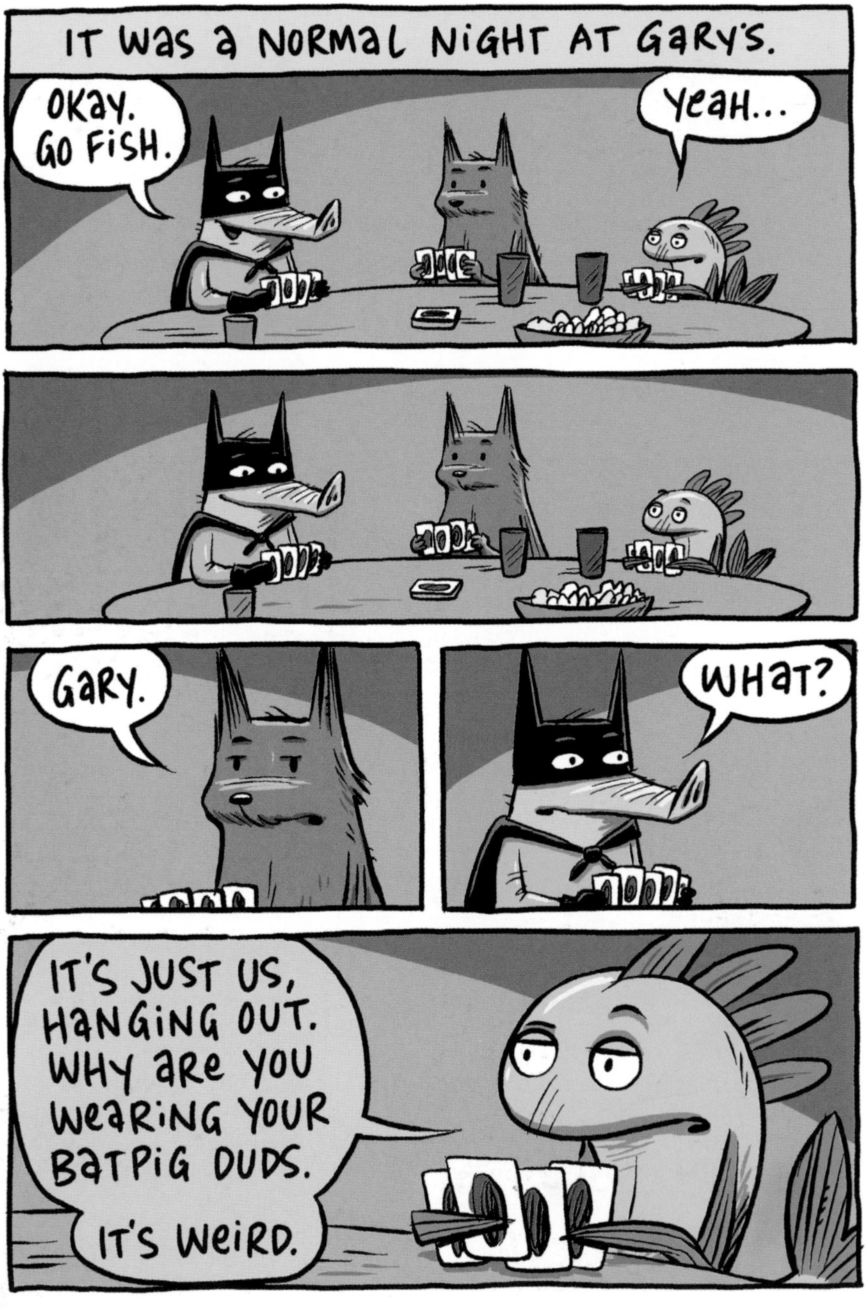
IT WAS A NORMAL NIGHT AT GARY'S.
OKAY. GO FISH.
YEAH...
GARY.
WHAT?
IT'S JUST US, HANGING OUT. WHY ARE YOU WEARING YOUR BATPIG DUDS.
IT'S WEIRD.

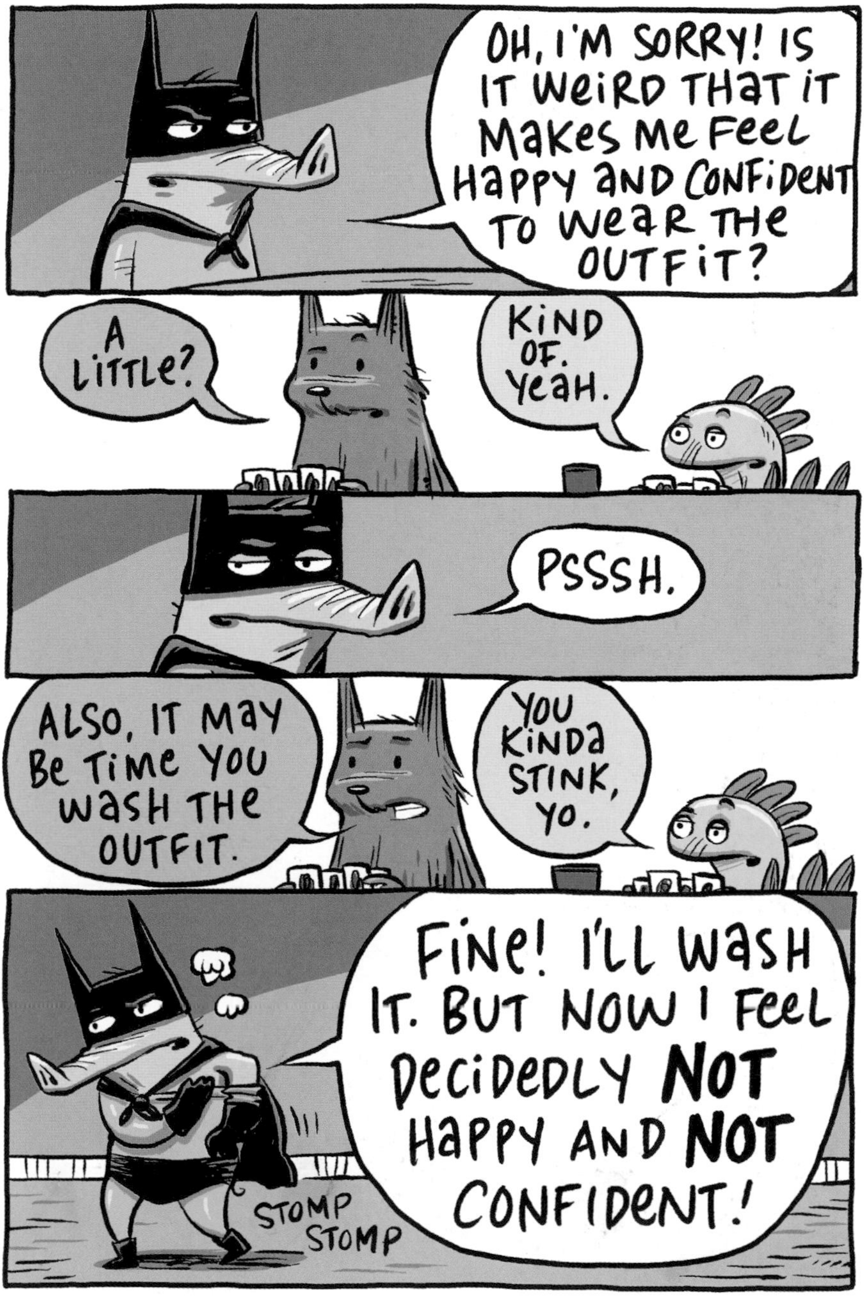
OH, I'M SORRY! IS IT WEIRD THAT IT MAKES ME FEEL HAPPY AND CONFIDENT TO WEAR THE OUTFIT?
A LITTLE?
KIND OF. YEAH.
PSSSH.
ALSO, IT MAY BE TIME YOU WASH THE OUTFIT.
YOU KINDA STINK, YO.
FINE! I'LL WASH IT. BUT NOW I FEEL DECIDEDLY **NOT** HAPPY AND **NOT** CONFIDENT!
STOMP STOMP

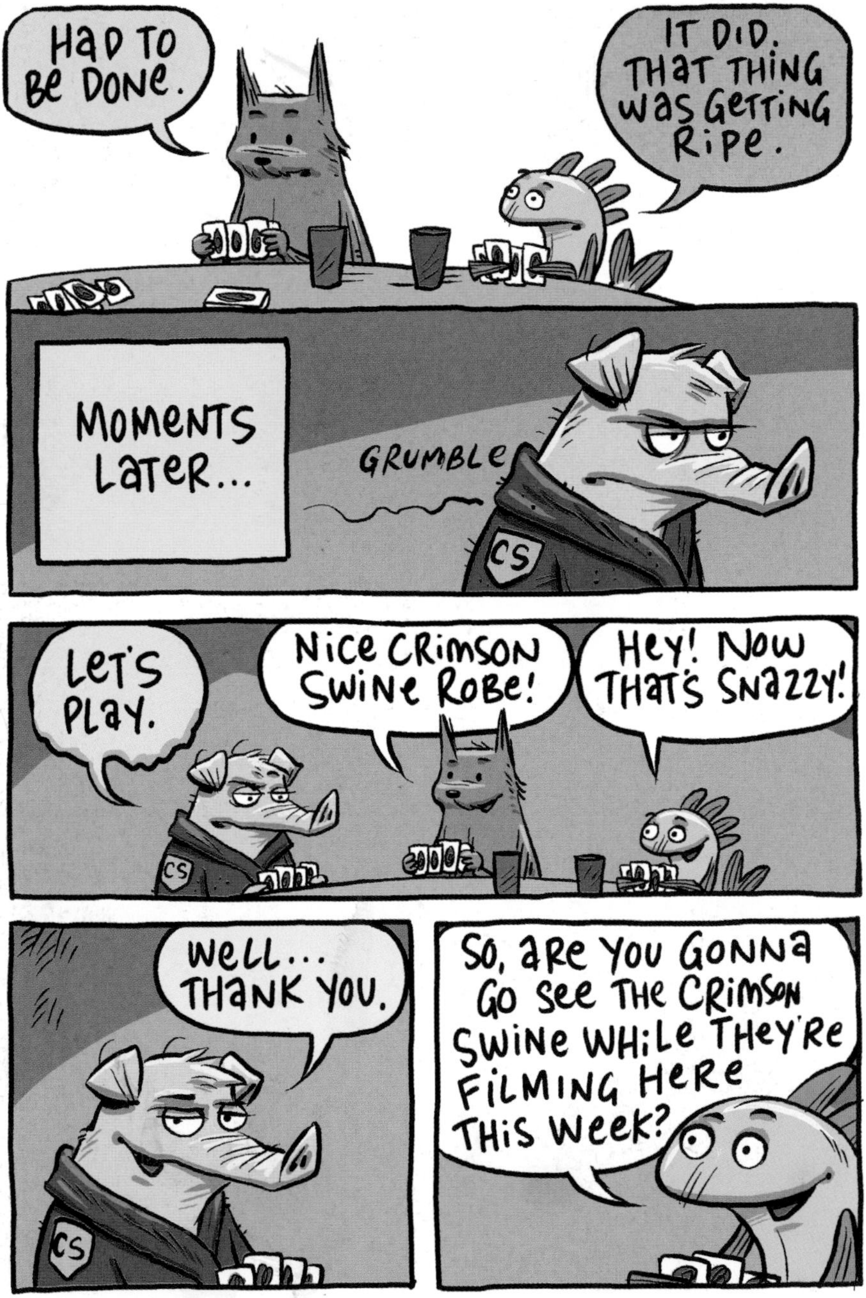
HAD TO BE DONE.
IT DID. THAT THING WAS GETTING RIPE.
MOMENTS LATER...
GRUMBLE
LET'S PLAY.
NICE CRIMSON SWINE ROBE!
HEY! NOW THAT'S SNAZZY!
WELL... THANK YOU.
SO, ARE YOU GONNA GO SEE THE CRIMSON SWINE WHILE THEY'RE FILMING HERE THIS WEEK?

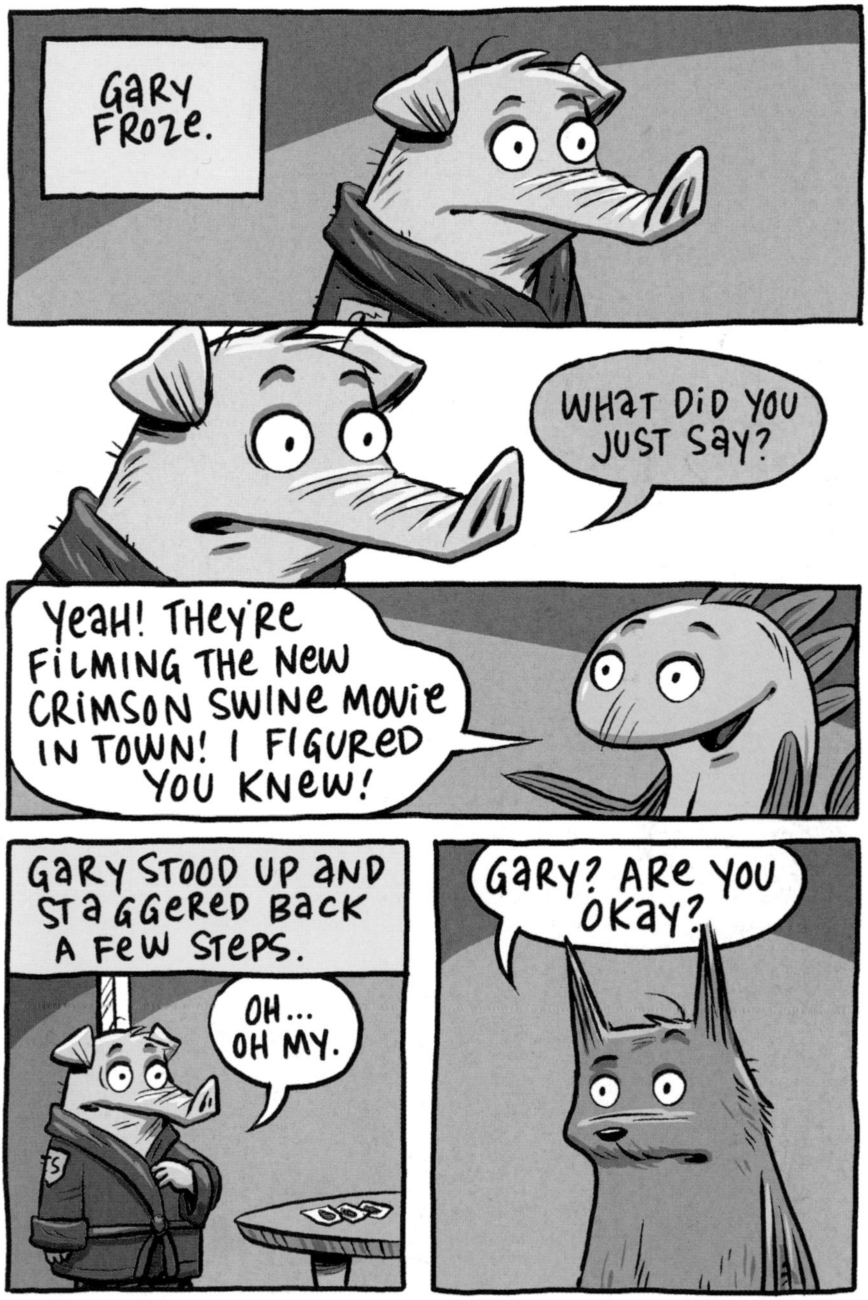
GaRY FROZE.
WHaT DiD YOU JUST SaY?
YeaH! THey'Re FiLMING THe New CRiMSON SWiNe MOVie IN TOWN! I FIGUReD YOU KNeW!
GaRY STOOD UP aND STaGGeReD BaCK a Few STePS.
OH... OH MY.
GaRY? ARe YOU OKaY?

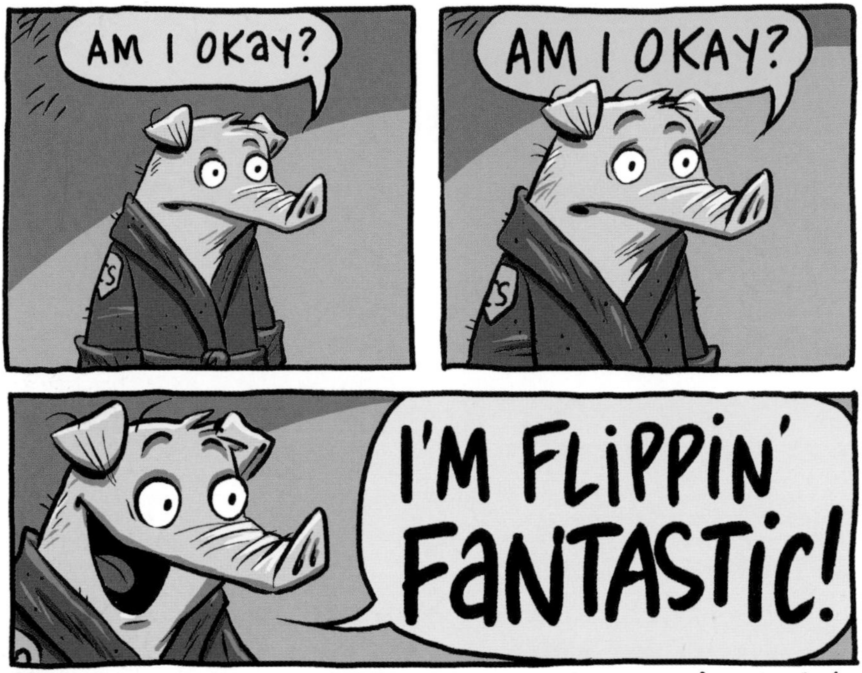
AM I OKAY?
AM I OKAY?
I'M FLIPPIN' FANTASTIC!

TO BE CLEAR, THE CRIMSON SWINE IS GARY'S FAVORITE SUPERHERO, AND MAYBE HIS FAVORITE THING PERIOD.

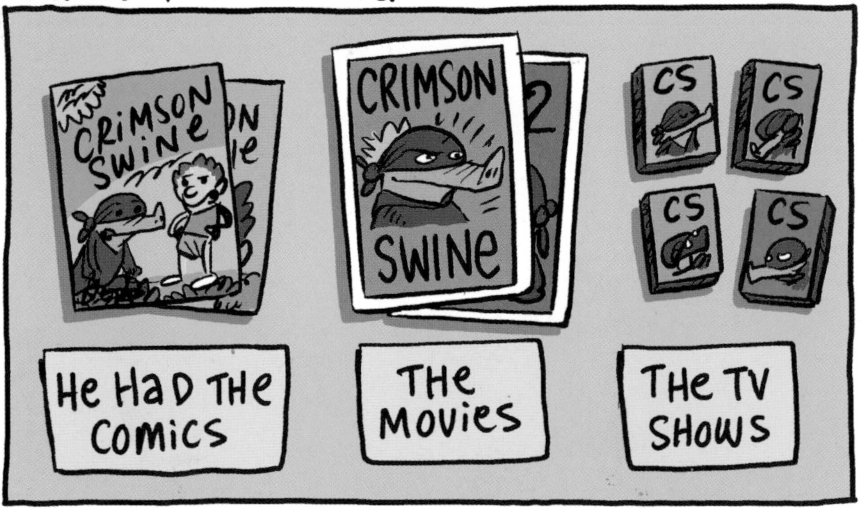
CRIMSON SWINE
CRIMSON SWINE
CS
CS
CS
CS
HE HAD THE COMICS
THE MOVIES
THE TV SHOWS

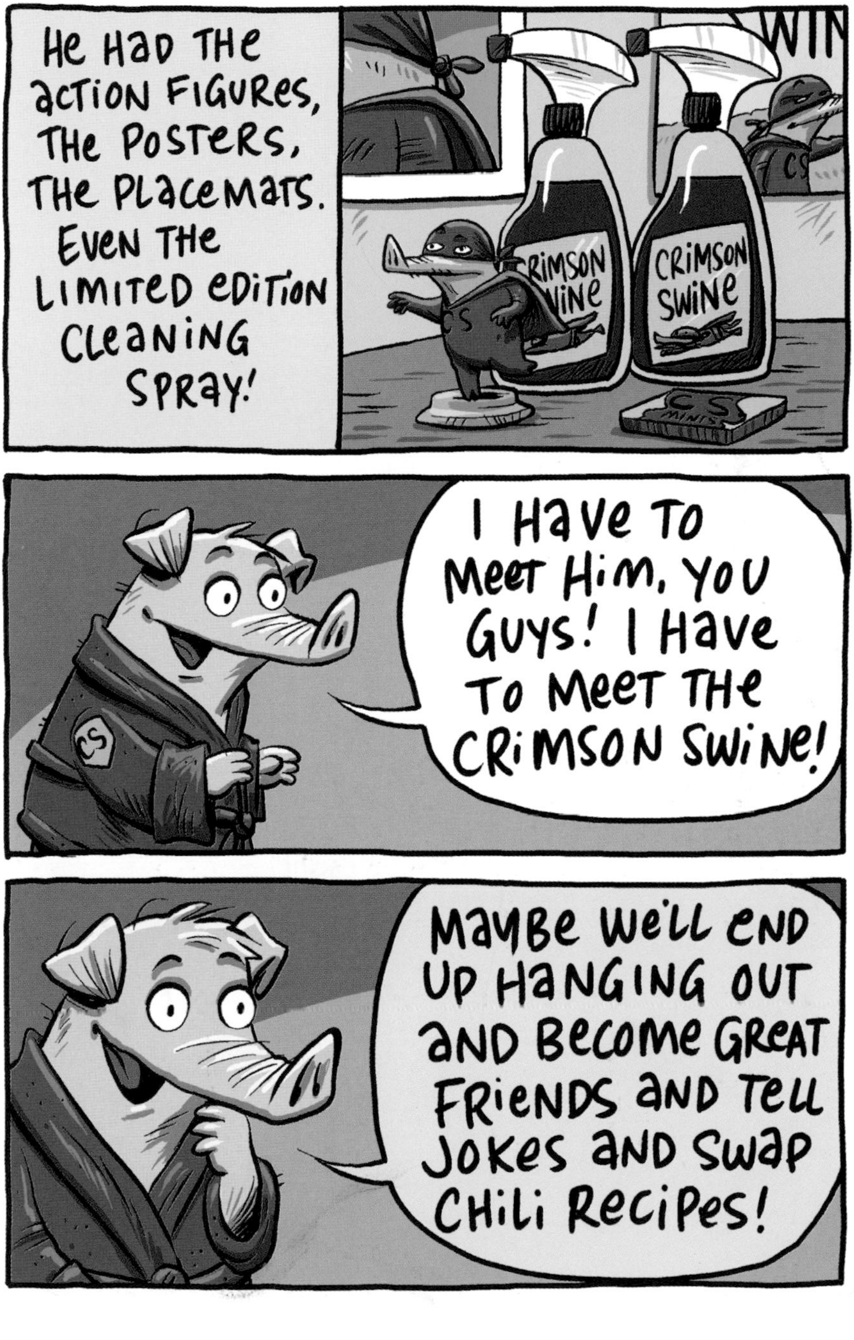
HE HAD THE ACTION FIGURES, THE POSTERS, THE PLACEMATS. EVEN THE LIMITED EDITION CLEANING SPRAY!
CRIMSON SWINE
CS MINTS
I HAVE TO MEET HIM, YOU GUYS! I HAVE TO MEET THE CRIMSON SWINE!
MAYBE WE'LL END UP HANGING OUT AND BECOME GREAT FRIENDS AND TELL JOKES AND SWAP CHILI RECIPES!

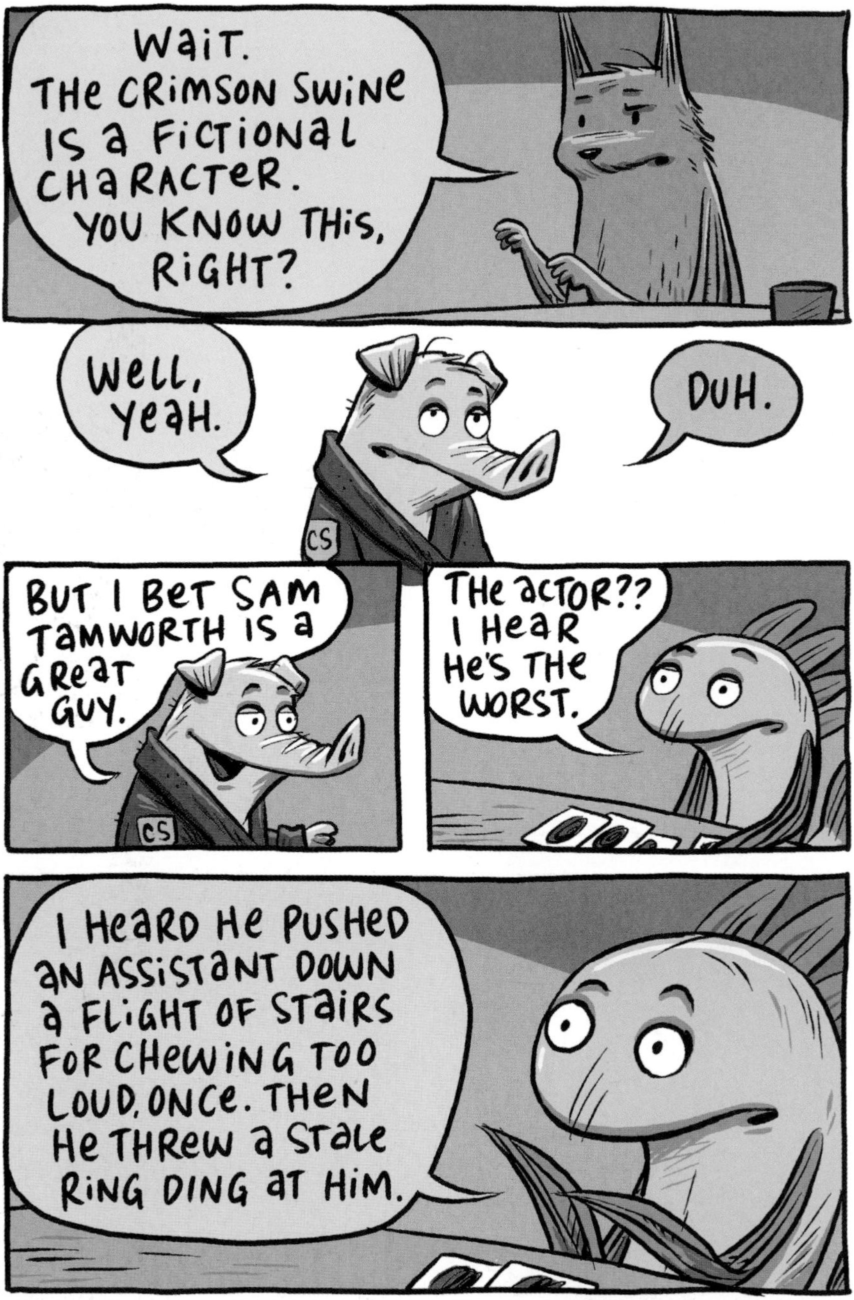
WAIT. THE CRIMSON SWINE IS A FICTIONAL CHARACTER. YOU KNOW THIS, RIGHT?
WELL, YEAH.
DUH.
CS
BUT I BET SAM TAMWORTH IS A GREAT GUY.
CS
THE ACTOR?? I HEAR HE'S THE WORST.
I HEARD HE PUSHED AN ASSISTANT DOWN A FLIGHT OF STAIRS FOR CHEWING TOO LOUD, ONCE. THEN HE THREW A STALE RING DING AT HIM.

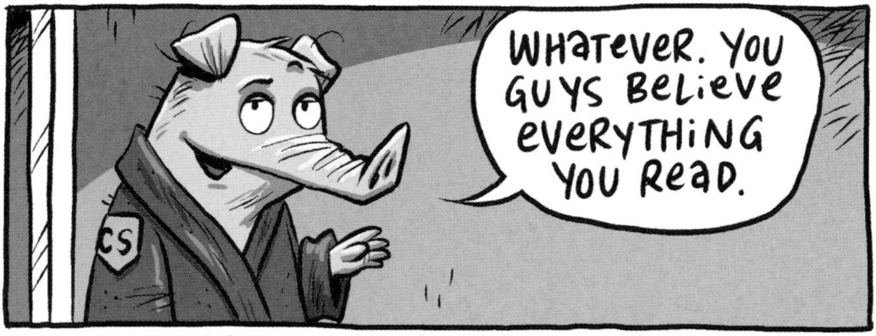
WHATEVER. YOU GUYS BELIEVE EVERYTHING YOU READ.

SAM TAMWORTH WAS, IN FACT, THE VERY AWFUL-EST.

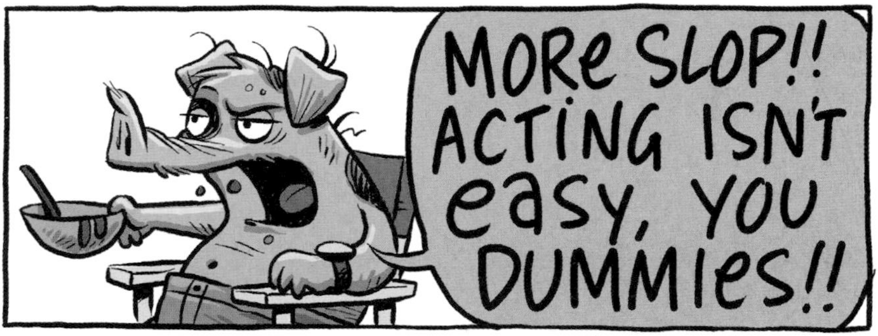
MORE SLOP!! ACTING ISN'T EASY, YOU DUMMIES!!

THE ACTOR'S SHENANIGANS WERE LEGENDARY. HIS TEMPER WAS FEARED FROM COAST TO COAST.

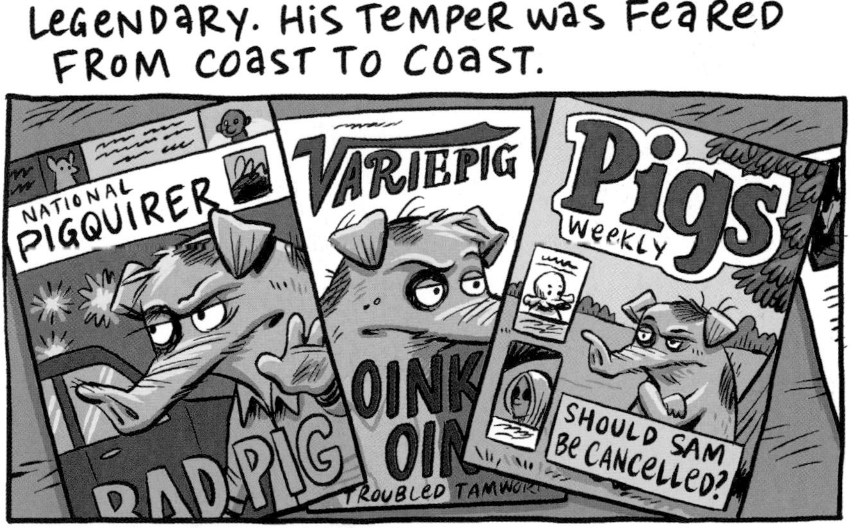
NATIONAL PIGQUIRER
PIG
VARIEPIG
Pigs
WEEKLY
SHOULD SAM BE CANCELLED?

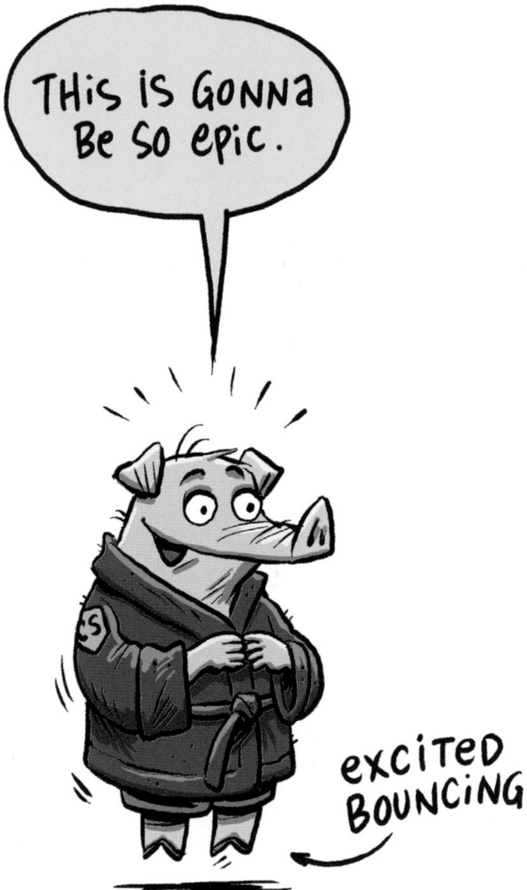
THIS IS GONNA
BE SO EPIC.
EXCITED
BOUNCING

CHAPTER THREE

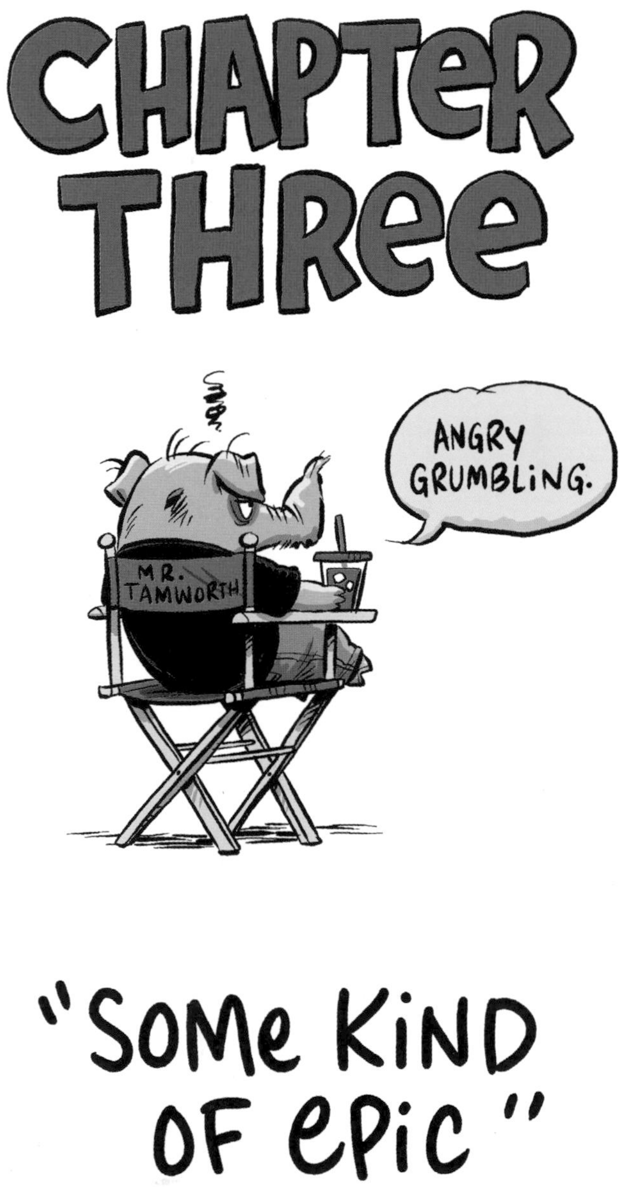
ANGRY GRUMBLING.
MR. TAMWORTH

"SOME KIND OF EPIC"

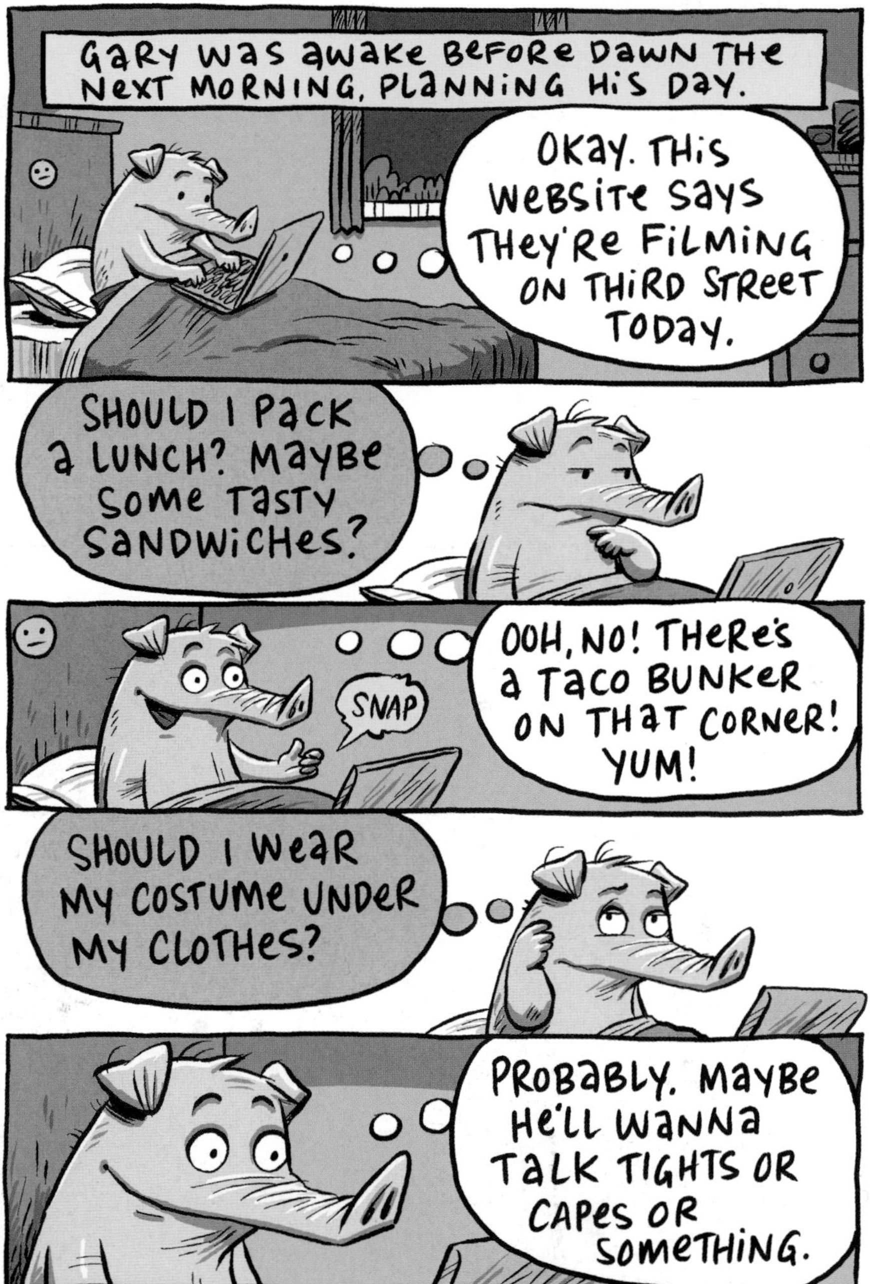
GARY WAS AWAKE BEFORE DAWN THE NEXT MORNING, PLANNING HIS DAY.
OKAY. THIS WEBSITE SAYS THEY'RE FILMING ON THIRD STREET TODAY.
SHOULD I PACK A LUNCH? MAYBE SOME TASTY SANDWICHES?
SNAP
OOH, NO! THERE'S A TACO BUNKER ON THAT CORNER! YUM!
SHOULD I WEAR MY COSTUME UNDER MY CLOTHES?
PROBABLY. MAYBE HE'LL WANNA TALK TIGHTS OR CAPES OR SOMETHING.

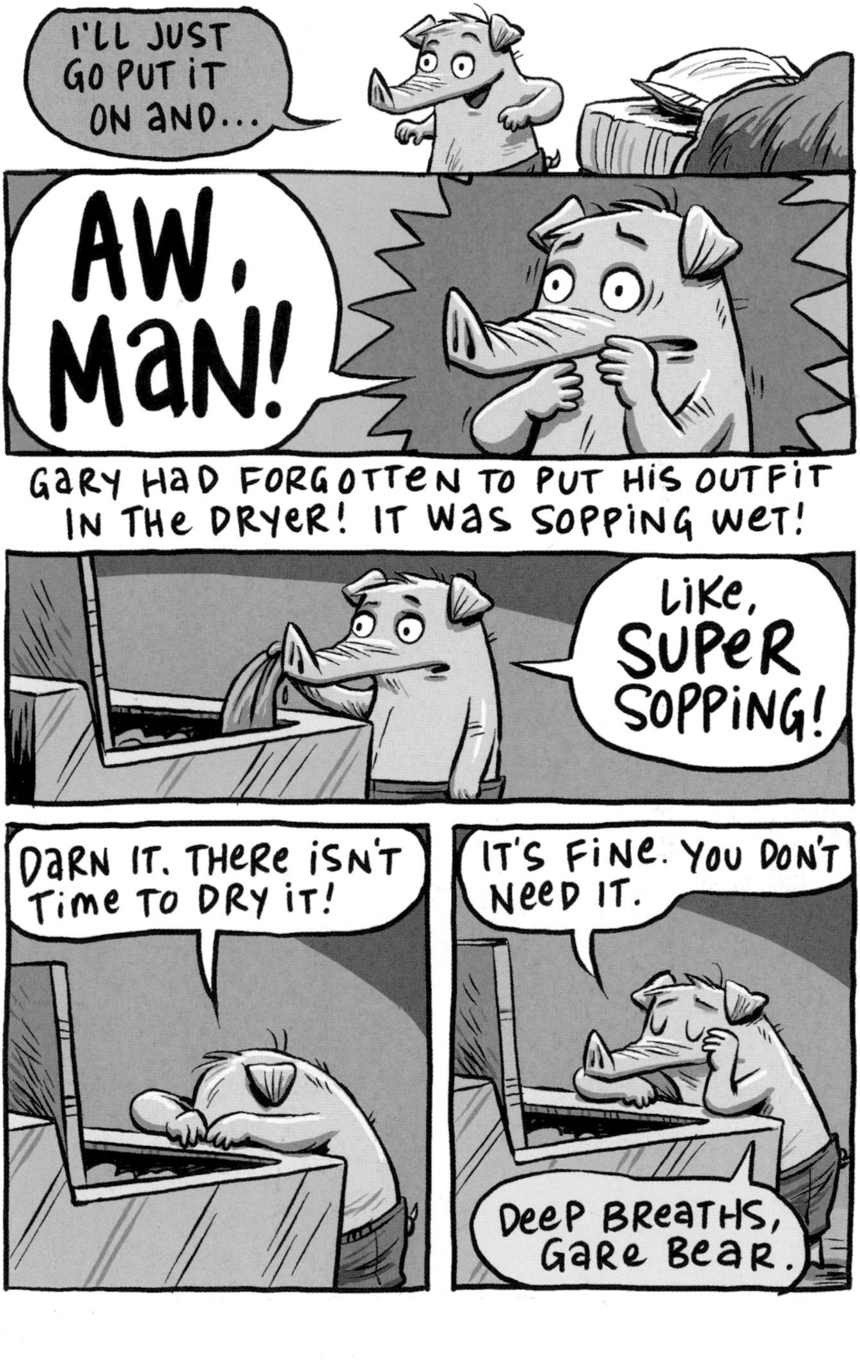
I'LL JUST GO PUT IT ON AND...
AW, MAN!
GARY HAD FORGOTTEN TO PUT HIS OUTFIT IN THE DRYER! IT WAS SOPPING WET!
LIKE, SUPER SOPPING!
DARN IT. THERE ISN'T TIME TO DRY IT!
IT'S FINE. YOU DON'T NEED IT.
DEEP BREATHS, GARE BEAR.

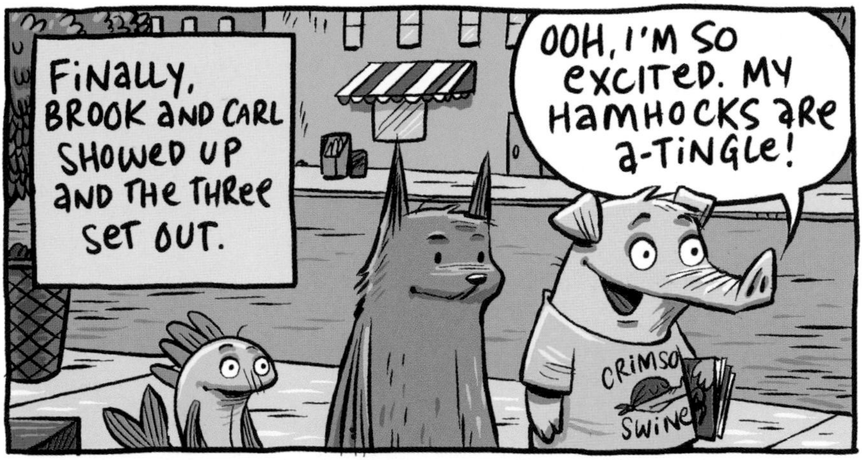
FINALLY, BROOK AND CARL SHOWED UP AND THE THREE SET OUT.
OOH, I'M SO EXCITED. MY HAMHOCKS ARE A-TINGLE!
CRIMSO
SWINE

AS THEY GOT CLOSE TO THE SET, THEY STARTED SEEING TRUCKS AND LIGHTING AND CREW AND MOVIE STUFF.

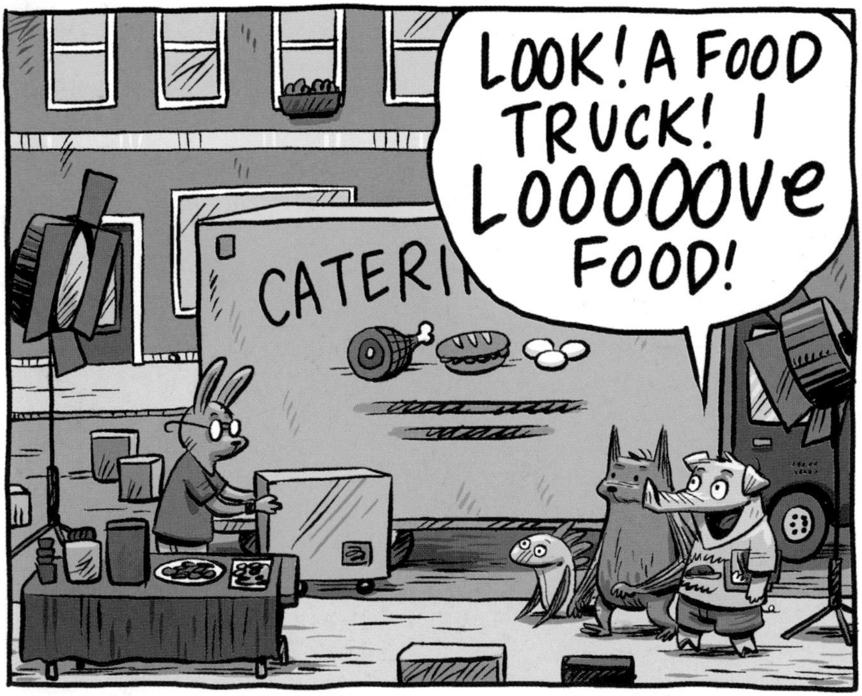
CATERI
LOOK! A FOOD TRUCK! I LOOOOOVE FOOD!

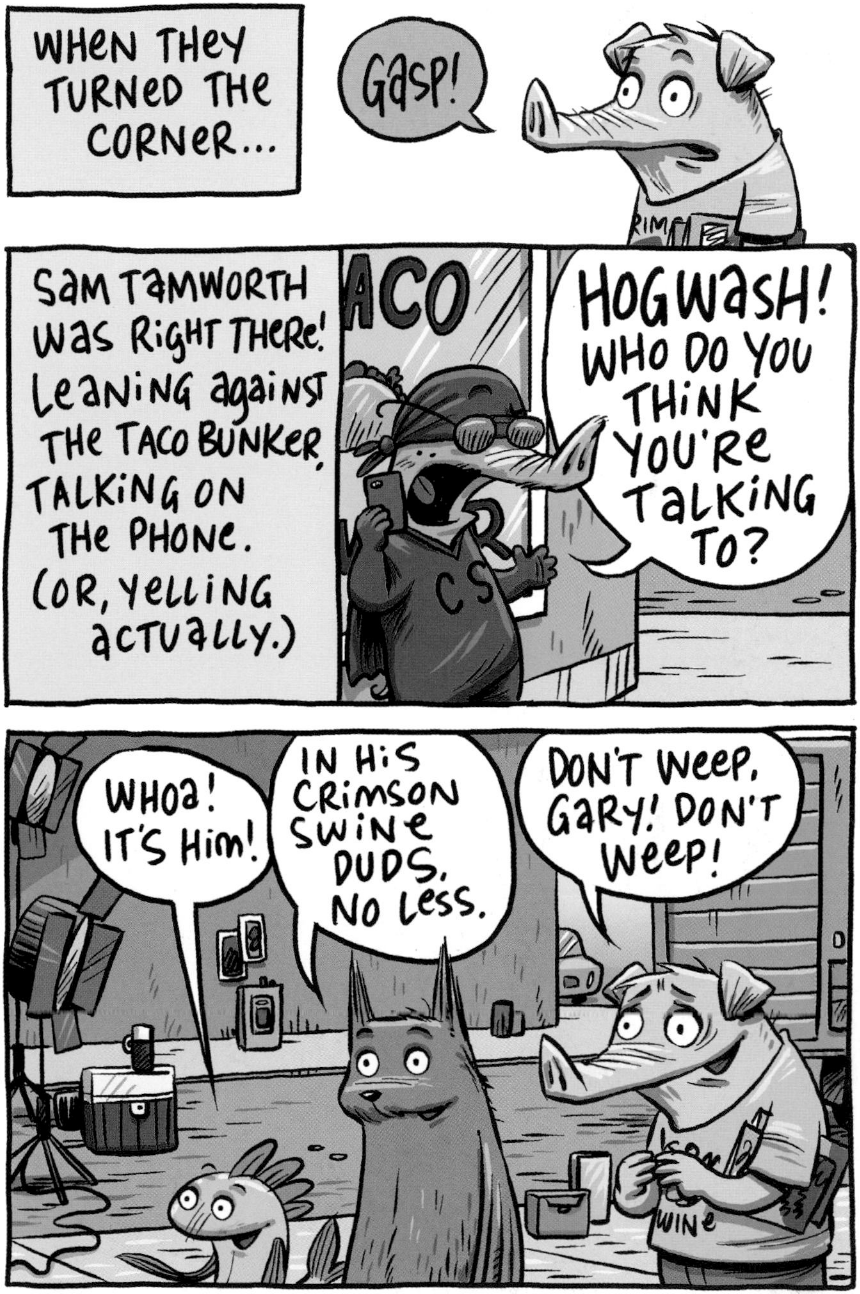
WHEN THEY TURNED THE CORNER...
GASP!
SAM TAMWORTH WAS RIGHT THERE! LEANING AGAINST THE TACO BUNKER, TALKING ON THE PHONE. (OR, YELLING ACTUALLY.)
ACO
HOGWASH! WHO DO YOU THINK YOU'RE TALKING TO?
WHOA! IT'S HIM!
IN HIS CRIMSON SWINE DUDS, NO LESS.
DON'T WEEP, GARY! DON'T WEEP!

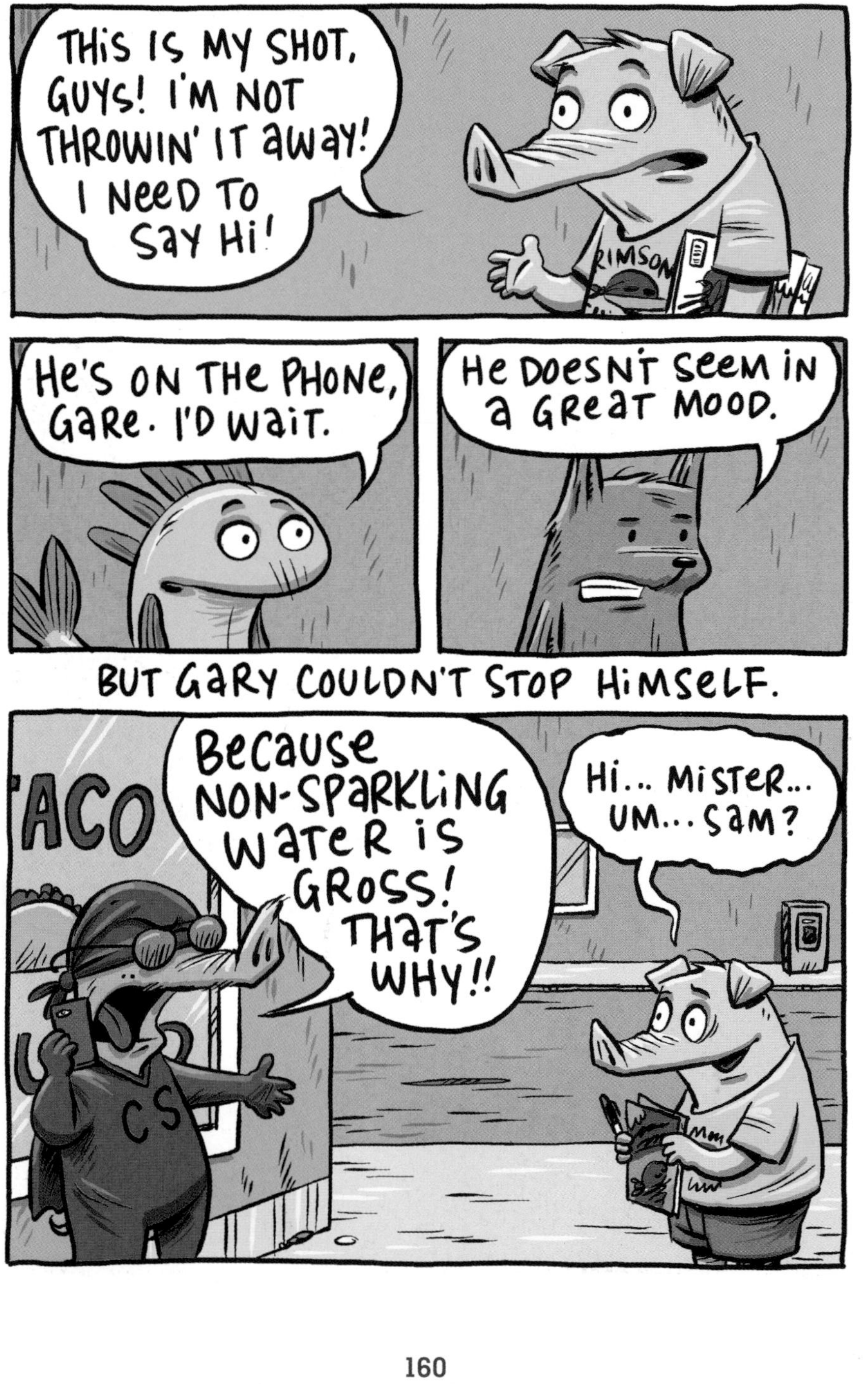
THIS IS MY SHOT, GUYS! I'M NOT THROWIN' IT AWAY! I NEED TO SAY HI!
HE'S ON THE PHONE, GARE. I'D WAIT.
HE DOESN'T SEEM IN A GREAT MOOD.
BUT GARY COULDN'T STOP HIMSELF.
TACO
BECAUSE NON-SPARKLING WATER IS GROSS! THAT'S WHY!!
HI... MISTER... UM... SAM?
CS

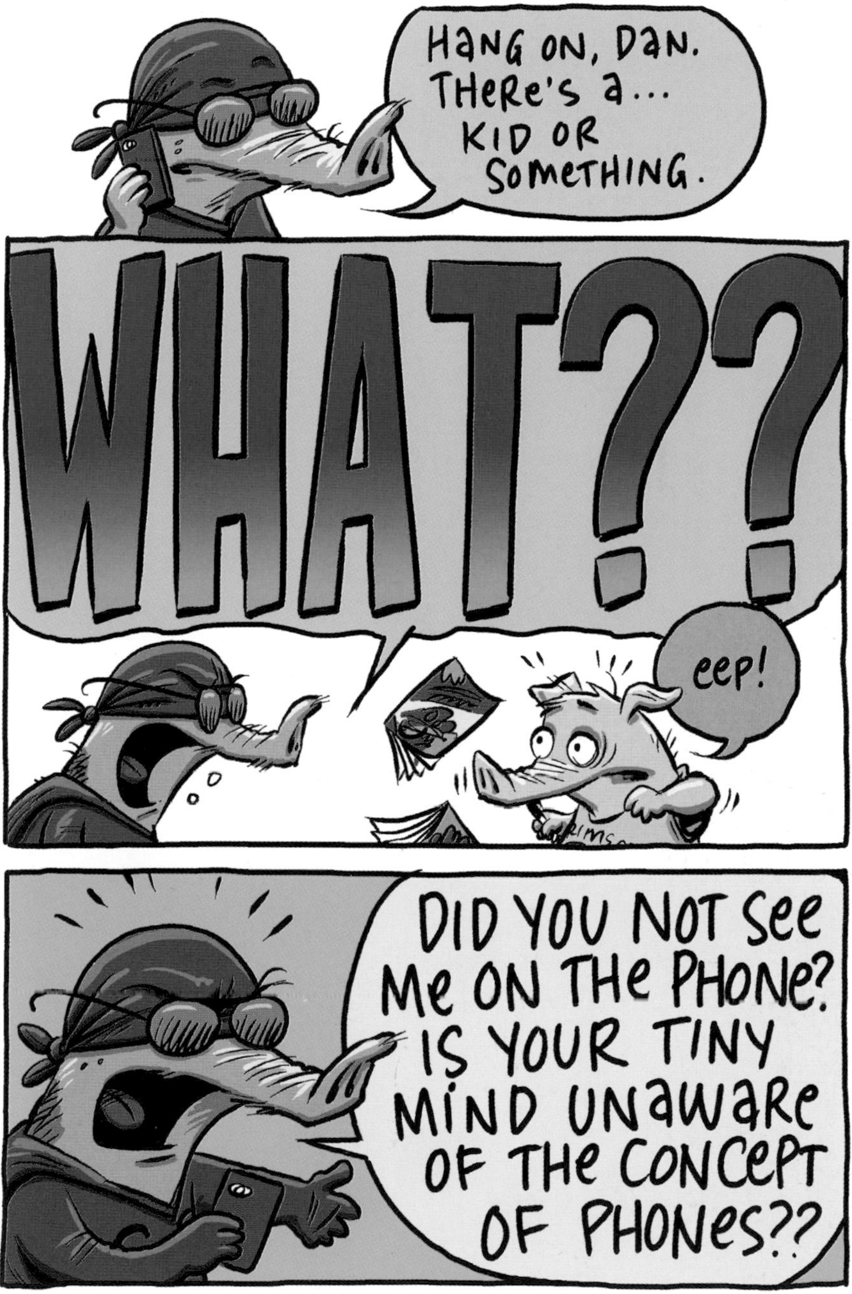
HANG ON, DAN. THERE'S A... KID OR SOMETHING.
WHAT??
eep!
DID YOU NOT SEE ME ON THE PHONE? IS YOUR TINY MIND UNAWARE OF THE CONCEPT OF PHONES??

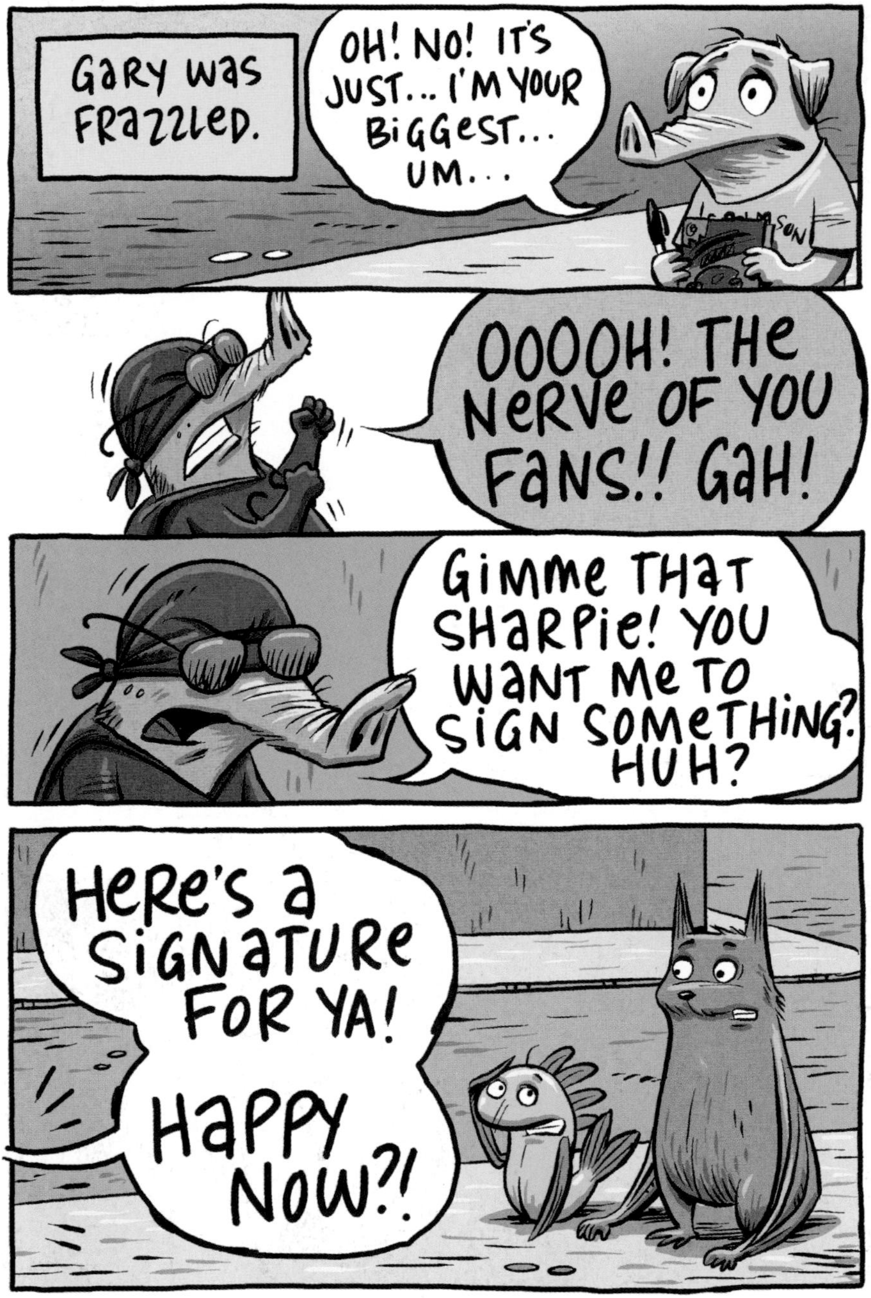
Gary was frazzled.
OH! NO! IT'S JUST... I'M YOUR BIGGEST... UM...
OOOOH! THE NERVE OF YOU FANS!! GAH!
GIMME THAT SHARPIE! YOU WANT ME TO SIGN SOMETHING? HUH?
HERE'S A SIGNATURE FOR YA!
HAPPY NOW?!

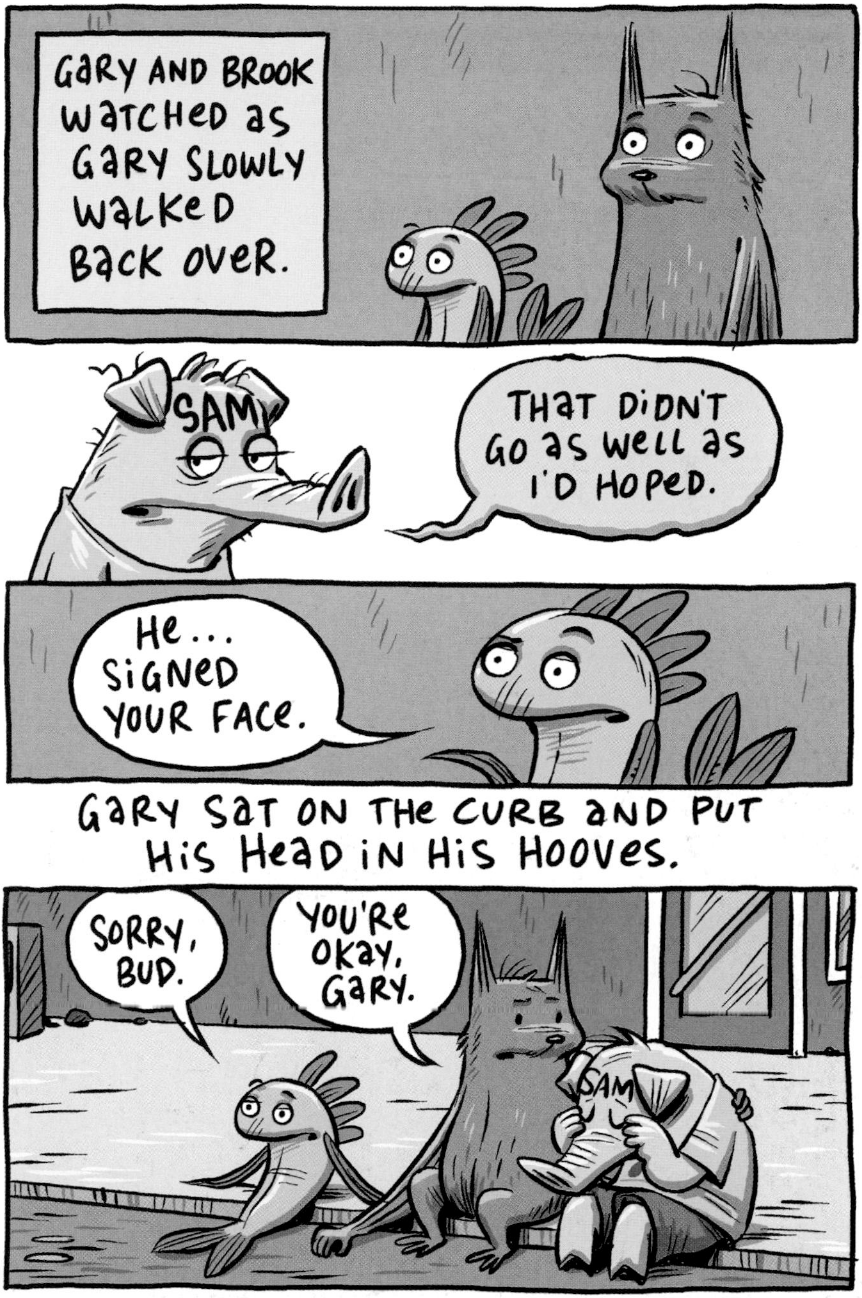
GARY AND BROOK WATCHED AS GARY SLOWLY WALKED BACK OVER.
SAM
THAT DIDN'T GO AS WELL AS I'D HOPED.
HE... SIGNED YOUR FACE.
GARY SAT ON THE CURB AND PUT HIS HEAD IN HIS HOOVES.
SORRY, BUD.
YOU'RE OKAY, GARY.
SAM

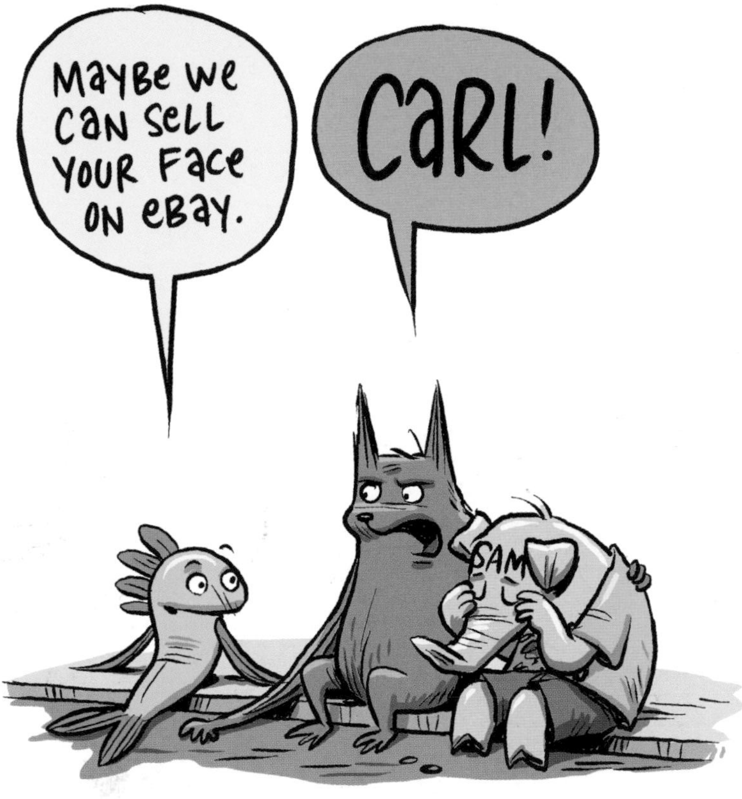
Maybe we can sell your face on eBay.
CARL!
SAM

CHAPTER FOUR

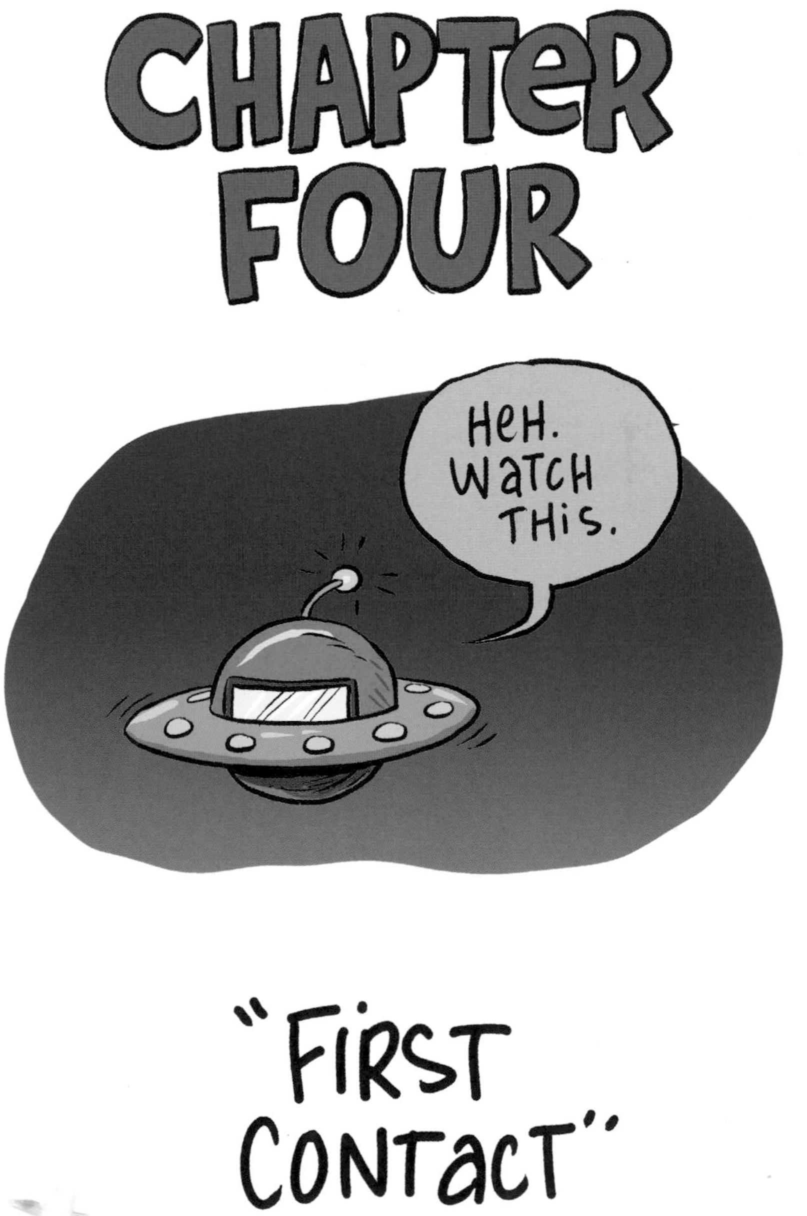
HEH. WATCH THIS.

"FIRST CONTACT"

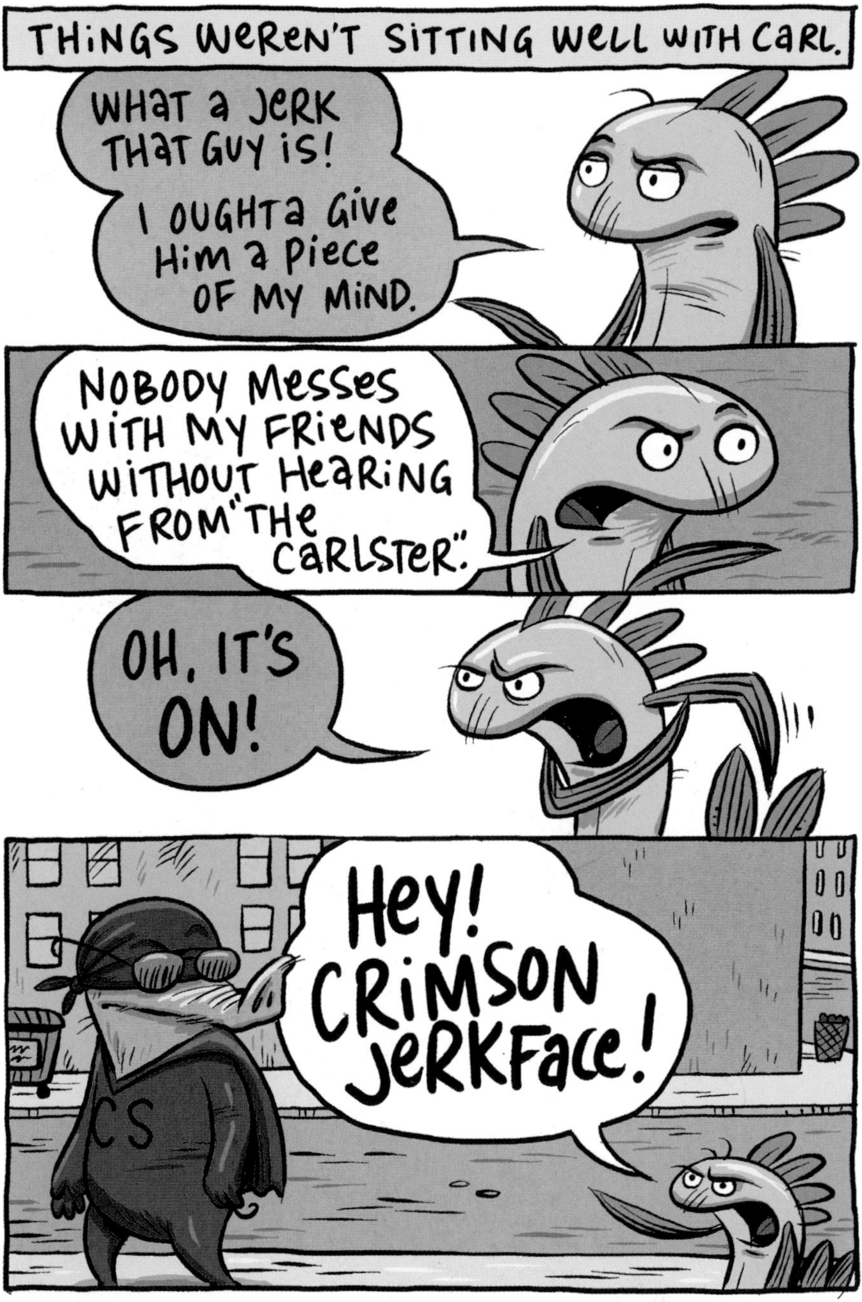
THINGS WEREN'T SITTING WELL WITH CARL.
WHAT A JERK THAT GUY IS!
I OUGHTA GIVE HIM A PIECE OF MY MIND.
NOBODY MESSES WITH MY FRIENDS WITHOUT HEARING FROM "THE CARLSTER."
OH, IT'S ON!
HEY! CRIMSON JERKFACE!
CS

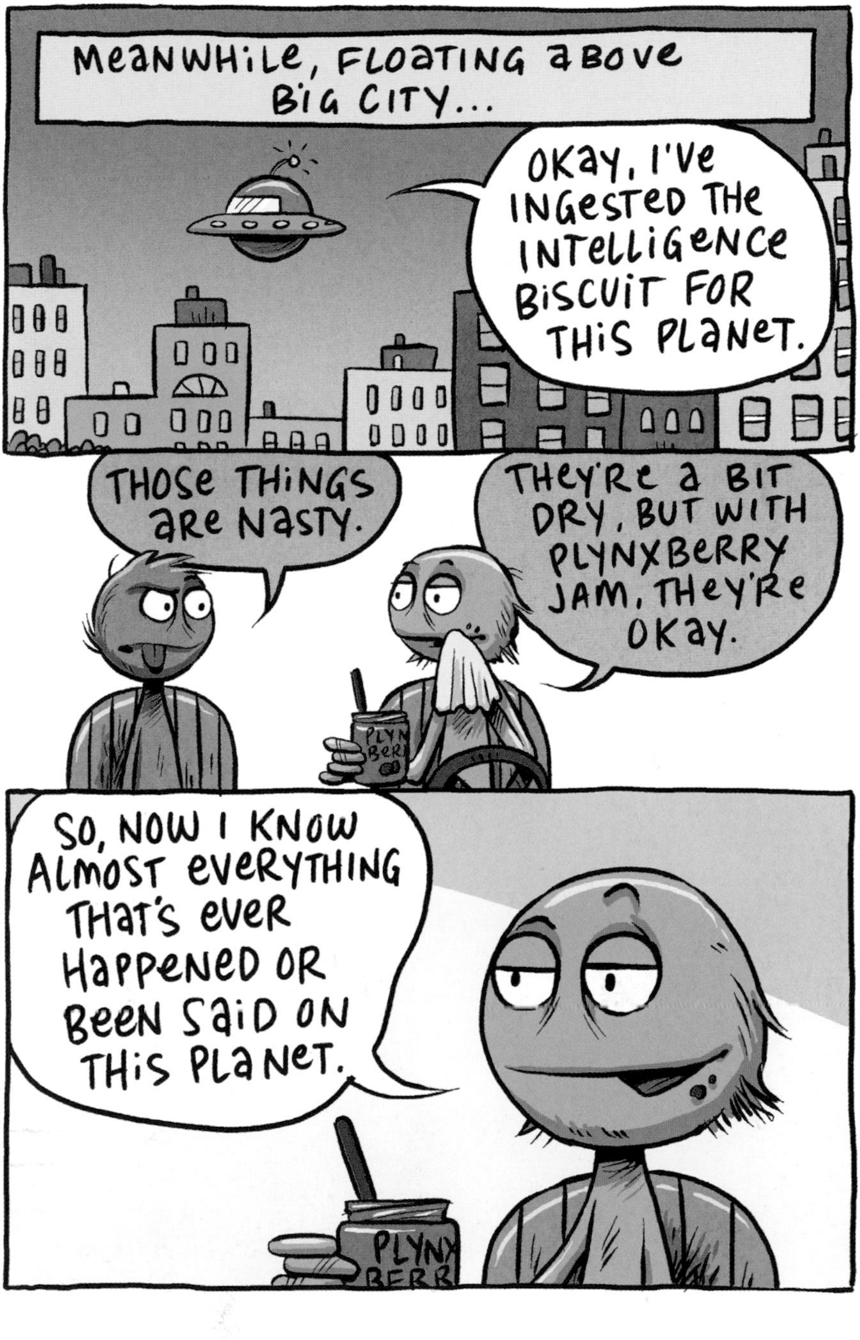
MEANWHILE, FLOATING ABOVE BIG CITY...
OKAY, I'VE INGESTED THE INTELLIGENCE BISCUIT FOR THIS PLANET.
THOSE THINGS ARE NASTY.
THEY'RE A BIT DRY, BUT WITH PLYNXBERRY JAM, THEY'RE OKAY.
SO, NOW I KNOW ALMOST EVERYTHING THAT'S EVER HAPPENED OR BEEN SAID ON THIS PLANET.

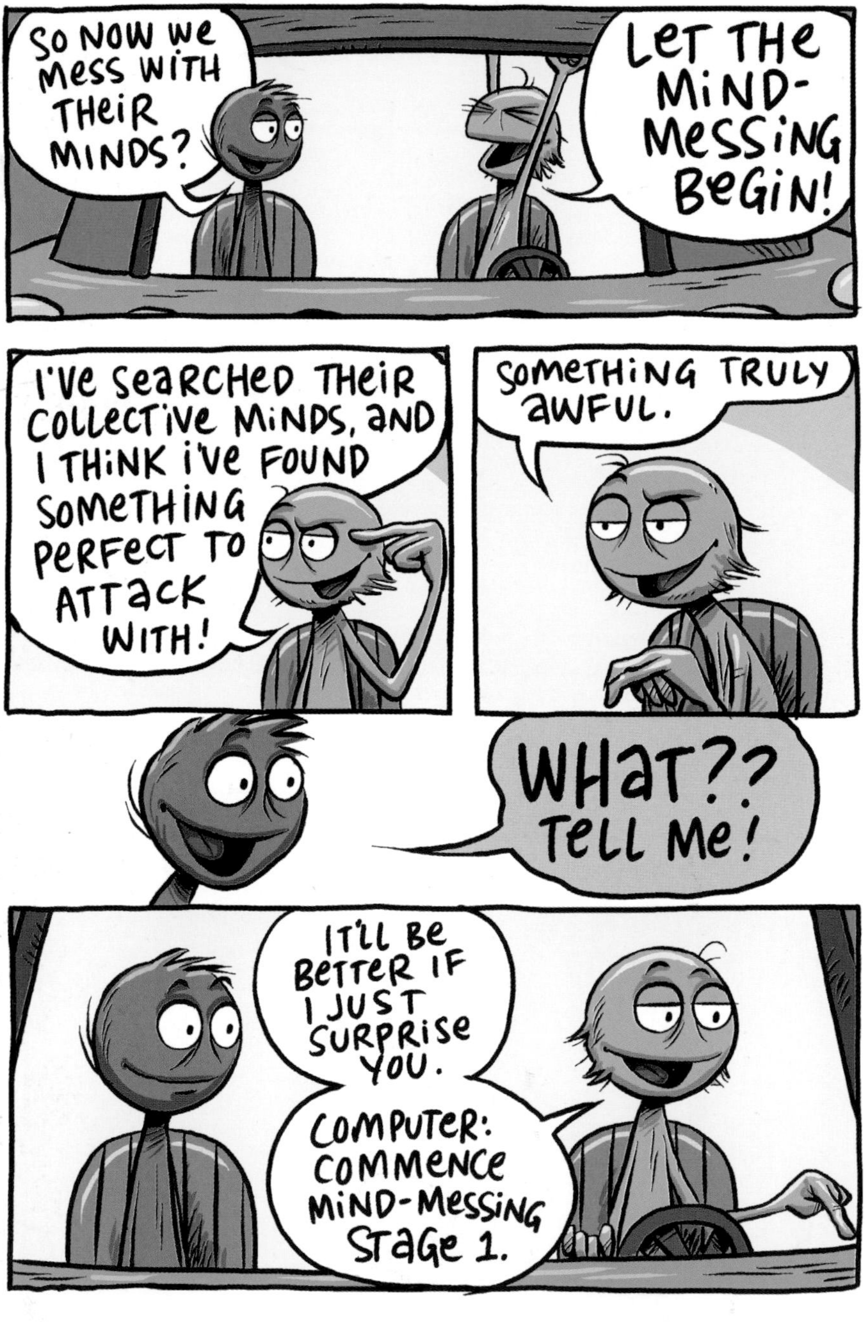
SO NOW WE MESS WITH THEIR MINDS?
LET THE MIND-MESSING BEGIN!
I'VE SEARCHED THEIR COLLECTIVE MINDS, AND I THINK I'VE FOUND SOMETHING PERFECT TO ATTACK WITH!
SOMETHING TRULY AWFUL.
WHAT?? TELL ME!
IT'LL BE BETTER IF I JUST SURPRISE YOU.
COMPUTER: COMMENCE MIND-MESSING STAGE 1.

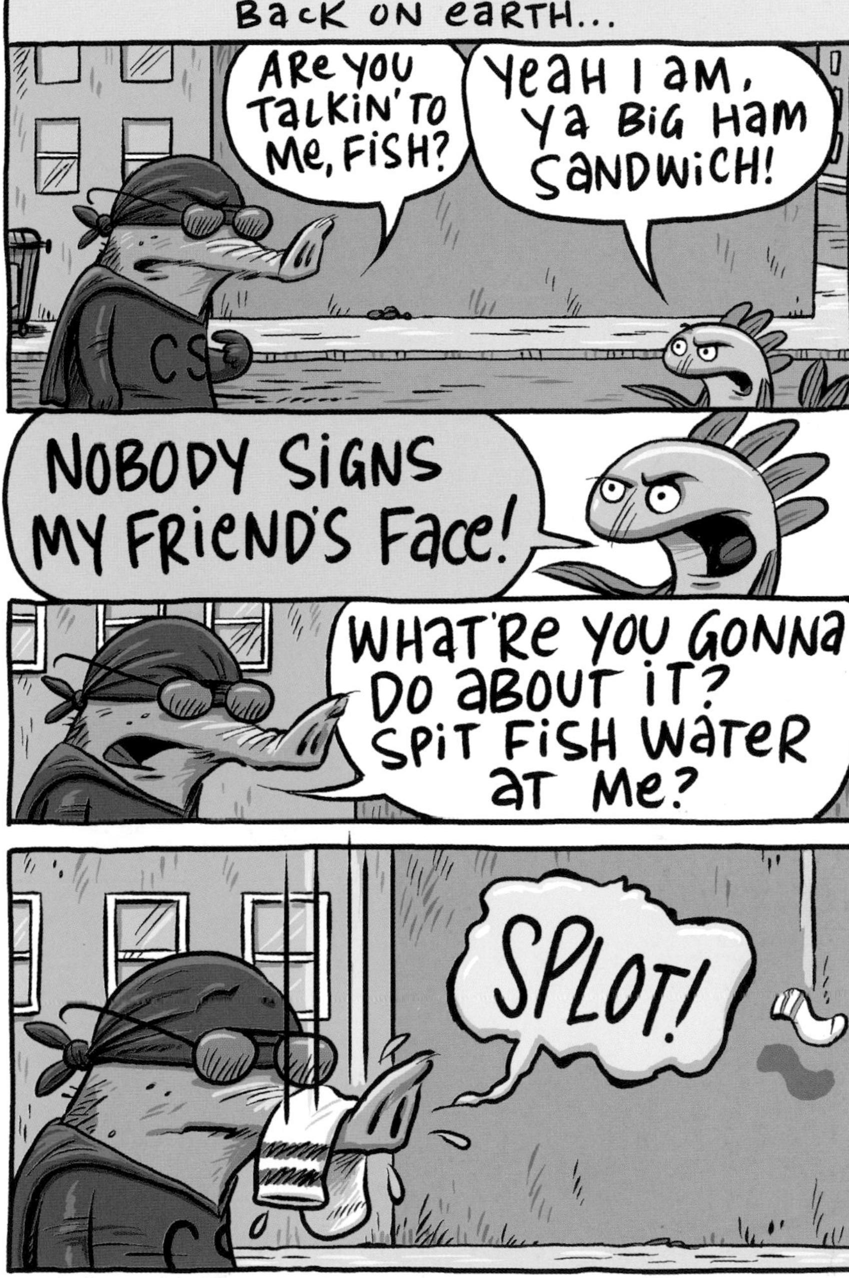
BACK ON EARTH...
ARE YOU TALKIN' TO ME, FISH?
YEAH I AM, YA BIG HAM SANDWICH!
CS
NOBODY SIGNS MY FRIEND'S FACE!
WHAT'RE YOU GONNA DO ABOUT IT? SPIT FISH WATER AT ME?
SPLOT!

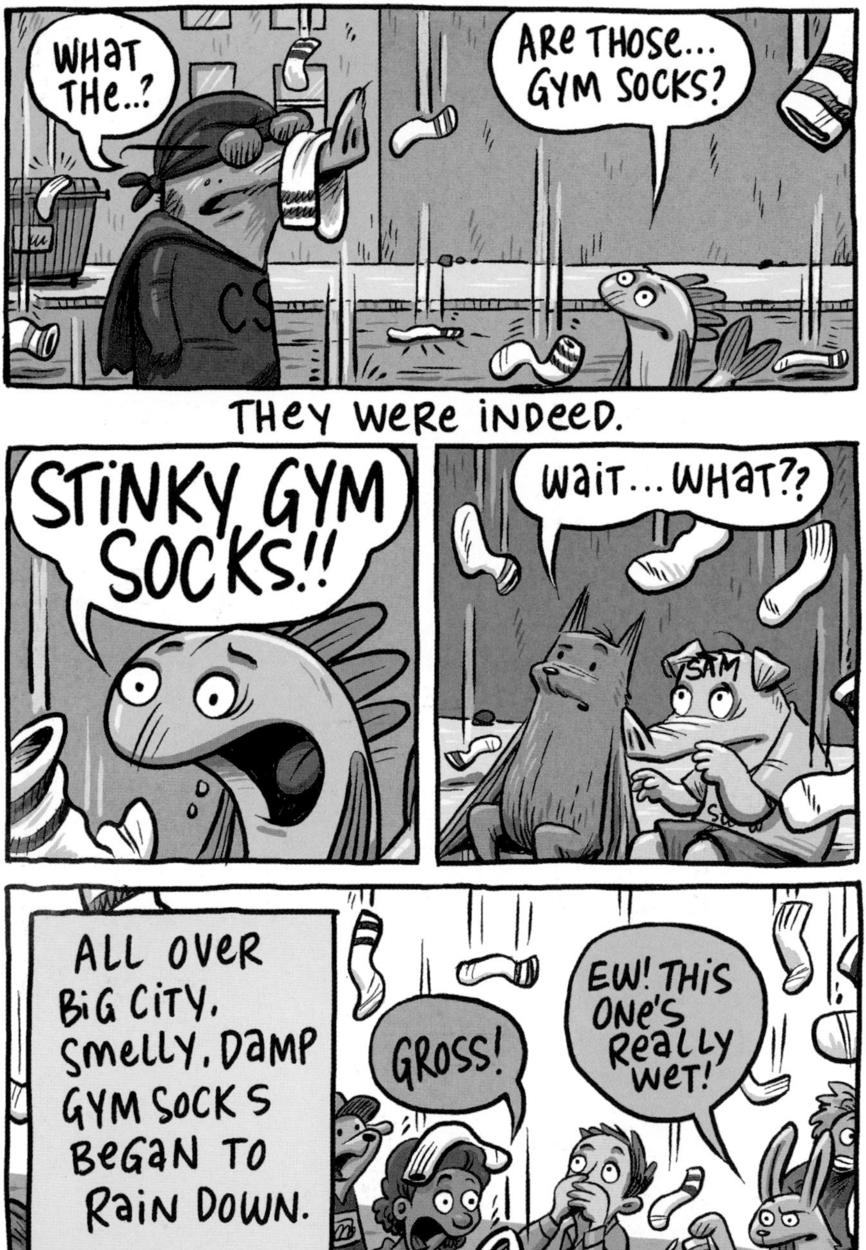
WHAT THE..?
ARE THOSE... GYM SOCKS?
THEY WERE INDEED.
STINKY GYM SOCKS!!
WAIT... WHAT??
SAM
ALL OVER BIG CITY, SMELLY, DAMP GYM SOCKS BEGAN TO RAIN DOWN.
GROSS!
EW! THIS ONE'S REALLY WET!

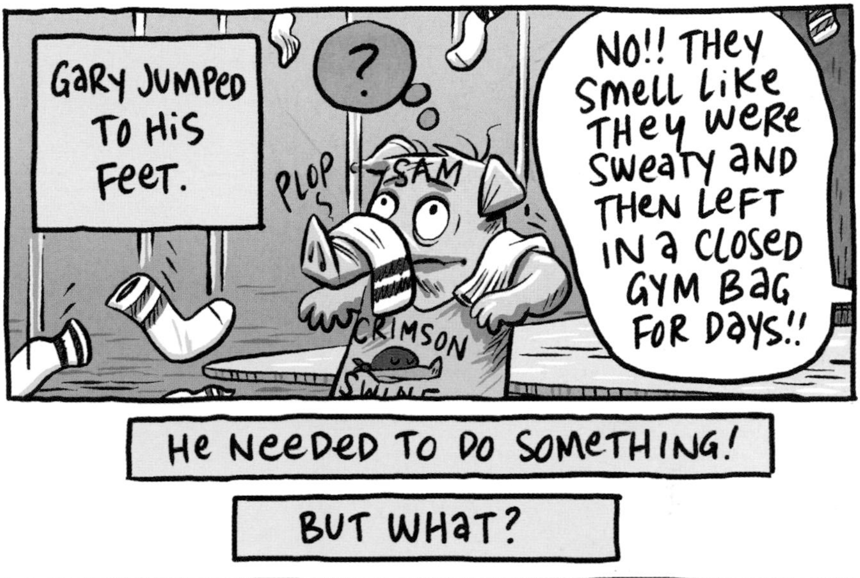
GARY JUMPED TO HIS FEET.
?
PLOP
SAM
CRIMSON
NO!! THEY SMELL LIKE THEY WERE SWEATY AND THEN LEFT IN A CLOSED GYM BAG FOR DAYS!!

HE NEEDED TO DO SOMETHING!

BUT WHAT?

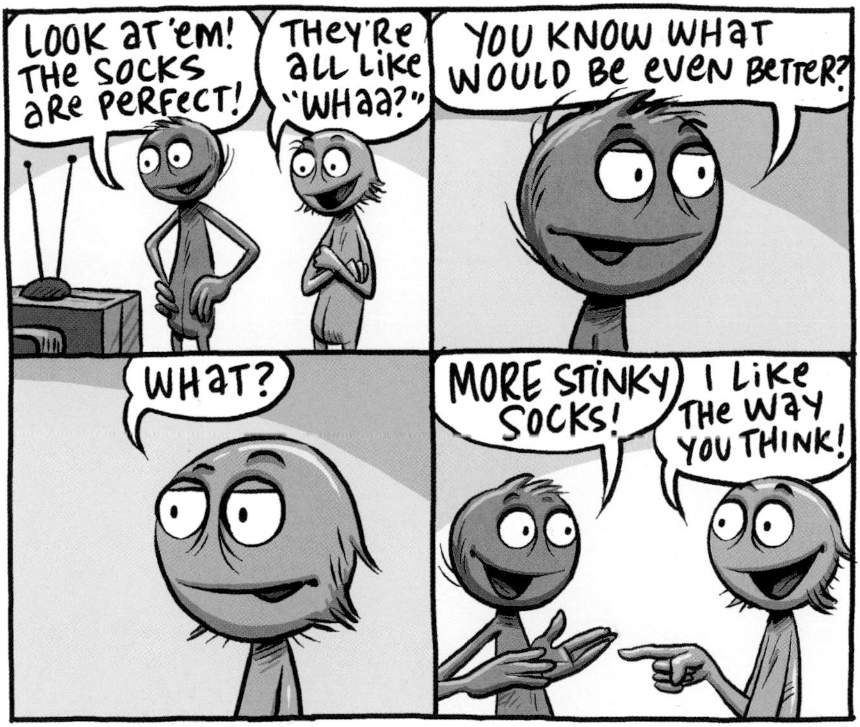
LOOK AT 'EM! THE SOCKS ARE PERFECT!
THEY'RE ALL LIKE "WHAA?"
YOU KNOW WHAT WOULD BE EVEN BETTER?
WHAT?
MORE STINKY SOCKS!
I LIKE THE WAY YOU THINK!

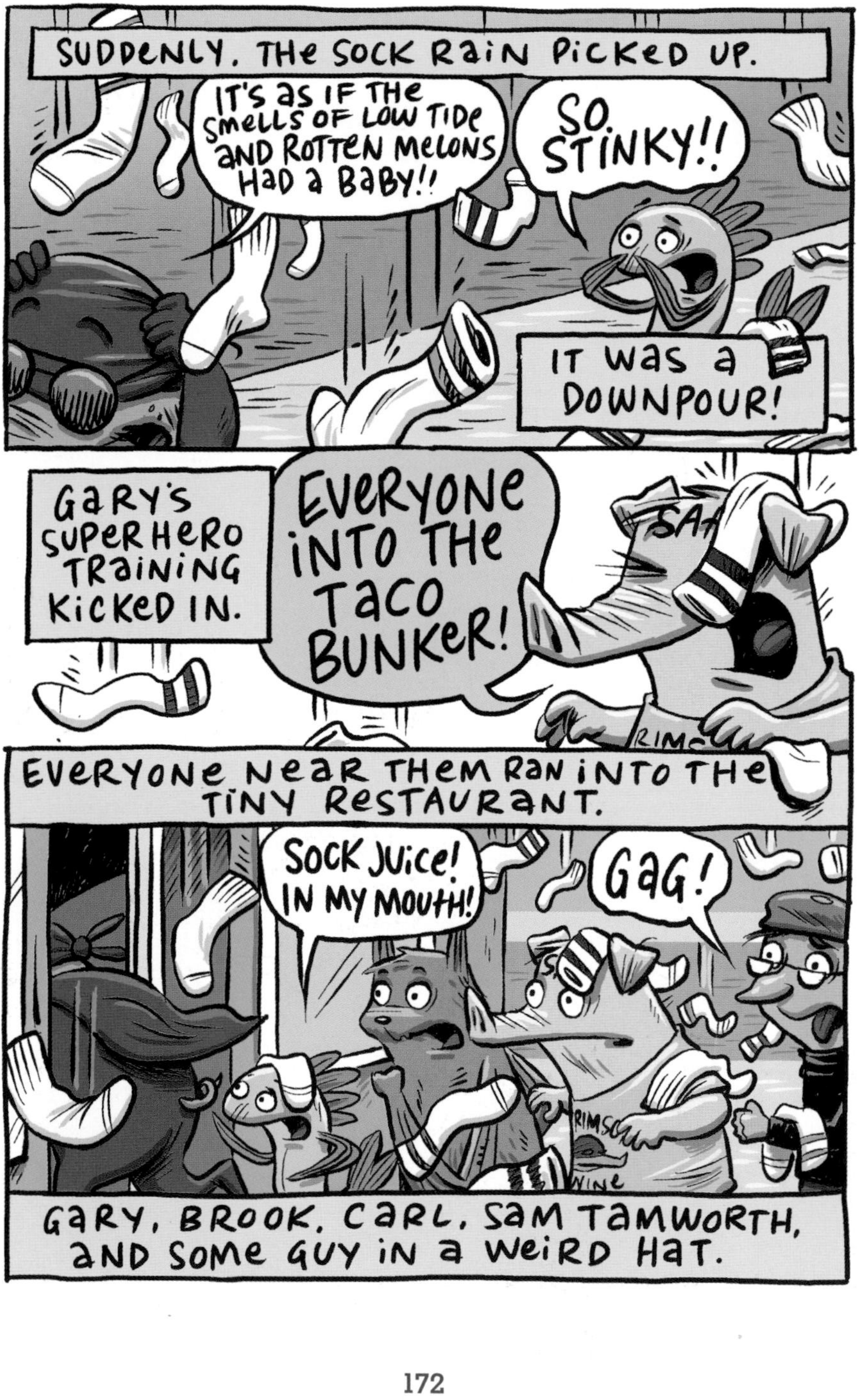
SUDDENLY, THE SOCK RAIN PICKED UP.
IT'S AS IF THE SMELLS OF LOW TIDE AND ROTTEN MELONS HAD A BABY!!
SO. STINKY!!
IT WAS A DOWNPOUR!
GARY'S SUPERHERO TRAINING KICKED IN.
EVERYONE INTO THE TACO BUNKER!
EVERYONE NEAR THEM RAN INTO THE TINY RESTAURANT.
SOCK JUICE! IN MY MOUTH!
GAG!
GARY, BROOK, CARL, SAM TAMWORTH, AND SOME GUY IN A WEIRD HAT.

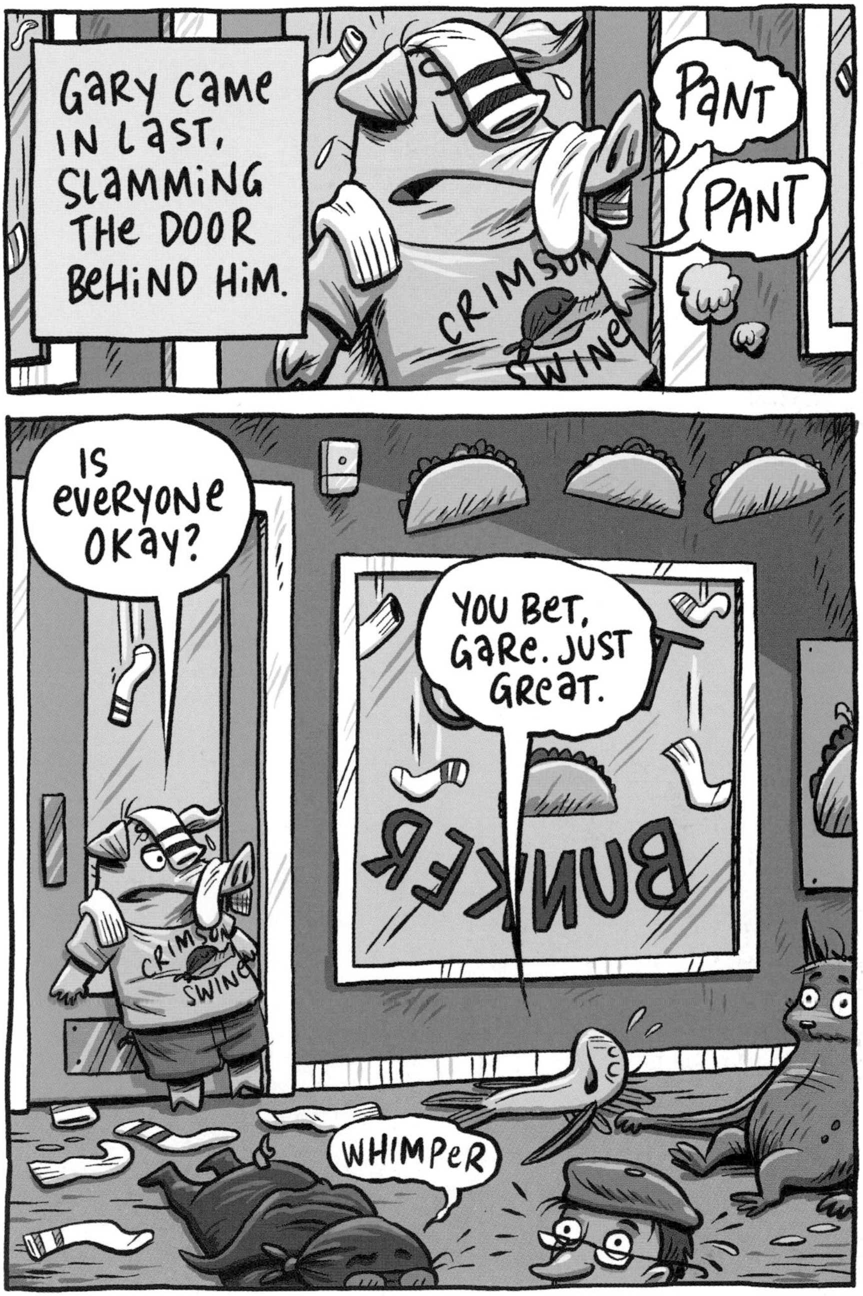
GARY CAME IN LAST, SLAMMING THE DOOR BEHIND HIM.
PANT
PANT
CRIMSON SWINE
IS EVERYONE OKAY?
YOU BET, GARE. JUST GREAT.
BUNKER
WHIMPER

CHAPTER FIVE

"BUNKERED DOWN"

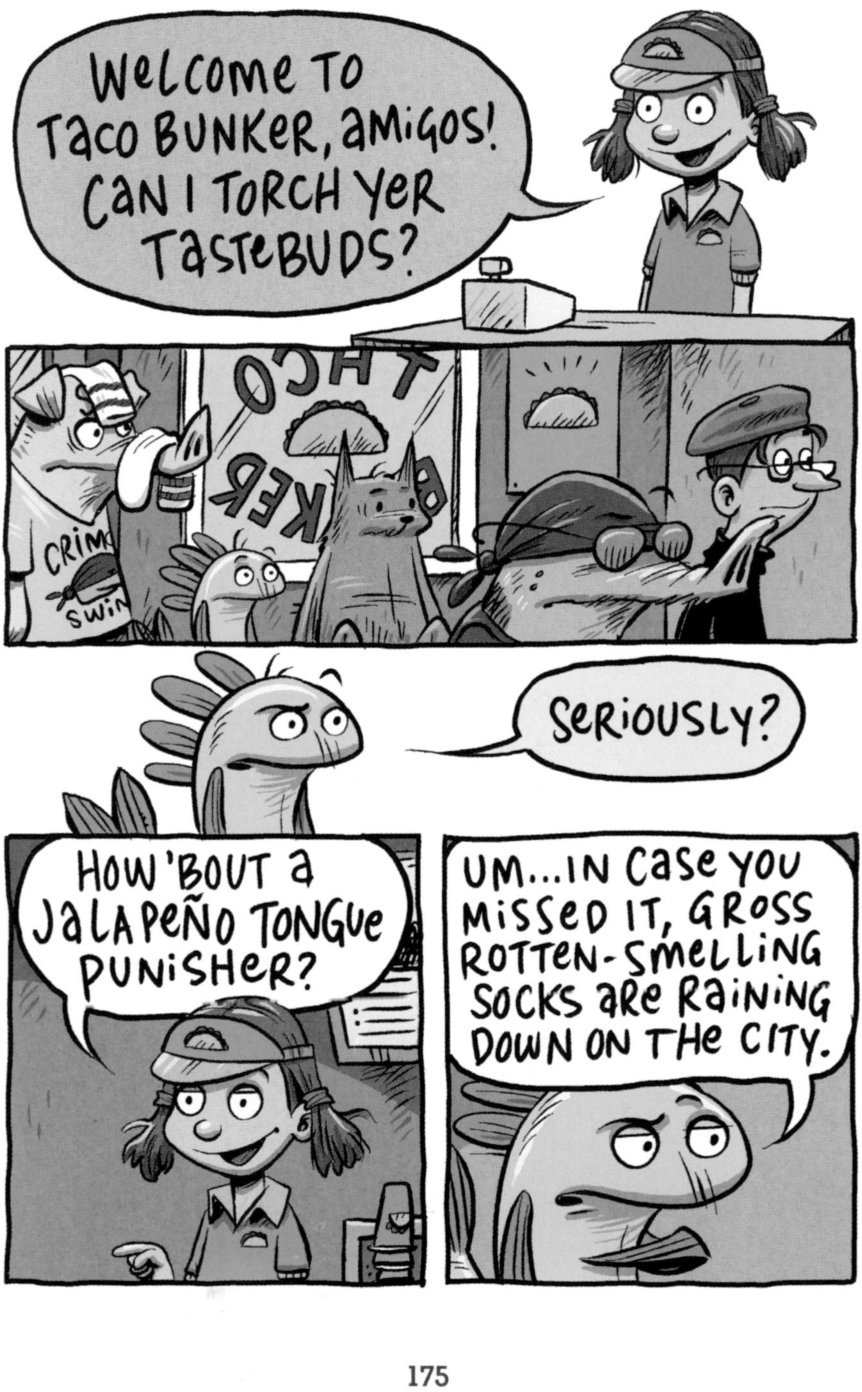
WELCOME TO TACO BUNKER, AMIGOS! CAN I TORCH YER TASTEBUDS?
TACO BUNKER
CRIM
SWIN
SERIOUSLY?
HOW 'BOUT A JALAPEÑO TONGUE PUNISHER?
UM...IN CASE YOU MISSED IT, GROSS ROTTEN-SMELLING SOCKS ARE RAINING DOWN ON THE CITY.

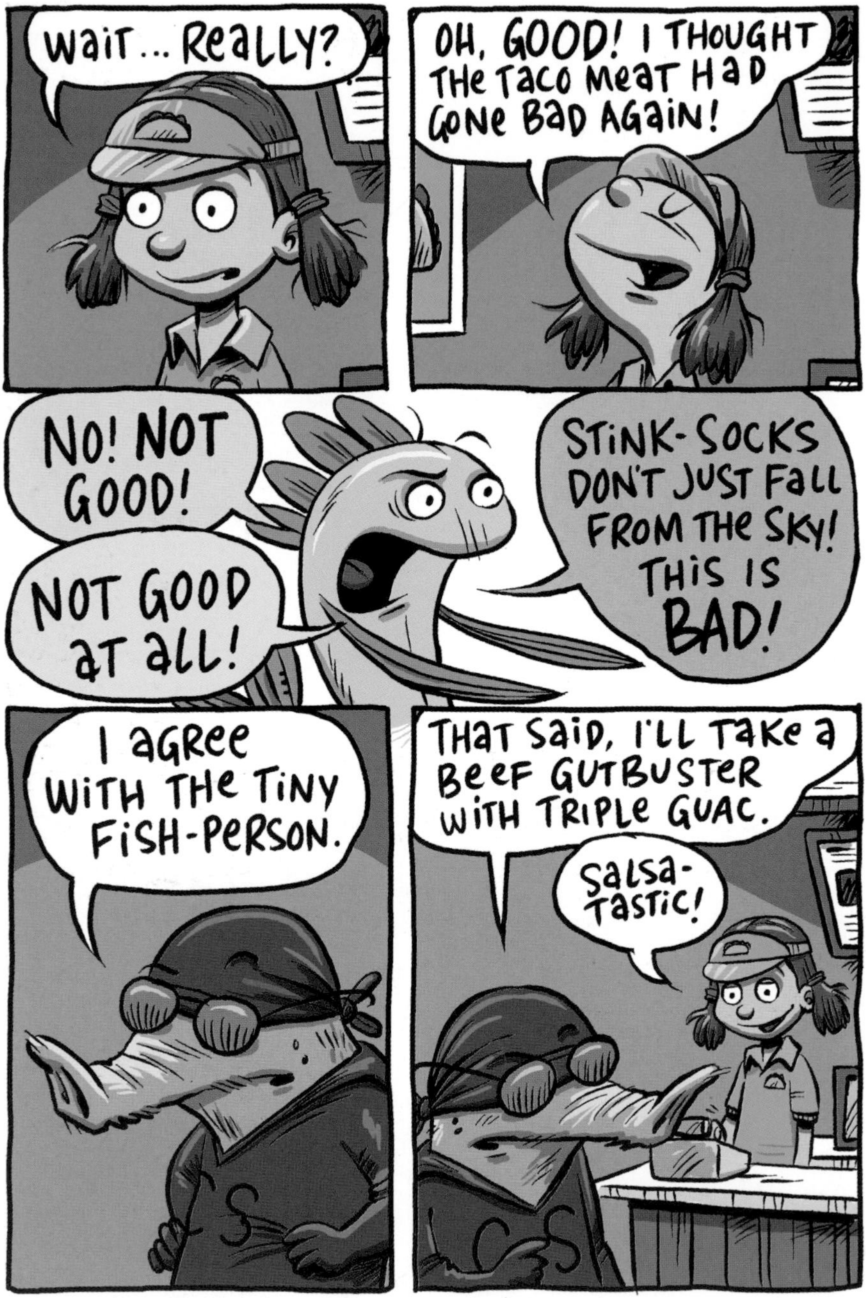
WAIT... REALLY?
OH, GOOD! I THOUGHT THE TACO MEAT HAD GONE BAD AGAIN!
NO! NOT GOOD!
NOT GOOD AT ALL!
STINK-SOCKS DON'T JUST FALL FROM THE SKY! THIS IS BAD!
I AGREE WITH THE TINY FISH-PERSON.
THAT SAID, I'LL TAKE A BEEF GUTBUSTER WITH TRIPLE GUAC.
SALSA-TASTIC!

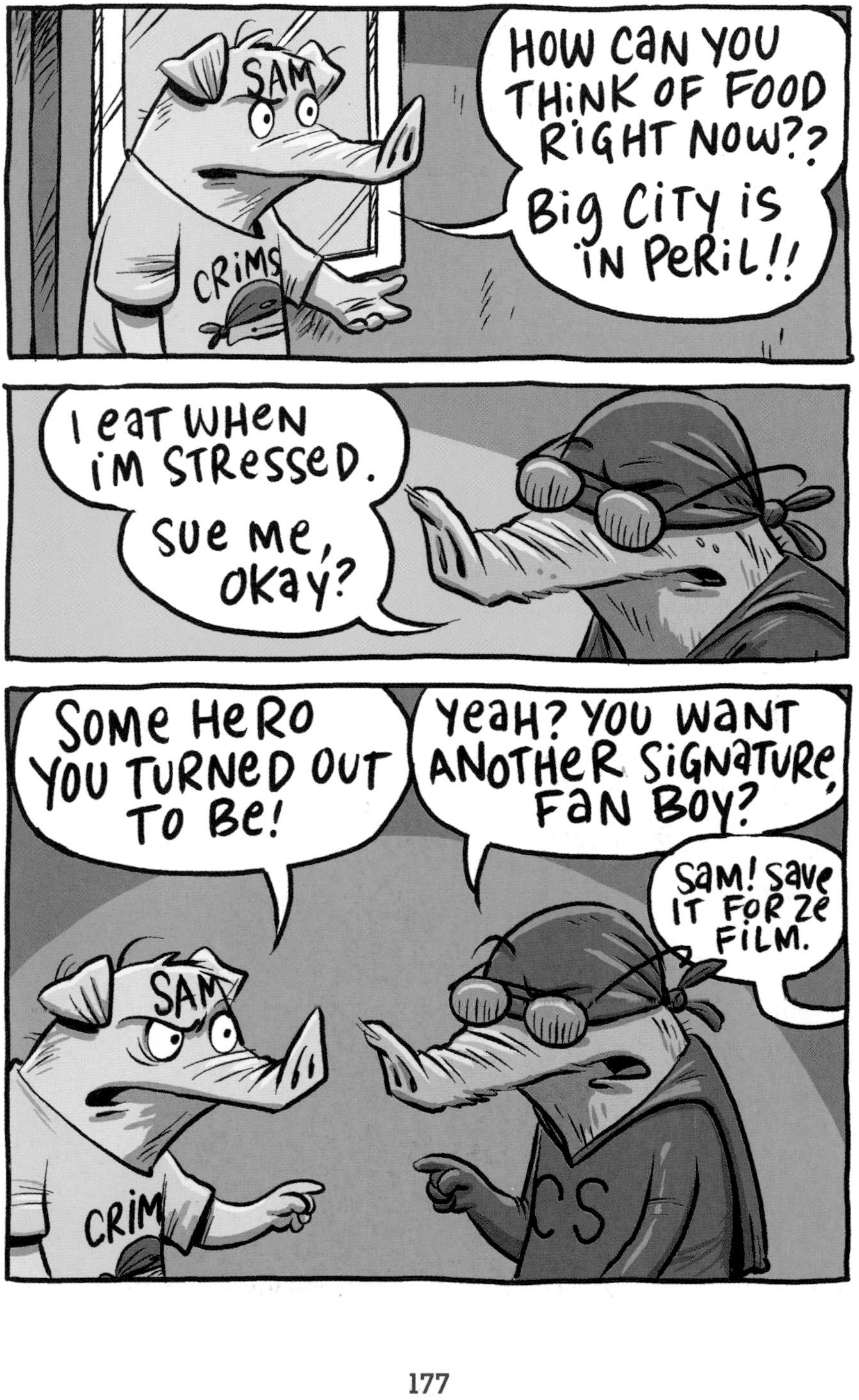
SAM
HOW CAN YOU THINK OF FOOD RIGHT NOW?? Big CITY is in PERIL!!
CRIMS
I eat WHEN I'M STRESSED. Sue me, okay?
Some HeRO YOU TURNED OUT TO Be!
Yeah? YOU WANT ANOTHER SIGNATURE, FAN BOY?
SAM! Save IT FOR ze FILM.
SAM
CRIM
CS

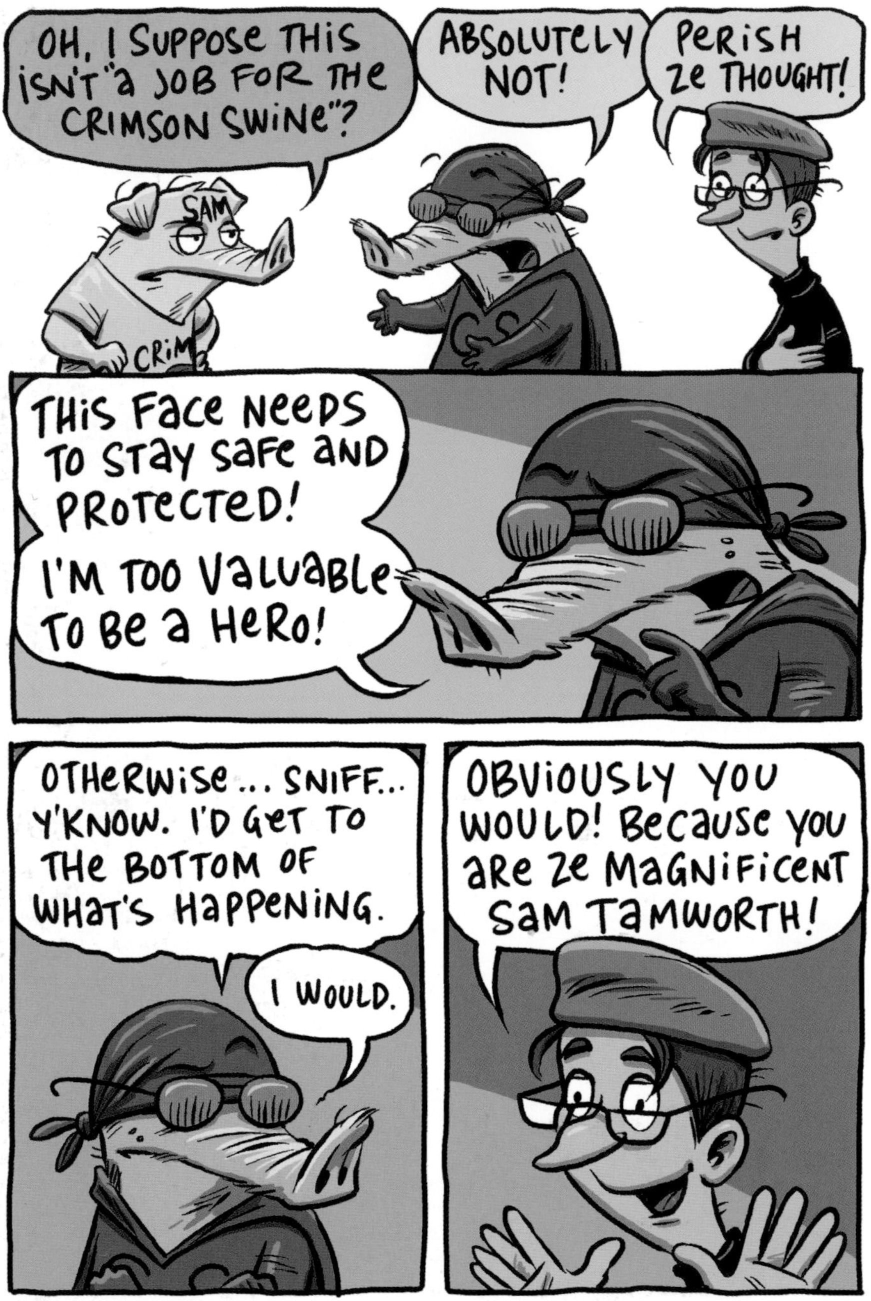
OH, I SUPPOSE THIS ISN'T "A JOB FOR THE CRIMSON SWINE"?
SAM
CRIM
ABSOLUTELY NOT!
PERISH ZE THOUGHT!
THIS FACE NEEDS TO STAY SAFE AND PROTECTED!
I'M TOO VALUABLE TO BE A HERO!
OTHERWISE... SNIFF... Y'KNOW. I'D GET TO THE BOTTOM OF WHAT'S HAPPENING.
I WOULD.
OBVIOUSLY YOU WOULD! BECAUSE YOU ARE ZE MAGNIFICENT SAM TAMWORTH!

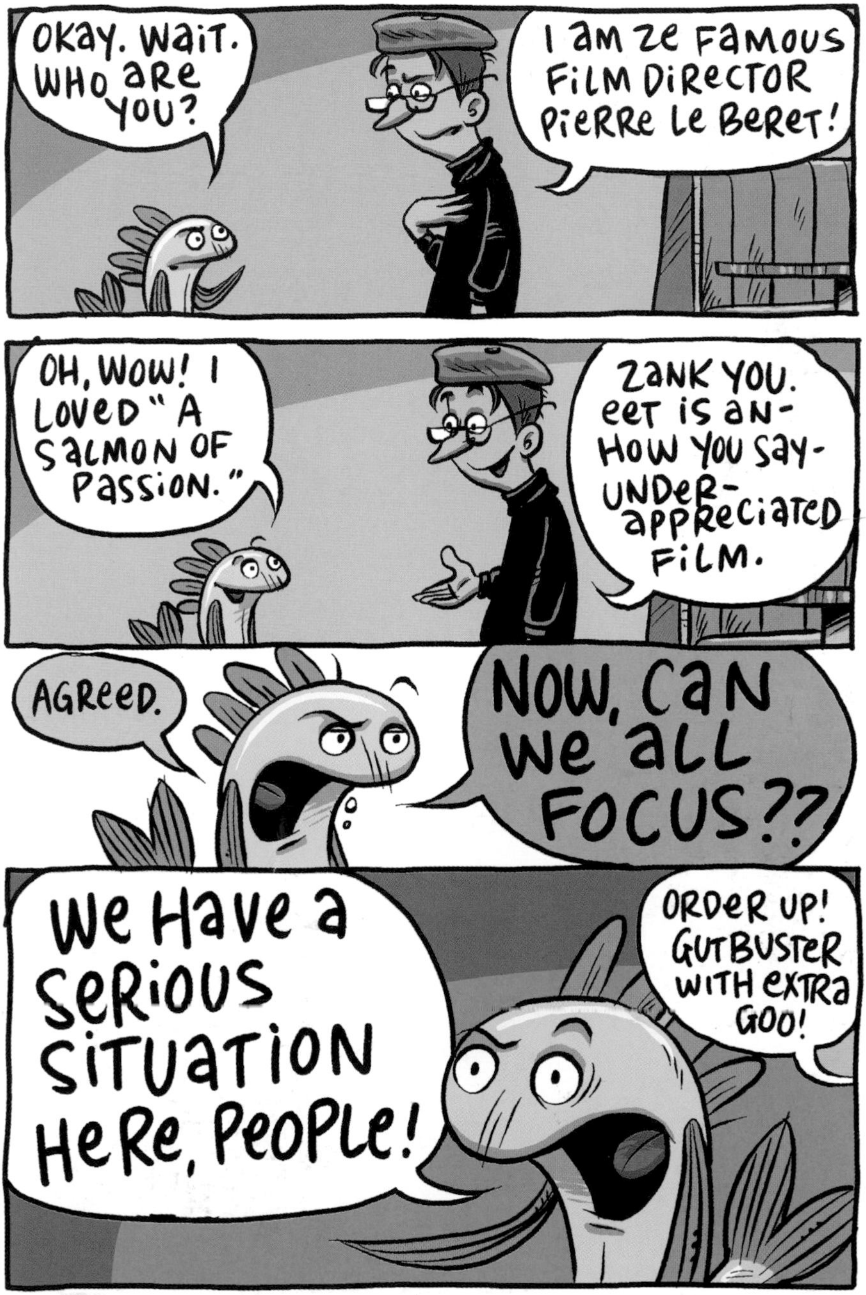
OKAY. WAIT. WHO ARE YOU?
I AM ZE FAMOUS FILM DIRECTOR PIERRE LE BERET!
OH, WOW! I LOVED "A SALMON OF PASSION."
ZANK YOU. EET IS AN- HOW YOU SAY- UNDER-APPRECIATED FILM.
AGREED.
NOW, CAN WE ALL FOCUS??
WE HAVE A SERIOUS SITUATION HERE, PEOPLE!
ORDER UP! GUTBUSTER WITH EXTRA GOO!

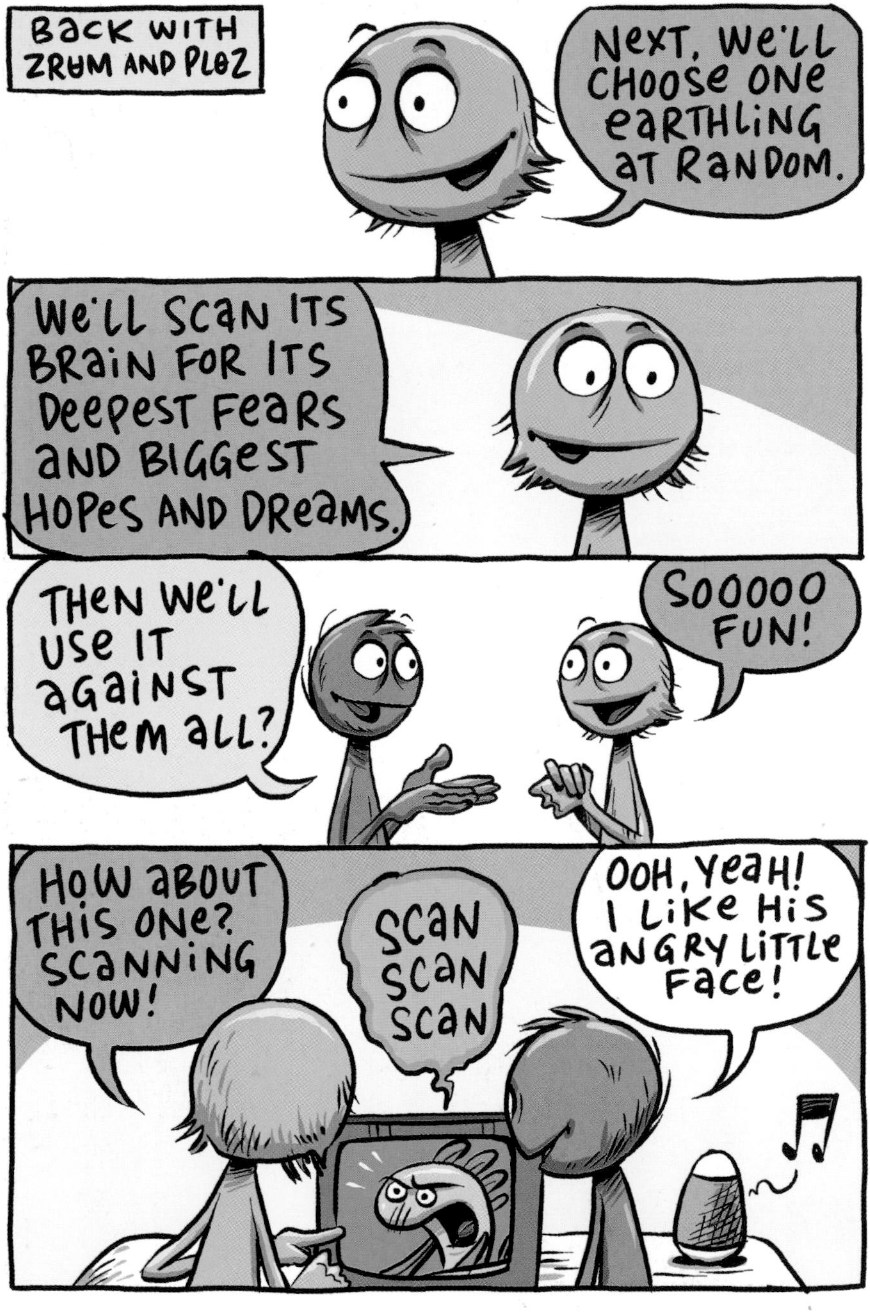
BACK WITH ZRUM AND PLOZ
NEXT, WE'LL CHOOSE ONE EARTHLING AT RANDOM.
WE'LL SCAN ITS BRAIN FOR ITS DEEPEST FEARS AND BIGGEST HOPES AND DREAMS.
THEN WE'LL USE IT AGAINST THEM ALL?
SOOOOO FUN!
HOW ABOUT THIS ONE? SCANNING NOW!
SCAN SCAN SCAN
OOH, YEAH! I LIKE HIS ANGRY LITTLE FACE!

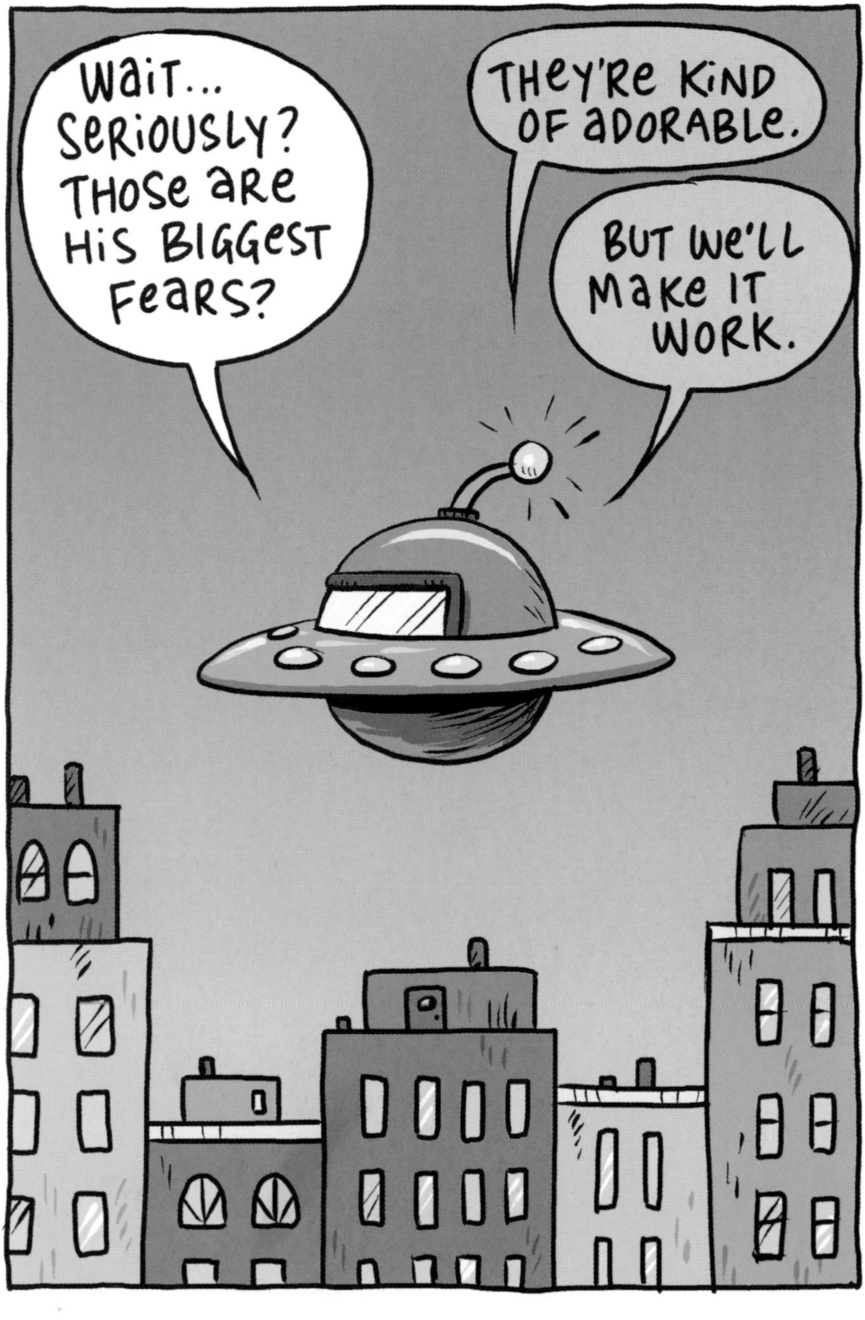
WAIT... SERIOUSLY? THOSE ARE HIS BIGGEST FEARS?
THEY'RE KIND OF ADORABLE.
BUT WE'LL MAKE IT WORK.

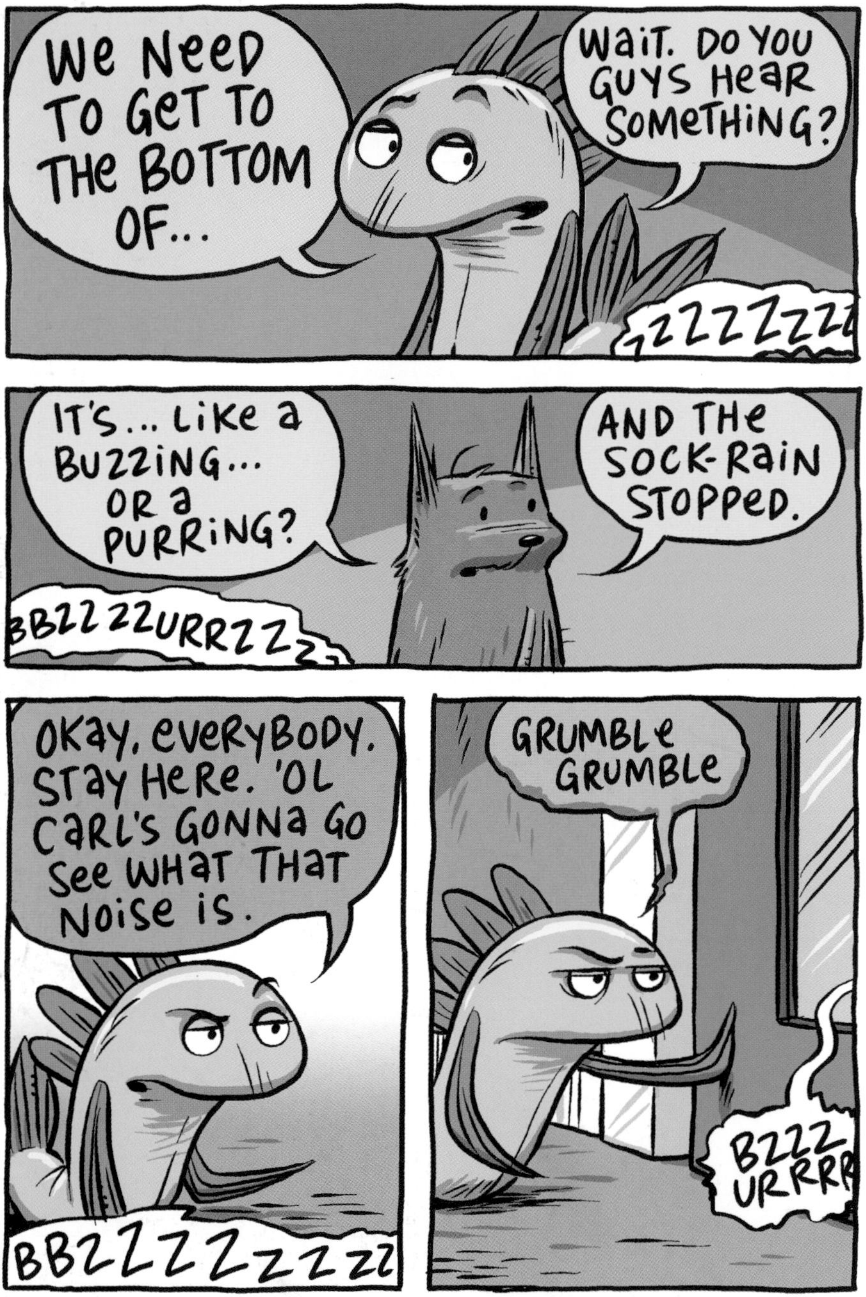
WE NEED TO GET TO THE BOTTOM OF...
WAIT. DO YOU GUYS HEAR SOMETHING?
ZZZZZZZZ
IT'S... LIKE A BUZZING... OR A PURRING?
AND THE SOCK-RAIN STOPPED.
BBZZZZZURRZZZ
OKAY, EVERYBODY. STAY HERE. 'OL CARL'S GONNA GO SEE WHAT THAT NOISE IS.
BBZZZZZZZZZ
GRUMBLE GRUMBLE
BZZZ URRR

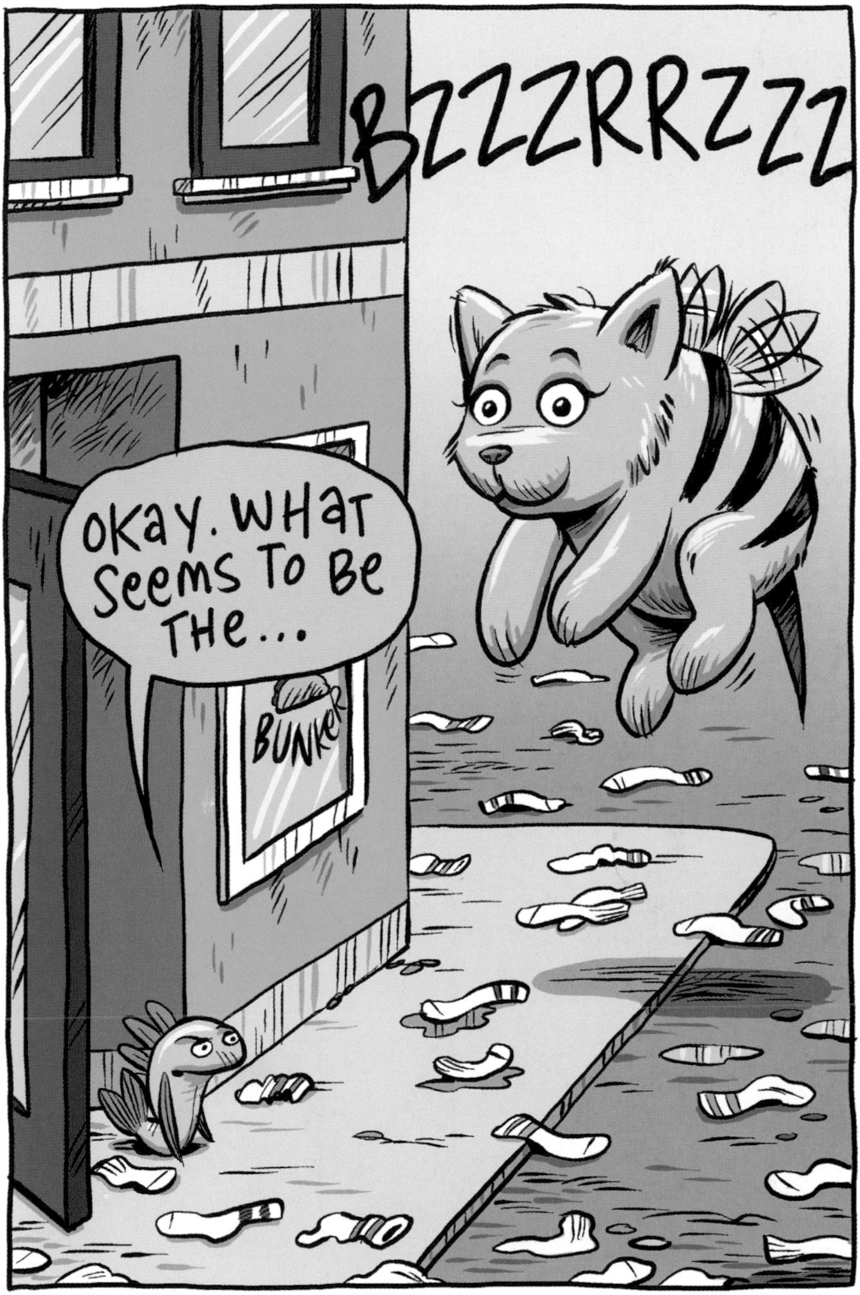
BZZZRRZZZ
OKAY. WHAT SEEMS TO BE THE...
BUNKER

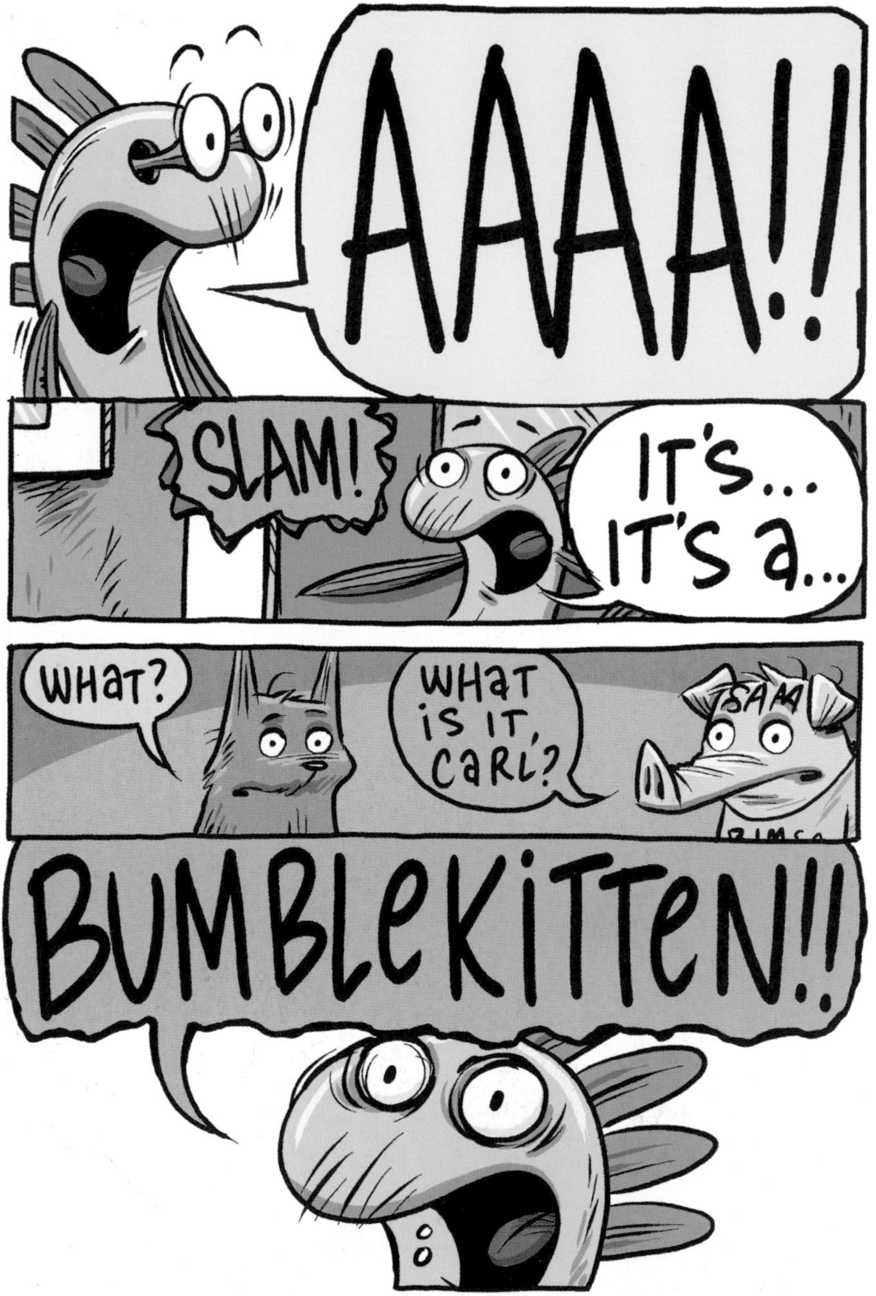
AAAA!!
SLAM!
IT'S... IT'S a...
WHAT?
WHAT IS IT, CARL?
BUMBLEKITTEN!!

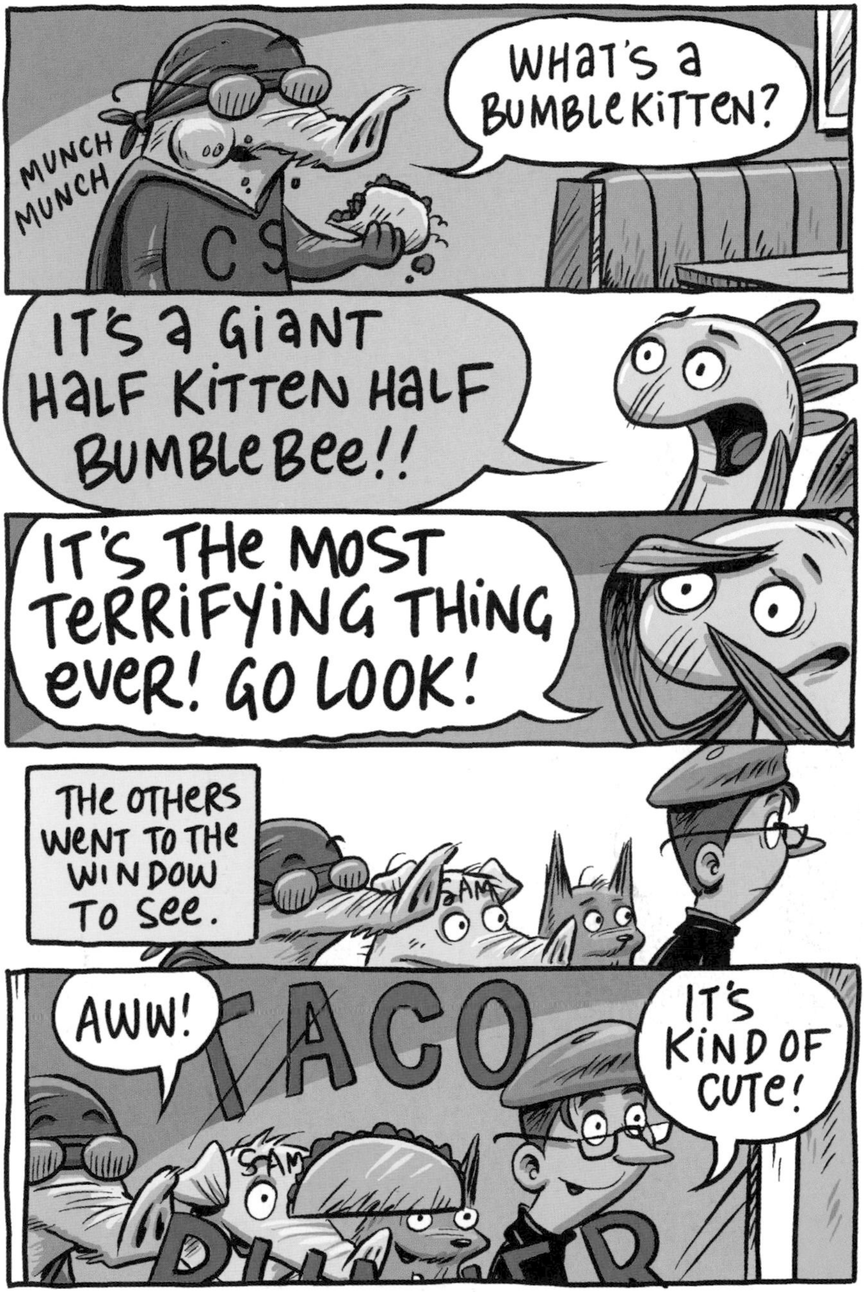
MUNCH MUNCH
WHAT'S A BUMBLEKITTEN?
IT'S A GIANT HALF KITTEN HALF BUMBLEBEE!!
IT'S THE MOST TERRIFYING THING EVER! GO LOOK!
THE OTHERS WENT TO THE WINDOW TO SEE.
AWW!
IT'S KIND OF CUTE!
TACO

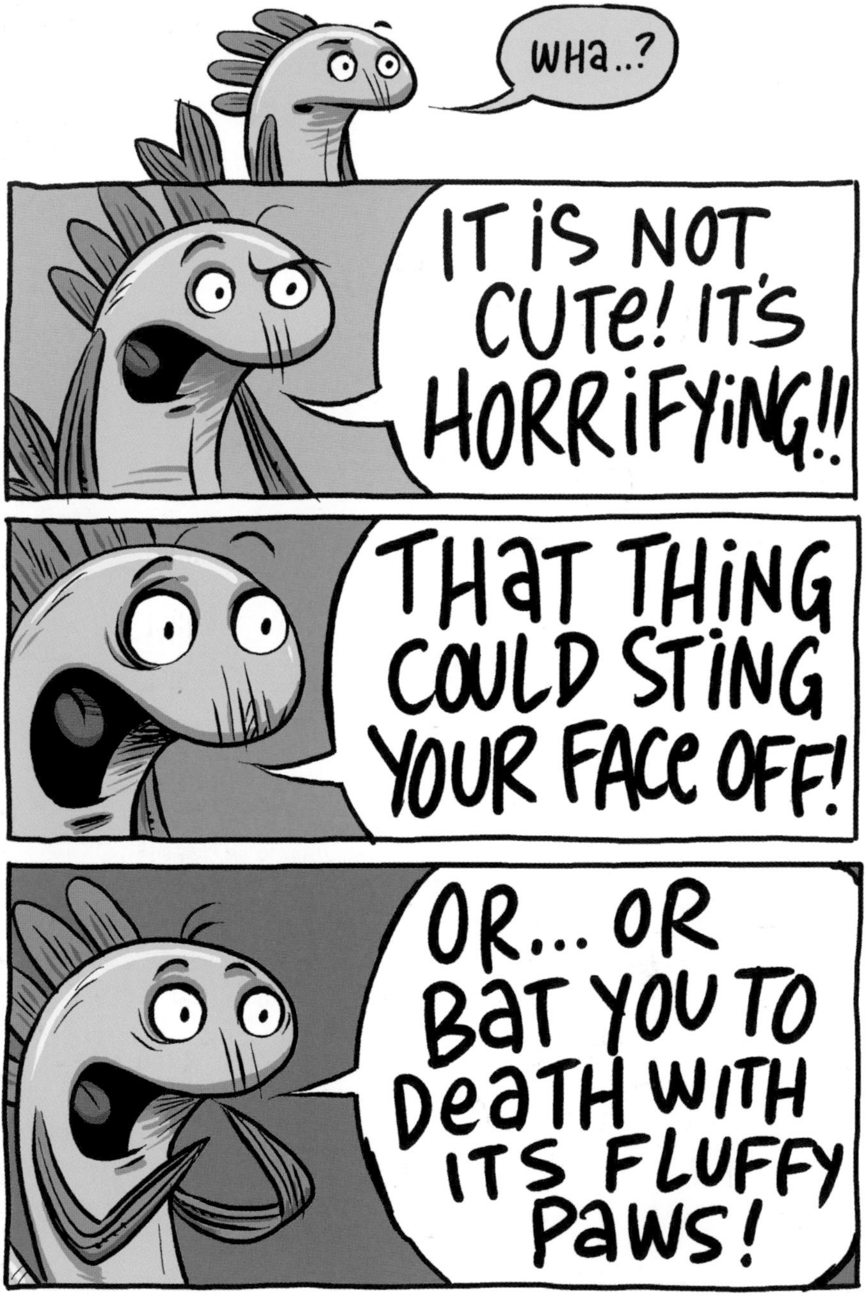
WHa...?
IT iS NOT CUTe! IT'S HORRiFYiNG!!
THaT THiNG COULD STiNG YOUR FACe OFF!
OR... OR BaT YOU TO DeaTH WITH ITS FLUFFY PaWS!

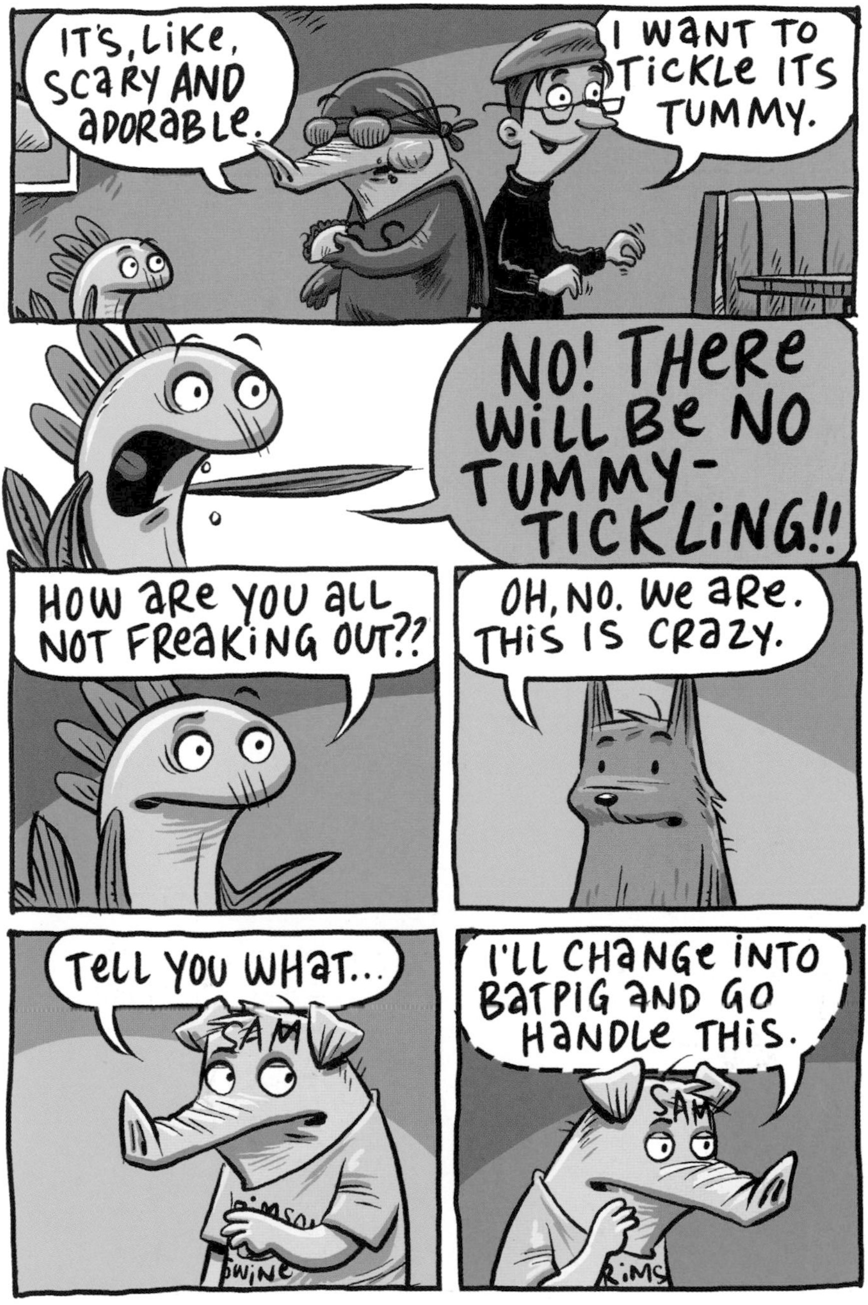
IT'S, LIKE, SCARY AND ADORABLE.
I WANT TO TICKLE ITS TUMMY.
NO! THERE WILL BE NO TUMMY-TICKLING!!
HOW ARE YOU ALL NOT FREAKING OUT??
OH, NO. WE ARE. THIS IS CRAZY.
TELL YOU WHAT...
SAM
I'LL CHANGE INTO BATPIG AND GO HANDLE THIS.
SAM

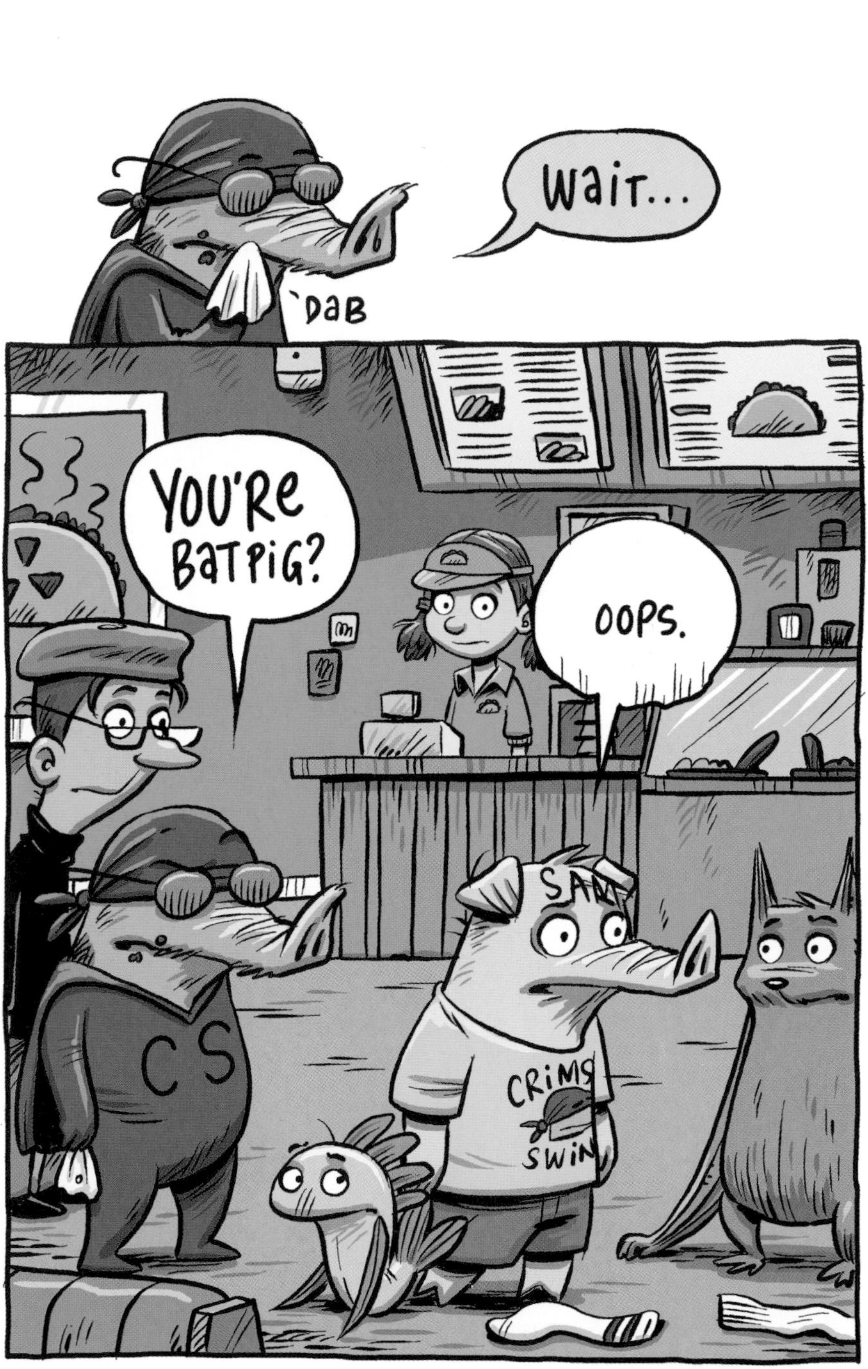
WAIT...
`DAB
YOU'RE BATPIG?
OOPS.
CS

CHAPTER SIX

SHH!

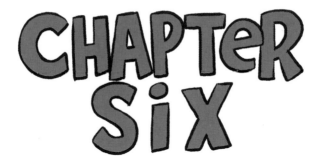

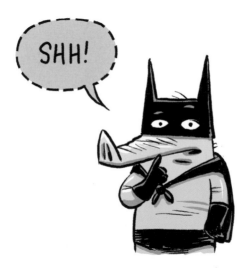

"SECRETS"

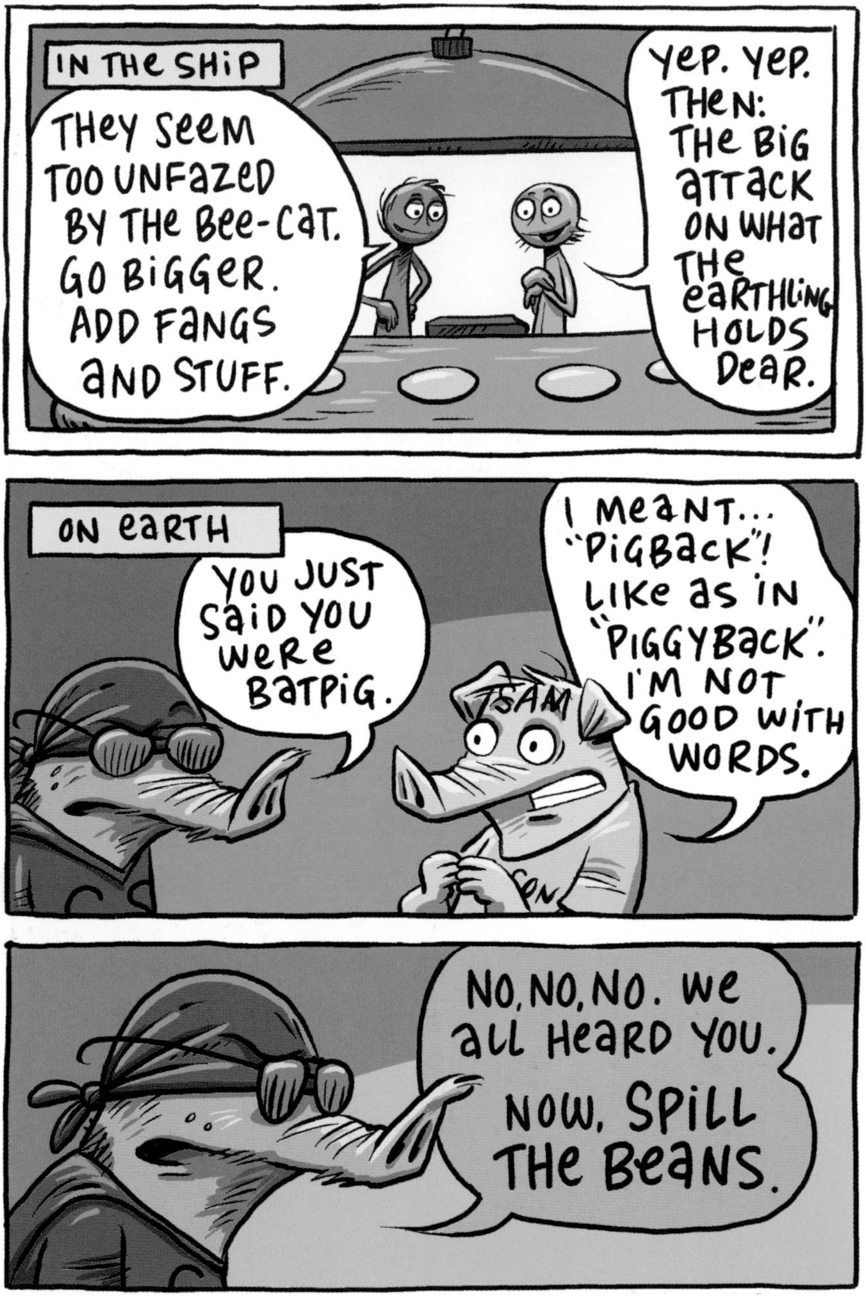
IN THE SHIP
THEY SEEM TOO UNFAZED BY THE BEE-CAT. GO BIGGER. ADD FANGS AND STUFF.
YEP. YEP. THEN: THE BIG ATTACK ON WHAT THE EARTHLING HOLDS DEAR.
ON EARTH
YOU JUST SAID YOU WERE BATPIG.
I MEANT... "PIGBACK"! LIKE AS IN "PIGGYBACK". I'M NOT GOOD WITH WORDS.
NO, NO, NO. WE ALL HEARD YOU.
NOW, SPILL THE BEANS.

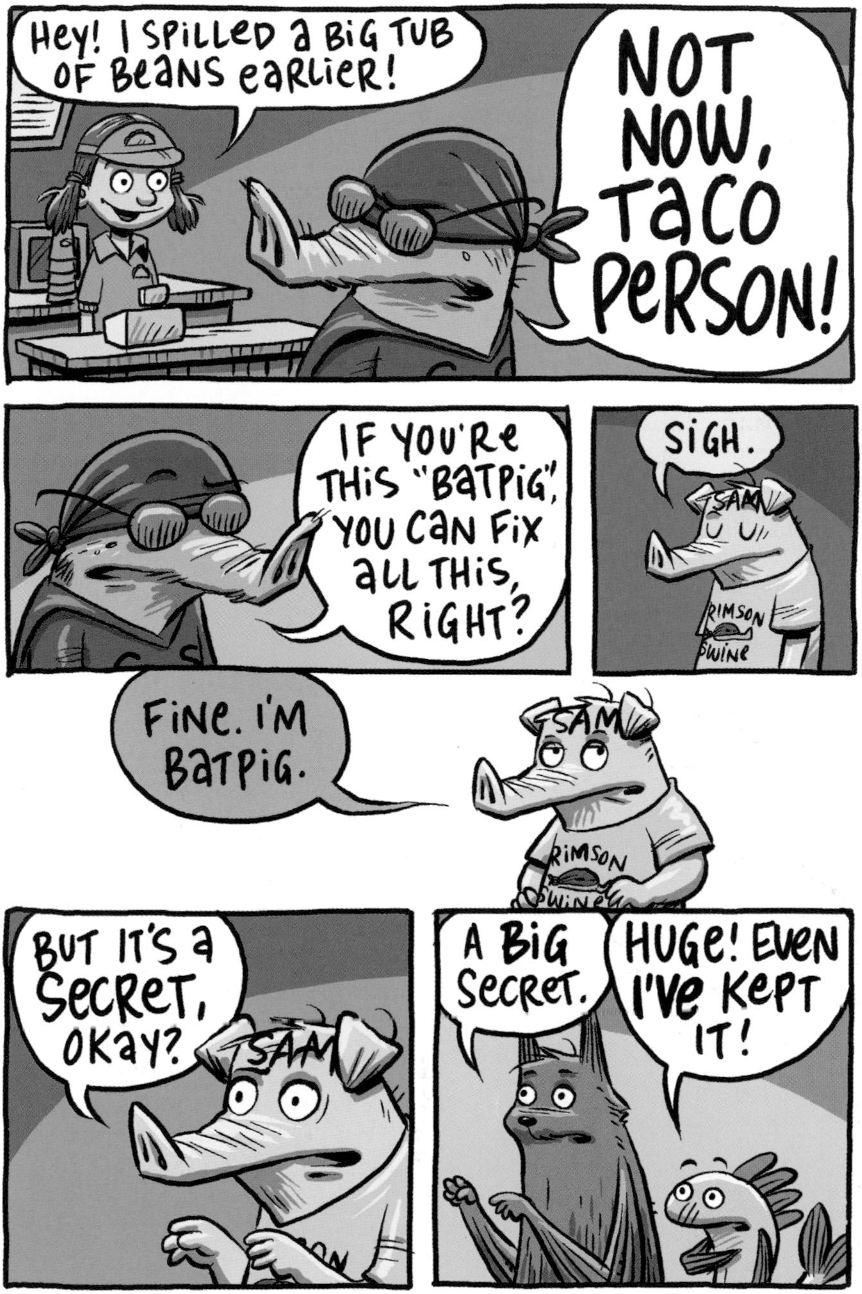
Hey! I SPILLED a BIG TUB OF BEANS earlier!
NOT NOW, TACO PERSON!
IF YOU'RE THIS "BATPIG", YOU CAN FIX ALL THIS, RIGHT?
SIGH.
SAM
RIMSON SWINE
FINE. I'M BATPIG.
BUT IT'S a SECRET, OKAY?
A BIG SECRET.
HUGE! EVEN I'VE KEPT IT!

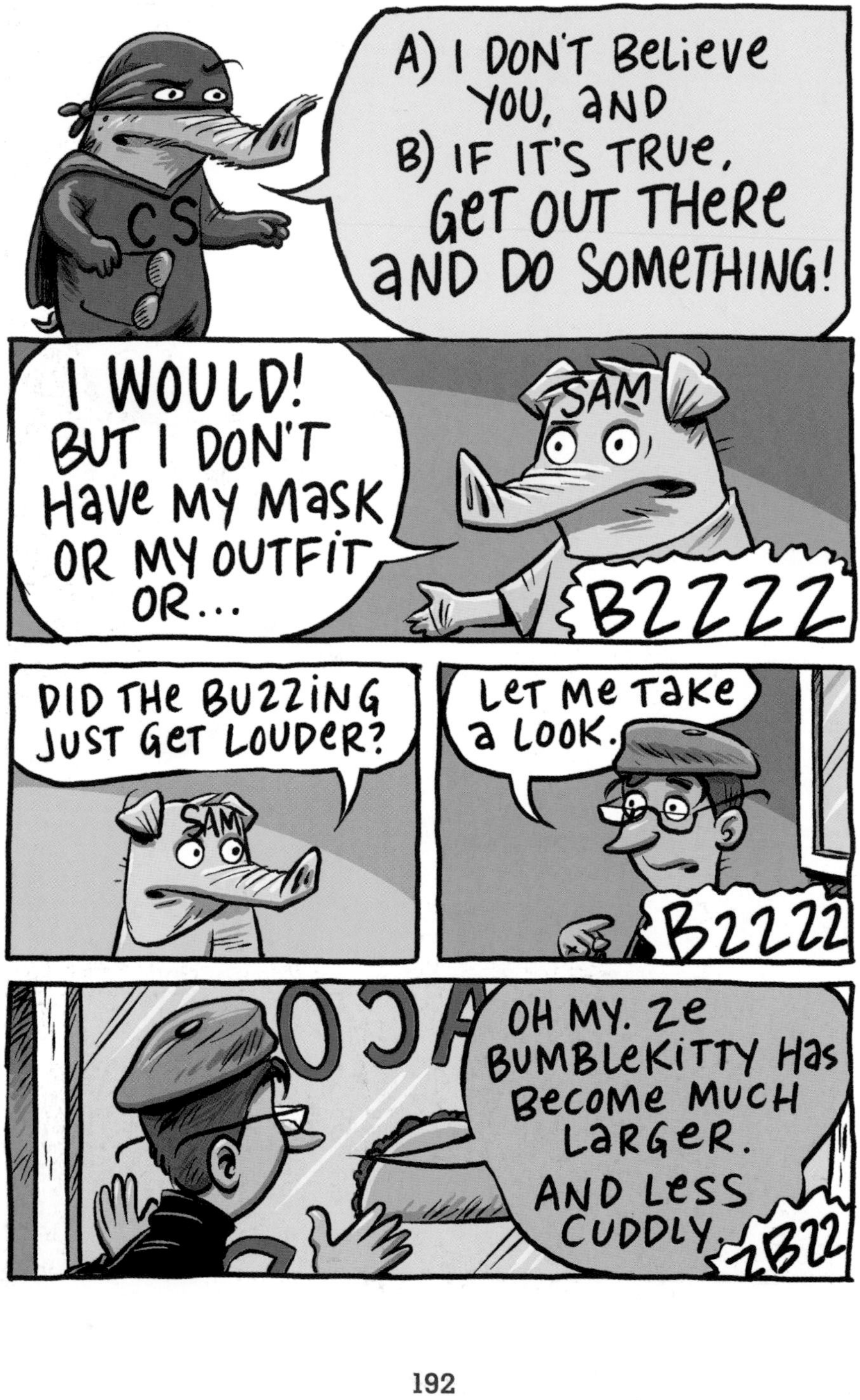
A) I DON'T BELIEVE YOU, AND B) IF IT'S TRUE, GET OUT THERE AND DO SOMETHING!
CS
SAM
I WOULD! BUT I DON'T HAVE MY MASK OR MY OUTFIT OR...
BZZZZ
DID THE BUZZING JUST GET LOUDER?
SAM
LET ME TAKE A LOOK.
BZZZZ
OH MY. ZE BUMBLEKITTY HAS BECOME MUCH LARGER.
AND LESS CUDDLY.
BZZ

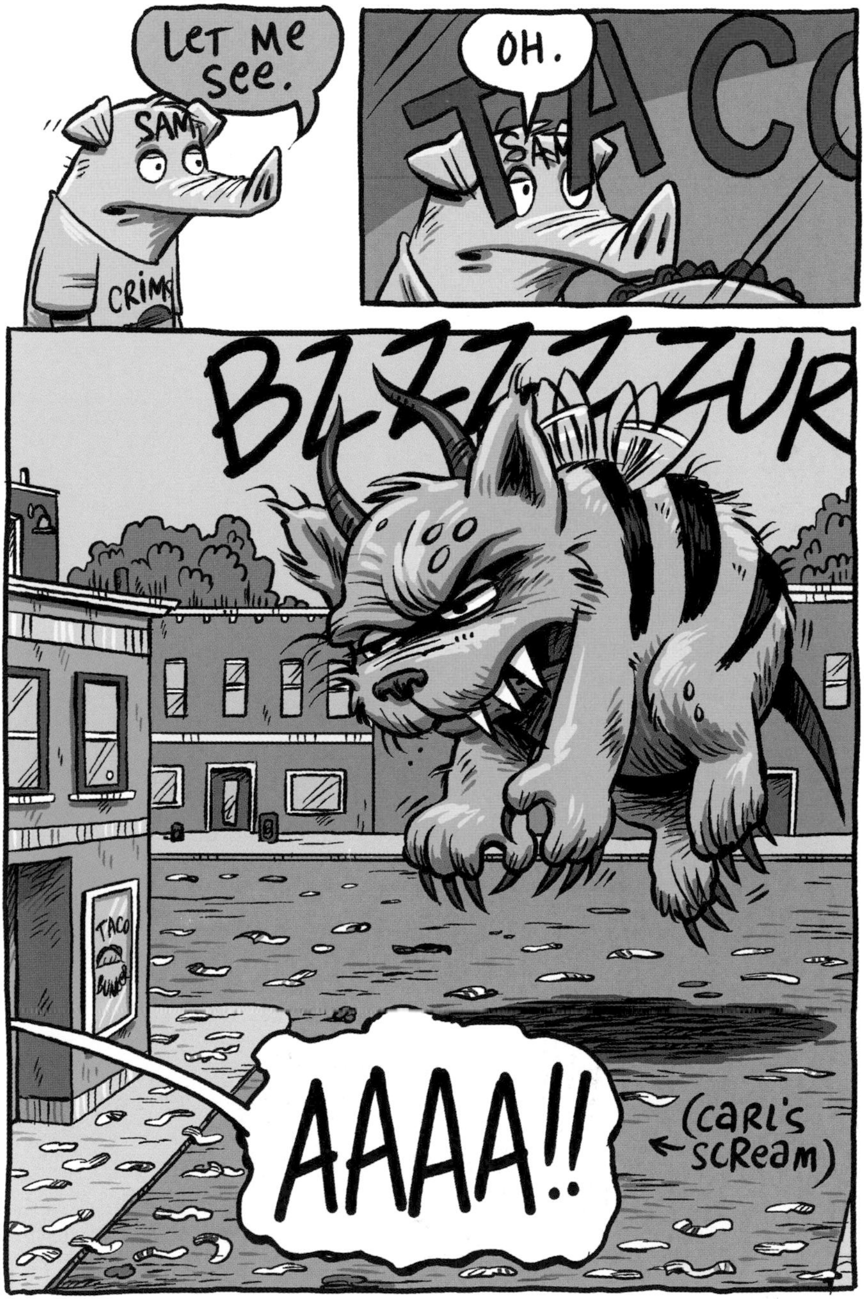

LET ME SEE.
SAM
CRIM
OH.
TACO
SAM
BZZZZZZUR
TACO
AAAA!!
(CARL'S SCREAM)

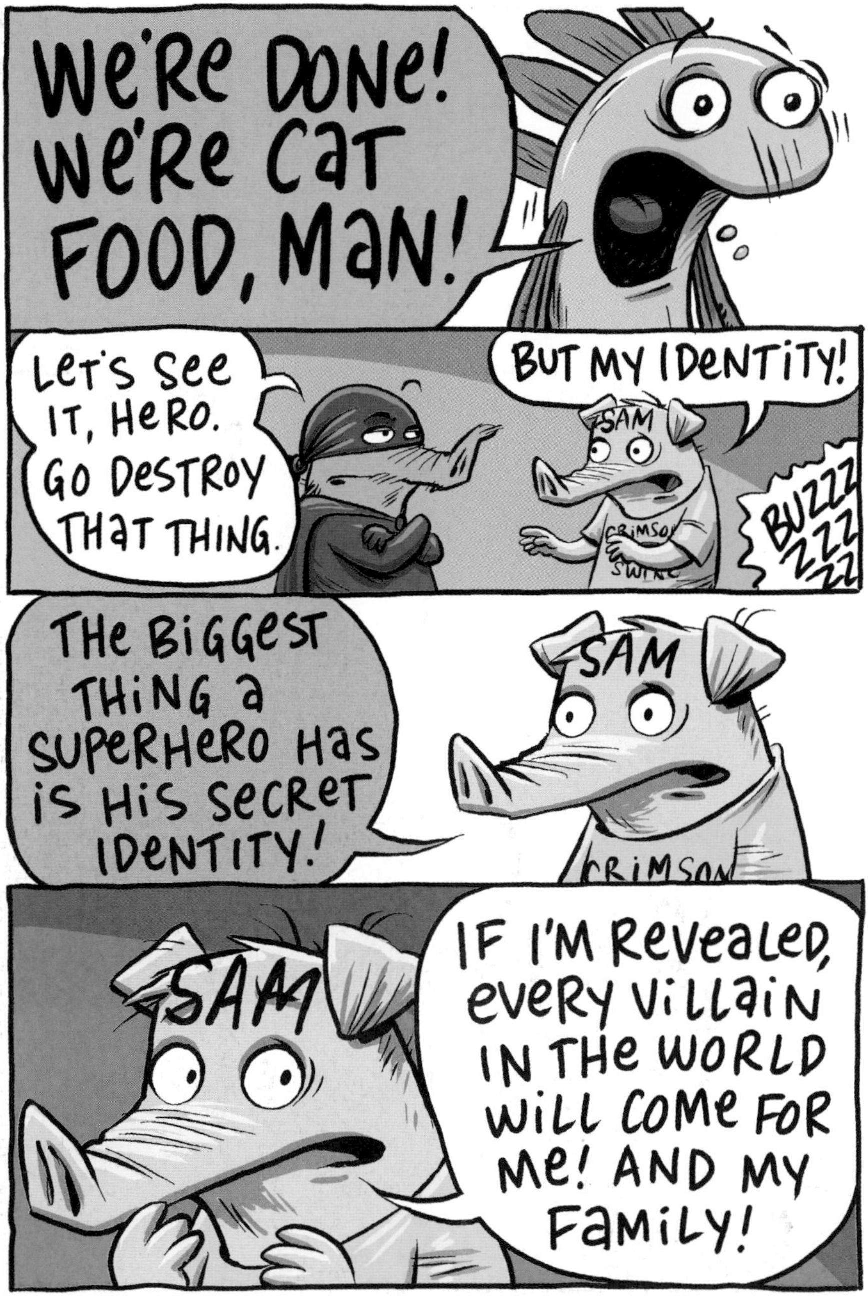
WE'RE DONE! WE'RE CAT FOOD, MAN!
LET'S SEE IT, HERO. GO DESTROY THAT THING.
BUT MY IDENTITY!
BUZZZZZZZZZ
THE BIGGEST THING A SUPERHERO HAS IS HIS SECRET IDENTITY!
IF I'M REVEALED, EVERY VILLAIN IN THE WORLD WILL COME FOR ME! AND MY FAMILY!

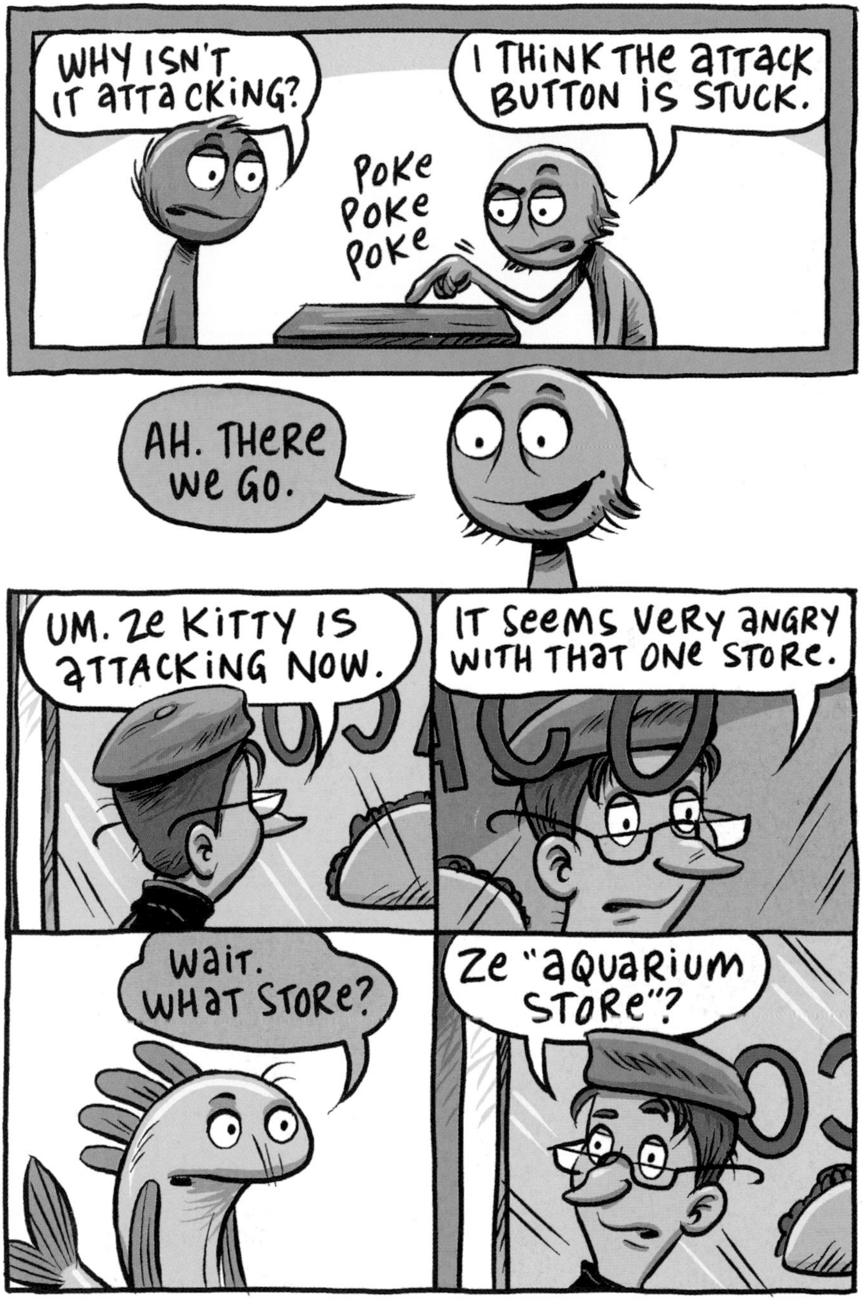
WHY ISN'T IT ATTACKING?
I THINK THE ATTACK BUTTON IS STUCK.
POKE POKE POKE
AH. THERE WE GO.
UM. ZE KITTY IS ATTACKING NOW.
IT SEEMS VERY ANGRY WITH THAT ONE STORE.
WAIT. WHAT STORE?
ZE "AQUARIUM STORE"?

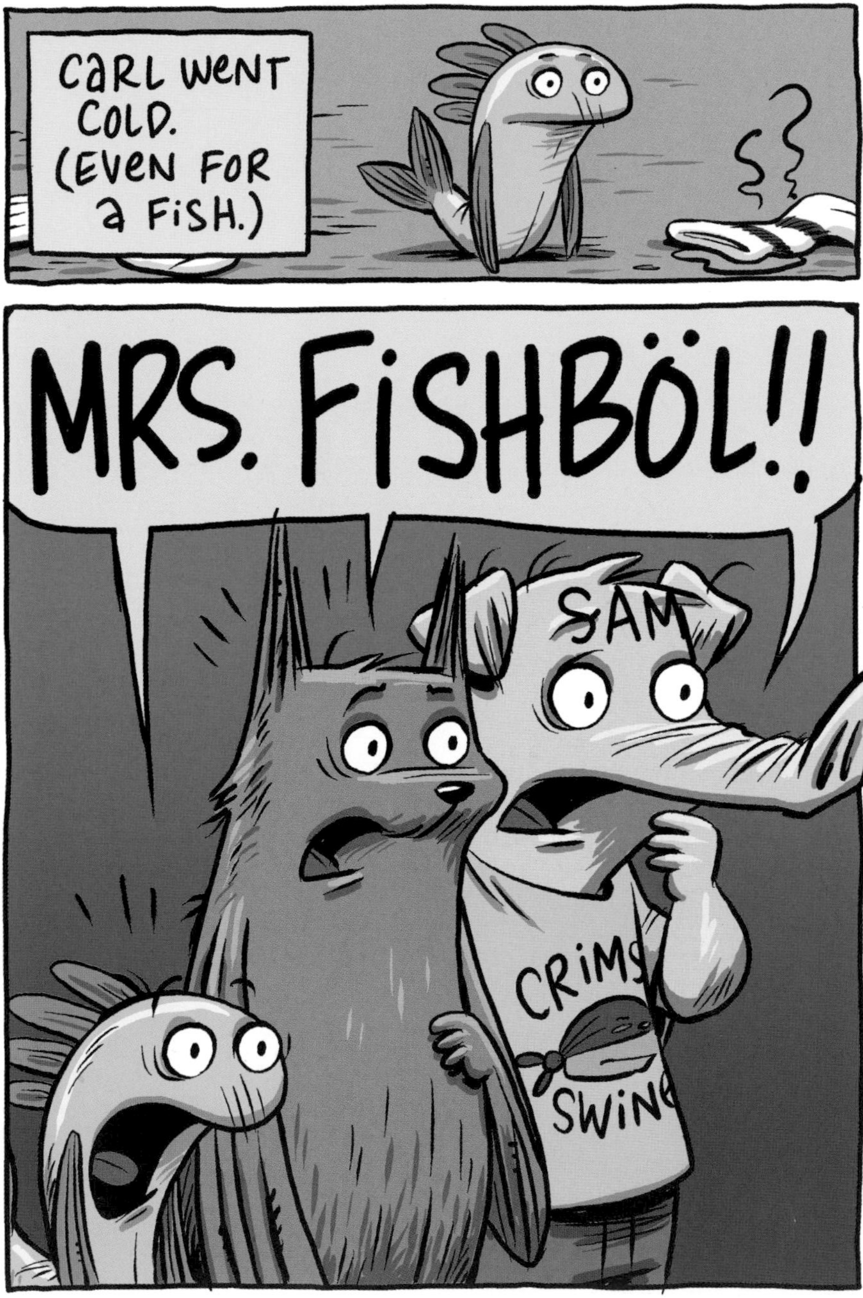
CARL WENT COLD. (EVEN FOR A FISH.)
MRS. FISHBÖL!!
SAM
CRIMS
SWIN

CHAPTER SEVEN

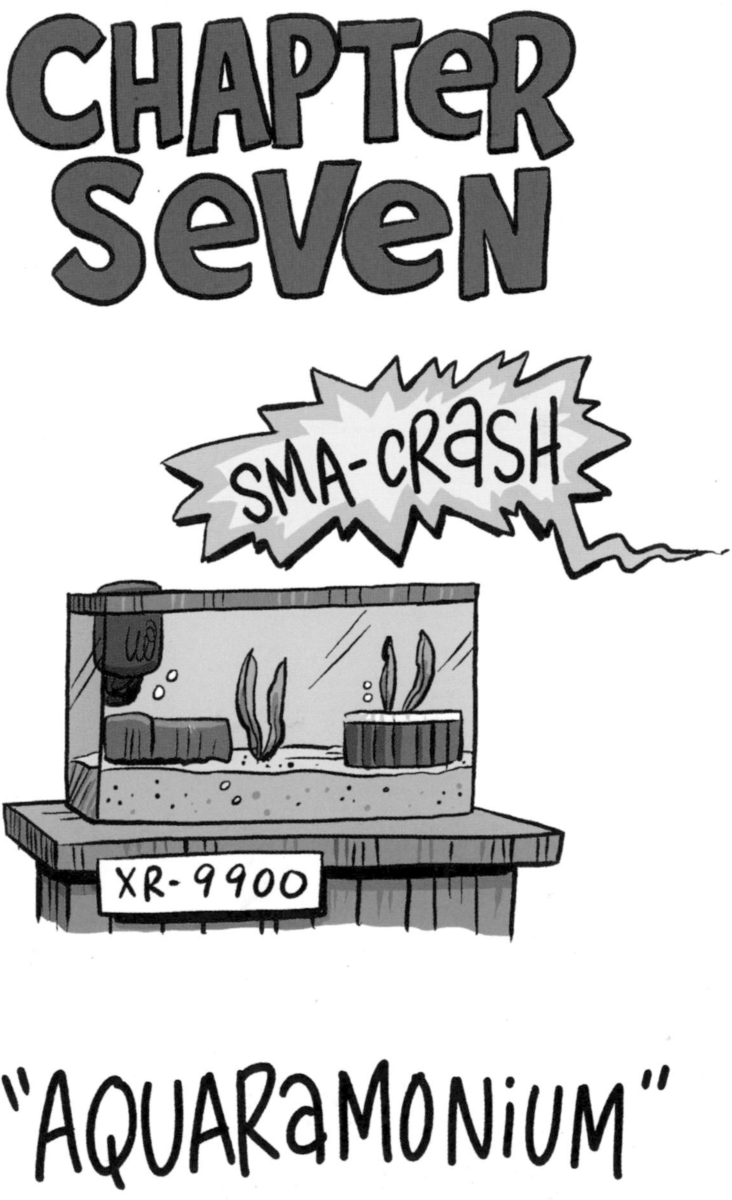
SMA-CRASH
XR-9900

"AQUARAMONIUM"

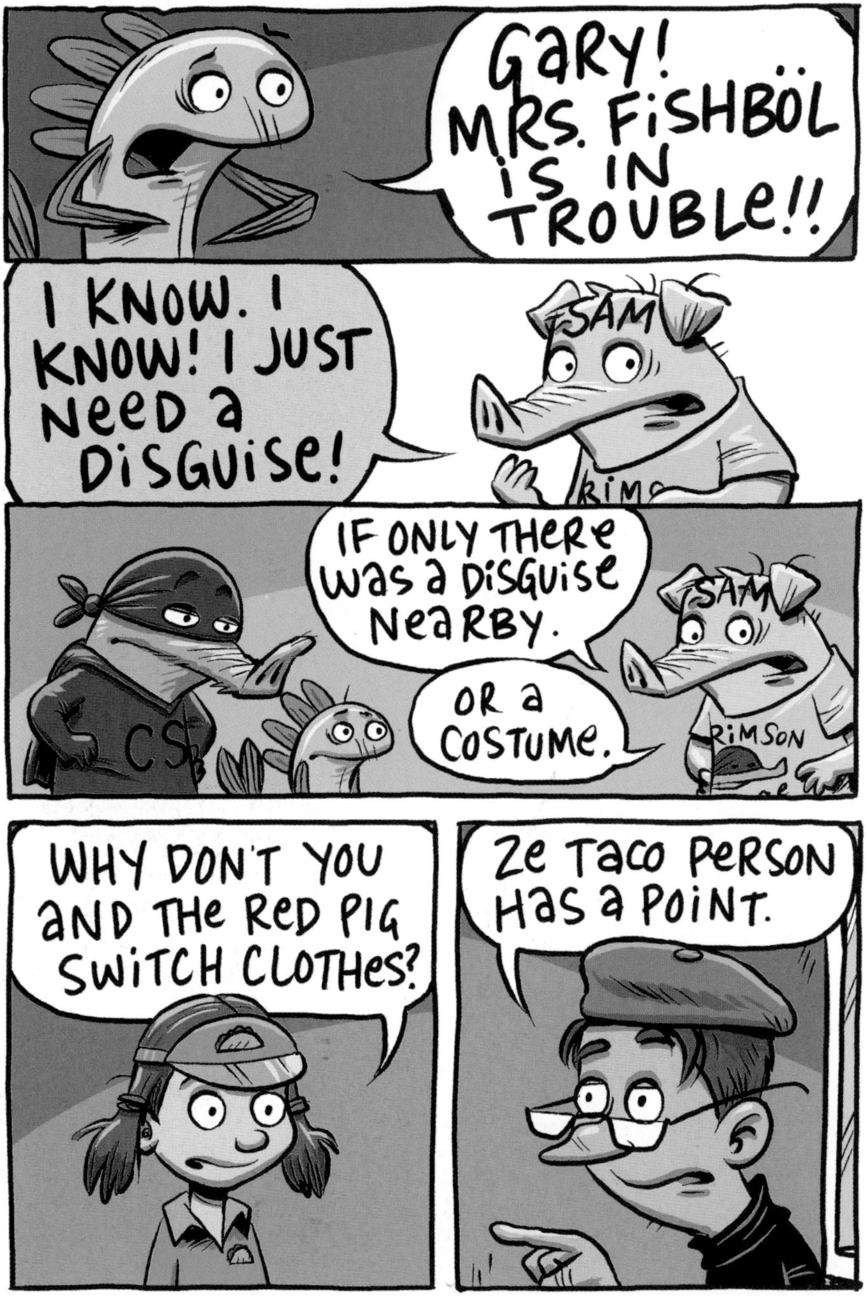
GARY! MRS. FISHBÖL IS IN TROUBLE!!
I KNOW. I KNOW! I JUST NEED A DISGUISE!
SAM
RIMS
IF ONLY THERE WAS A DISGUISE NEARBY.
OR A COSTUME.
CS
SAM
RIMSON
WHY DON'T YOU AND THE RED PIG SWITCH CLOTHES?
ZE TACO PERSON HAS A POINT.

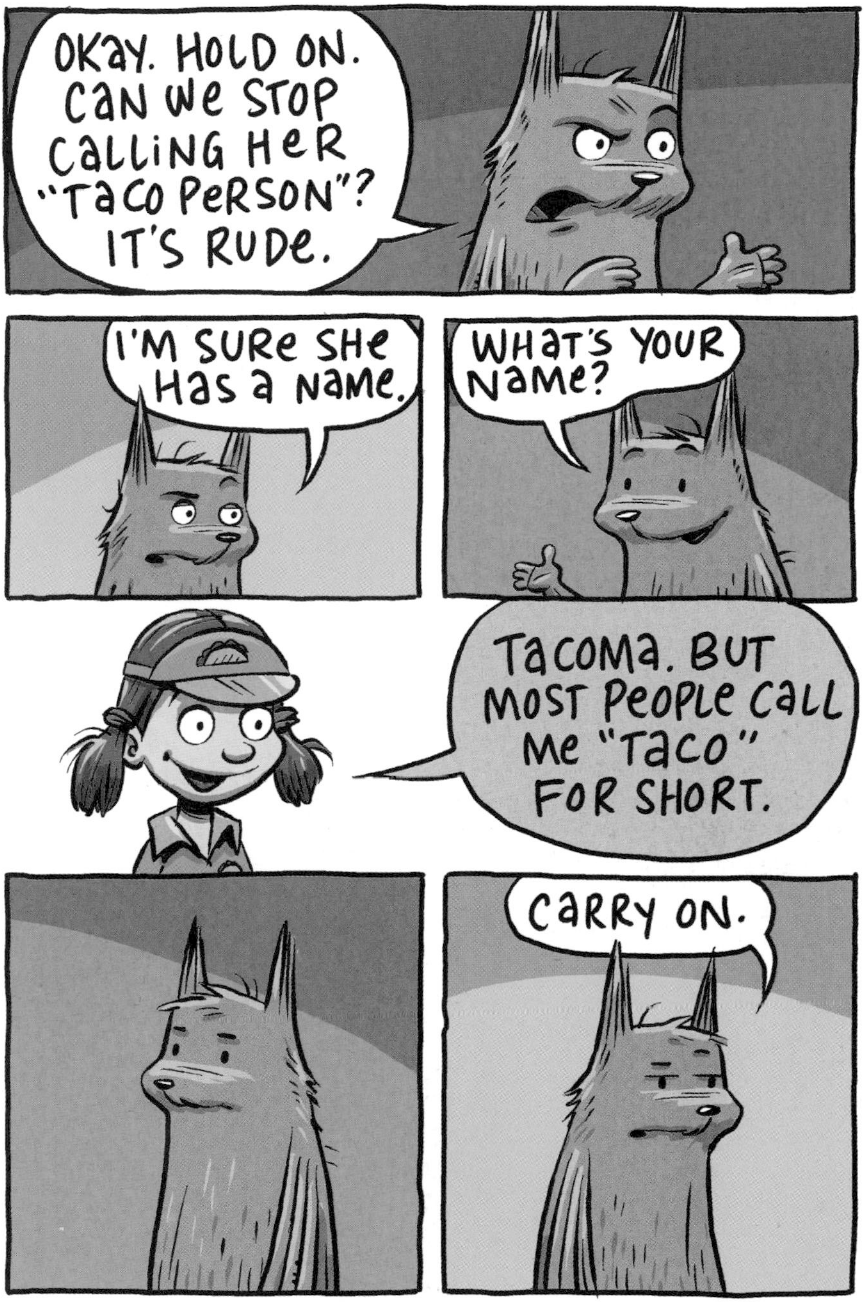
OKAY. HOLD ON. CAN WE STOP CALLING HER "TACO PERSON"? IT'S RUDE.
I'M SURE SHE HAS A NAME.
WHAT'S YOUR NAME?
TACOMA. BUT MOST PEOPLE CALL ME "TACO" FOR SHORT.
CARRY ON.

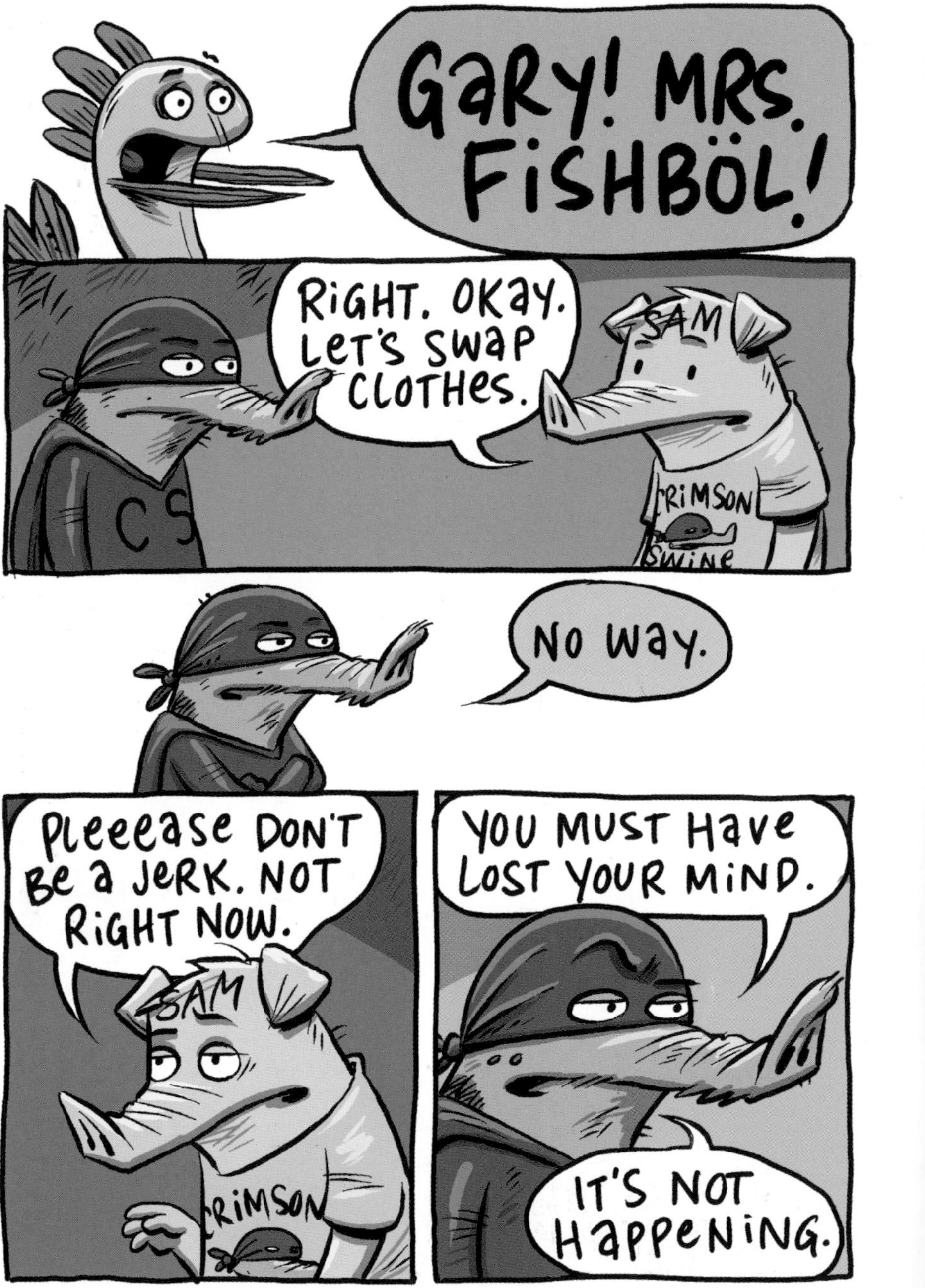
GARY! MRS. FISHBÖL!
RIGHT. OKAY. LET'S SWAP CLOTHES.
SAM
CS
CRIMSON SWINE
NO WAY.
PLEEEASE DON'T BE A JERK. NOT RIGHT NOW.
SAM
CRIMSON
YOU MUST HAVE LOST YOUR MIND.
IT'S NOT HAPPENING.

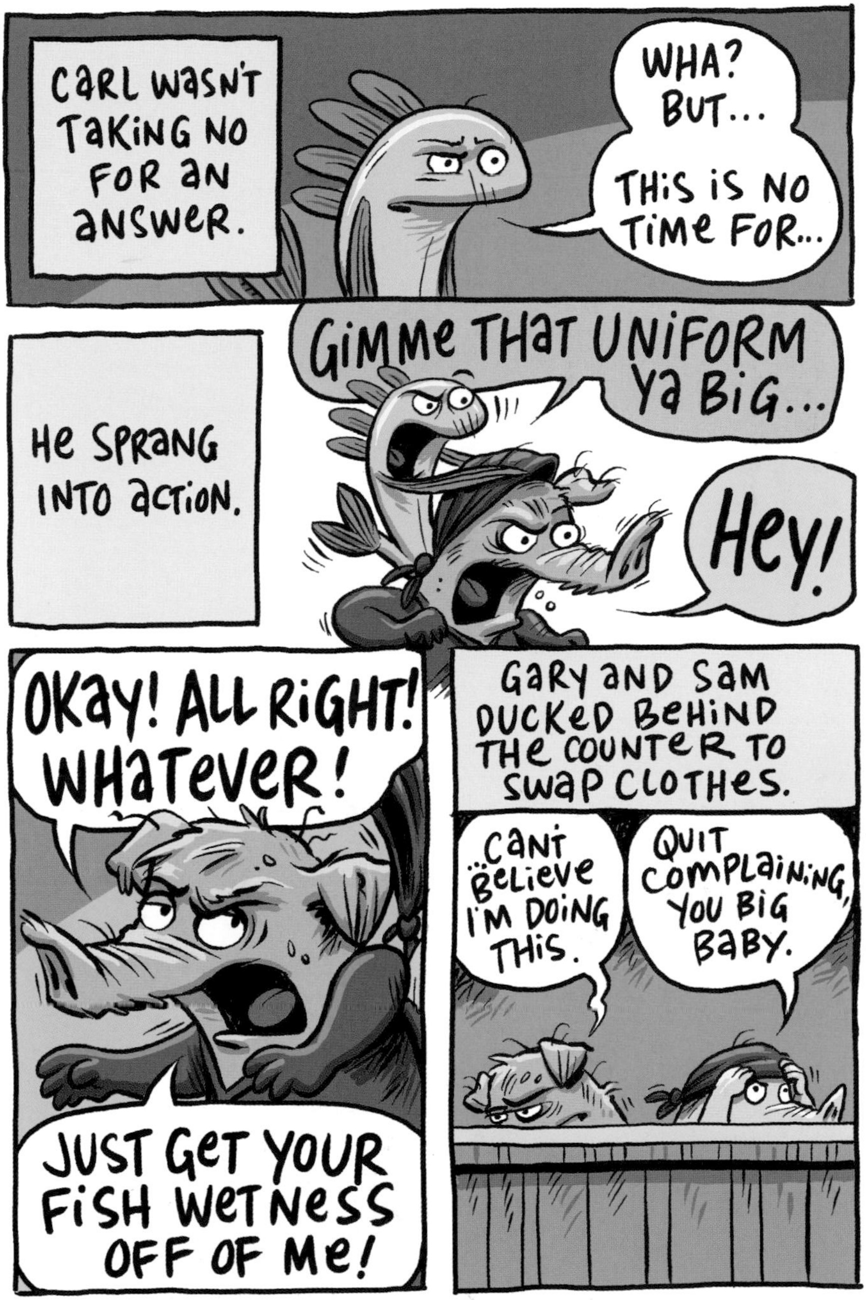
CARL WASN'T TAKING NO FOR AN ANSWER.
WHA? BUT...
THIS IS NO TIME FOR...
HE SPRANG INTO ACTION.
GIMME THAT UNIFORM YA BIG...
HEY!
OKAY! ALL RIGHT! WHATEVER!
JUST GET YOUR FISH WETNESS OFF OF ME!
GARY AND SAM DUCKED BEHIND THE COUNTER TO SWAP CLOTHES.
...CAN'T BELIEVE I'M DOING THIS.
QUIT COMPLAINING, YOU BIG BABY.

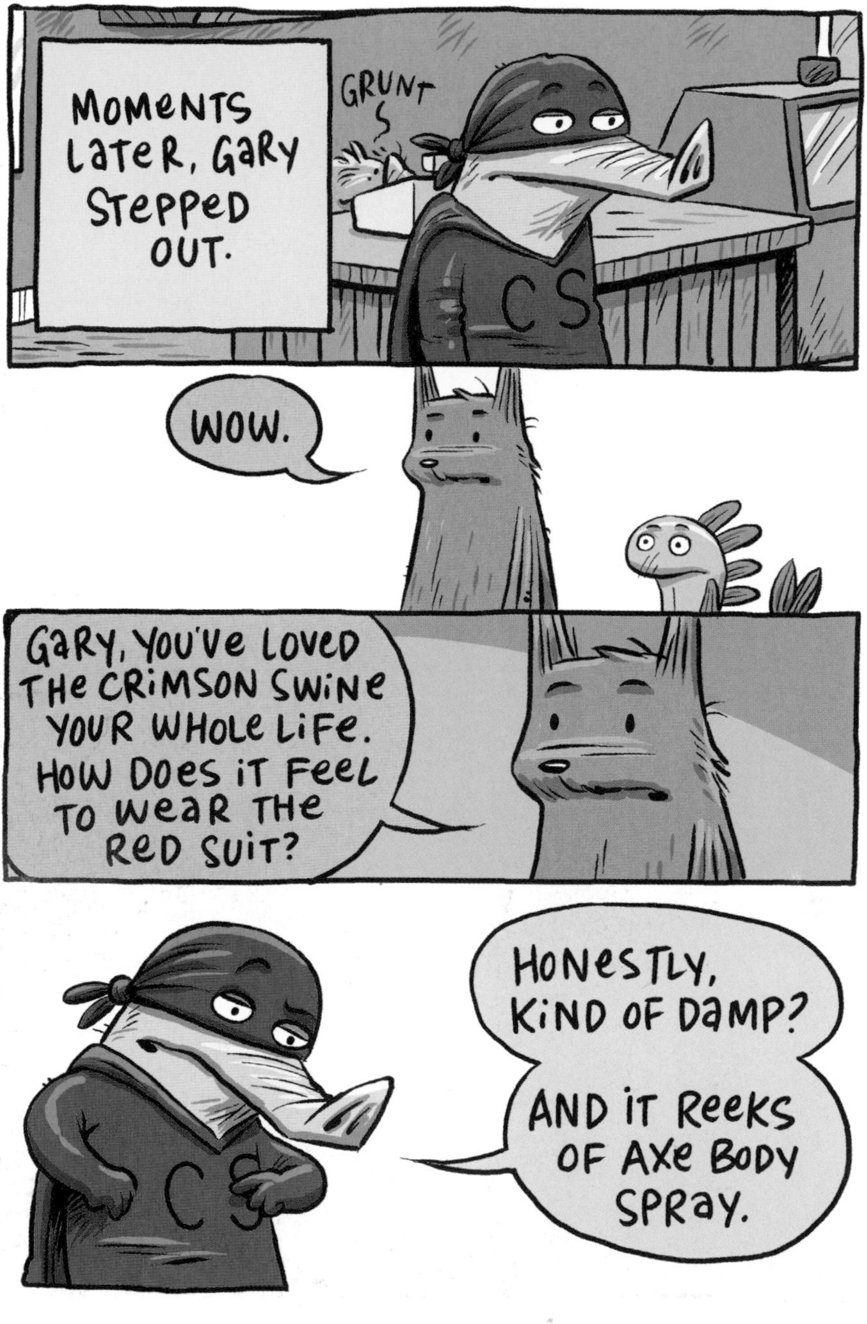
MOMENTS LATER, GARY STEPPED OUT.
GRUNT
WOW.
GARY, YOU'VE LOVED THE CRIMSON SWINE YOUR WHOLE LIFE. HOW DOES IT FEEL TO WEAR THE RED SUIT?
HONESTLY, KIND OF DAMP?
AND IT REEKS OF AXE BODY SPRAY.

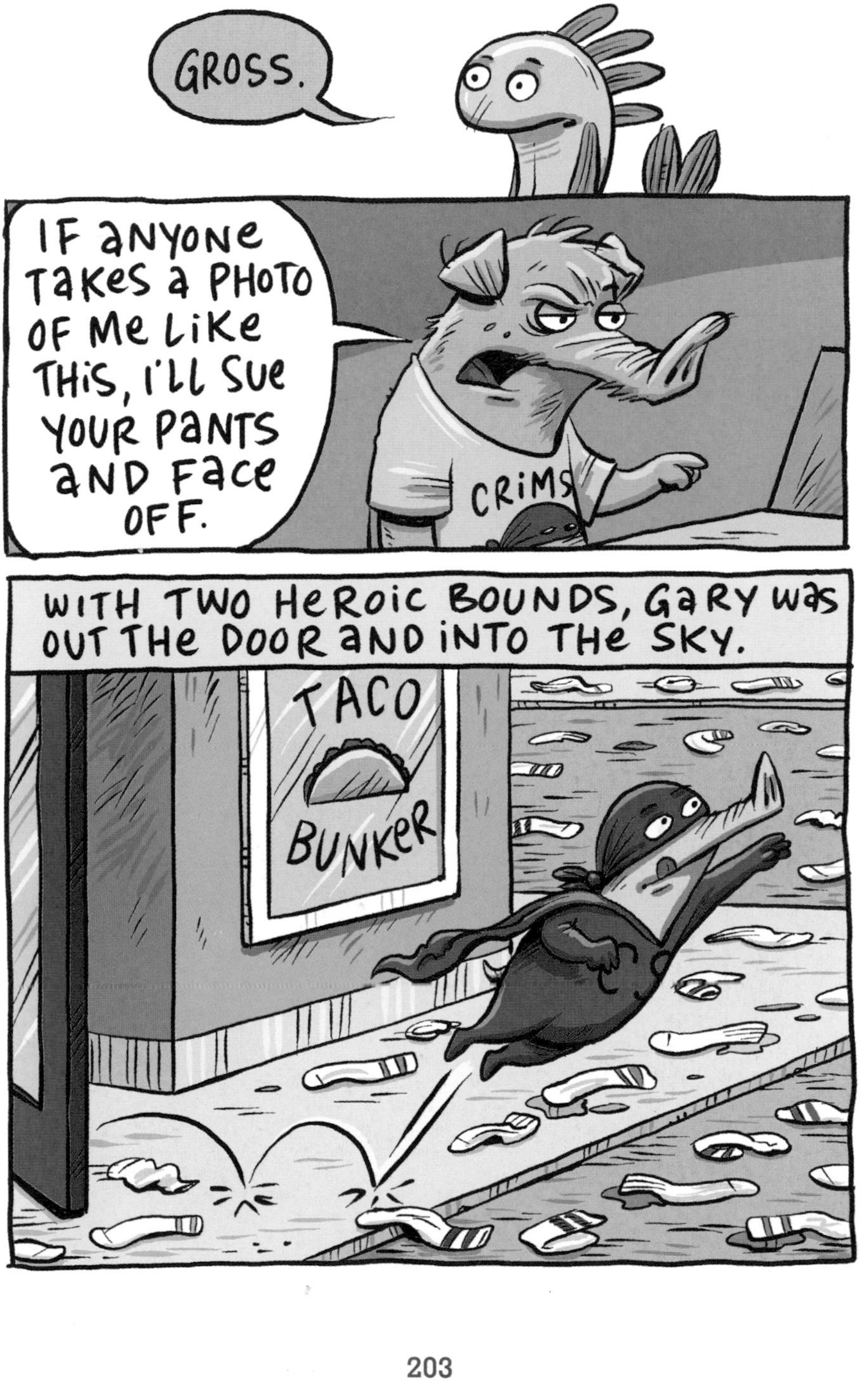
GROSS.
IF ANYONE TAKES A PHOTO OF ME LIKE THIS, I'LL SUE YOUR PANTS AND FACE OFF.
CRIMS
WITH TWO HEROIC BOUNDS, GARY WAS OUT THE DOOR AND INTO THE SKY.
TACO BUNKER

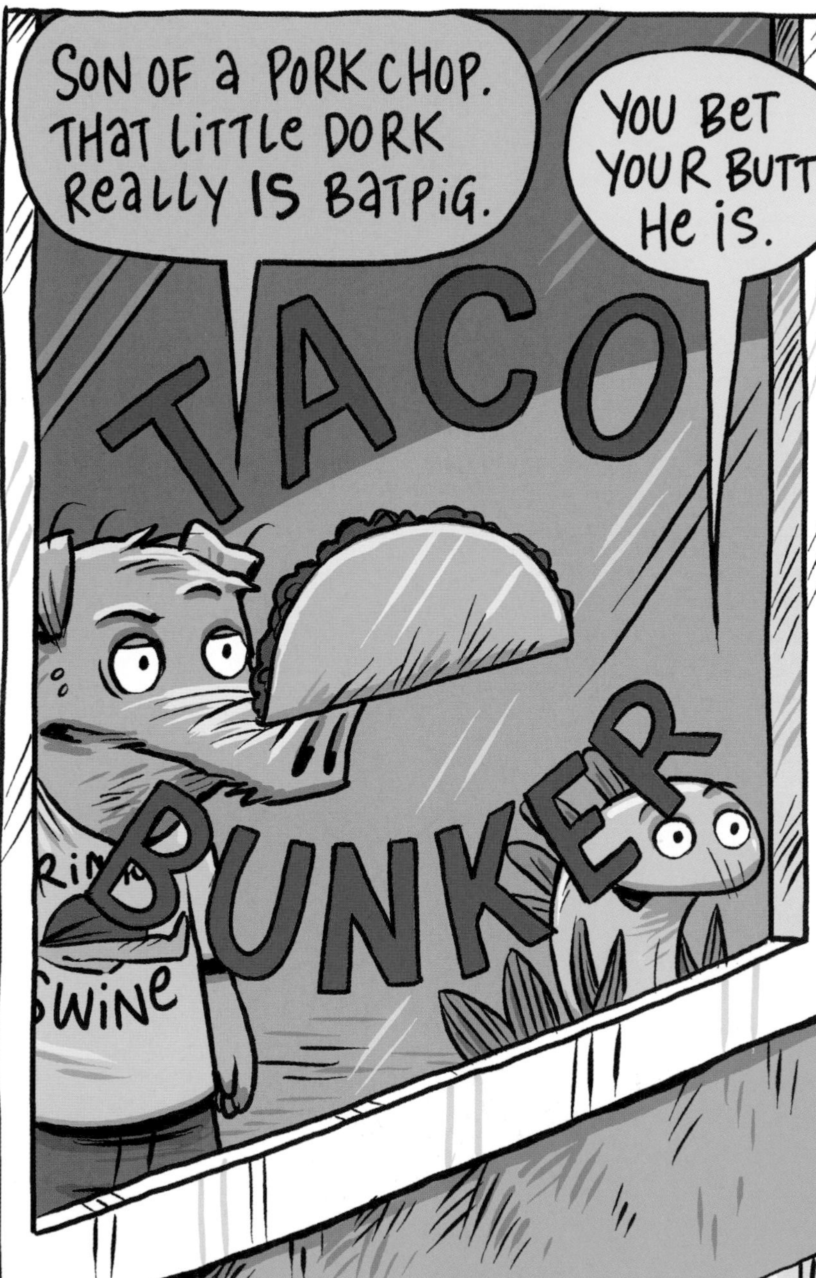
SON OF a PORK CHOP. THAT LITTLE DORK REALLY IS BATPIG.
YOU BET YOUR BUTT HE IS.
TACO BUNKER
SWINE

CHAPTER EIGHT

"CAT SCRATCH
FEVER"

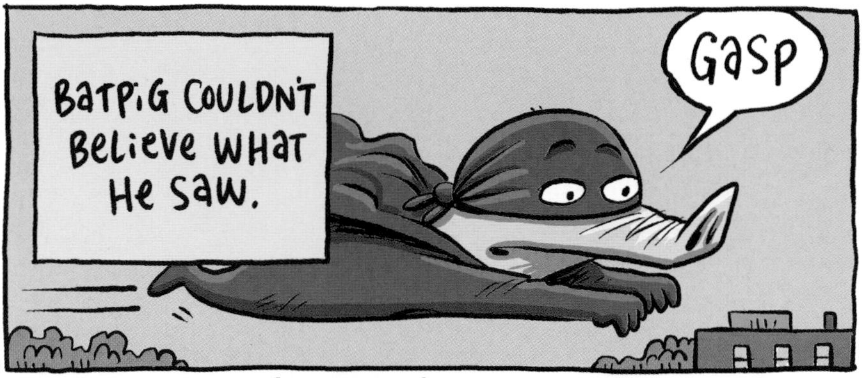
BATPIG COULDN'T BELIEVE WHAT HE SAW.
GASP

THE GIANT BUMBLEKITTEN WAS REALLY GOING AFTER MRS. FISHBÖL'S SHOP. HOPEFULLY SHE WAS GOOD AT HIDING.

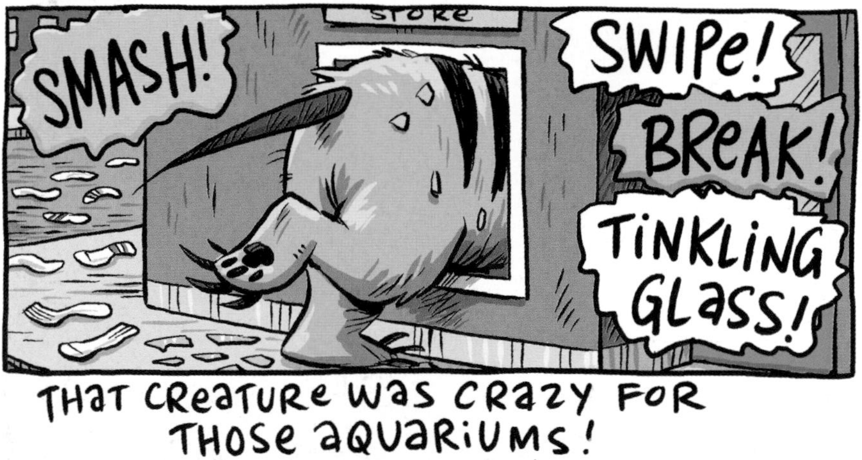
SMASH!
SWIPE!
BREAK!
TINKLING GLASS!

THAT CREATURE WAS CRAZY FOR THOSE AQUARIUMS!

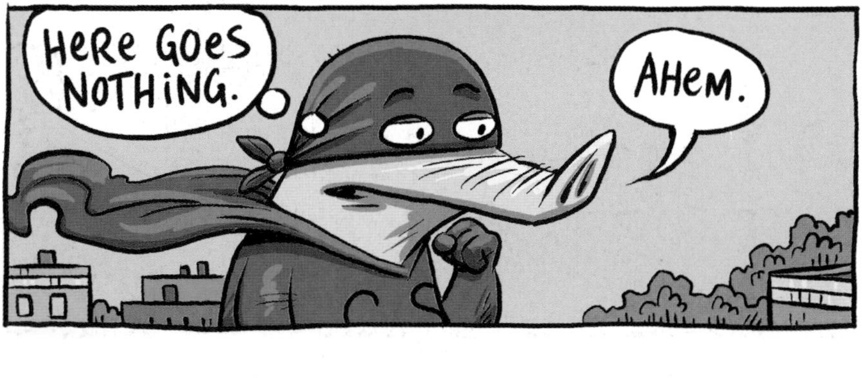
HERE GOES NOTHING.
AHEM.

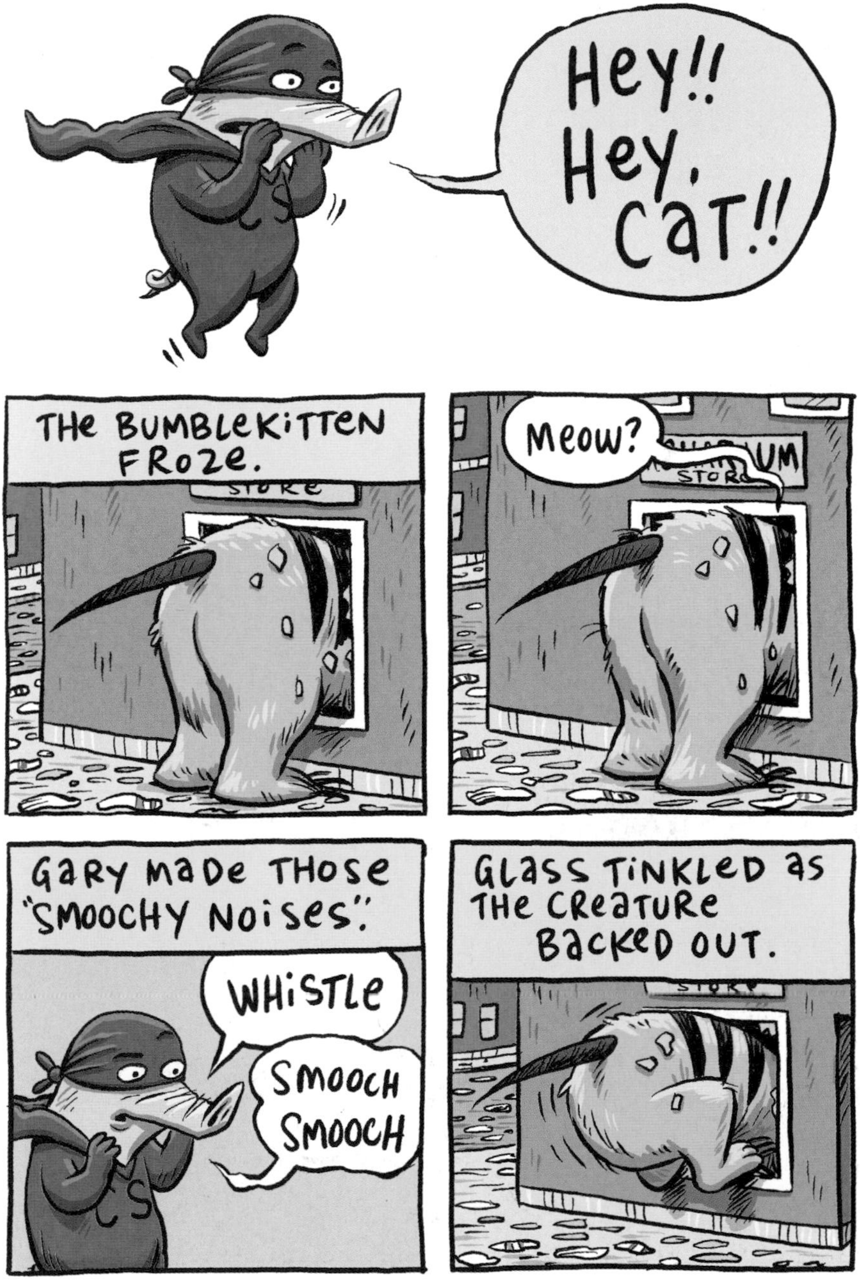
Hey!! Hey, Cat!!
The Bumblekitten froze.
Meow?
Gary made those "smoochy noises".
WHISTLE
SMOOCH SMOOCH
Glass tinkled as the creature backed out.

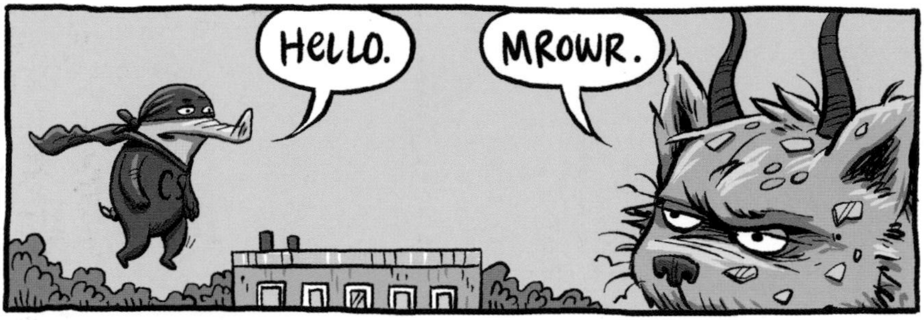
HELLO.
MROWR.

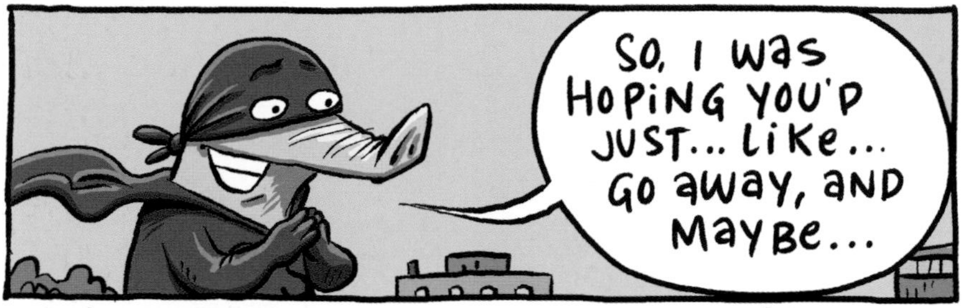
SO, I WAS HOPING YOU'D JUST... LIKE... GO AWAY, AND MAYBE...

WITH THAT, THE GIANT FELINE INSECT SWATTED OUT AND SMACKED THE ABSOLUTE STUFFING OUT OF OUR HERO.

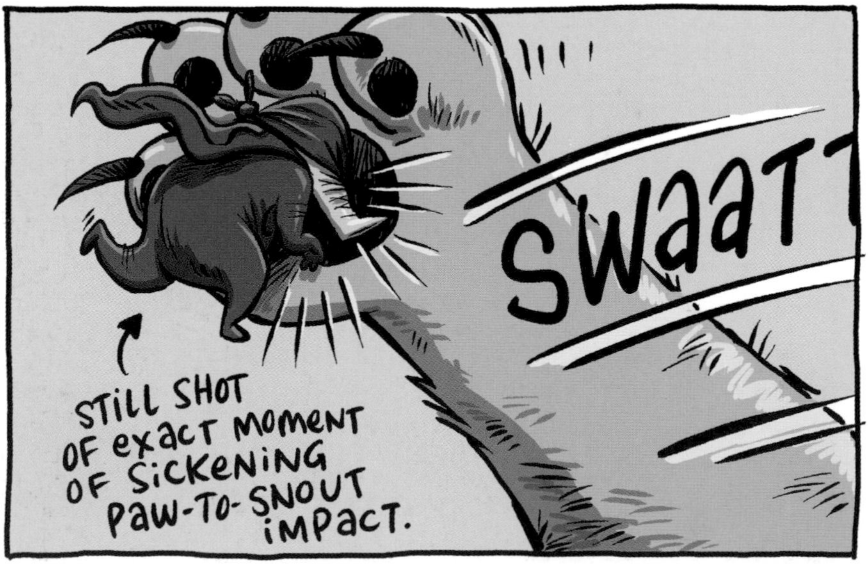
SWAAT
STILL SHOT OF EXACT MOMENT OF SICKENING PAW-TO-SNOUT IMPACT.

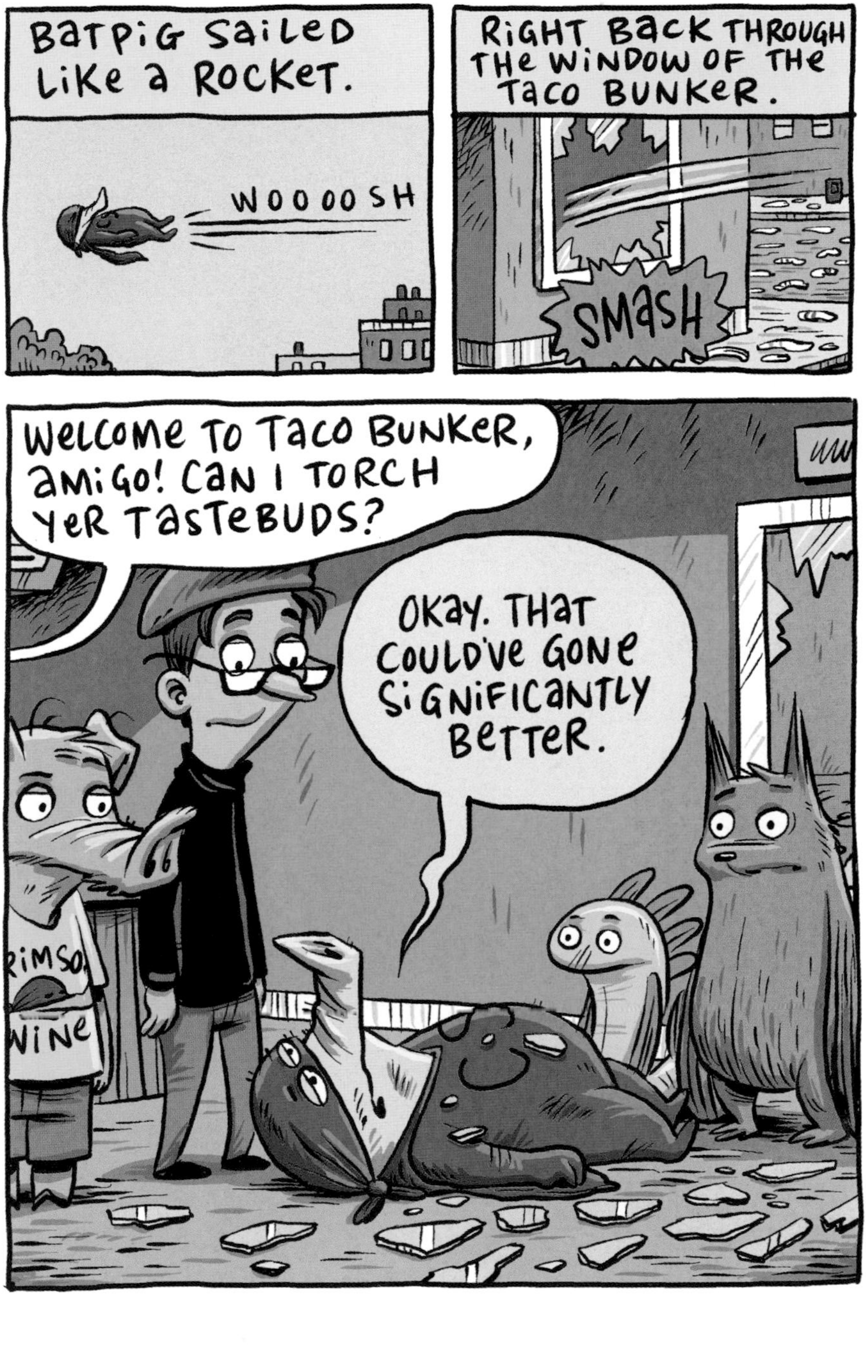
BATPIG SAILED LIKE A ROCKET.
WOOOOOSH
RIGHT BACK THROUGH THE WINDOW OF THE TACO BUNKER.
SMASH
WELCOME TO TACO BUNKER, AMIGO! CAN I TORCH YER TASTEBUDS?
OKAY. THAT COULD'VE GONE SIGNIFICANTLY BETTER.
RIMSO
WINE

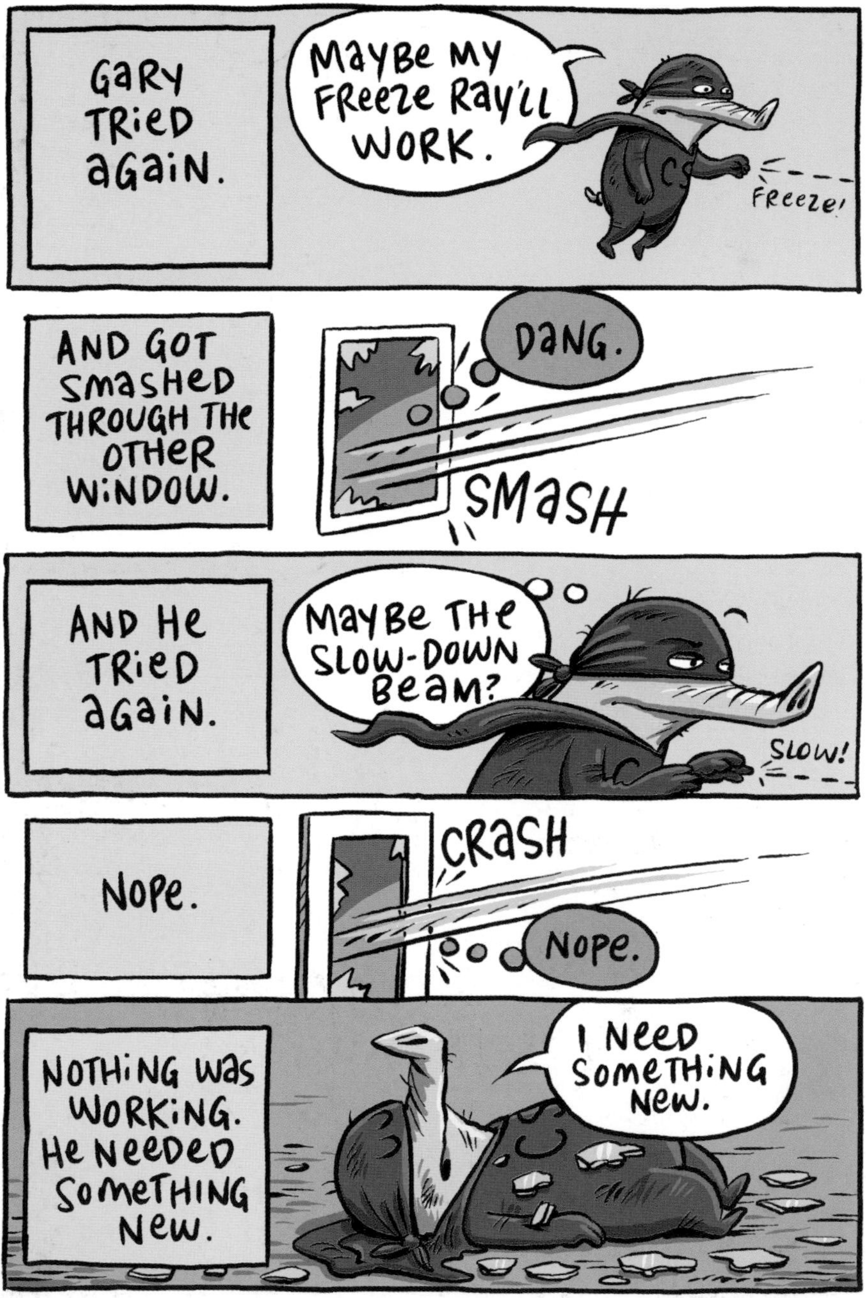

Gary tried again.
Maybe my freeze ray'll work.
Freeze!
And got smashed through the other window.
Dang.
SMASH
And he tried again.
Maybe the slow-down beam?
SLOW!
Nope.
CRASH
Nope.
Nothing was working. He needed something new.
I need something new.

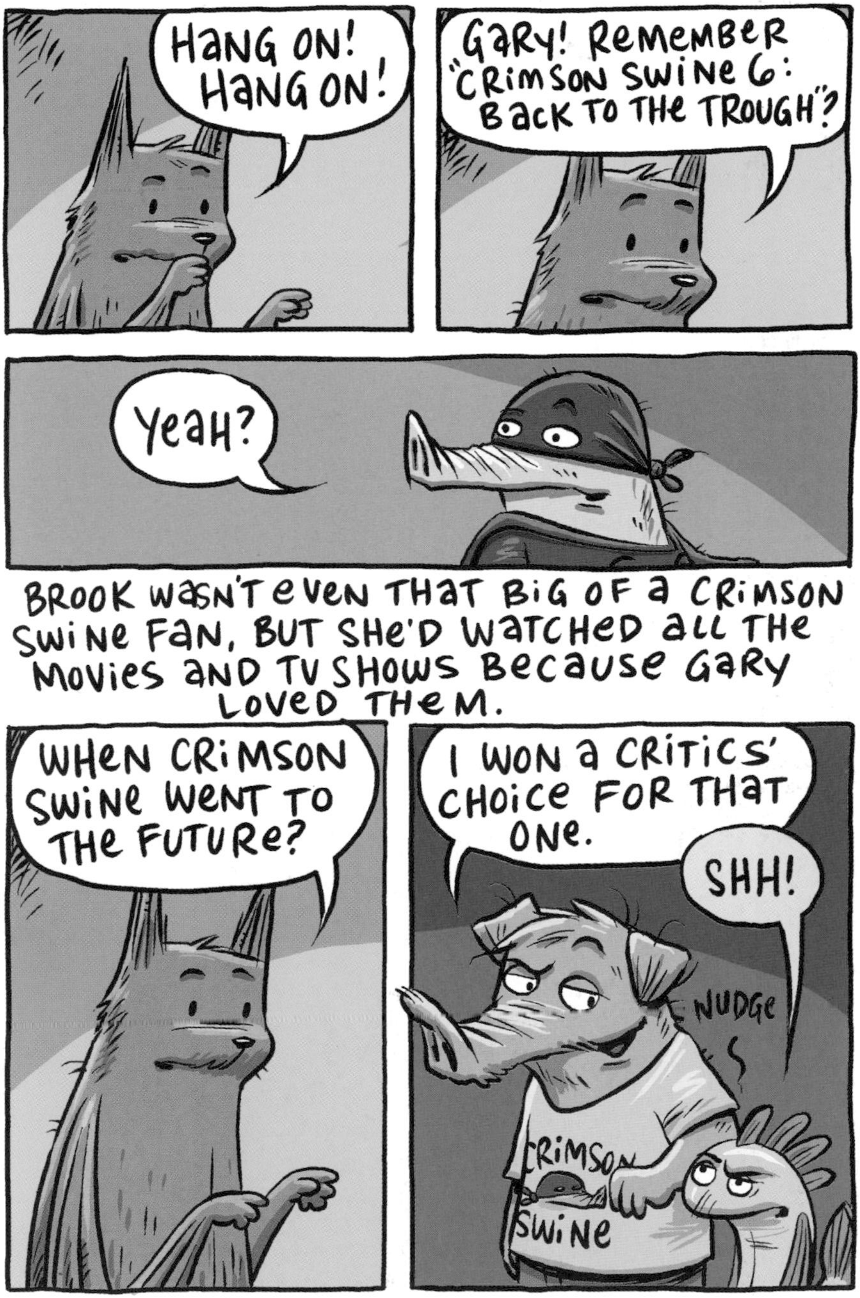
HANG ON! HANG ON!
GARY! REMEMBER "CRIMSON SWINE 6: BACK TO THE TROUGH"?
YEAH?
BROOK WASN'T EVEN THAT BIG OF A CRIMSON SWINE FAN, BUT SHE'D WATCHED ALL THE MOVIES AND TV SHOWS BECAUSE GARY LOVED THEM.
WHEN CRIMSON SWINE WENT TO THE FUTURE?
I WON A CRITICS' CHOICE FOR THAT ONE.
SHH!
NUDGE
CRIMSON SWINE

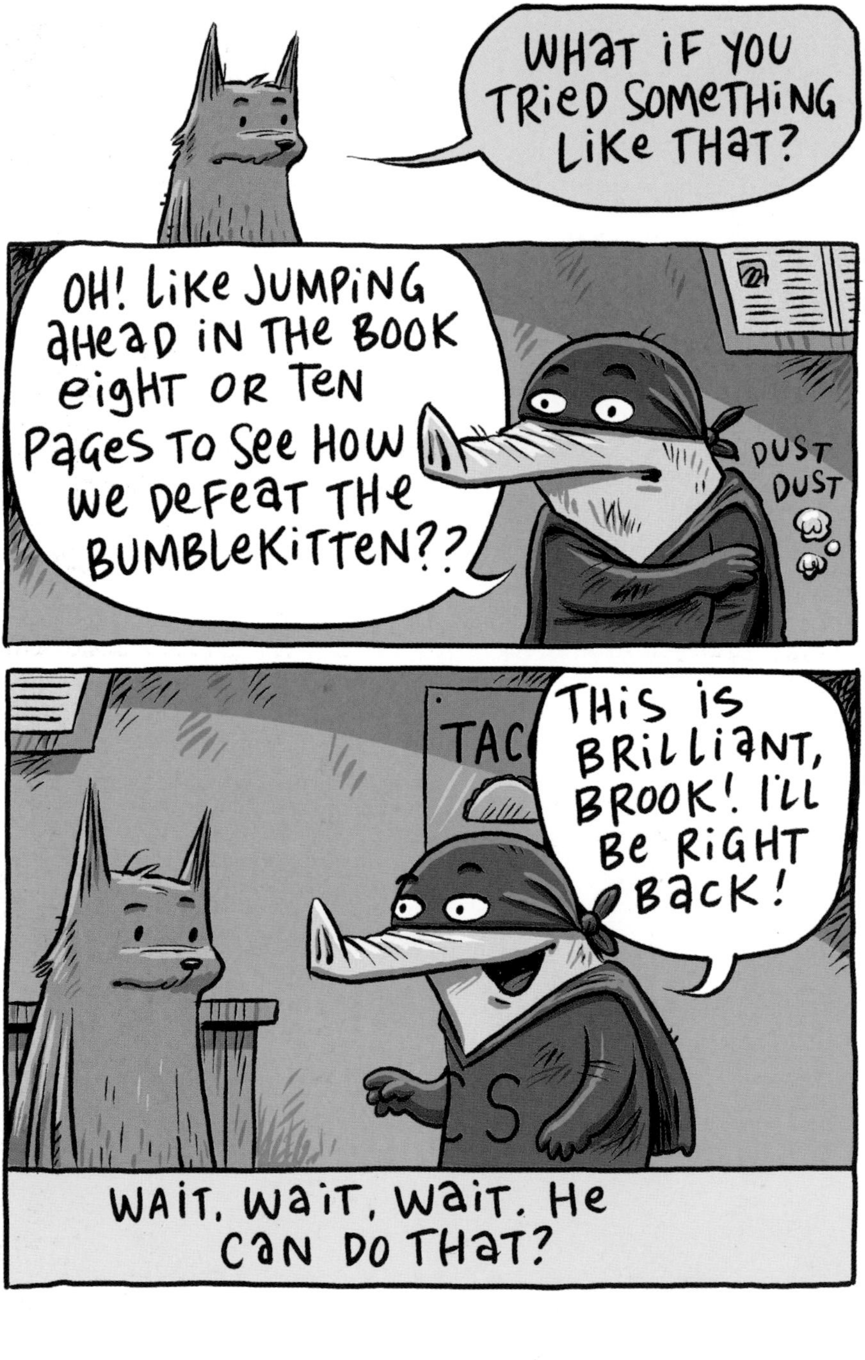
WHAT IF YOU TRIED SOMETHING LIKE THAT?
OH! LIKE JUMPING AHEAD IN THE BOOK EIGHT OR TEN PAGES TO SEE HOW WE DEFEAT THE BUMBLEKITTEN??
DUST DUST
TAC
THIS IS BRILLIANT, BROOK! I'LL BE RIGHT BACK!
WAIT. WAIT, WAIT. HE CAN DO THAT?

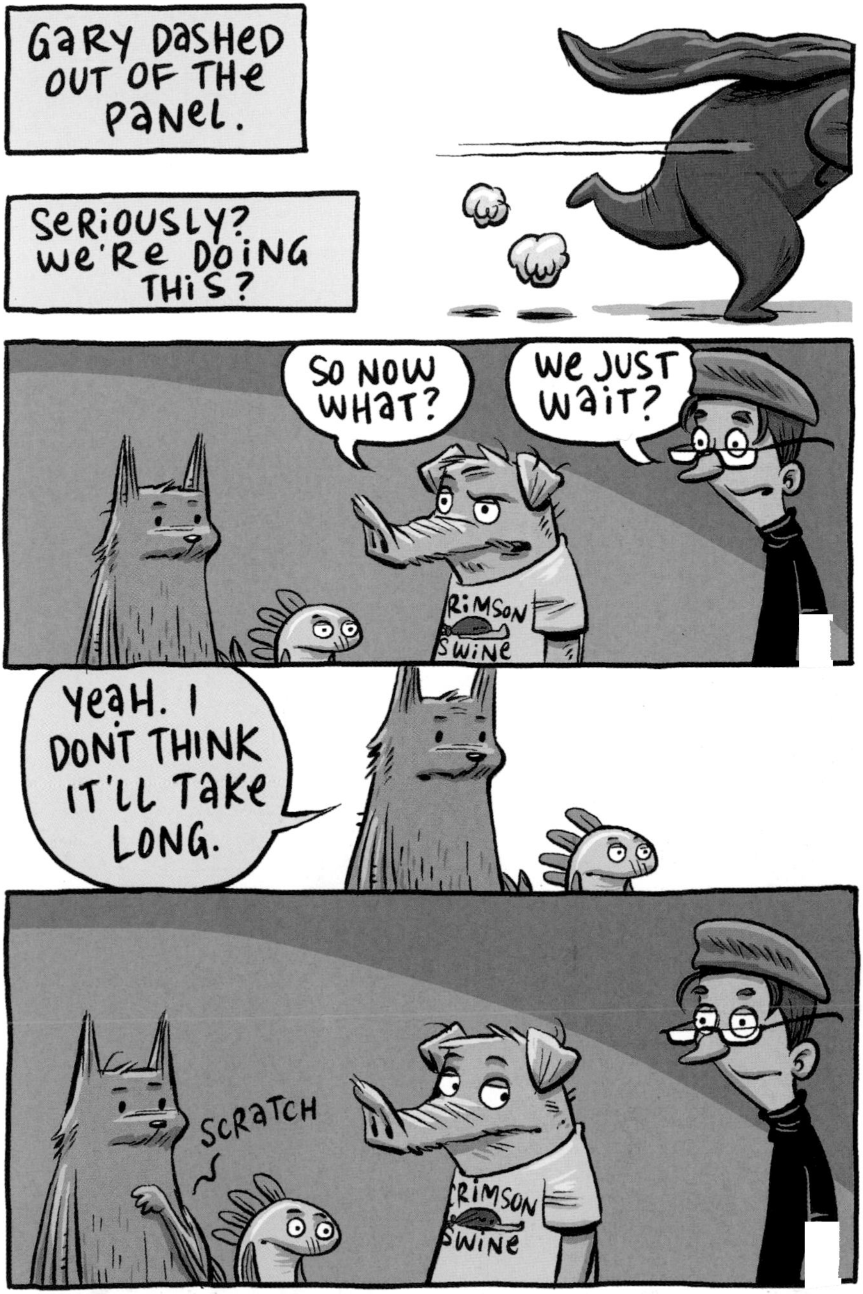
GaRY DaSHED OUT OF THE PaNEL.
SERIOUSLY? WE'RE DOING THIS?
SO NOW WHaT?
WE JUST WaIT?
RIMSON SWINE
YEaH. I DON'T THINK IT'LL TaKE LONG.
SCRaTCH
RIMSON SWINE

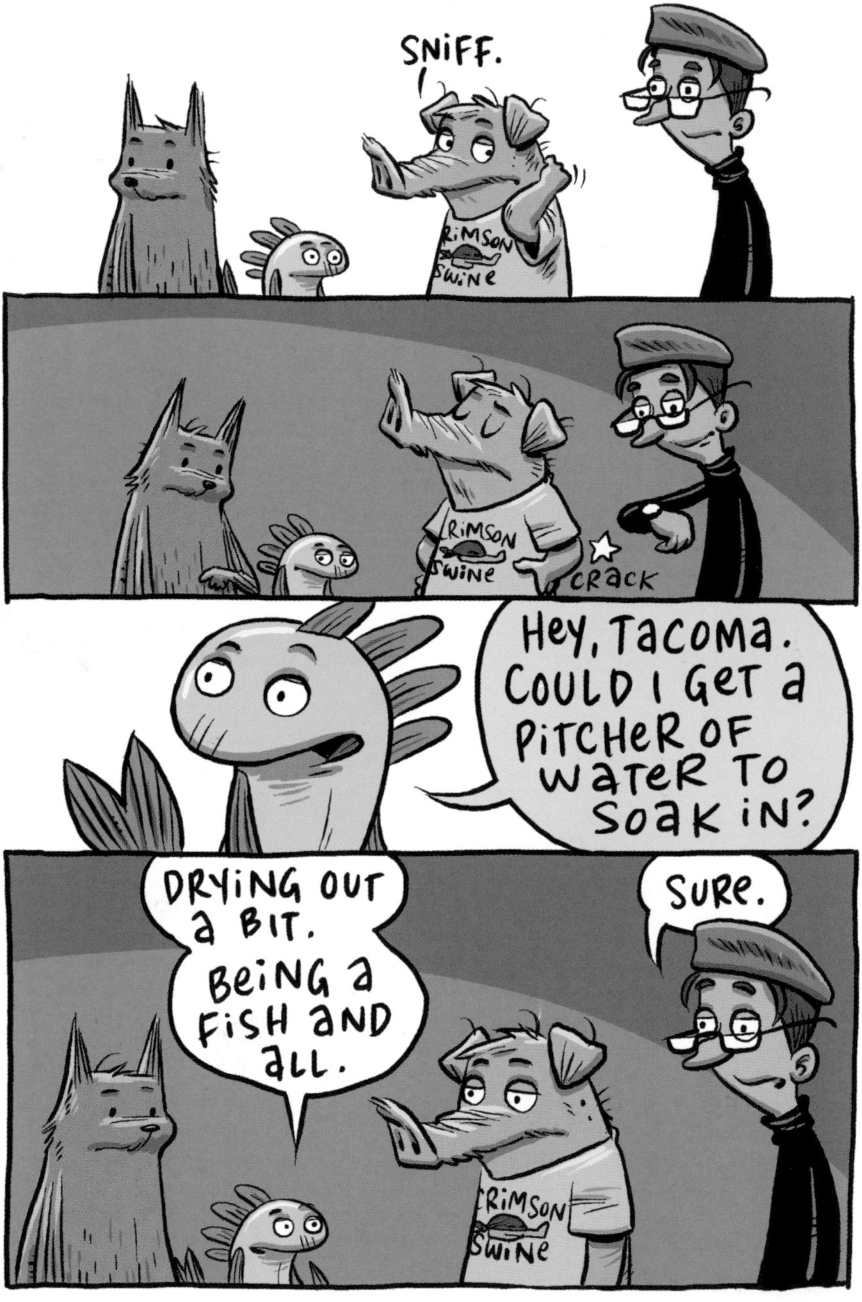
SNIFF.
CRIMSON SWINE
CRIMSON SWINE
CRACK
Hey, Tacoma. Could I get a pitcher of water to soak in?
Drying out a bit. Being a fish and all.
Sure.
CRIMSON SWINE

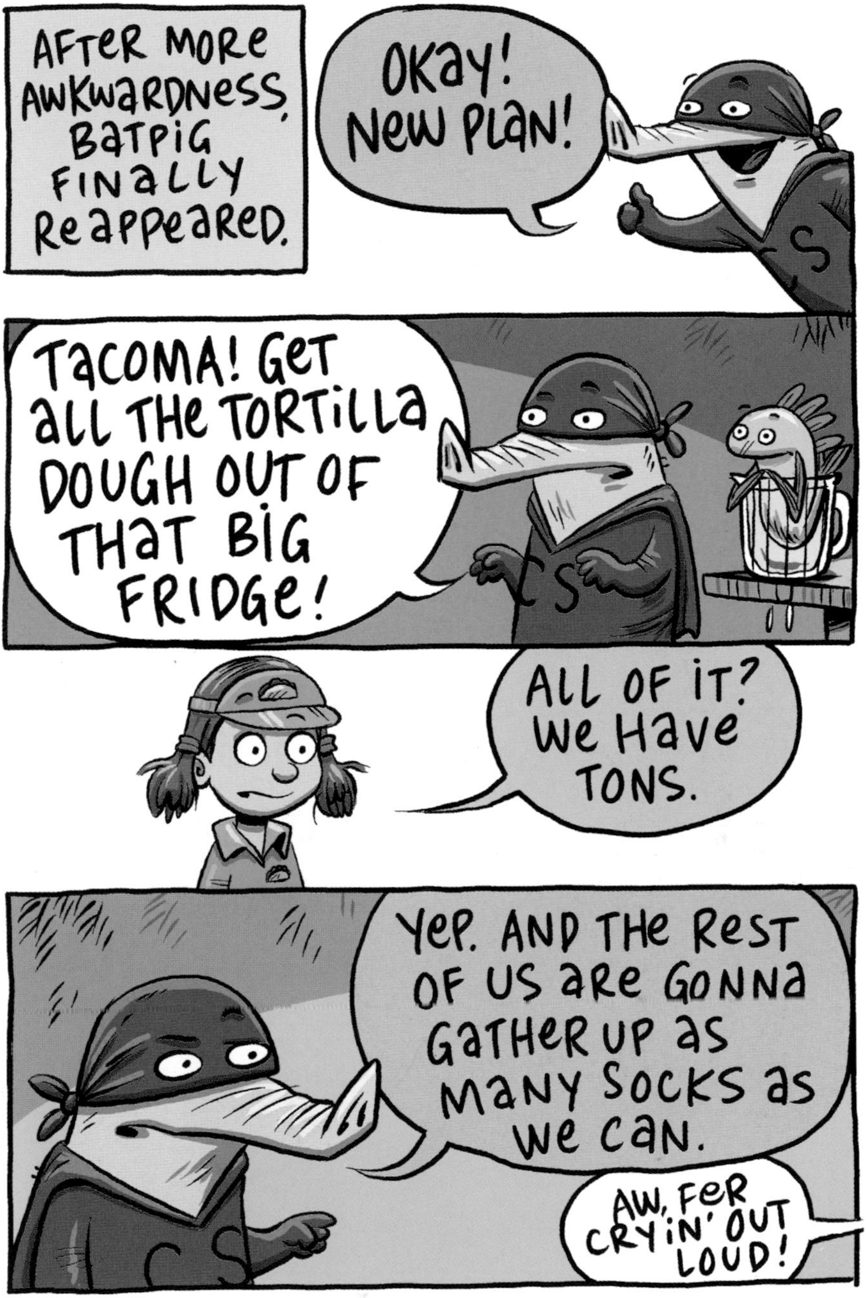
AFTER MORE AWKWARDNESS, BATPIG FINALLY REAPPEARED.
OKAY! NEW PLAN!
TACOMA! GET ALL THE TORTILLA DOUGH OUT OF THAT BIG FRIDGE!
ALL OF IT? WE HAVE TONS.
YEP. AND THE REST OF US ARE GONNA GATHER UP AS MANY SOCKS AS WE CAN.
AW, FER CRYIN' OUT LOUD!

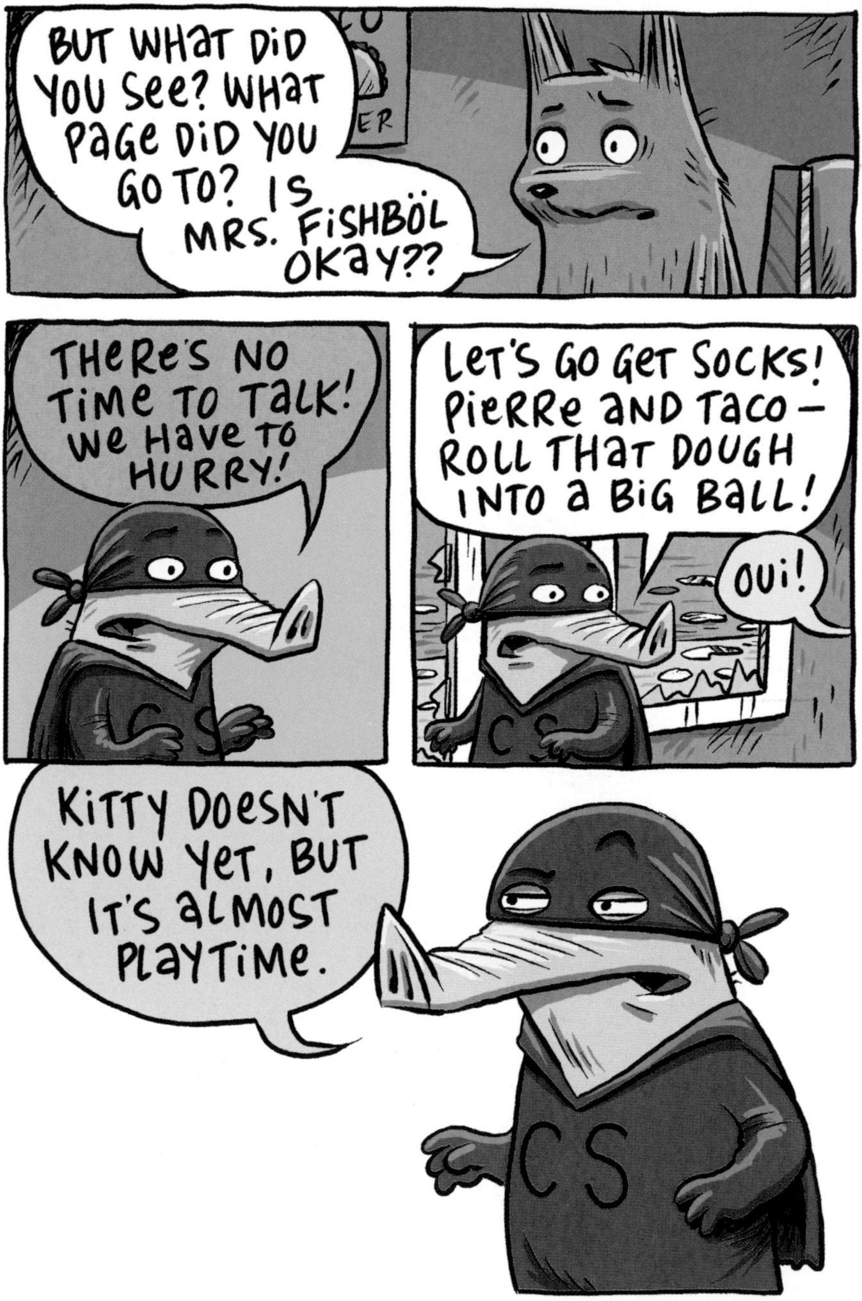
BUT WHAT DID YOU SEE? WHAT PAGE DID YOU GO TO? IS MRS. FISHBÖL OKAY??
THERE'S NO TIME TO TALK! WE HAVE TO HURRY!
LET'S GO GET SOCKS! PIERRE AND TACO— ROLL THAT DOUGH INTO A BIG BALL!
OUI!
KITTY DOESN'T KNOW YET, BUT IT'S ALMOST PLAYTIME.

CHAPTER NINE

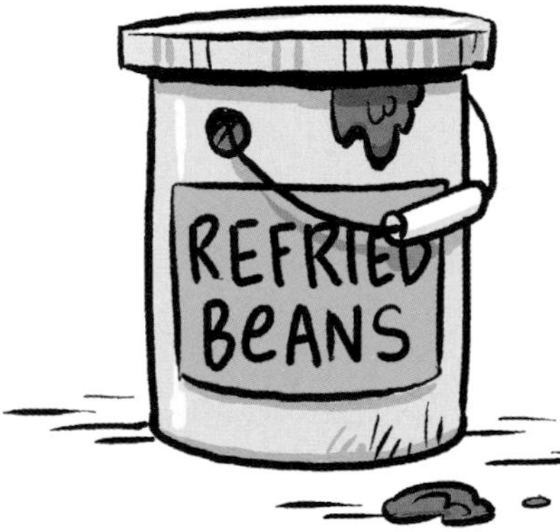
REFRIED
BEANS

"THE MAGICAL FRUIT"

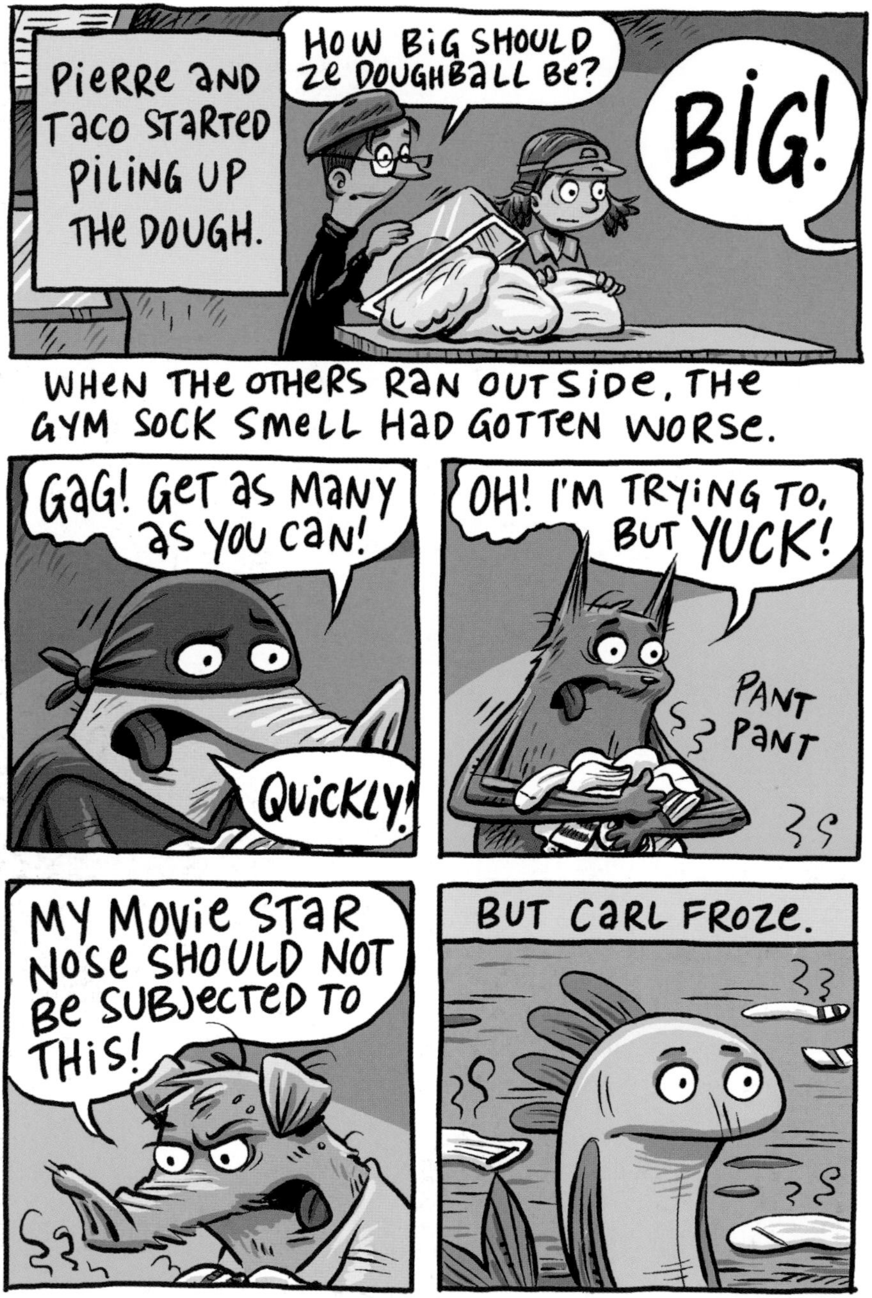
PIERRE AND TACO STARTED PILING UP THE DOUGH.
HOW BIG SHOULD ZE DOUGHBALL BE?
BIG!
WHEN THE OTHERS RAN OUTSIDE, THE GYM SOCK SMELL HAD GOTTEN WORSE.
GAG! GET AS MANY AS YOU CAN!
QUICKLY!
OH! I'M TRYING TO, BUT YUCK!
PANT PANT
MY MOVIE STAR NOSE SHOULD NOT BE SUBJECTED TO THIS!
BUT CARL FROZE.

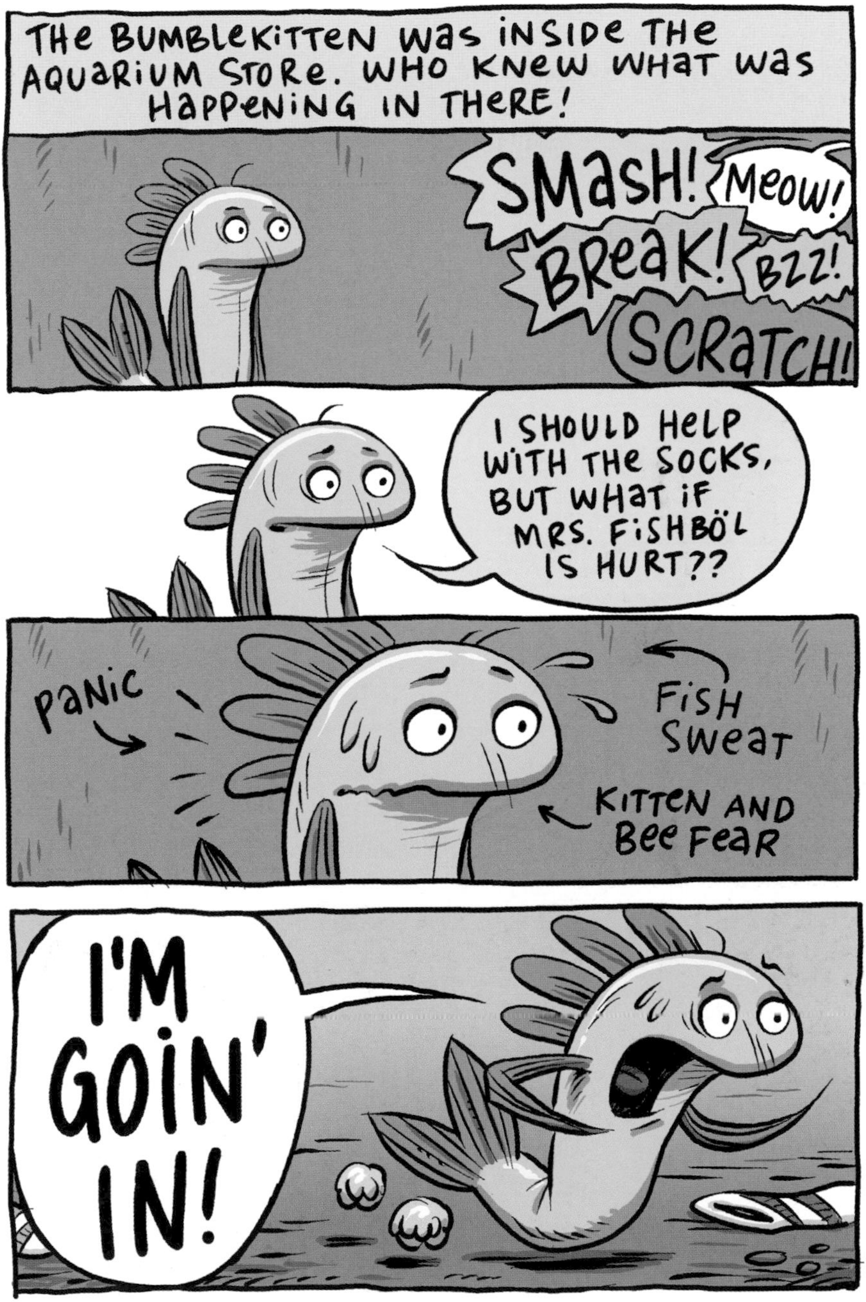
THE BUMBLEKITTEN WAS INSIDE THE AQUARIUM STORE. WHO KNEW WHAT WAS HAPPENING IN THERE!
SMASH!
MEOW!
BREAK!
BZZ!
SCRATCH!
I SHOULD HELP WITH THE SOCKS, BUT WHAT IF MRS. FISHBÖL IS HURT??
PANIC
FISH SWEAT
KITTEN AND BEE FEAR
I'M GOIN' IN!

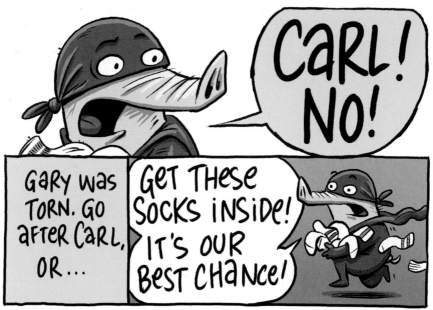

CARL! NO!
GARY WAS TORN. GO AFTER CARL, OR...
GET THESE SOCKS INSIDE! IT'S OUR BEST CHANCE!
AS THEY DASHED INSIDE, SEVERAL BYSTANDERS SAW IT ALL.
I TOLD YOU I SAW THE CRIMSON SWINE FLYING BY EARLIER!
HE'S REAL!
HE'S SAVING US!
AW, MAN.

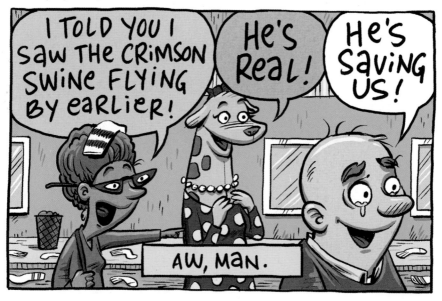

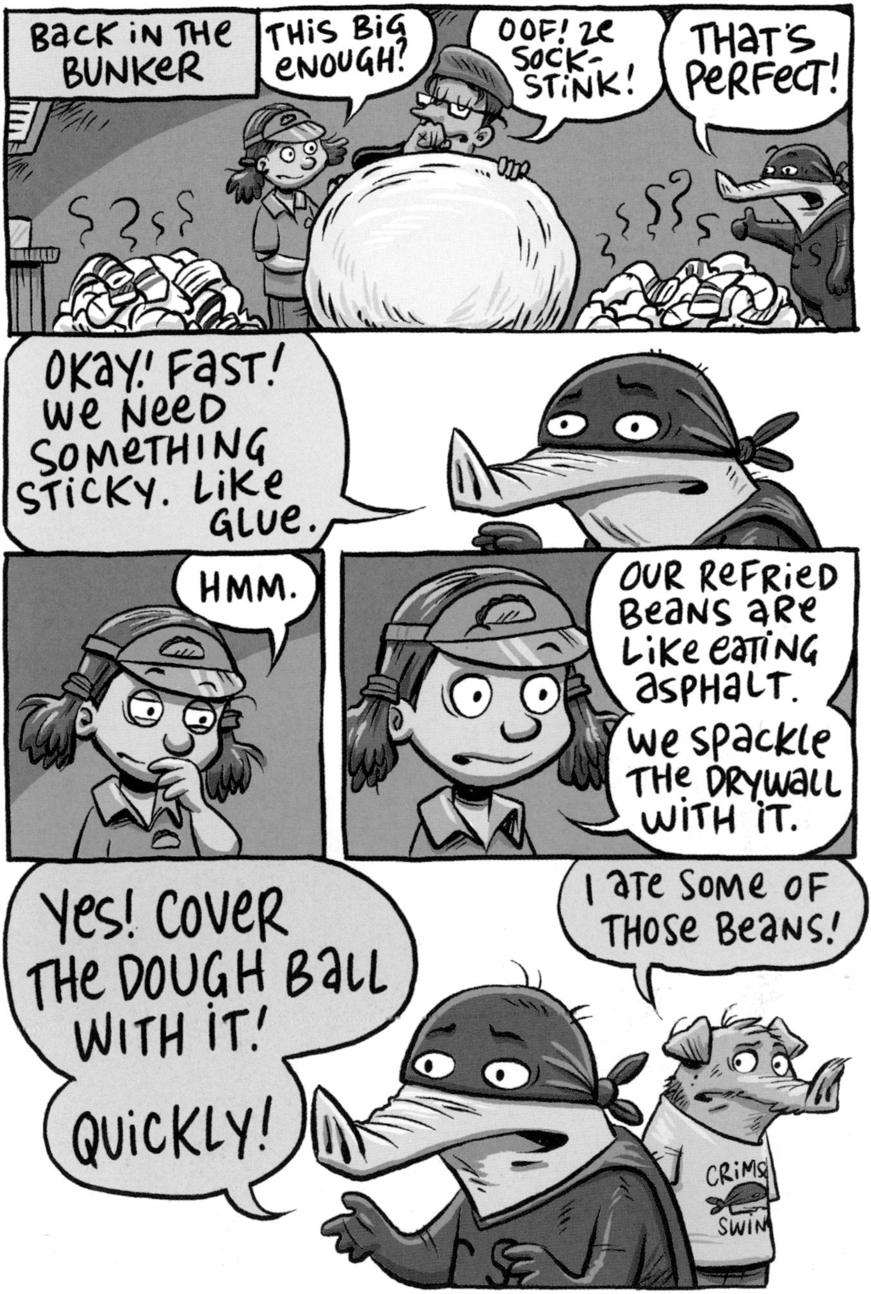
BACK IN THE BUNKER
THIS BIG ENOUGH?
OOF! ZE SOCK-STINK!
THAT'S PERFECT!
OKAY! FAST! WE NEED SOMETHING STICKY. LIKE GLUE.
HMM.
OUR REFRIED BEANS ARE LIKE EATING ASPHALT.
WE SPACKLE THE DRYWALL WITH IT.
YES! COVER THE DOUGH BALL WITH IT!
QUICKLY!
I ATE SOME OF THOSE BEANS!

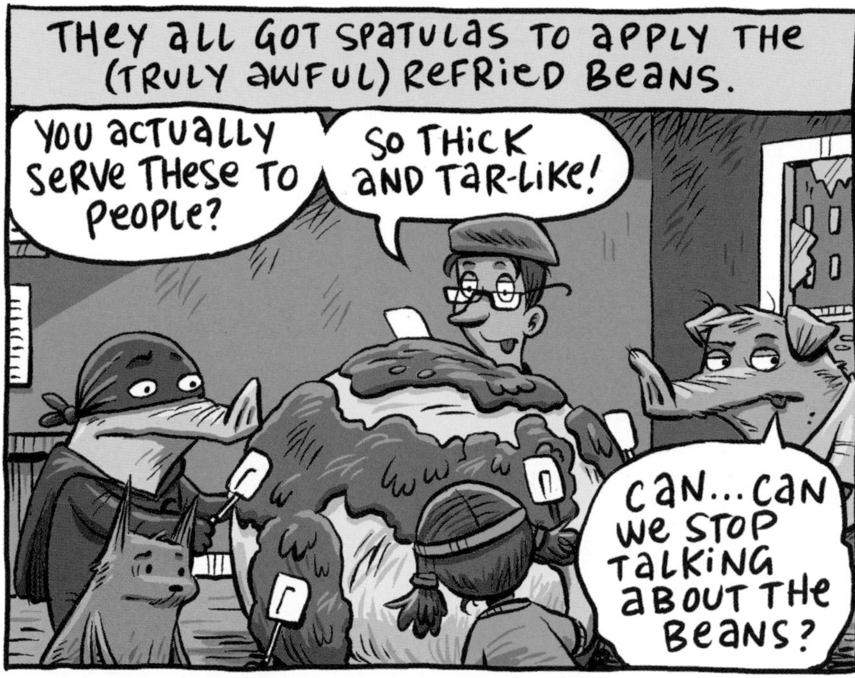
THEY ALL GOT SPATULAS TO APPLY THE (TRULY AWFUL) REFRIED BEANS.
YOU ACTUALLY SERVE THESE TO PEOPLE?
SO THICK AND TAR-LIKE!
CAN... CAN WE STOP TALKING ABOUT THE BEANS?

THEN GARY GRABBED SOME SOCKS.

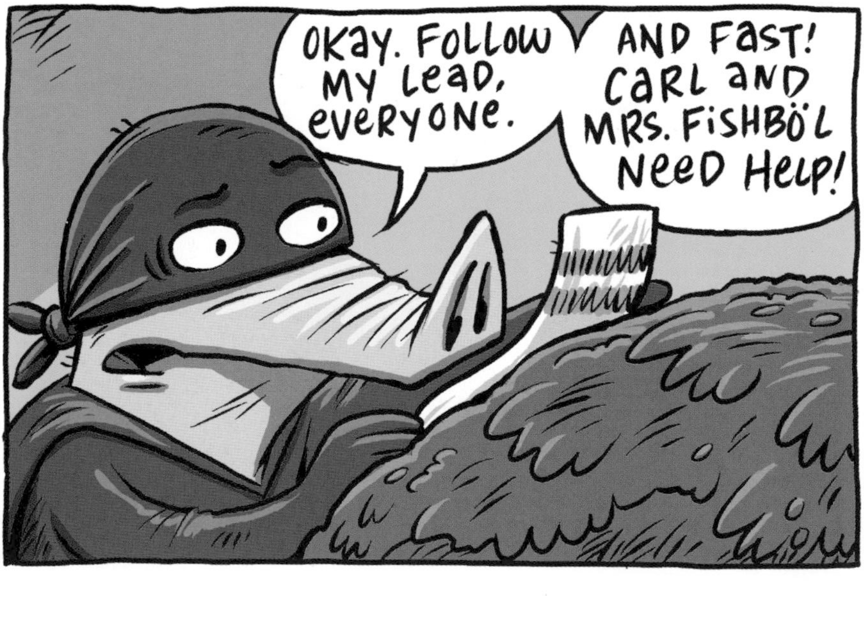
OKAY. FOLLOW MY LEAD, EVERYONE.
AND FAST! CARL AND MRS. FISHBÖL NEED HELP!

CHAPTER TEN

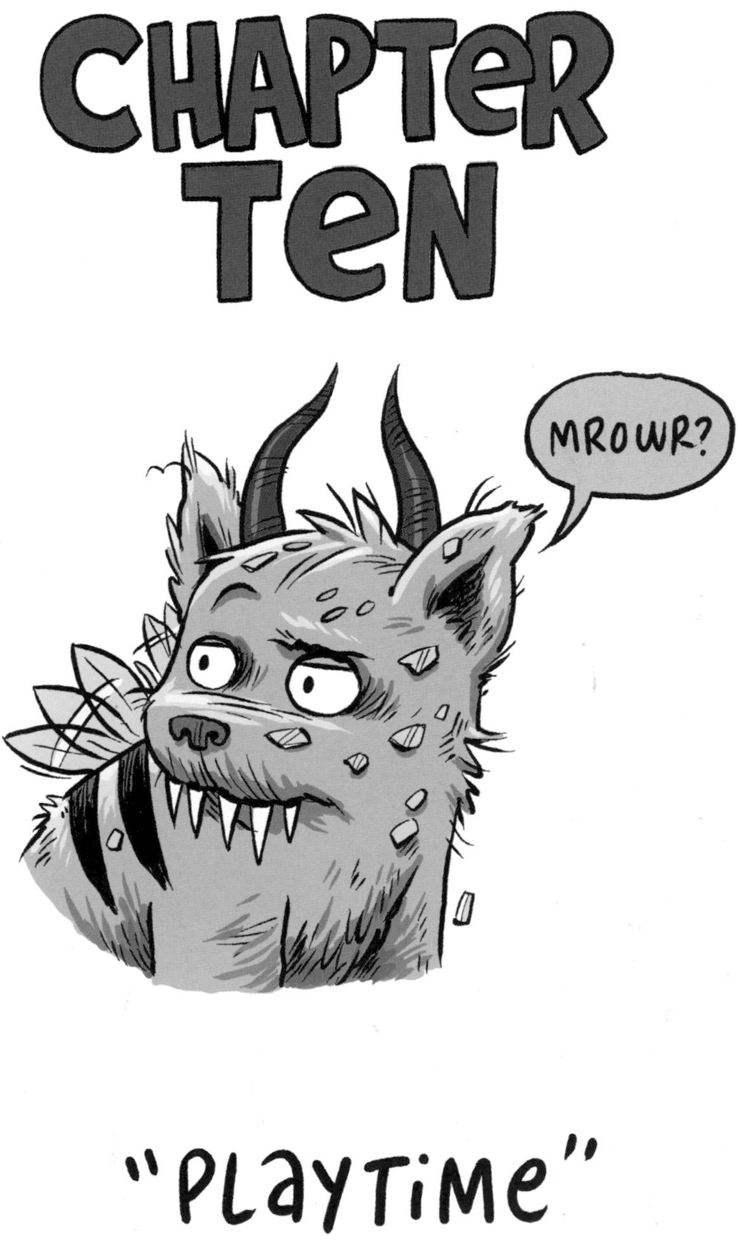
MROWR?

"PLAYTIME"

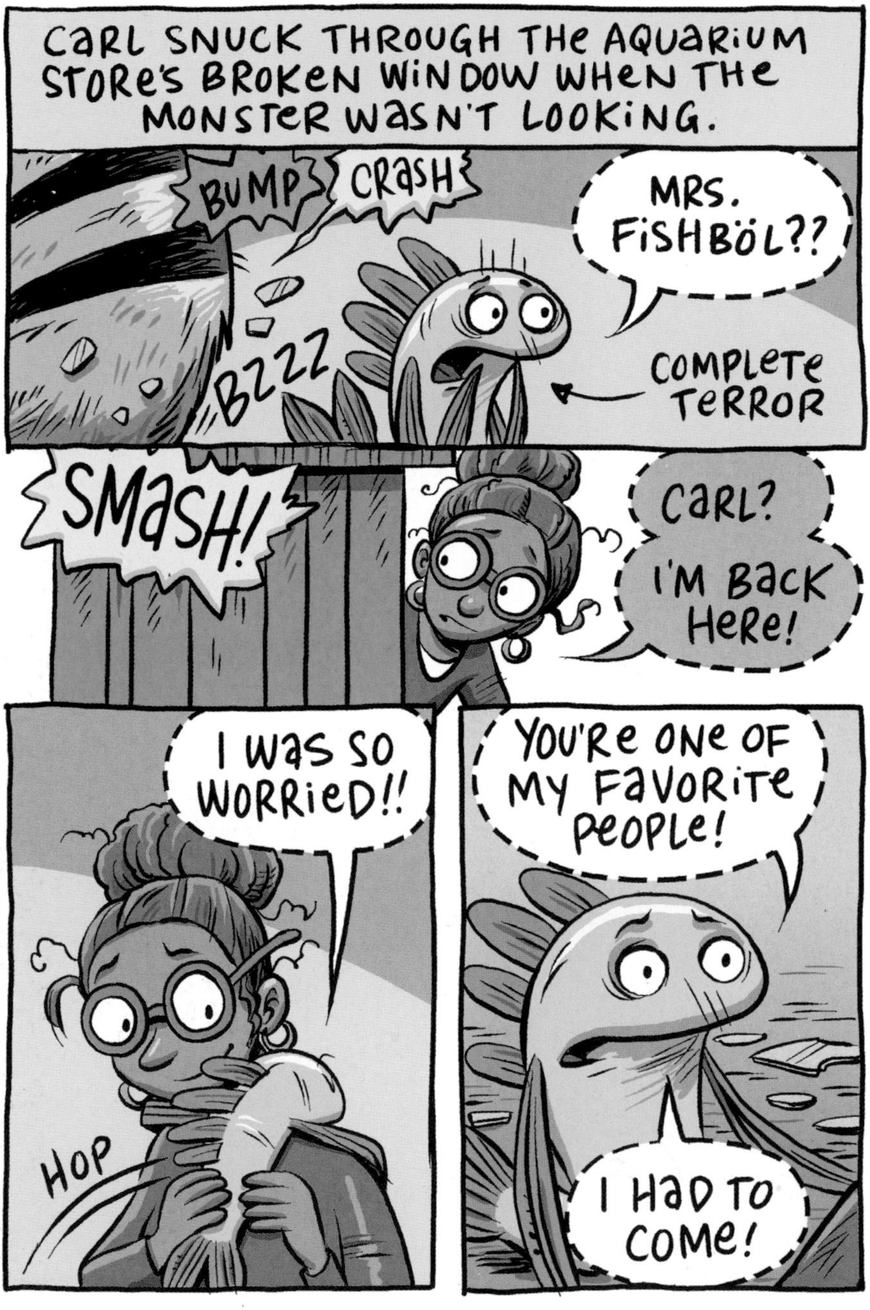
CARL SNUCK THROUGH THE AQUARIUM STORE'S BROKEN WINDOW WHEN THE MONSTER WASN'T LOOKING.
BUMP
CRASH
MRS. FISHBÖL??
BZZZ
COMPLETE TERROR
SMASH!
CARL?
I'M BACK HERE!
I WAS SO WORRIED!!
HOP
YOU'RE ONE OF MY FAVORITE PEOPLE!
I HAD TO COME!

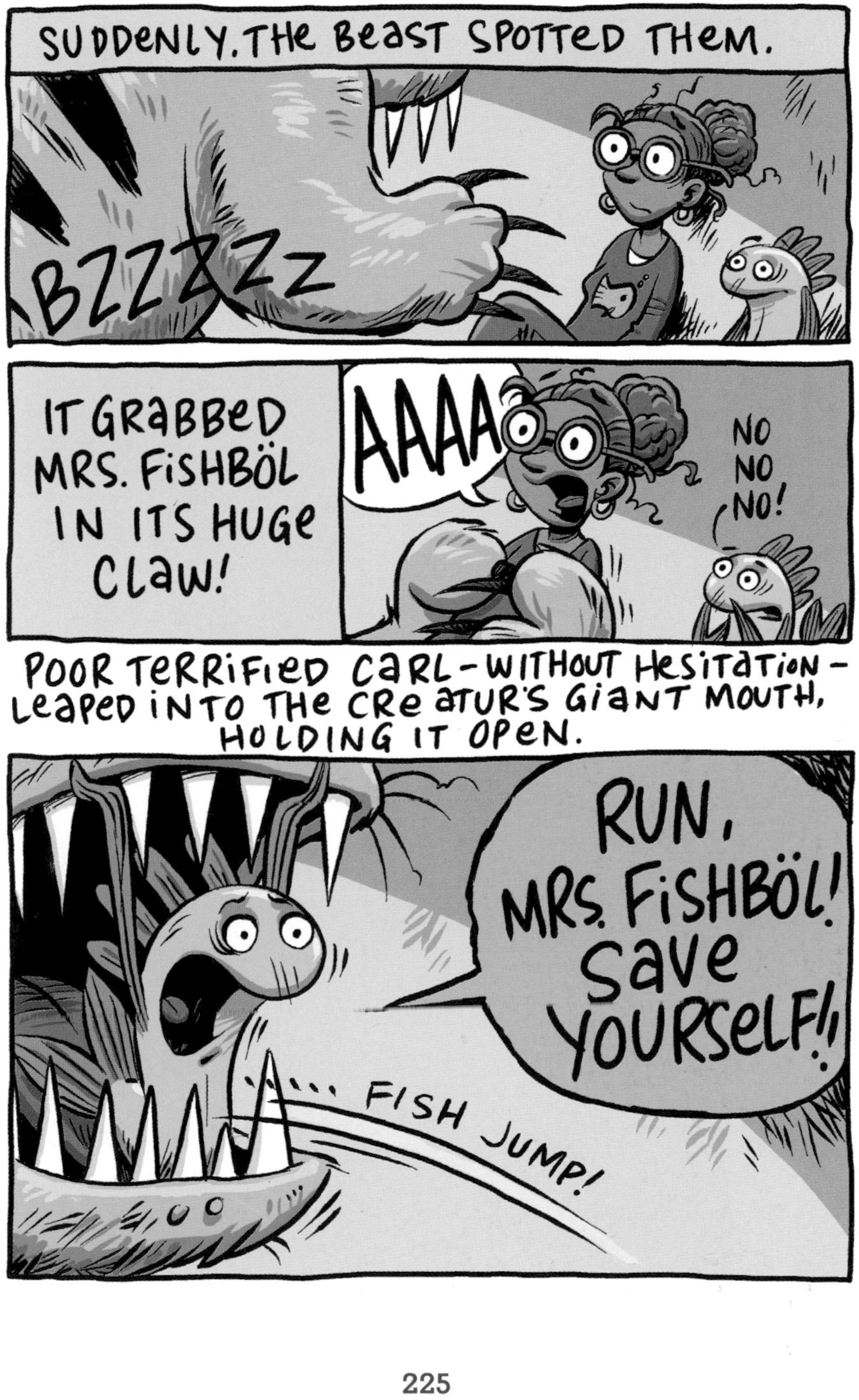
SUDDENLY. THE BEAST SPOTTED THEM.
BZZZZZz
IT GRABBED MRS. FISHBÖL IN ITS HUGE CLAW!
AAAA
NO NO NO!
POOR TERRIFIED CARL - WITHOUT HESITATION - LEAPED INTO THE CREATUR'S GIANT MOUTH, HOLDING IT OPEN.
RUN, MRS. FISHBÖL! SAVE YOURSELF!
... FISH JUMP!

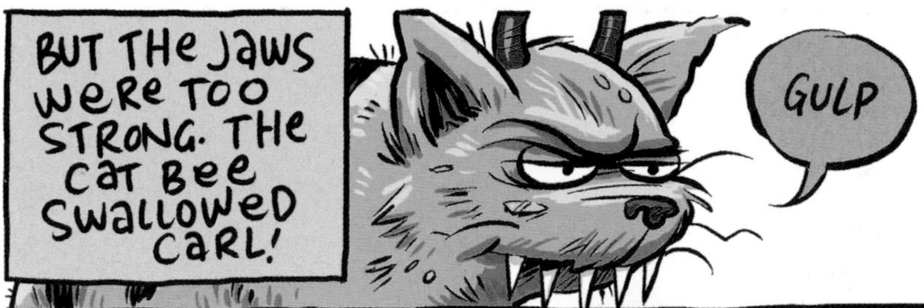
BUT THE JAWS WERE TOO STRONG. THE CAT BEE SWALLOWED CARL!
GULP

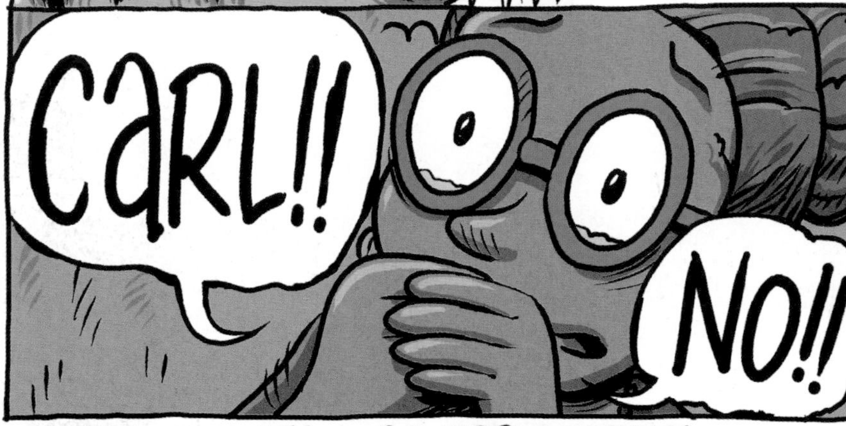
CARL!!
NO!!

MRS. FISHBÖL WAS FRANTICALLY SCRAMBLING AWAY FROM THE BUMBLE-KITTEN, WHEN...

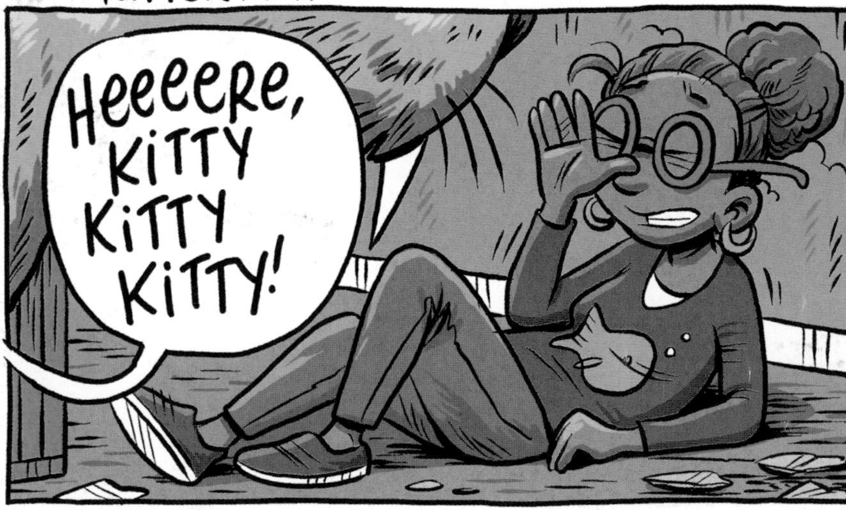
HEEEERE, KITTY KITTY KITTY!

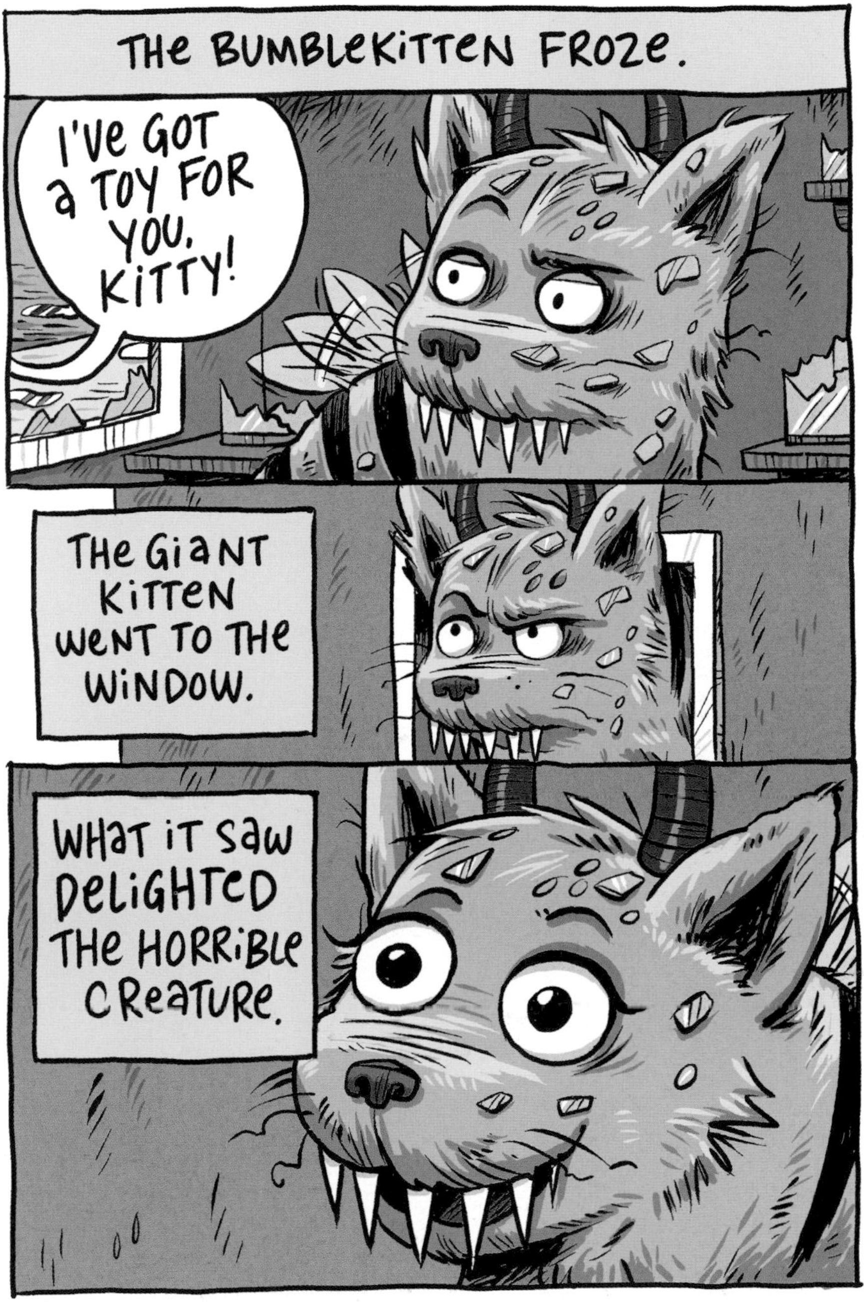
THE BUMBLEKITTEN FROZE.
I'VE GOT A TOY FOR YOU, KITTY!
THE GIANT KITTEN WENT TO THE WINDOW.
WHAT IT SAW DELIGHTED THE HORRIBLE CREATURE.

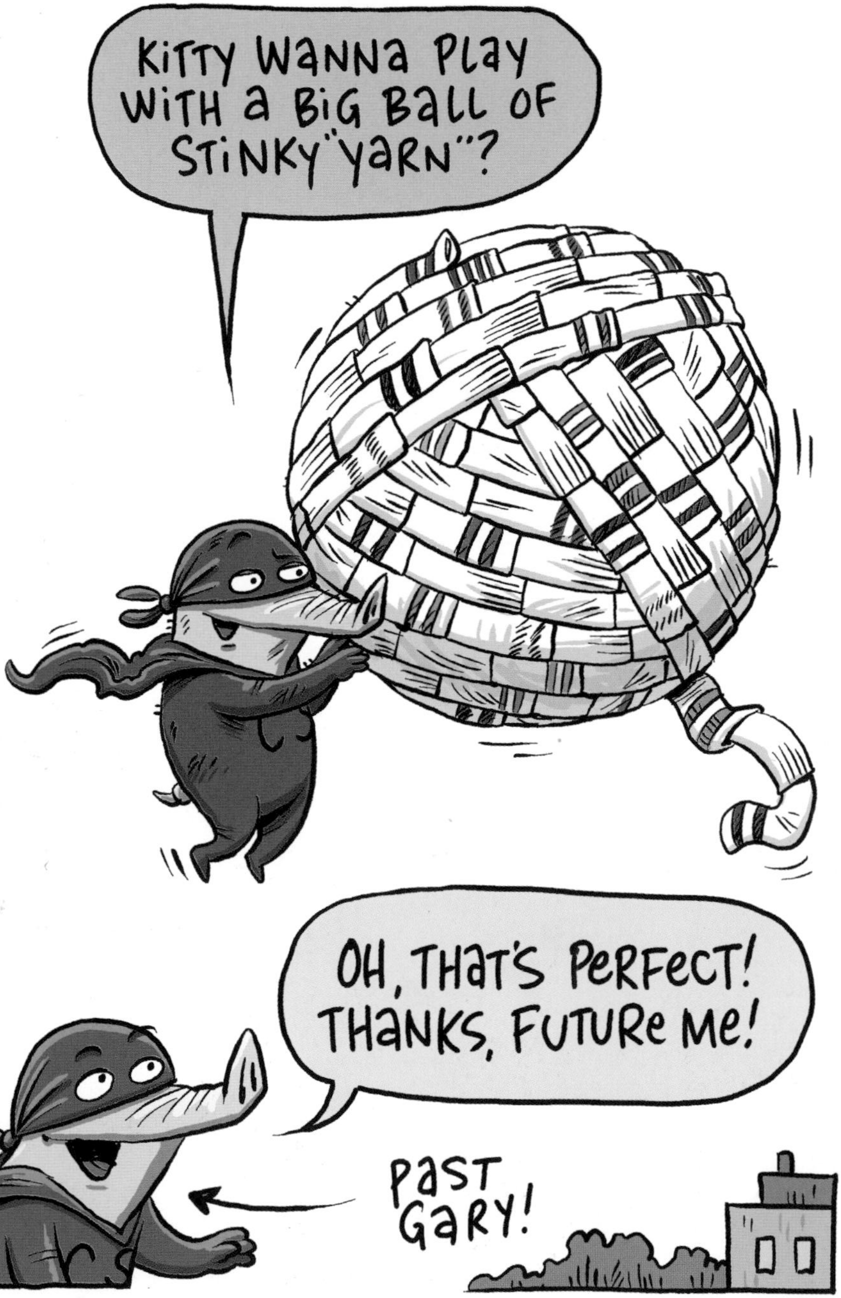
KITTY WANNA PLAY WITH A BIG BALL OF STINKY "YARN"?
OH, THAT'S PERFECT! THANKS, FUTURE ME!
PAST GARY!

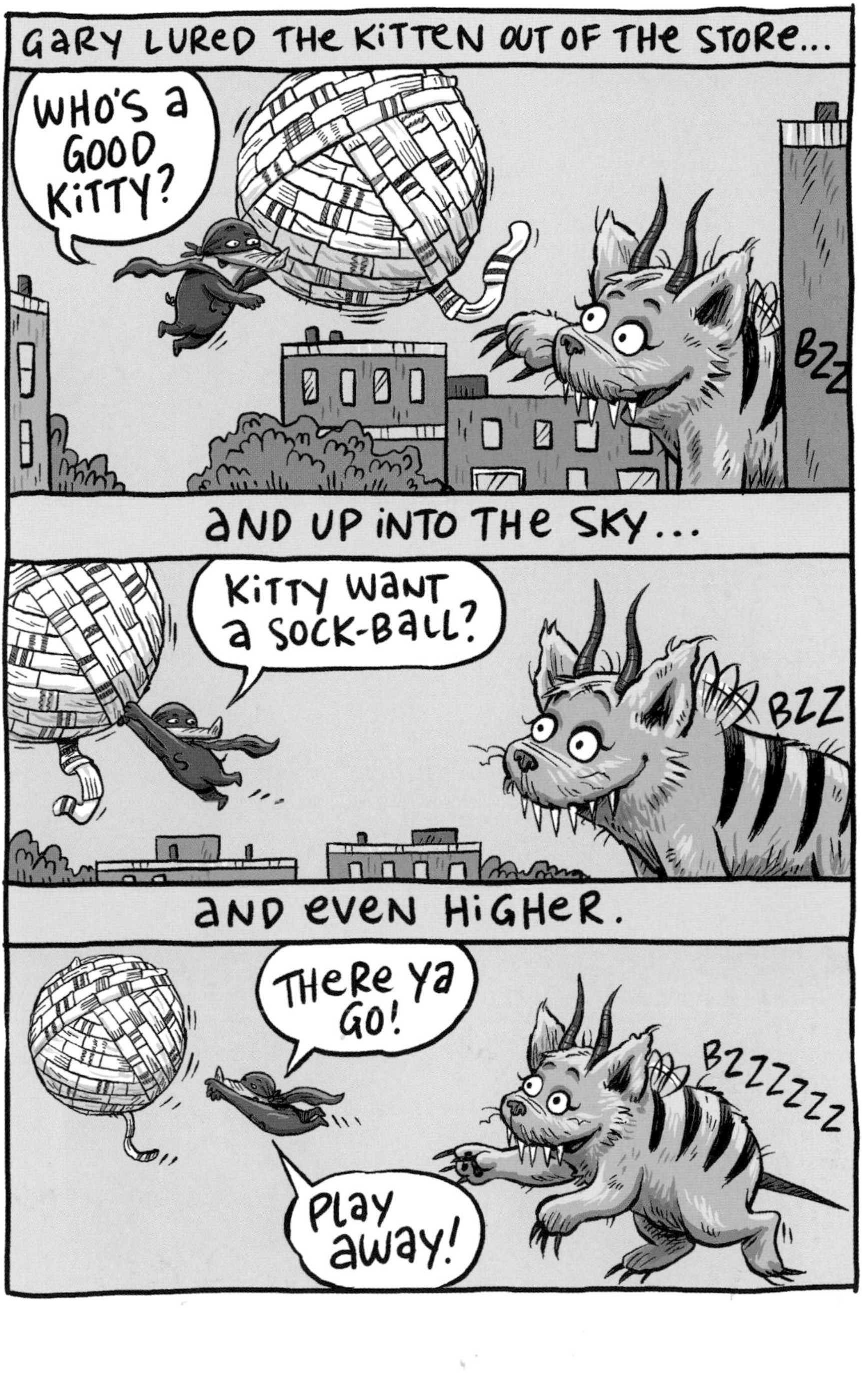
GARY LURED THE KITTEN OUT OF THE STORE...
WHO'S A GOOD KITTY?
BZZ
AND UP INTO THE SKY...
KITTY WANT A SOCK-BALL?
BZZ
AND EVEN HIGHER.
THERE YA GO!
BZZZZZZZ
PLAY AWAY!

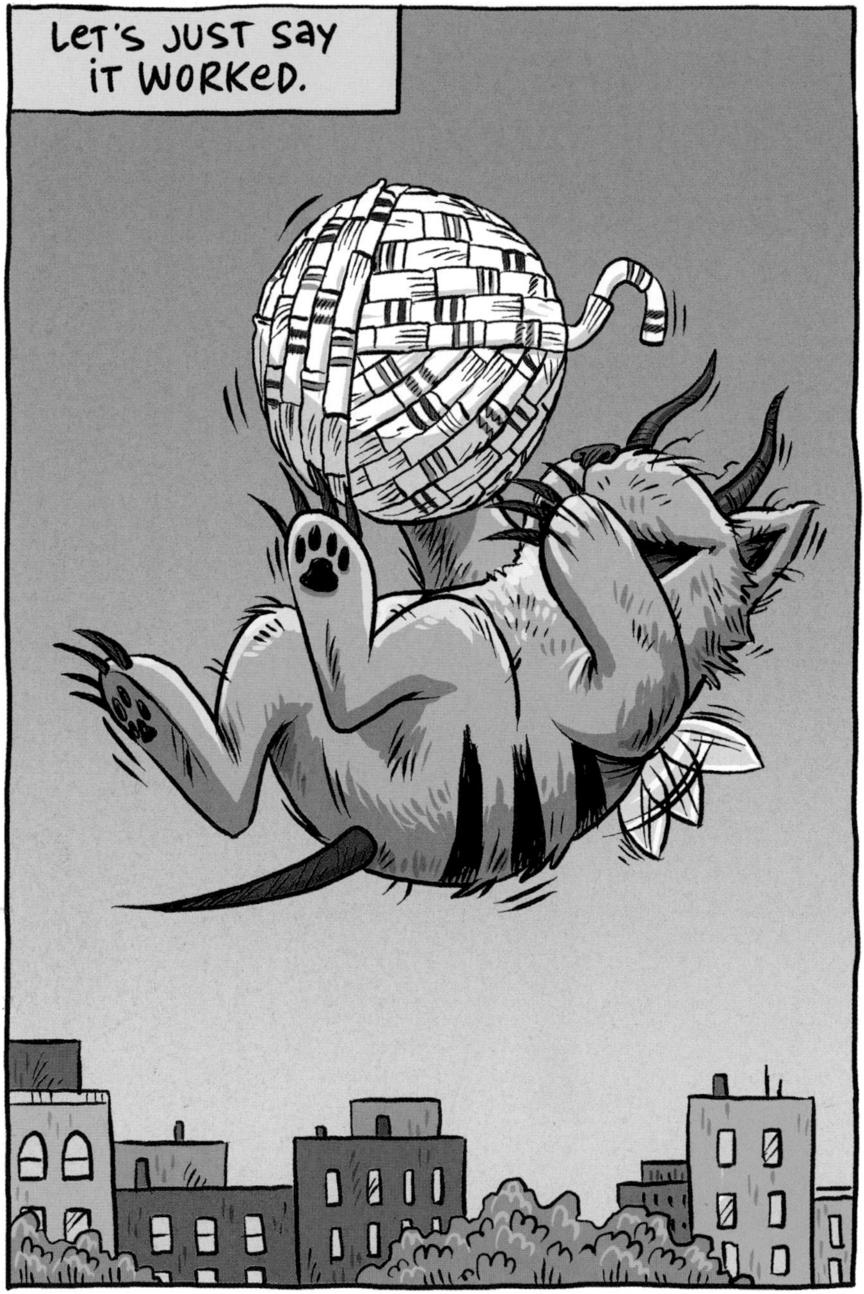
LET'S JUST SAY IT WORKED.

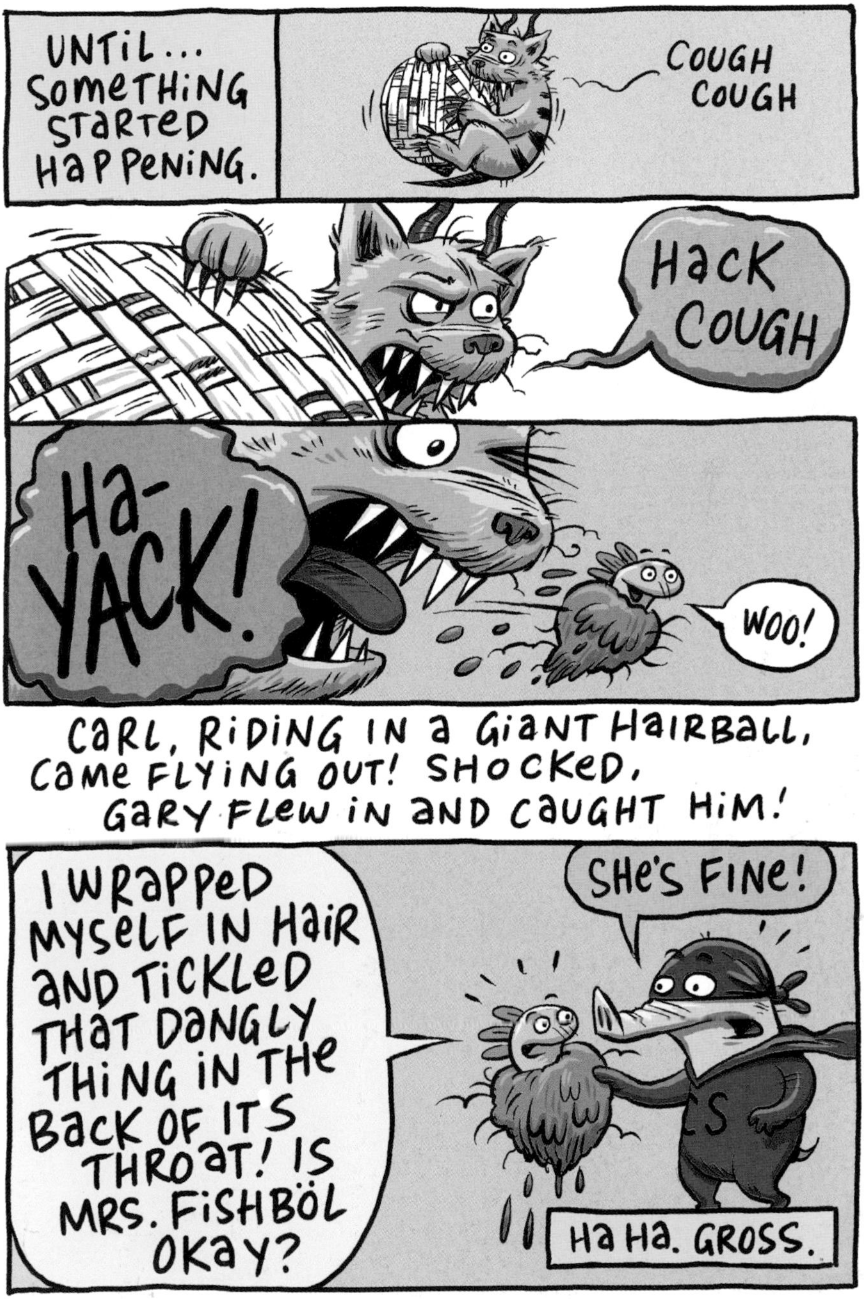
UNTIL... SOMETHING STARTED HAPPENING.
COUGH COUGH
HACK COUGH
HA-YACK!
WOO!
CARL, RIDING IN A GIANT HAIRBALL, CAME FLYING OUT! SHOCKED, GARY FLEW IN AND CAUGHT HIM!
I WRAPPED MYSELF IN HAIR AND TICKLED THAT DANGLY THING IN THE BACK OF ITS THROAT! IS MRS. FISHBÖL OKAY?
SHE'S FINE!
HA HA. GROSS.

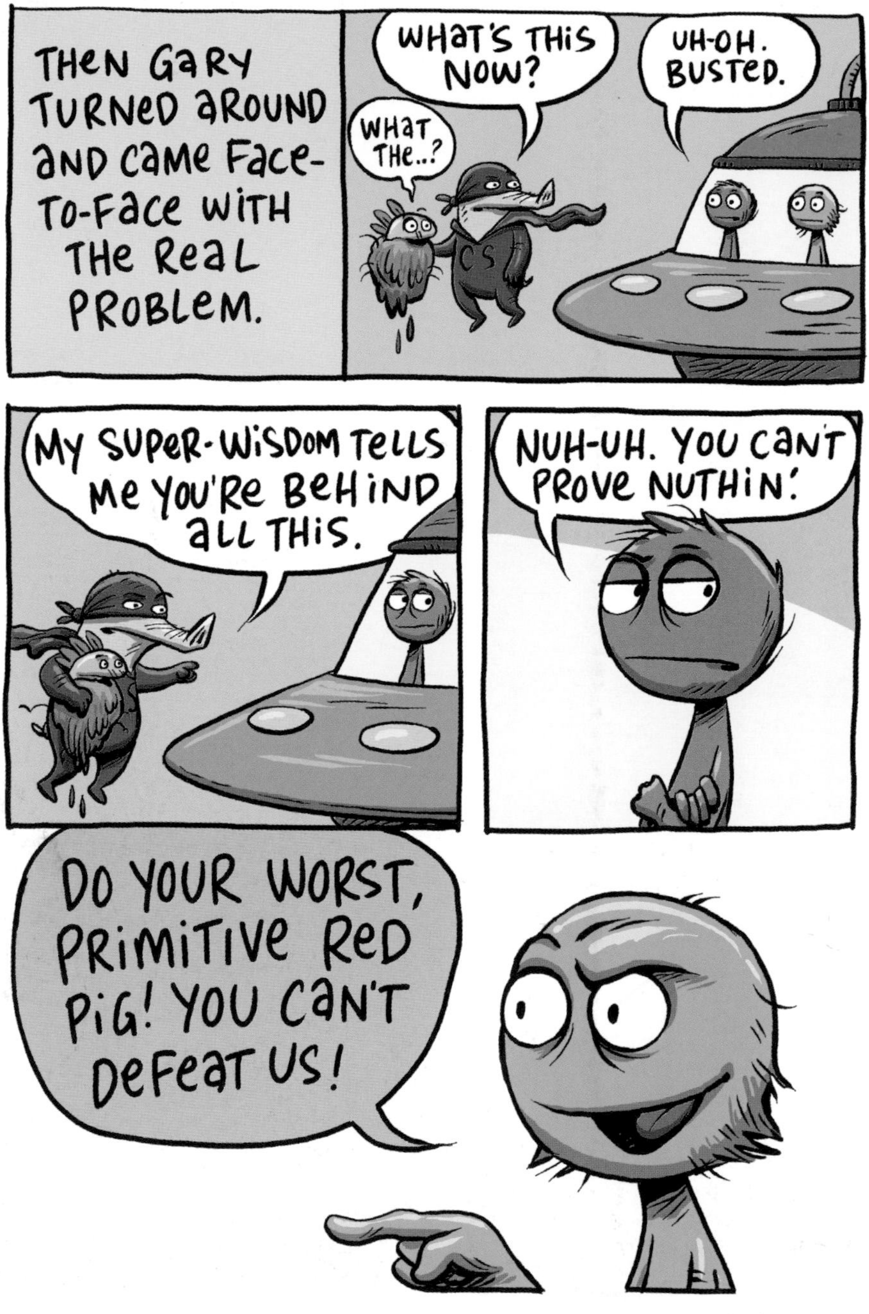
THEN GARY TURNED AROUND AND CAME FACE-TO-FACE WITH THE REAL PROBLEM.
WHAT'S THIS NOW?
WHAT THE..?
UH-OH. BUSTED.
MY SUPER-WISDOM TELLS ME YOU'RE BEHIND ALL THIS.
NUH-UH. YOU CAN'T PROVE NUTHIN'.
DO YOUR WORST, PRIMITIVE RED PIG! YOU CAN'T DEFEAT US!

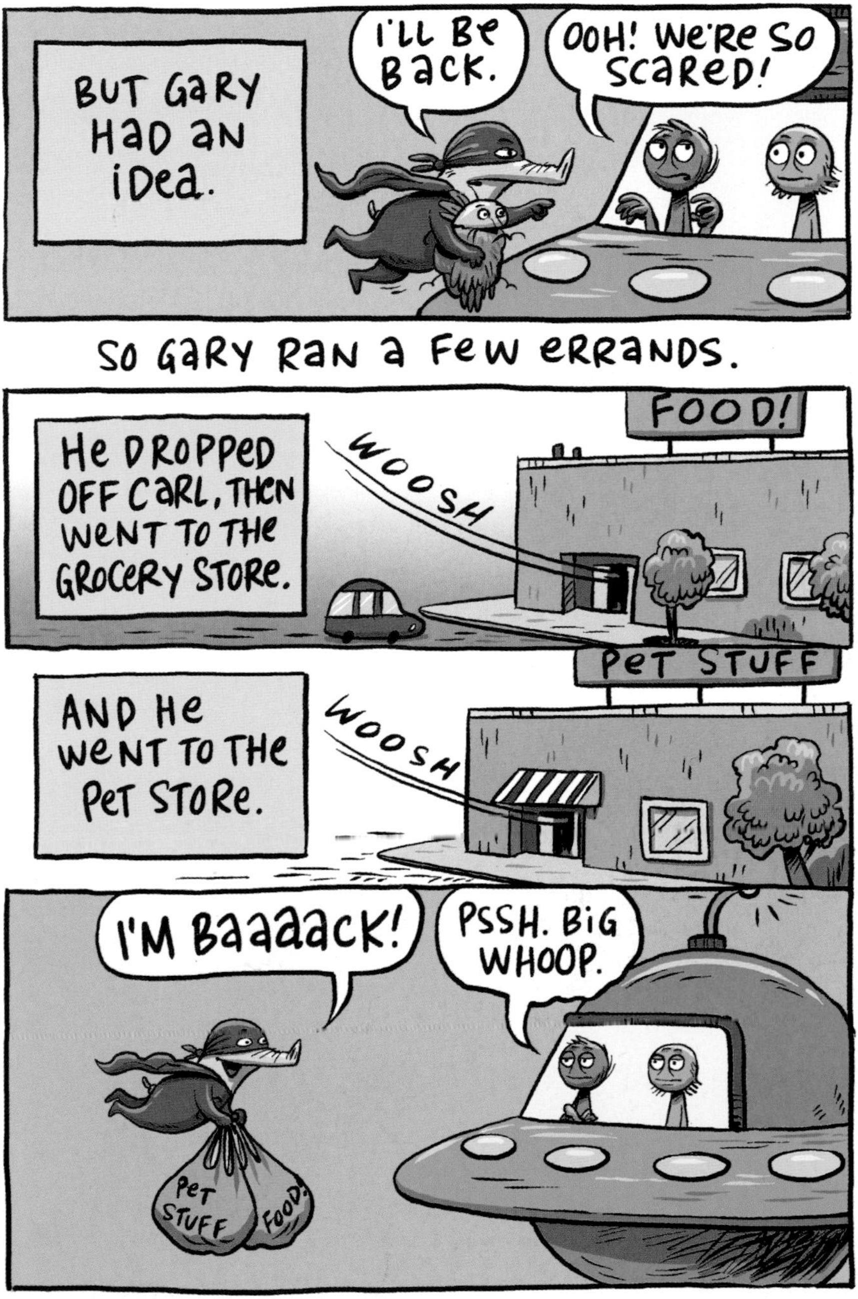
BUT GARY HAD AN IDEA.
I'LL BE BACK.
OOH! WE'RE SO SCARED!
SO GARY RAN A FEW ERRANDS.
HE DROPPED OFF CARL, THEN WENT TO THE GROCERY STORE.
FOOD!
WOOSH
PET STUFF
AND HE WENT TO THE PET STORE.
WOOSH
I'M BAAAACK!
PSSH. BIG WHOOP.
PET STUFF
FOOD!

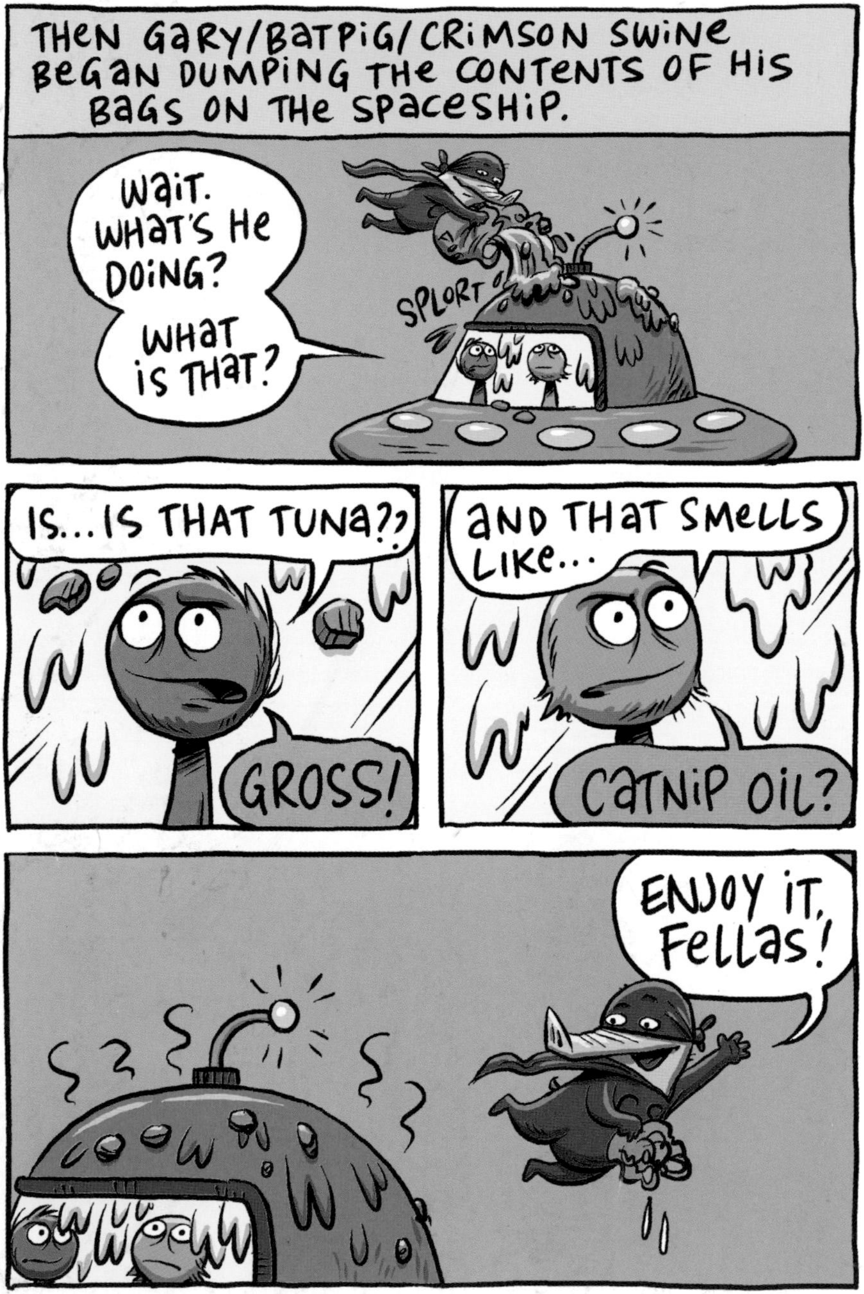
THEN GARY/BATPIG/CRIMSON SWINE BEGAN DUMPING THE CONTENTS OF HIS BAGS ON THE SPACESHIP.
WAIT. WHAT'S HE DOING?
WHAT IS THAT?
SPLORT
IS...IS THAT TUNA??
GROSS!
AND THAT SMELLS LIKE...
CATNIP OIL?
ENJOY IT, FELLAS!

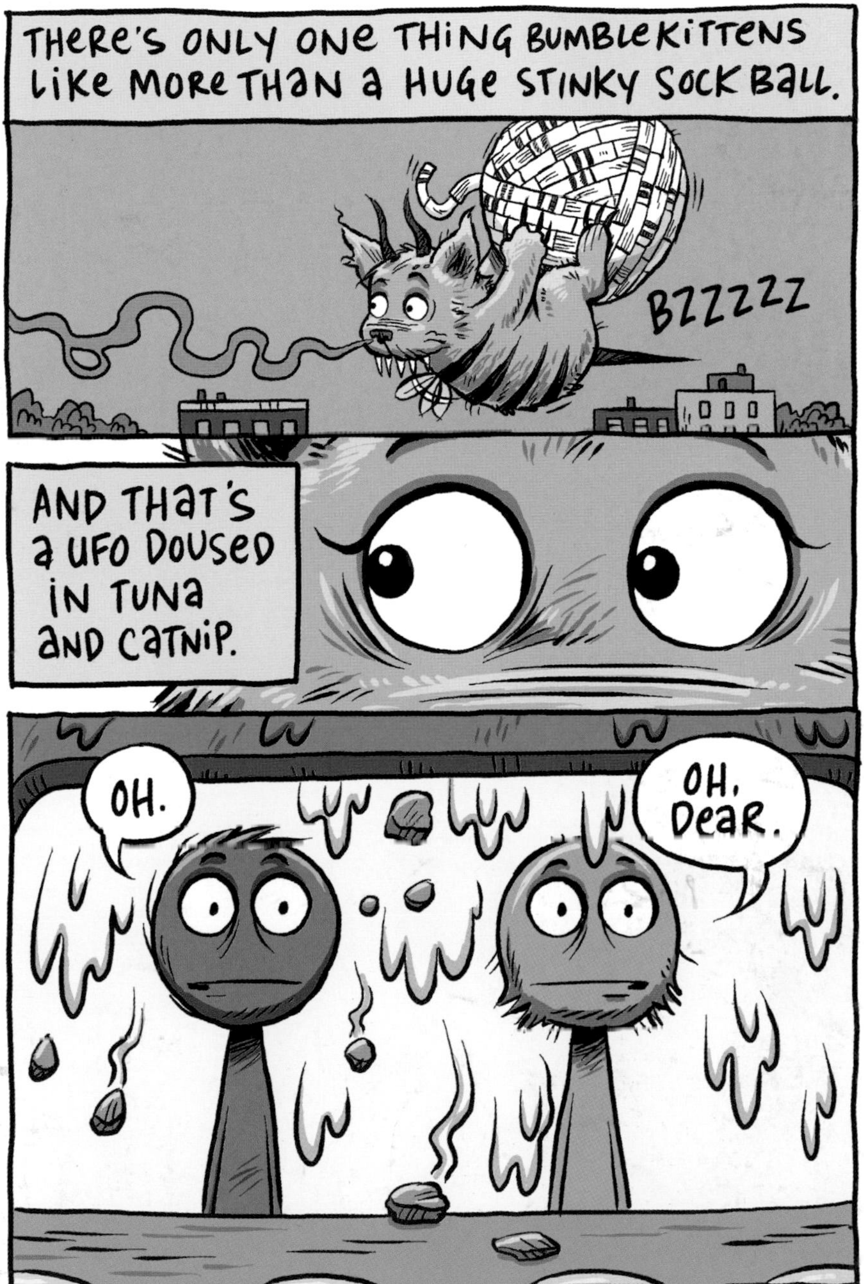
THERE'S ONLY ONE THING BUMBLEKITTENS LIKE MORE THAN A HUGE STINKY SOCK BALL.
BZZZZZ
AND THAT'S A UFO DOUSED IN TUNA AND CATNIP.
OH.
OH, DEAR.

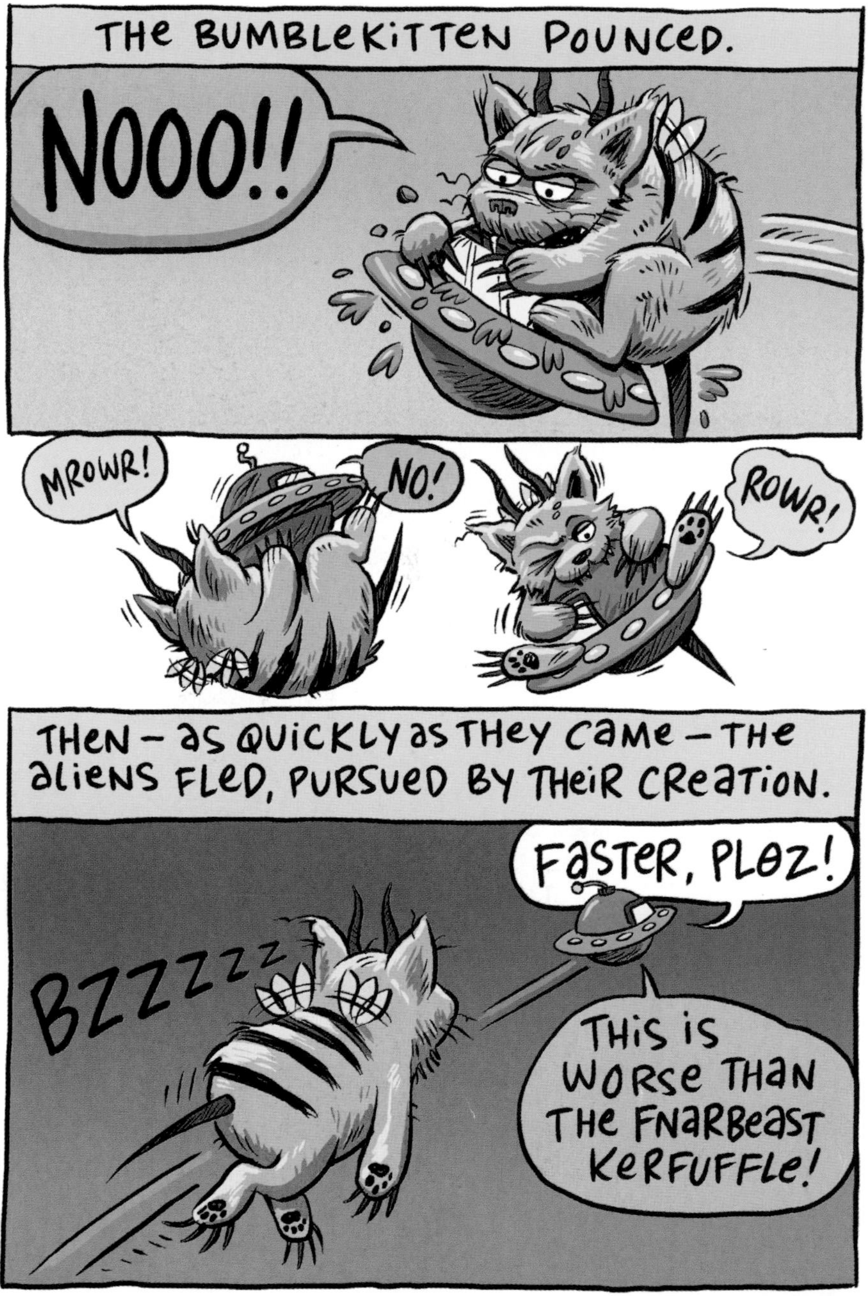
THE BUMBLEKITTEN POUNCED.
NOOO!!
MROWR!
NO!
ROWR!
THEN – AS QUICKLY AS THEY CAME – THE ALIENS FLED, PURSUED BY THEIR CREATION.
FASTER, PLOZ!
BZZZZZZ
THIS IS WORSE THAN THE FNARBEAST KERFUFFLE!

CHAPTER ELEVEN

"WHEW"

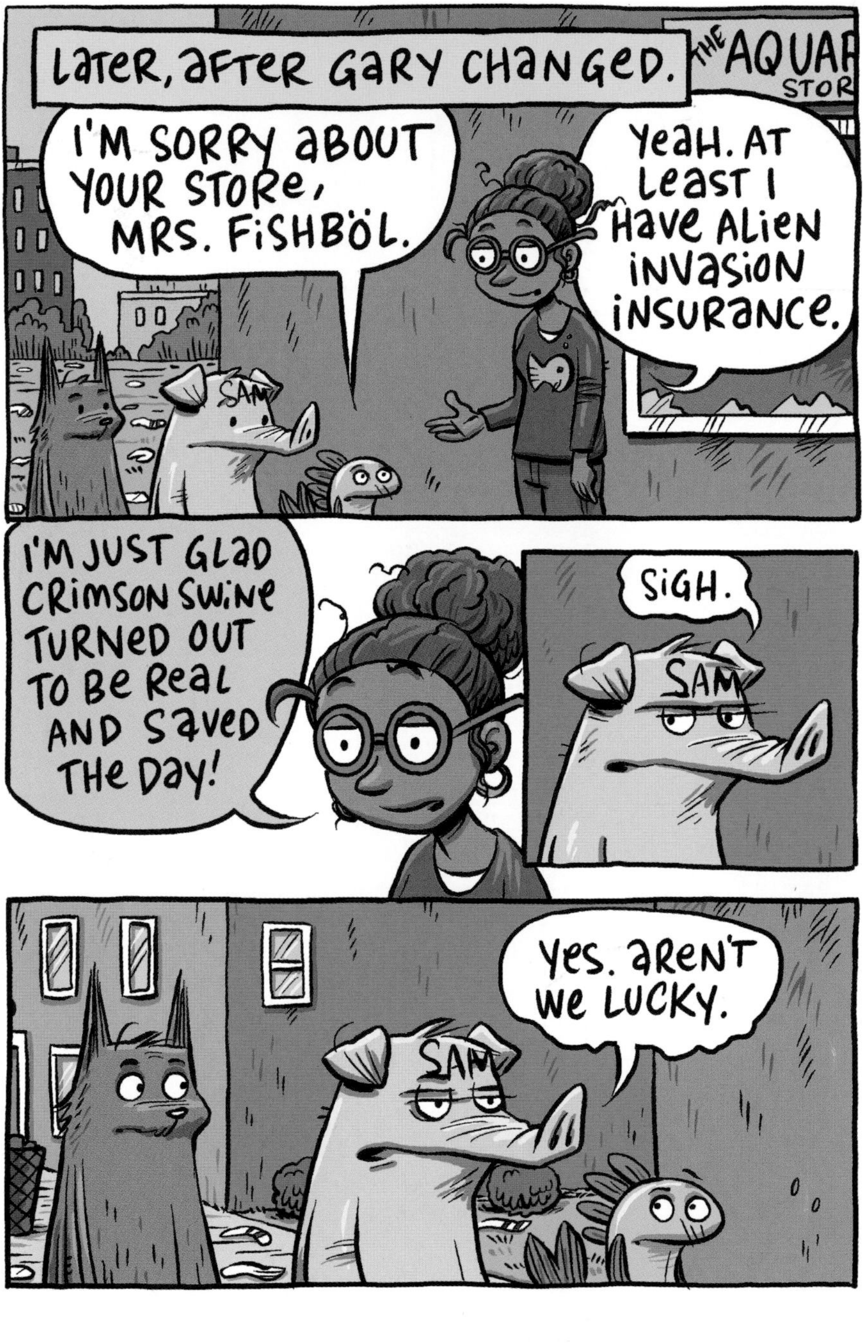
LATER, AFTER GARY CHANGED.
THE AQUAR
STOR
I'M SORRY ABOUT YOUR STORE, MRS. FISHBÖL.
YEAH. AT LEAST I HAVE ALIEN INVASION INSURANCE.
SAM
I'M JUST GLAD CRIMSON SWINE TURNED OUT TO BE REAL AND SAVED THE DAY!
SIGH.
SAM
YES. AREN'T WE LUCKY.
SAM

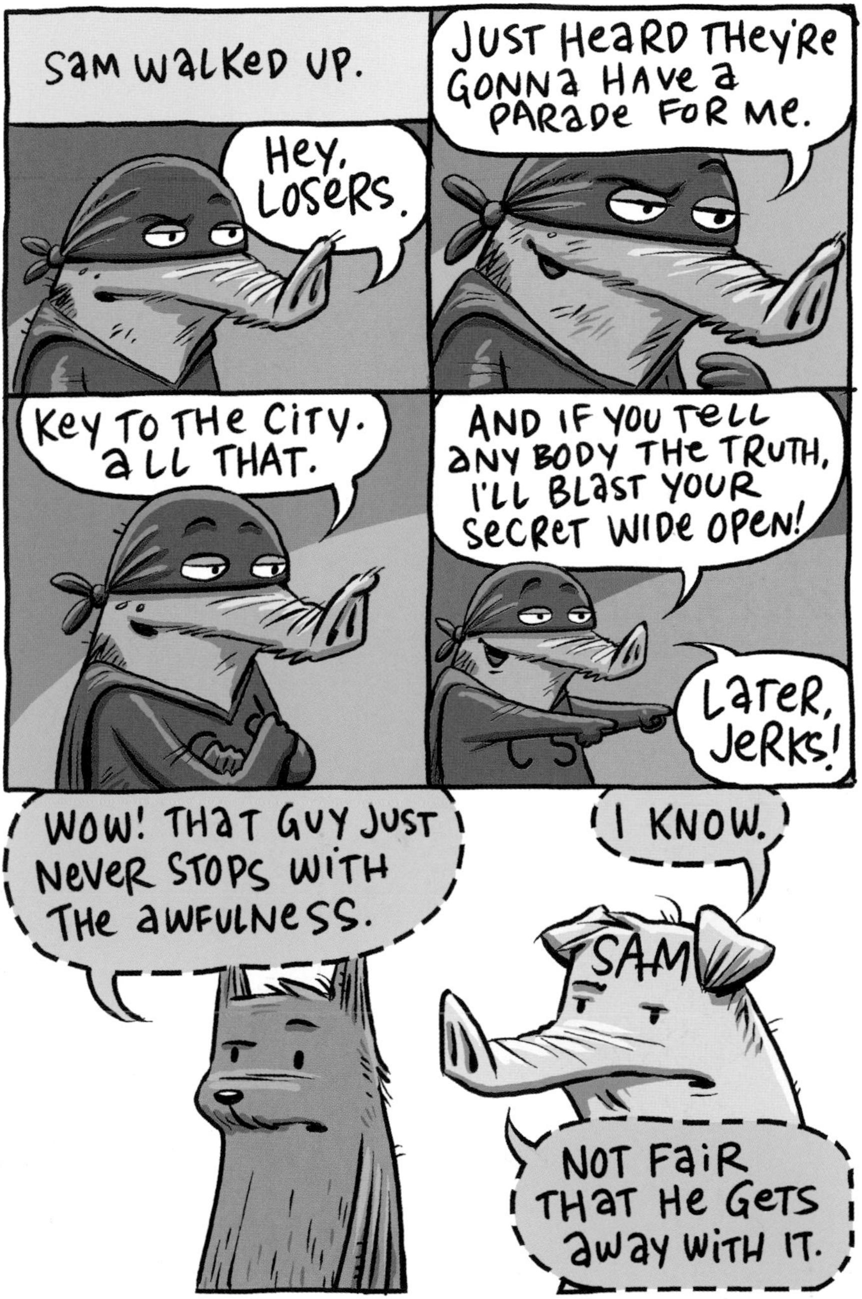
SAM WALKED UP.
HEY, LOSERS.
JUST HEARD THEY'RE GONNA HAVE A PARADE FOR ME.
KEY TO THE CITY. ALL THAT.
AND IF YOU TELL ANYBODY THE TRUTH, I'LL BLAST YOUR SECRET WIDE OPEN!
LATER, JERKS!
WOW! THAT GUY JUST NEVER STOPS WITH THE AWFULNESS.
I KNOW.
SAM
NOT FAIR THAT HE GETS AWAY WITH IT.

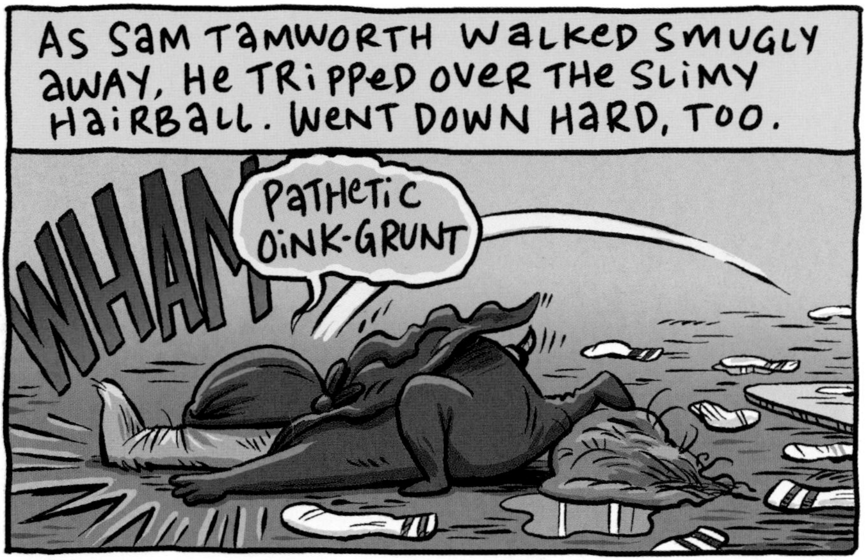
AS SAM TAMWORTH WALKED SMUGLY AWAY, HE TRIPPED OVER THE SLIMY HAIRBALL. WENT DOWN HARD, TOO.
WHAM
PATHETIC OINK-GRUNT

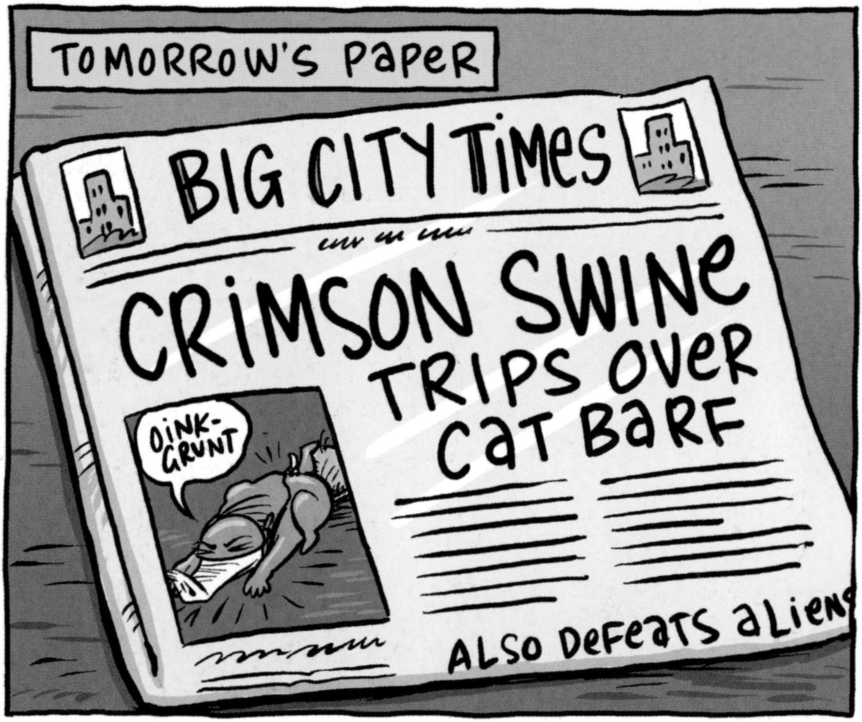
TOMORROW'S PAPER
BIG CITY TIMES
CRIMSON SWINE TRIPS OVER CAT BARF
OINK-GRUNT
ALSO DEFEATS ALIENS

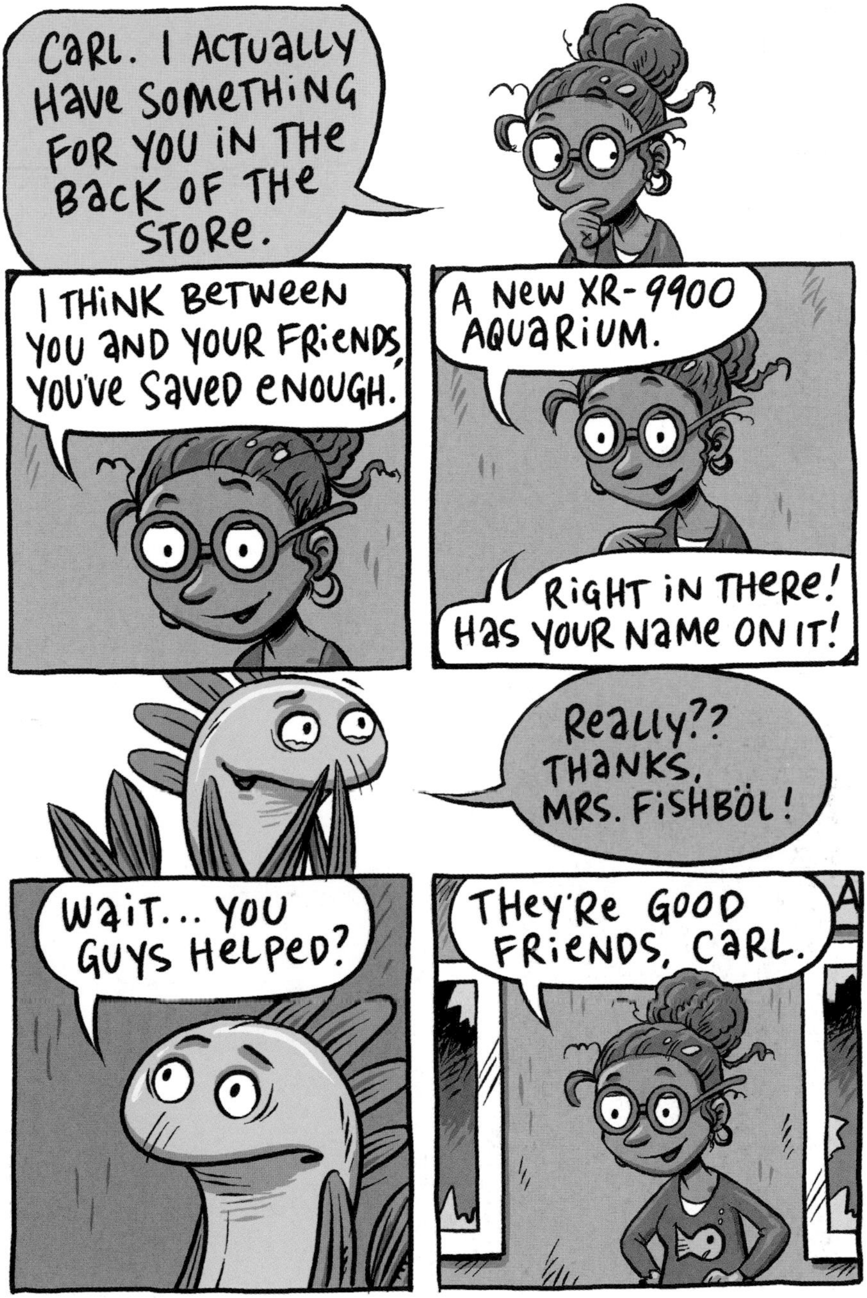
CARL. I ACTUALLY HAVE SOMETHING FOR YOU IN THE BACK OF THE STORE.
I THINK BETWEEN YOU AND YOUR FRIENDS, YOU'VE SAVED ENOUGH.
A NEW XR-9900 AQUARIUM.
RIGHT IN THERE! HAS YOUR NAME ON IT!
REALLY?? THANKS, MRS. FISHBÖL!
WAIT... YOU GUYS HELPED?
THEY'RE GOOD FRIENDS, CARL.

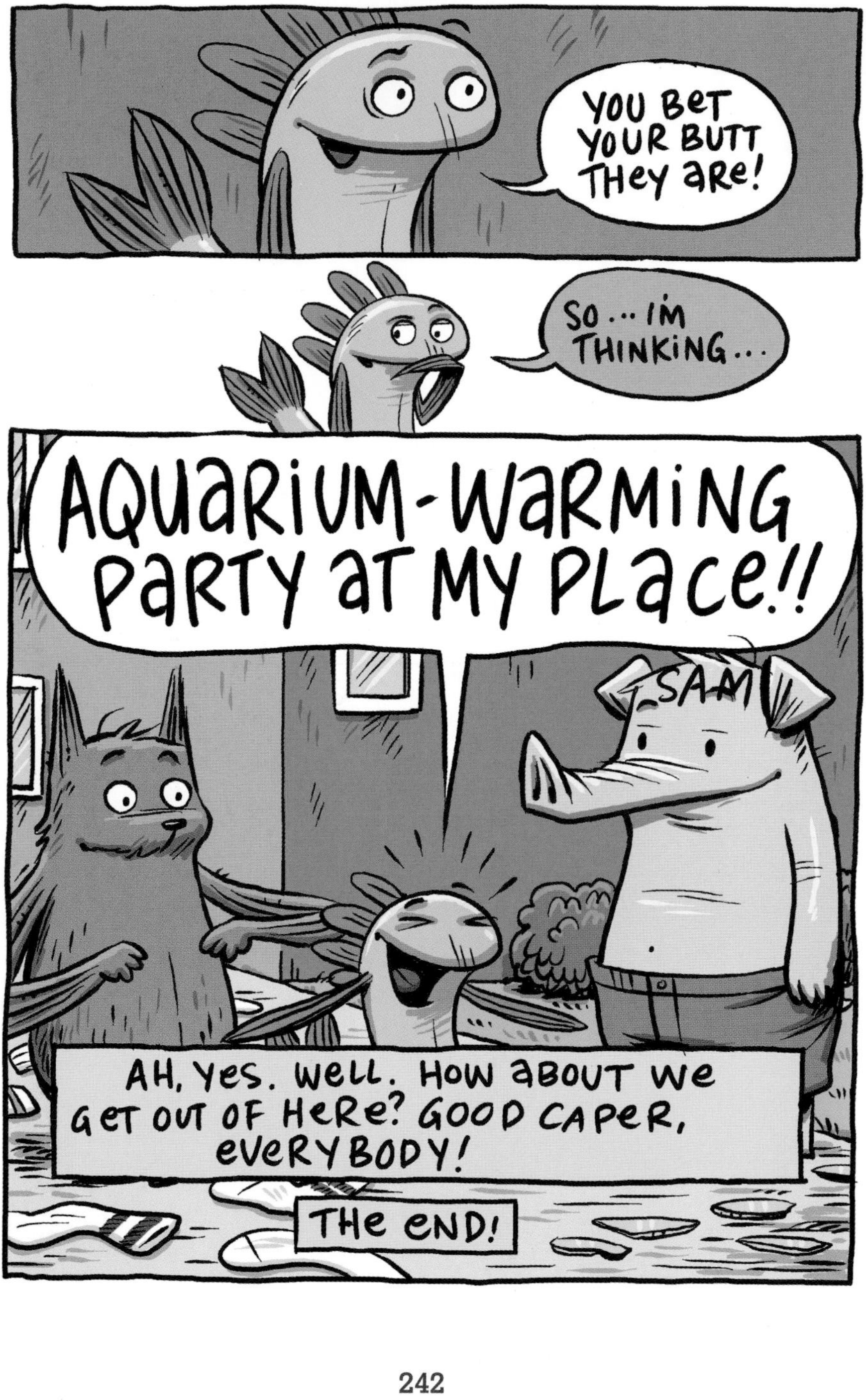
YOU BET YOUR BUTT THEY ARE!
SO... I'M THINKING...
AQUARIUM-WARMING PARTY AT MY PLACE!!
SAM
AH, YES. WELL. HOW ABOUT WE GET OUT OF HERE? GOOD CAPER, EVERYBODY!
THE END!

HEY YOU!

You look like you need more Batpig! Never fear, the next book will be coming soon. Stay tuned for:

GO PIG OR GO HOME!

AND CHECK OUT THE FIRST BATPIG BOOK:

A **BATPIG** BOOK

WHEN PIGS FLY

AUTHOR OF WINK
ROB HARRELL

★ "This is an absolute must-read for fans of Dav Pilkey's Dog Man series. Readers will go hog wild for this lovable hero." —*Kirkus*, starred review

"Action-packed, clever, and uproariously funny— kids will go hog wild for Batpig!" —Lincoln Peirce, *New York Times* bestselling author of the Big Nate series

DON'T MISS ROB HARRELL'S **WINK**, WITH SPECIAL APPEARANCES FROM BATPIG!

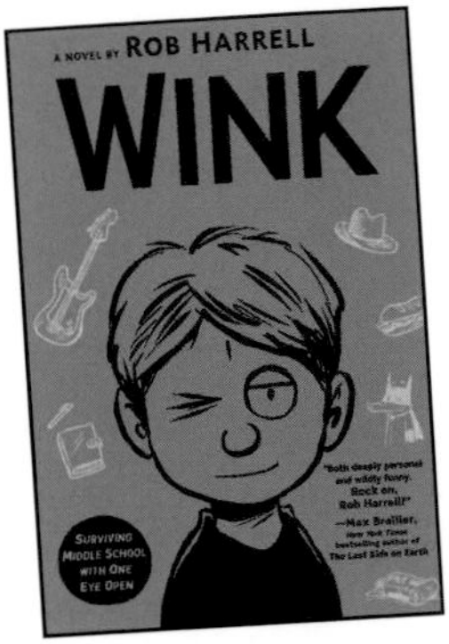
A NOVEL BY ROB HARRELL
WINK
SURVIVING MIDDLE SCHOOL WITH ONE EYE OPEN

TIME Best Book of the Year

Barnes & Noble Children's Book Award Shortlist

NYPL Best Book for Kids

NPR's Book Concierge Pick

Evanston Public Library Great Books for Kids

A Texas Lone Star Reading List Selection

An ALSC Notable Children's Book

"Harrell's genius is making all of it feel authentic for a seventh grader, a teenager who, like countless others, just wants to be normal . . . Bodies change, people change, life continues. It's a lesson a lot of us have been learning, and relearning, in recent days." —*New York Times Book Review*

★ "Filled with the same sardonic humor and celebration of atypical friendships as his Life of Zarf series, [*Wink*] draws from [Harrell's] personal experience to track the wild emotional roller coaster a seventh-grader rides after being diagnosed with a rare tear duct cancer." —*Booklist*, starred review

★ "This page-turner is not to be missed."
—*School Library Connection*, starred review

★ "This lively novel showcases the author's understanding of middle school angst amid the protagonist's experience with a serious illness." —*Publishers Weekly*, starred review

ALSO BY

ROB HARRELL

Life of Zarf: The Trouble with Weasels

Life of Zarf: The Troll Who Cried Wolf

Life of Zarf: Troll Overboard

Monster on the Hill

LIFE OF ZARF
THE TROUBLE WITH WEASELS
ROB HARRELL

LIFE OF ZARF
THE TROLL WHO CRIED WOLF
ROB HARRELL

LIFE OF ZARF
TROLL OVERBOARD
ROB HARRELL

MONSTER ON THE HILL
THE GRAPHIC NOVEL THAT INSPIRED THE THEATRICAL FILM
RUMBLE
EXPANDED WITH A NEW EPILOGUE!
ROB HARRELL

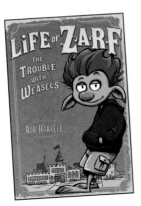

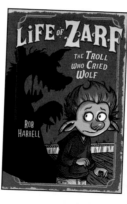

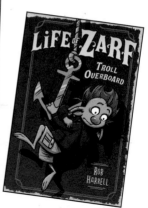

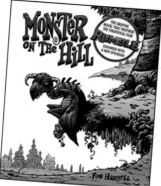

ROB HARRELL (www.robharrell.com) is the creator of the Batpig and Life of Zarf series, as well as *Wink* and *Monster on the Hill*. He also writes and draws the long-running daily comic strip *Adam@Home*, which appears in more than 140 papers worldwide. He lives with his wife in Indiana.